"Matchar's debut novel is a richly layered and beautifully written tale that immerses the reader into a sweeping saga set in the picturesque backdrop of the lush West Virginia mountains' legendary Greenbrier resort, and its fascinating, secret history. Utterly captivating, *In the Shadow of the Greenbrier* is unforgettable."

—Kim Michele Richardson, author of *The Book Woman of Troublesome Creek*

"Careful research, vivid description, and a solid historical basis are the scaffold on which this novel is built. But it's the characters, with all their longings and disappointments, their flaws and their triumphs, who will steal your heart and not give it back; they'll stay with you long after the last page is turned."

—Kitty Zeldis, author of *The Dressmakers of Prospect Heights*

ALSO BY EMILY MATCHAR

Homeward Bound

In the Shadow
of the Greenbrier

A NOVEL

Emily Matchar

G. P. PUTNAM'S SONS · NEW YORK

PUTNAM
— EST. 1838 —
G. P. PUTNAM'S SONS
Publishers Since 1838
An imprint of Penguin Random House LLC
penguinrandomhouse.com

Library of Congress Cataloging-in-Publication Data

Names: Matchar, Emily, author.
Title: In the shadow of the Greenbrier: a novel / Emily Matchar.
Description: New York: G. P. Putnam's Sons, 2024.
Identifiers: LCCN 2023057054 (print) | LCCN 2023057055 (ebook) |
ISBN 9780593713969 (trade paperback) | ISBN 9780593713976 (ebook)
Subjects: LCGFT: Novels.
Classification: LCC PS3613.A8237 I5 2024 (print) | LCC PS3613.A8237 (ebook) |
DDC 813/.6—dc23/eng/20231208
LC record available at https://lccn.loc.gov/2023057054
LC ebook record available at https://lccn.loc.gov/2023057055
p.   cm.

Printed in the United States of America
1st Printing

Book design by Elke Sigal

To Charlie and Sid

In the Shadow
of the Greenbrier

CHAPTER I

※

Jordan

WASHINGTON, DC

JANUARY 1992

*W*hen the letter arrived, Jordan Barber was sitting at his desk eyeing the cuffs of his chinos, wondering if he could hem them with a stapler. If he did it from the inside out, maybe the little folded silver legs of the staples would look like fancy stitching.

A minute before, Rick Lowell from the National News desk had walked by and made a wisecrack about Jordan wearing his dad's clothes. Jordan wanted to shoot back that he was actually taller than his dad, but even he knew this was not the right way to do newsroom banter. So he just stared down at his feet, noticing how the pants puddled around the tops of his brown wingtips, which had felt so sharp when his mom bought them at Hecht's the month before but now seemed too shiny, as if announcing "I'm brand-new."

All the top reporters at the *Post*—the ones whose names appeared above the fold, who talked about having drinks "at Ben's," who'd flown on Air Force One—dressed like they'd slept at their desks all night: rumpled oxford shirts, loafers worn down to the color and texture of cardboard. Nobody else's shoes were shiny. No one else ironed their chinos.

Maybe Scotch Tape would work better than a stapler? Or masking tape? Jordan began rummaging in his desk drawer.

Just then, the mail cart clattered through, pushed by Alice the intern, who wore a plaid headband and a thousand-yard stare. She tossed a letter on Jordan's desk without turning her head.

"Thanks!" Jordan called, but Alice didn't look back.

He looked down at the letter.

> *Jordan Barber*
> *Local and Regional News Desk*
> *The Washington Post*

Weird. He'd only been at the desk for four months, and he'd never had a letter personally addressed to him before. He was about to tear it open when he remembered his letter opener, the one his granddad had given him for college graduation. He plucked it from the University of Maryland mug where he kept his pens. It was brass and felt good in his hand, cool and heavy and professional. He slid it under the letter's flap, noting the West Virginia postmark. Unfolding the paper, he began to read. Then his eyes caught a name, and he stopped.

The Greenbrier.

The words sounded like a gong somewhere deep and primal in his brain, sound waves rippling outward. *The Greenbrier.*

There's something underneath the Greenbrier Resort, the letter read. *It's time for people to know.*

His mother had rarely referred to it as "the Greenbrier." It was simply "the resort."

Other children were told bedtime stories about princes or

talking bunnies or teddy bear picnics. Jordan and his twin sister had been raised on tales of the Greenbrier: The green hotel Rolls-Royces that used to meet the trains. The movie stars hanging out by the pool. The doormen who all knew their mother's name, even though she was just a townie kid, not a guest. Jordan always imagined the resort as a fairy-tale castle atop a hill, with the village of White Sulphur Springs—his mother's hometown—in its shadow.

Their mother and their uncle Pete would go on and on about the annual Greenbrier employee Christmas parties—*Remember that gingerbread house that was a perfect scale model of the resort? Remember the time Dewey Burdette broke Santa's throne?* This would annoy Jordan's sister, since Jordan and Jessica were never allowed to so much as watch a Christmas movie. (*That's how assimilation starts,* their father would say, as if there were a slippery chute from *It's a Wonderful Life* straight to accepting Jesus Christ as your Lord and Savior.)

Yet the Greenbrier was also somehow related to the other part of their mother's life, the part she didn't talk about. The part about her mother and her other brother, Alan. About what had happened to them. *There was an incident* with a car. Her mother and Alan had died and it had been *terribly sad.* That's all Jordan's mother would say. A *terribly sad incident.* Everything Jordan knew was gleaned from snatches of conversation overheard late at night, when Uncle Pete was in town.

He couldn't leave it alone. All that blood.

Their mother wouldn't tell them more. If Jessica pressed, Mom would sigh and turn away and let her eyes fill with tears.

Jordan never pressed. He hated to be the One Who Made His Mother Cry. But he did imagine. He pictured long, snouty, sinister cars full of anti-Semites, of course—as a child he misheard the word (*ant-i-Semites*), and imagined enormous ants, with shiny dark carapace-like armor.

Now a stranger was offering information about this black hole at the center of his childhood. Not only that, but the stranger was offering him a *story*. Maybe a big story. Jordan might not have the right pants or the right shoes, but he knew how to follow a lead as well as any of the A1 guys. Maybe this would be his chance.

Doree

*W*hen people heard she was from West Virginia and raised their eyebrows a little—a look that said they were thinking of tar paper shacks and toothless snake handlers and black lung—Doree wished she could walk them through the Greenbrier Resort in the winter of 1958.

In fact, she had an exact date in mind. December 13. The day of the employees' Christmas party.

The resort gleamed like a cruise ship on the horizon. The acres of lawns as pampered as a starlet's hair. The fleet of bottle-green Rolls-Royces. The dining room so big waiters used to ride horses through it. The Swiss chefs who flambeed crêpes suzette tableside, just like in Monte Carlo. The crisp *G* stamped in the fresh white sand of every ashtray. The massive brass lobby doors swinging open and welcoming her inside.

Doree and her younger brothers, Alan and Pete, walked west along White Sulphur Springs's stunted Main Street, stopping at the corner of Surber Road to meet Patty and Tommy Curry. Pete and Tommy raced ahead, kicking stones with the toes of their dress shoes. Alan, as usual, trailed behind.

"I love that coat!" Patty said, reaching out to pet the shoulder of Doree's new tartan cape coat. "Did your mom do that?"

Doree nodded. "I like your new hat."

"It's going to squash my hair, though," Patty said.

Arms linked, they crossed the invisible line dividing town from resort and came to the entrance gate, where the younger boys were waiting, leaning against the brick. The driveway was flanked by tall white pillars topped with Grecian urns. From each pillar hung a wrought iron lantern, and beneath the lantern, in curling script, the words THE GREENBRIER.

Normally, when Doree and other townies visited the Greenbrier, they'd cut across the bridge over Howard's Creek and come in the lower North Entrance. But not today.

"We get to go in the big entrance today!" called Pete. "Like the Duke of York!"

"Duke of *Windsor*," muttered Alan.

On they walked, past the guardhouse, waving to Mr. Sammy in his forest-green suit and cap. They passed the South Carolina Cottages on their right, with their identical American flags hanging stiffly in the cold air. The younger boys picked up sticks on the hillside and began sword fighting. Then they turned the bend in the drive, and even Pete and Tommy stopped messing around for a minute because there it was, at the head of the oval lawn, seeming to glow in the pinkening dusk.

The resort.

It was a palace as large and white and splendid as anything in their history books, sitting tall on a gentle rise in the valley floor, the dark ridgeline of the Alleghenies its backdrop. Hundreds of windows—the resort had more than seven hundred guest rooms,

Alan had told her—seemed to twinkle like stars. Front and center was an immense portico in the style of a Greek temple, a single oval pane set in its pediment like an all-seeing eye. The building was surrounded by widening circles of lawns, then formal gardens, then rows of nineteenth-century gingerbread cottages, a remnant of the resort's days as the Old White, when the aristocracy of Richmond and Atlanta and Charleston would come to take the waters.

With two weeks to Christmas, the building was festooned and beribboned from bottom to top. Swags of fir branches overhung the arches of the lower arcade, while the towering white columns of the portico had been wound with golden twinkle lights. More lights glittered from the laurel trees flanking the front lawn. On the balcony was a Christmas tree lavished with tinsel and crowned with a single gold star.

Looking at the resort always gave Doree the same warm flush she got when singing "The Star-Spangled Banner" before Little League games. Like something bigger than her belonged to her alone. It made White Sulphur Springs different from all the little West Virginia towns clinging to the hillsides and hollows of the Alleghenies. *Bluefield and Welch will be in trouble when the coal mines play out*, her father always said. *But we've got the Greenbrier.*

At the motor entrance, the doormen stood stoic in the cold. "Young ladies, young gentlemen," said Leon, the head doorman, pulling open the heavy brass door. They stepped inside with a whoosh of warm air. It was check-in time, and the Motor Lobby was thick with smoke and perfume. Bellboys glided back and forth to the elevators with trolleys of luggage as men in flannel suits stood waiting at the front desk, rubbing the impressions of their hats from their hair, bleary from whiskey and sodas on the Chesapeake and Ohio *George Washington* from DC. "Now, let me tell you the thing," said a man with a Yankee accent, leaning over the concierge desk.

"Billy! Where are you, Billy?" called a woman with the face of a movie star, as a little boy in short pants stood giggling behind a potted fern.

Doree did a careful sweep of the room. You never knew who you'd see. Patty had spotted Debbie Reynolds once, sitting on the front steps in Bermuda shorts, as normal as could be. Bob Hope had been here just last summer.

"There's Mama!" called Patty.

Evangeline Curry was standing by the elevators, waving. She'd put on a green wool party dress but was still wearing her stubby-heeled brown housekeeper's shoes.

"Girls, you both look so pretty!" she said, reaching out to squeeze their arms.

Even though Doree was nearly eighteen, the Greenbrier employees' children's Christmas party was still exciting. She'd gone every year since kindergarten, thanks to Patty. Mrs. Curry was the head housekeeper at the Greenbrier, so she was allowed guest tickets. Patty and Tommy always brought Doree and Pete and Alan. Patty and Doree had been best friends since they were five; so had Tommy and Pete. And Mrs. Curry wouldn't have let Alan be left out, of course.

The group of them headed back towards the theater. Carol VanDonk, who was a classmate of Doree and Patty's, was taking tickets at the door; her father ran the resort print shop, where he set the dining room menus every day on heavy cream-colored card stock with gold embossing. The younger boys threw their coats on the table and ran into the theater, and Mrs. Curry dissolved into a group of other Greenbrier mothers. Alan hung back, waiting for Doree. "Go on, Alan," she said impatiently. Why couldn't Pete invite Alan to tag along for once? It would be nice to have just one event where he wasn't her responsibility.

"That is such a cute coat," Carol said to Doree. "I wish my mama could sew."

Patty leaned over the table and faux whispered to Carol, "Are you-know-who here yet?"

"Lee Burdette and them?" Carol said, putting the coats on hangers and hanging them from the bellboy rail. "I saw Dewey, but nobody from our year."

Lee Burdette was the captain of the basketball team and had a dirty blond pompadour and heavy-lidded blue eyes, like Elvis. He drove an old army jeep from back when the Greenbrier was a war hospital. His father, Johnny Burdette, was the resort's head groundskeeper.

"Well, when you see Lee, tell him Doree's gonna get him under the mistletoe!" Patty said.

"Y'all are too boy crazy!"

The girls went inside, Alan trailing silently behind. The gold and pink theater was set up like an indoor carnival, and it was as noisy and wild as any fair on a Saturday night. The little kids were streaming between card tables set up with games—ring toss, balloon and darts, cover the spot—or waiting in line to see Santa, their mouths slack with anticipation. At the head of the Santa line, a doorman dressed as an elf was doing card tricks. Santa himself was Jim Wiley, the assistant to the manager. His beard was made of pulled cotton balls glued to felt, but his belly was entirely real. He sat in the same gold foil throne Doree had seen every year since she was five. She'd never sat in Santa's lap, though. That would have been a step too far.

Dewey Burdette and a gaggle of freshman boys were taking turns at the Strongman, peacocking back and forth with the rubber mallet and making muscle arms when they hit the bell. The other teenagers were gathered around the refreshments table, drinking ginger ale punch and eating pinwheels and little merengue cookies tinted red and green.

"Go get something to eat, Alan," Doree told her brother. If she didn't tell him something he'd stand behind her like a shadow for the whole party. *You'd think he was four, not two days from turning sixteen*, she thought. "But not the pinwheels."

"Why not?"

"Ham."

"I like ham."

"Suit yourself. But don't tell Mama."

Doree and Patty filled their plates and sat down at one of the card tables on the stage with Louise Level and Patty's cousins Wanda and Annette. The room was warm from the rising heat of dozens of excited children, and Doree felt flushed in her wool skirt and sweater set. She could feel her hair, carefully styled in a ponytail with side curled bangs, beginning to wilt.

"Look," said Patty. "Lee and them are here."

Framed in the light of the open door were Lee Burdette; Vance Calwell; and Jack and Edisto Level, Louise's cousins. The starting lineup of the White Sulphur Springs High basketball team, minus Davey-John Newsome, who was probably freezing his behind off on the golf course caddying for some Yankee guest. Seeing them, Doree checked her posture and pretended to be laughing at something Louise said. Boys liked girls who smiled a lot.

"Okay, y'all," said Patty, looking around the table and raising her eyebrows wickedly. "Let's get this straight in advance. Doree's gonna marry Lee, Wanda can have Edisto, and Annette gets Vance."

"Ewww," said Wanda. "I'm not marrying anybody who chews tobacco."

"Who do I get to marry?" said Louise Level.

"I'm sorry to say you might have to be an old maid," said Patty, sipping her punch. "You can wear all purple clothes and work at the Doll House shop with Miss Cricket."

"I'm not gonna be an old maid," said Louise, indignant. She was pretty and used to people telling her so, which made it easy for Patty to get her goat.

"I guess you can marry a Carper," Patty said. "Be a mountain wife with twelve kids and eat possums."

"Patty!" Louise's pretty face was red.

Patty shrugged, pleased with herself.

The girls watched in silence as the boys made their way through the theater. They were all dressed up—nobody's mama would let them go to the Greenbrier without a tie—and the slight discomfort of the fancy clothes made them strut even more cockily, just to show they didn't care. They stopped for a ring toss, and when Lee won a chocolate Christmas tree, he handed it to a little girl standing in the Santa line. His smile was as white and even as Pat Boone's. Doree imagined his arm around her as they—dressed to the nines and on a proper date—swanned into the Greenbrier dining room, a maître d' leading them to the best table, the one directly beneath the chandelier.

"Doesn't Doree have to marry a Jew?" said Louise suddenly.

Doree felt an angry prickle at the back of her neck, but she kept smiling.

"Be polite, Louise," said Wanda.

"I'm being polite. I'm just saying."

"Doree can marry whoever she feels like marrying," Patty said crisply. "But not until we're both done with college."

That shut Louise up. Louise didn't have the grades for college, and the Levels didn't have the money either. Louise would go work at the resort too, along with most of the high school's graduating class.

Doree reached up and touched her ponytail. The curls had gone flat—nothing she could do about that now. But the ribbon was slipping. That needed fixing.

"Excuse me." She got up and picked her way through the carnival games and out to the ladies' room.

*T*he calamine pink–painted ladies' room was silent and heavy with the fragrance of the tall vases of lilies on either side of the sink. Doree moved slowly, washing her hands twice with glossy pink soap and drying them with a white hand towel from the top of a pyramid of rolled-up towels in a wicker basket. She untied her yellow hair ribbon and tied it again, pulling it into an even bow.

She gave herself a long look. She was pretty too, she knew that. Slender neck, big light brown eyes. Her nose wasn't any bigger than any other girl's.

Doesn't Doree have to marry a Jew?

The Zelners were the only Jews in White Sulphur Springs. Until a few years ago there had been Matthew Portnoff, the Greenbrier's dinnertime organist, too. But he retired and moved to Florida. So now it was just the Zelners. They were the only Jews all the way to Lewisburg, where Mr. Saltzman was a timekeeper for the C&O Railway. The nearest synagogue was in Beckley, so that's where they went on the High Holidays. A traveling rabbi came every two weeks to help Pete with his bar mitzvah lessons. Other than that, they were pretty much the same as anyone else in White Sulphur Springs, except they kept two sets of dishes and they didn't eat pork. Except Alan, who never followed a rule that didn't make sense to him personally.

Squaring her shoulders and tossing her hair, Doree put on her biggest smile as she walked back into the party.

*T*he noise seemed to have doubled by the time Doree got inside. Half a dozen Level kids were racing around the stage with the rubber mallets from the beanbag launcher. A little girl in a velvet-trimmed bonnet was perched on Santa's knee, screaming, her body straining desperately towards her mother. The Chipmunk song came on, and Dewey and the other freshmen started shrieking along comically.

Where is Alan? Doree spotted Pete and Tommy sitting on the stage steps, plates of cookies balanced on their knobby twelve-year-old knees.

"Have you seen Alan?" she asked. "And go easy on the cookies—they're for everyone, not just y'all."

Pete and Tommy shrugged. Doree backed out of the theater and looked down the hallway. Nothing. She stood next to the coat table, chatting with Carol for a few minutes in case he'd gone to the restroom and was going to come back. But she didn't see him anywhere.

"I've got to go find Alan," Doree told Carol. "It was really loud in there. You know how he gets when it's loud."

She hurried down the glossy green-painted hallway, peeking into any partially open door. She passed a private dining room, where a chef was carving a glossy mahogany-colored duck atop a wheeled cart. On the veranda, a knot of men in flannel suits were smoking cigars, coatless despite the cold. In the Greenbrier Shops corridor, she nearly bumped into a couple coming out of the jewelry store, the man holding a beribboned box, the woman resting her head against his shoulder.

Sometimes Alan liked to come to the newsstand to look at stamps. But no one was browsing the racks of pipes and tobacco and magazines today except a man with an old-fashioned waxed mustache.

Sometimes Alan liked to talk to Joe the shoeshine man, who was always happy to listen to him ramble on about car engines or carnivorous plants. But Joe had already packed up his kit and gone home.

Finally, just as the anxiety was beginning to rise in Doree's throat, she found Alan. He was standing by the French doors in the mostly empty West Lobby, looking down on the grounds. Doree came up and stood beside him. It was dark already, and the lawns were lit with spotlights. Hundreds of tiny lanterns illuminated the paths that led to the golf course and spring house and cottages. Beyond, on Copeland Hill, the windows in the employee dormitories glowed yellow.

"Alan, what are you doing? Did you eat?"

Alan didn't turn. "Look what they're doing."

"Who? Doing what?"

"They're digging something."

Doree looked. The lawn below the back veranda was marked off with orange surveyor's tape. At the near corner, a diesel motor shovel sat in shadows. Below it was a hole. A square-shaped hole with neat corners.

"They're adding a wing, Mrs. Curry said," she told him. "Neat, huh?"

"But why is that hole so deep?"

"I don't know, Alan, I can't tell how deep it is."

"Deeper than a normal foundation."

"How do you know?" Doree knew how he knew, of course. Alan had gone through a phase of fascination with construction and mining equipment that had lasted nearly up to his bar mitzvah. He could identify any machine from a block away. Everyone figured he was going to be an engineer. But then he'd abruptly dropped the interest before his birthday and requested stamp-collecting books for gifts. Now, at nearly sixteen, plants had become his latest fascination. He could identify every living thing along Howard's Creek and in the Greenbrier Forest. But who cared about the difference between a swamp white oak and a sugar maple? Nobody, not unless they wanted to tap for maple syrup.

"Gotta be fifty feet deep," he said. His face was so close to the French doors his breath steamed the glass.

"So what? Let's go back to the party." Lee and them probably wouldn't stay long.

"Why would they need a fifty-foot-deep foundation?" Alan said, not moving.

"Ask Mrs. Curry to ask Johnny Burdette. Come on."

"I already ate."

"We're not here just to eat. There's going to be a Christmas cake soon. And then there's a raffle. First prize is a BB gun, so I know Pete will want to stay for that."

"Mama doesn't like us playing with BB guns."

"Yes, well, Mama doesn't like us eating ham, but you had about two platefuls of pinwheels from the looks of you."

Alan gave her a blank stare. His tie was smeared with cream cheese.

Doree felt a flash of impatience. "I just want to have fun with my friends for a little bit. Come on."

"How many minutes is 'a little bit'?"

Doree sighed. "We'll leave right after the raffle, okay?"

As they walked back to the party, Doree saw Lee leaving the

ballroom with the rest of the basketball boys. She tried to catch his eye, but he slipped around the corner too quickly. Suddenly, out of nowhere, Edisto Level's pointy face was close to hers and her nose filled with the sharp odor of sweat and carbolic soap.

"Real Americans first, weirdo," he said, elbowing Alan and pushing ahead. Edisto had been taunting Alan ever since Alan got called to the principal's office for refusing to say the Pledge of Allegiance. ("How can you have allegiance to a flag?" Alan had said, baffled. "It's an inanimate object. It doesn't make sense.")

"Grow up, Edisto," Doree hissed.

Honestly, those boys were such children. Not Lee, though. Lee was all right. At least he never gave Alan a hard time.

*D*oree, Alan, and Pete left through the North Entrance and walked home in the dark. It was cold and silent, and Doree felt the high spirits of the party draining as she picked her way across Howard's Creek in her kitten heels. Pete was also quiet, disappointed he hadn't won the BB gun and queasy from platefuls of meringues and gingerbread men. He slouched along, swinging his red sateen loot bag and dragging his feet through the damp leaves. Only Alan was peppy, talking to himself about the hole behind the West Lobby—was it really fifty feet, or only forty-five? Where had the digger come from? Could they be burying new power cables? Doree ignored him.

As they turned onto Spring Street and approached the porch of the narrow blue house, Doree went through her checklist. Was her hair a mess? Had the boys torn or stained anything? She'd already dabbed at Alan's cream cheese–smeared tie with a wet napkin.

"Pete, wipe your shoes," she whispered, as the porch light illuminated the leaves plastered to the front of Pete's black dress shoes.

Pete gave her a sullen glance and scraped his feet against the steps.

Before she could give Pete a final look, he was already through the front door. Doree followed. The entranceway was unlit, and the door to Grandpa's room was closed—he went to sleep so early these days, almost as early as Grandma, who was tucked away up in the old nursery where she lived now. On the hall table, the china bird with the glued-on head stared at her with its blank little eyes. She sniffed the air. Mama *could* have cooked—the Sabbath, with its prohibition on cooking, would have ended long before suppertime because of the early winter dark. But Doree couldn't smell any food, so her parents and grandparents must have had a cold supper. A bit of tinny TV music wafted through the house, and Doree felt herself relax. Her father must be in his easy chair in the back parlor watching *People Are Funny*. Doree would make herself a plate from the fridge and go join him, curling up on the settee in the golden light of the stained glass lamp. Perry Como would come on next.

As her brothers disappeared upstairs, Doree slipped off her heels and opened the fridge, pulling out a platter of cold sliced lamb and a jar of her mother's beet pickles. She put them on a plate along with a slice of white bread from the bread box and poured herself a glass of orange juice.

She was about to go into the hall to the back parlor when she heard the floorboard squeak, which meant someone was about to come down the stairs. Then footsteps. Her mother appeared in the arched kitchen doorway.

Mama's hair was in curlers, and she wore a white nightgown

with a scalloped hem. Even with her face scrubbed clean, her lips were still a bitten red.

"What are you doing?" Sylvia looked at her daughter with narrowed eyes.

"Getting some supper." Doree closed the refrigerator and stood looking across the table at her mother, plate in hands. The slice of bread was quickly turning a wet pink from the beet juice.

"They didn't feed you at your party?" *Zey didn't feed you.* Even after all these years in America, Mama's *th* still sometimes came out as a *z*.

"They had food, but I didn't get a chance to eat very much."

"I should think such a fancy *Christmas*"—her voice deepened with disgust—"party with the goyim would have so much nice food."

"The food was nice. I just didn't get a chance to eat very much."

Even in her nightgown and curlers, Sylvia was still as beautiful as the most rouged and spa-treated Greenbrier guest. Some people said she looked like the actress Ruth Roman. She had Ruth Roman's high arched brows and almond eyes, and the flared nostrils that made her look angry even on the rare occasion she wasn't.

Doree picked up her glass of juice. Sylvia didn't move from the doorway.

"You think you will eat in the parlor?"

"Mama, I'm not going to spill anything." She was almost eighteen!

"You will eat in the kitchen," Sylvia said, taking a step forward.

"Fine."

"Good." Sylvia gave her daughter a long look. "You're not as clever as you think, remember this," she said. Then she turned around and walked slowly up the stairs.

Doree looked down at her plate. The bread was beginning to

come apart in sodden pink clumps, and the lamb had an oily sheen under the bluish kitchen light. She drank her juice, then scrapped the plate into the trash and headed down the hall to the parlor. But by the time she got there, her father had already turned off the TV and disappeared upstairs, and the room was dark and silent except for the wheeze of the radiator.

Doree walked upstairs feeling limp and deflated. Why could she not have the simplest thing for herself? An hour at the Christmas party without worrying about Alan. A sandwich in front of the television. Alan didn't mean to spoil things; it was just his nature. But her mother—it was as if her mother's only goal in life was keeping Doree from what she wanted.

CHAPTER 3

❧

Sylvia

*T*he Italians arrived at the Greenbrier the day Carole Lombard died. Her plane had taken off from Las Vegas and never arrived in California. The radio repeated the story every hour with the rest of the news bulletin: British retreat in Malaya. More U-boats sunk. The Pan-American conference proving a tremendous success. They said Clark Gable had chartered a private plane to find the crash site, that he was beside himself with grief.

Sylvia had only seen one Carole Lombard film—*Mr. & Mrs. Smith*, at the Greenbrier cinema with Louis last winter. Doree had been a week overdue then and was rolling with such vigor beneath Sylvia's box-pleated dress that Sylvia could barely get a breath. She hardly looked at the screen the entire film. She didn't know Carole Lombard from Jean Arthur or Rosalind Russell.

Yet every hour, when the horns of the news bulletin began to sound on the store radio, Sylvia would relax her shoulders and allow the tears to begin.

"It's so sad, isn't it?" asked a customer, a middle-aged woman with a face as white and lumpy as cheese curds, hearing the bulletin and noting Sylvia's glazed pink eyes. "She was such a pretty girl."

It was a relief, having something official to cry about. It made the great swell of tears inside her feel less like private insanity. A woman with a husband and a new baby and a successful business should be happy—or at least cheerful—even if there was a war on. But Sylvia wasn't. She was wretched.

They had no idea, these customers. They had such pride in their horrid little mud-splattered town. *Home of the world-famous Greenbrier.* Feh! It felt like just a minute ago Sylvia had been flouncing down Piotrkowska Street in Lodz—a *real* city—arms linked with her best friend, Ewa, satin ribbons from her father's factory in her hair. Then she'd blinked and found herself in these dark mountains, in this strange land, a shopkeeper's wife, stocking shelves in a daze, nodding numbly as her husband—her *husband*! How was it possible that this man was her husband?—droned on about inventory and discounts. Some days she could straighten her back and bear the misery and unfairness of it all. But not today.

Easier to say you were crying over poor Carole what's-her-name.

During the afternoon lull, Sylvia allowed herself to weep freely while rearranging the stock ahead of the payday rush. Louis was in the back, working on the books, and Martin, the clerk, didn't come in until three. She stacked folded dungarees into a pyramid shape and put a SPECIAL SALE! sign on the rack of brassieres. She moved the baskets of ladies' notions away from the cash register—nobody wanted to mend seams on a payday—and replaced them with a tray of Bakelite bangles. Then she rearranged the heavy glass candy jars—licorice laces, horehound drops, chocolate Tootsie Rolls, paper-wrapped hunks of Turkish taffy, wax bottles full of sinisterly colored sugar water. The more feral of the town children would decapitate the bottles with their incisors and spit the tops directly on the store's wooden floor.

On Friday paydays, the Greenbrier day shift employees would stream out the back gates and down Main Street at six, eager to try on new hats and buy bags of candies for their sweethearts. By then Sylvia would be gone, walking home in the cold to light the Shabbos candles and put the baby to bed. It would hardly be a real Shabbos, not with Louis working, but things were different here in America. You can't shut the store on payday evening just because you're Jewish, not when everyone else in town is a gentile with a hot handful of money to spend.

The door jingled and Martin came in, rubbing his dented egg of a head. He'd just woken up, probably—he often stayed up all night studying for his correspondence degree in accounting. Soon he'd go back to Baltimore and they'd have to find a new shop clerk.

"How you doing, Mrs. Zelner?" he asked, shuffling behind the counter.

"It could be worse," said Sylvia. "I am going home now. Louis is in the back."

"Another bunch is coming to the Greenbrier tonight," Martin called, as Sylvia scooped up a bag of clothes to take home for alterations. "Everyone's going to the train station to see. More Krauts, I guess."

More Krauts.

"Hmmm," said Sylvia, dismissing Martin with a half wave. She pushed open the front door with ZELNER'S LOW PRICE STORE printed in gold letters and stood on the sidewalk.

More Krauts.

Their precious resort. The pride of Greenbrier County. The vast white wedding cake of a building that dominated the coal-black hills. The reason this miserable town even existed at all.

Now it was full of Nazis.

When America had declared war the month before, Washington rounded up the German diplomats and embassy workers. But no one knew what to do with them. They couldn't let them run loose in America, and they couldn't put them in prison—that was against international law, as Louis explained to Sylvia many times. So someone had called up the manager of the Greenbrier, and, not two weeks after the Pearl Harbor bombings, they'd begun sending detained diplomats and their families to White Sulphur Springs.

It had been a slushy gray December morning when a special all-Pullman train pulled up at White Sulphur Springs Station. Fifty or so townspeople gathered on the road across from the tracks. The men were stoic, faces white with cold and anger. The women whispered to one another in loud hisses. Several of the children gathered small rocks in their pockets. Sylvia was there on her own, with Doree in the carriage. She'd told Louis she was going for a walk.

As the first Germans stepped down from the train, the crowd began to murmur. There were men in rumpled suits and bowler hats, women in fox fur–trimmed wool, their hair undone, clutching hatboxes or children's hands.

"They look *regular*," said one little boy in wonder.

Sylvia, of course, already knew that Nazis looked regular. What, Americans thought they'd look like the villains in Detective Comics?

That night, Sylvia and Louis had had a screaming fight. Well, Sylvia screamed.

"Nazis! Getting into Greenbrier Rolls-Royce cars! Something so disgusting I've never seen!"

"What should we do with enemy diplomats, Sylvia?" Louis said, sitting in his easy chair, continuing to sip an after-supper coffee. "We can't put them in prison."

"We can't put them in prison, so we should put them in the Greenbrier? The Greenbrier that is so beautiful—so *luxurious*—this is where American presidents go? The Nazis should go where the presidents go?"

"As far as I understand, the Greenbrier was chosen because it's remote," Louis said. "The Germans can't go sending messages to their allies by Morse code and so forth. I heard they're even going to take the newspapers out of the newsstand."

"Remote? They want remote, they should put them in Carper's."

Carper's Travel Paradise was a tourist camp of dingy clapboard cabins in a field at the far end of Main Street. The only people who ever stayed there were fishermen, and the assorted male Carpers who used it as a drinking spot.

"These people are diplomats, Sylvia."

"These people are Nazis, *Louis!*"

"There's a tit for tat here, you know. If we put their diplomats in a filthy hovel, what will they do to ours?"

"You think we put their people in the Greenbrier and this means they'll put the Americans in the Potsdam palace? Ha! They'll do what they want. They don't follow rules—they make rules."

"Not in America, Sylvia," Louis said, with that look of awful reasonableness. She wanted to slap it right off his face. He had no idea what the world was really like. None!

"Not in America. Ha! Not in Poland? Not in France?"

Louis's parents, Pauline and Sol, came into the parlor. "So much noise!" said Sol, who was carrying a cup of tea.

"We're just discussing where the government should send the German diplomats. Sylvia doesn't think they should stay somewhere so nice as the Greenbrier."

"They should stay in a hole in the ground!"

"That's not how we treat even our enemies in America," said Pauline, her thin lips set primly in her pointy little fox face. "We're not animals." She sat down on the sofa with her cross-stitch. She pretended to begin embroidering, but Sylvia could tell she was waiting, anticipating.

Sylvia felt her nostrils flare. Her arms itched. How she longed to reach out and fling the stained glass lamp across the parlor. How satisfying it would be to see it smash on the fireplace tiles and watch Pauline's shriveled mouth tighten in shock.

"They'll be here for a little while only, Sylvie," Sol said soothingly. "Just until the governments can work out a way to trade them. You know what Lyle VanDonk tells me?"—Lyle VanDonk, the chief handyman at the Greenbrier, was more of a gossip than any Polish yenta—"He says the waiters will spit in the Nazis' soup at dinner—maybe even worse!"

"I'm certain that's not true," Pauline said.

Sol shrugged and gave Sylvia a wink.

Sylvia sighed and shook her head. Sol always knew how to make her feel better, even just a little.

On New Year's Eve, a few weeks after the first detainees had appeared, more Germans arrived. Then came the staff of the Hungarian and Bulgarian embassies. Now, barely two weeks into January, they were bringing more?

Sylvia stood outside Zelner's in the pale winter sunlight, fury throbbing in the pit of her belly. Nazis, lounging on crisp white resort sheets. Nazis, swimming in the indoor pool. Nazis, breakfasting on strawberries and cream. Sickening. Unfathomable. America was supposed to be fair and strong. The poster in the post office showed the boot of Uncle Sam crushing a three-headed snake: Hitler, Mussolini, Hirohito. *Stamp 'Em Out*. She hadn't understood the pun; Louis had to explain. But where was the boot of Uncle Sam now? Strawberries and cream. Feh!

She turned towards home, then turned back again. Why go home? The narrow house, its paint the faint blue-gray of a corpse flesh, was always cold. Pauline would be in the kitchen, feeding Doree supper with her horrifying efficiency. For Pauline, Doree would open her little mouth for the spoon like a bird taking a worm. For Sylvia, she would only cry and smear cereal in her hair.

So she walked the other way down Main Street, pulling her coat tighter as a stabbing mountain wind drove leaves around her ankles. A farmer rumbled by in a truck loaded with cabbages. This truly was *hotseplots*—the middle of nowhere. Not what she'd imagined when Louis had proposed back in Baltimore. *Charming*, he'd said. *And right in the shadow of one of America's most famous resorts*. She'd imagined Ciechocinek, where she'd gone to take the waters with her mother and aunts several times, with its villas and gardens and cafés along the river.

Ha!

As Sylvia approached the station, she could see that there was indeed a crowd. A line of Greenbrier bellhops stood at attention in front of a fleet of green resort Rolls-Royces. Could the Nazis not walk up the resort driveway by themselves?

Sylvia joined the crowd at the back. A woman turned to her. It was one of the councilmen's wives, a woman with a name like a bird's chirp, but Sylvia couldn't remember exactly what. Sylvia had sewn a dress for her. Green cotton, with a heart-shaped neckline and gathered bodice. It had come out nicely.

"They say it's not Krauts this time," the woman said.

"Oh?"

"You reckon it's Japs?" the woman said. She had lipstick on her teeth and an air of excitement, as if this were a party.

"I wouldn't know."

"Naw," said a second woman, a bony blonde with a flushed, shiny face. "They sent all the Japs to the Homestead over yonder in Hot Springs."

Sylvia had heard this already. The Japanese diplomats and their families were being kept at the Homestead Resort across the Virginia state line. Sol said the Homestead was just as grand as the Greenbrier, but it was gentiles only and didn't have so many movie stars, so some of the more hoity-toity Southerners thought it was classier.

"Train's comin'," called a child.

The dark green snout of the C&O *George Washington* appeared, sheets of oily black smoke billowing in its wake. It came to a stop at the station with a painfully loud hiss. Immediately, the platform was a whirr of energy, with baggagemen alighting and handing off trunk after trunk to the waiting bellmen. Several soldiers followed, shouting instructions Sylvia couldn't hear amid the commotion.

As the rush subsided, an old man stepped down from the train. He was short, with a scythe of a nose, hooded eyes, and sparse black hair slicked straight back. His bearing suggested importance—an ambassador, perhaps. He wore a three-piece suit, an overcoat folded sharply over one arm. He looked around slowly, then took out a cigarette. Before he could light it, a second man had stepped down from the train and reached out with a lighter. Several other men followed, all with black hair and three-piece suits. Even from a distance Sylvia could see their shoes were shiny enough to reflect the wooden beams of the train platform's ceiling.

"Lord have mercy, are those *Italians*?" exhaled the councilman's wife.

The words were barely out of her mouth before another several dozen people were streaming out of the train. More men in dark suits with unreadable faces. They descended the train steps and stretched their arms and necks, as casually as if they were arriving home after a long day at work. Then came women with brightly lipsticked mouths beneath tired eyes, prodding along little girls in dark braids and boys in short pants and vests. They carried hatboxes and furs—some had two or three furs piled in their arms. One older girl clutched an instrument case nearly as tall as she was.

"You live long enough you see everything, I reckon," the councilman's wife said.

Twila. That was her name.

"This is not everything," Sylvia said, fixing her eyes on Twila. "This is not half of everything. This is not even a tiny, tiny piece of everything."

Twila stared back at Sylvia, goggle-eyed.

Sylvia snorted, turned around, left.

*A*s she closed the front door, the eyes of the ceramic bird on the hallway table fixed on her accusingly, as if the little figurine was a stand-in for her mother-in-law.

Not a moment later, Pauline herself appeared in the kitchen doorway, frowning and wiping her hands on her frilled apron.

"Where were you? Doree is already asleep. She had a whole bowl of cereal and she was still hungry, so I gave her a bottle of Carnation—I didn't know if you'd be home to feed her or not."

"A baby does not need to be in bed by six o'clock. It's so early."

"It's healthiest."

The two women stared at each other from across the green enamel kitchen table. Sylvia hated that table, the chilly underwater color of hospital walls. But when Sylvia moved in, Pauline had made it clear there would be no redecorating, that *she* was still the lady of the house.

Pauline blinked first. "Sol's having his bath," she said. "We'll do Shabbos when he comes down. There's a chicken in the icebox."

We'll do Shabbos when he comes down. After nearly two years of living with these people, their attitude towards Jewish observance was still perplexing. You lit the Shabbos candles twenty minutes before dark, not whenever you were done with your bath! But if Sylvia complained to Pauline, Pauline would only laugh and call her a greenhorn. *You Galitzianers are so old-fashioned*, she loved to say. *Things are different here.*

How Sylvia would love to march her mother-in-law down Piotrkowska Street, with its merchants' mansions and glittering cafés. How Pauline would gawp at Sylvia's house in Lodz, twice as big as this one, with its wrought iron balcony and delicate floral molding around the windows. *Things are different in Poland*, Sylvia would say.

The floor creaked, and her father-in-law appeared in the kitchen doorway in his dressing gown.

"This is how you dress for Shabbos dinner?" Pauline said.

"What, you want I should wear a tuxedo?"

Sol was a tiny man, even smaller than Pauline. His back, bent from years of carrying a peddler's pack through the West Virginia coalfields, made him look smaller still. He had wet brown eyes and a large, rubbery nose. One of his stick-out ears was half the size of the other one, capped by a ridge of scar tissue. He smiled at Sylvia. She felt her anger ebb. It was hard not to feel better when Sol was around.

Pauline sniffed and began setting the table. Cold roast chicken, carrot salad, a loaf of homemade challah beneath a hand-embroidered cover. Then she covered her head with her white lace mantilla, lit the candles, and raised her hands to her eyes.

Baruch ata Adonai, Eloheinu melekh ha'olam

Asher kid'shanu b'mitzvotav v'tzivanu l'hadlik ner shel Shabbat

The familiar words, the smell of the challah beneath its fringed cover, and the lit match lingering in the air. Sylvia could see her own mother at the end of their long wooden dining table set with silver, her face glowing in candlelight. But while Sylvia's mother had sung the words, Pauline chanted them atonally. The loneliness sat heavily in the pit of Sylvia's stomach, as if she'd swallowed a cold stone.

When the prayers were done, Sol rubbed his hands together and began loading his plate.

"Your stomach, Sol," Pauline said. She pursed her lips and looked at Sylvia. "He won't live past sixty if we don't watch him."

"The ulcer won't kill me," Sol said. "It will only just make me miserable. You make it worse by trying to starve me!" He cut a thick slice of challah and began to slather it with oleomargarine. "How was the shop today?"

"Fine," Sylvia said. "No problems."

"I heard there would be some new arrivals at the Greenbrier today," Sol said. He gave Sylvia a long look. "Have you heard too?"

Sol knew her better than anyone. Was it because they were both strangers in this land?

"Yes. Italians."

"Italians. Ah. Interesting."

"Why interesting? More fascist rubbish who will eat nicer food and sleep in nicer beds than anyone else in this town."

"Yes," Sol said thoughtfully. "They are fascists. But I wonder. Is the Italian fascist the same as the German fascist? Or is he different?"

"Different? Different how? Fascist is fascist."

"I knew many Italians in the coalfields," Sol said. "Pick-and-shovel miners. Very dangerous job. The Americans, they worked the undercutting machines. For the Italians and the colored men, pick and shovel. They were very friendly to me. Always invite me to dinner when I come to town with my heavy pack, so scrawny. Us Jews, only the women cook. But the Italian men—they can cook too! Italians have helped me very much."

"So you met some nice Italians, and what?" Sylvia said. "There are nice German people, perhaps. But those ones in the resort? Those are enemies."

"I don't like this talk at dinner, not on the Sabbath—it's uncouth," Pauline said. "I'm going to take a plate down to Louis and Martin at the store."

"I will do it," Sylvia said, standing up abruptly. But just then, a muffled wail sounded from the upstairs.

"Better you go take care of your baby." Pauline smirked. "She probably wants her mother."

*T*he baby was sitting upright in her bassinet, her eyes shining in the dark like a cat's. She wore a white flannel gown Sylvia had sewn and embroidered with roses, and her feet were bare—she'd kicked off her socks again. The blankets were crumpled at the foot of the crib. Not yet one, and already so restless, so full of cleverness and desire. At the sight of Sylvia, she raised her arms and opened and closed her little fists. Want. Want.

Sylvia picked her up. "Shhhhshhhh, *zeeskeit*." She sat down in the rocking chair and unbuttoned her dress.

The baby latched on, and her body immediately relaxed into Sylvia's. Sylvia tucked the baby's bare feet into her armpit to keep them warm. She began to rock. After not nursing since lunchtime, the feeling of her breasts letting down their milk was a relief. She could hear the click, click, click of the baby's steady swallows.

Doreen Helen Zelner. Her daughter. Even after nearly a year, it felt so strange to say.

Louis had picked her first name. He heard it on a radio play and thought it sounded smart. Sylvia had chosen Helen, for her maternal grandmother, Chaja. Everyone assumed she was being sentimental, naming her baby after her beloved grandmother, dead for a decade back in Poland. But the truth was, Sylvia had no real fondness for Chaja. Chaja, a widow, had been half-deaf and spent most of her time in the back bedroom, mumbling over her battered copy of *Tseno Ureno*, the Yiddish women's Bible. Like many Galitzianers, she was immensely superstitious—if you called someone pretty or mentioned an upcoming birthday in her presence, she'd scream *kein ayin hara* to ward off the evil eye. She hated Litvaks, the Lithuanian Jews who'd begun streaming into Lodz after the pogroms. Chaja thought the Litvaks were no better than gypsies. The men, modern and clean-shaven in short coats, their women bareheaded, their observance of commandments haphazard: Were they even Jews? Once, when a Litvak neighbor asked to borrow a cooking pot, Chaja had slammed the door in her face. The Litvak would curse the pot, Chaja said, and all our food would curdle.

The Zelners were Litvaks.

If Pauline had come to Chaja's door looking to borrow a pot, Chaja would have slammed the door in her face. Sylvia kept this truth close to her heart, a secret lucky pebble to take out and rub between thumb and forefinger in times of strain.

Doree released Sylvia's breast with a sigh, and flopped backwards, asleep, a pearl of milk on her parted lips.

Sylvia looked down at her daughter's sleeping face. "When you grow big, if anyone is cruel, you will slam the door in their face too," she whispered.

CHAPTER 4

❧

Sol

*T*he knock on the door came two weeks after Sol's seventeenth birthday.

Yitzhak Rausk was married to one of Sol's cousins up in Rudamina. "It's time, Sol," Yitzhak said, twisting his cap in his fat hands.

Sol's mother came running from the kitchen. "Nonsense!" she cried. "He's only just seventeen! Boys must be eighteen for the tsar's army! Eighteen!"

Yitzhak shrugged and looked over his shoulder. "I'm only the messenger."

Sol's mother let out a wail. Dina, the youngest of his sisters, who'd crept up behind her mother and was watching Yitzhak with big round eyes, began to sob. Sol put his arm around her. "Shhh, *zeeskeit*, it's all right. It'll be fine."

Everyone knew what happened to Jewish boys drafted into the tsar's army. Some changed their names to avoid it. Some moved to Vilna with fake papers. The older brother of Sol's best friend had cut off his own right index finger. But he didn't cut off enough, and they took him anyway. No one had heard from him since.

Sol's mother wasn't taking any chances with her only son. Years before, she'd sewn a leather pouch, filled it with rubles, and hidden it in the rafters of the house. As soon as Yitzhak left, she went to get the ladder.

"You'll take the first wagon to Vilna in the morning," she told Sol. "Then the train west. A ship leaves from Bremen, in Germany."

Then she gave him his father's watch.

The pocket watch was silver, with a Star of David engraved on the back. The face had numbers in Hebrew on a glossy cream background. On the border was a raised braid pattern that reminded Sol of his sisters' hair or of the challah his mother baked on Fridays.

It was nicer, and undoubtably more expensive, than anything Sol had ever owned. Before his father died, the family had been quite comfortable—his father had been a timber merchant, earning enough to keep the family in beef and furnish the house with thick green velvet curtains. After he was gone, Sol's mother did what she could. There was the money from the ketubah, of course. She also kept chickens and sold their eggs, which were large and the light brown of milky tea. Sometimes she'd sell one of the family's goats. Still, the watch spoke to Sol of better times.

"If you need money, you sell that," his mother said, placing the watch in Sol's hand. "Don't be sentimental. Your father wasn't sentimental." Then she went to the kitchen to boil eggs for his journey.

All Sol knew about his father he'd heard from his three older sisters, Freya, Raisel, and Dina. Freya, seven years older than Sol, should have remembered the most, but all she ever talked about was a song their father would sing, about a little bird alighting on a branch. Raisel, though three years younger than Freya, remembered much more. She was the one who told Sol their father's eyes had been a rich gold-brown like the color of honey in the summer, when the bees fed on the flowering buckwheat. She was the one who talked about the sound of his voice as he said his prayers, so deep you could feel its rumble through the floorboards. How he used to pick the girls up and hang them upside down and tickle their stomachs until they cried. Once he held Raisel too close to the fire by accident and her hair was scorched.

Dina didn't say much, but Dina, barely a year older than Sol, couldn't talk much. She'd been born simple. She spent most of her time underfoot in the kitchen, playing with a ball of dough or a doll so old its button eyes had long since disappeared. She remembered their father, though; Sol could tell. When they visited the cemetery, she'd spend ages finding the roundest, most perfect pebbles to lay atop the grave, to show their father had not been forgotten.

When Sol left the following morning, Dina was the only one who didn't cry. *See you soon*, she said, waving over and over, as if Sol were just taking a goat to market and would be back in the evening.

As Sol climbed into the wagon, he wiped his own tears away with the cuff of his jacket. But there was another feeling underneath the sadness. Excitement. It came upon him in big shivery waves as he watched the shtetl disappear behind the pine trees. *Gam zu l'tova*, he whispered to himself. It was his favorite Talmud line (one of the only he remembered; Sol was no scholar). *Even this is for the best*. He was seventeen, he was leaving home, a whole new life lay ahead of him.

He was going to Amerika.

. . .

*T*he leather pouch made a bulge under Sol's shirt, though by the time he got on the ship at Bremen, he'd lost so much weight it fitted neatly into the hollow beneath his rib cage. He'd eaten all the boiled eggs and crackers and dried apples his mother had sent with him, and he'd been too afraid to take any money out of the pouch to buy more food from the shops along the train route.

He gained the weight back in the ten days it took to sail to Baltimore. Most of the other passengers in steerage found the food inedible and were seasick to boot. But Sol stuffed himself three times a day with brown bread and herring, salt meat and rice, liver and prunes. His bunkmates, a family of friendly Galitzianers, shared their mandelbrot with him. He never felt seasick, not even during a rolling storm that made the bunks creak and luggage crash to the floor. He was just lucky, he guessed.

Sitting on his bunk as his bunkmates retched and moaned, Sol examined the leather pouch. It was so carefully stitched. And all done in secret. His mother must have been worrying over it when Sol was still a little boy making mud pies behind the chicken coop, not a care in his head.

*S*ol disembarked at Locust Point on the most beautiful day he'd ever seen. It had still been winter in Europe, but in Baltimore, somehow, it was spring. Fingers of dawn light fell through the windows of the pier building where Sol waited to have his papers stamped. By the time he got outside, it was warm enough to take off his jacket. He stood there for a moment, watching the rising sun turn the bricks of Baltimore golden, just breathing in the air. American air.

Sol's mother had told him to ask the first Jew he saw where to find a synagogue. The rabbi would direct him to a relief society, who would help him find work and a place to live.

But as Sol stood, breathing, someone yelled at him: *"Hei, yid?"*

Sol turned and saw a boy of ten or twelve with a freckled face and bronze curls under a yarmulke. "Hey, kiddo," he called back in Yiddish. "Yep, I'm Jewish."

"Do you want a job?" the boy said. "I know a guy who can give you one."

Sol smiled and shrugged. Couldn't hurt to find out what the kid was offering. "Sure."

He picked up his bag and followed the boy through the morning streets of Baltimore, streets full of sights he'd never imagined. There was a man selling what looked like rocks from a wheelbarrow. He'd pop the rocks open with a knife, and customers would put them to their mouths and slurp. ("Oysters," the boy explained. "Tref.") A woman leaned from a second-story window, calling to someone in the street. Sol looked up and saw she had skin the dark brown of his hair. Most marvelous of all was the electric streetcar zipping down the tracks; even in Vilna the tram was still pulled by horses.

Finally, they came to a tall brick building with dozens of windows. Carts and motor trucks were unloading boxes and bales by a side door, and dozens of men in shirtsleeves were ferrying the goods inside.

"This is the Baltimore Bargain House," the boy said. "Come inside and I'll take you to Mr. Epstein."

Sol smiled. His very first day—his very first hour—in America, and already he was feeling lucky.

CHAPTER 5

Jordan

JANUARY 1992

*H*olding the letter, Jordan stood outside the corner office door. He was still gathering his nerve to knock when a voice from inside shouted, "You gonna come in or what?" Taking a deep breath, Jordan pushed the door open.

Jim Kelley, the *Washington Post*'s Local and Regional news chief, didn't look up from the proofs spread across his desk. His egg-bald head glinted in the fluorescent lights that made everyone in the newsroom look sallow and sickly.

Jordan shifted his weight from foot to foot. Was he supposed to just start talking? "Um, I just received a letter," he said finally. "From an anonymous source."

"An *anonymous source*, huh?" Kelley repeated, still not looking up.

"Yes," Jordan went on. "It's about the Greenbrier Resort, in West Virginia. The letter says there's something underneath it. People ought to know, it said."

"Intriguing."

"I think so? I mean, isn't it?"

"Let me guess," Kelley said, his right hand gliding across the proofs, red slashes blooming in its wake like flesh opening under a surgeon's scalpel. "You want to drive out there to West Virginia to investigate the lead?"

"That's right!" Jordan said, brightening.

Kelley raised his head, his mouth twisted at the corners into a faint smirk. "Look, kid," he said, eyeing Jordan. (Did Kelley think his pants were too long?) "You're new. You're not an Ivy guy. You're"—he squinted at Jordan, as if trying to come up with the right word (Jordan braced himself for "'chubby")—"you're *green*. This letter might be a bit of hazing."

"Hazing?"

Kelley leaned back in his chair. "We had a girl on the desk a few years ago. A *woman*, I guess I should say. Her first week here, the guys sent her a bogus tip about an illegal alligator farm down in St. Mary's County. She spent a couple days out there, confusing the heck out of locals before she figured it out. It's sort of a tradition."

Jordan thought. In high school, Jennifer Liebsky had asked him to meet her after school, and he had shown up holding a poem he'd written, only to get pantsed by Michael Blum. Was this like that?

But no.

A memory: his mother, on the phone to Uncle Pete, pulling the cord taut so she could stand in the pantry with the door half-shut. *If only Alan could have left it alone. We should have kept him away from that place.*

"What if it's not a joke, though?"

"Okay, let's play this out. Name ten things that could possibly be under a hotel."

Jordan did not do his best thinking on the spot. "Well," he said, stalling for time, "an Indian burial ground?"

Kelley gave a snort. "Let me guess—you read *Pet Sematary* when you were twelve?"

He'd been eleven, actually. Jordan blushed. "Something to do with the government? A black site?"

Kelley rolled his eyes. "You been hanging out with the Langley desk?" He finally put down his pen and looked right at Jordan. "Look, if this was real, why would they contact the guy who's been writing town council reports for Local and Regional for all of two months?"

I've been here four *months*, Jordan thought. Trying to formulate a response, he grasped at fragments of memories. *He just wanted to know what they were doing down there*, Uncle Pete had said. *But loose lips sink ships.*

"You want to go rooting around bumfuck, be my guest," Kelley went on. "But not for my section. Pitch something to Ladies. A travel piece. 'A trip back in time at the opulent Greenbrier' or what have you. Just make it back here in time for the county commissioner's meeting."

"Ladies?"

"Yeah, Ladies. You know, the Features section. Stuff ladies read. If you dig up anything real, you can always bring it back to me." Kelley stretched in his chair and gave Jordan a long look. "You ought to spend more time at the bar after work, Jordan. You'll pick up the culture a lot quicker. Maybe the guys won't give you such a hard time."

*T*he Ladies section! Jordan's neck was still hot and red with embarrassment. Not that there was anything wrong with ladies (*women*, seriously, Kelley, it's the nineties!), but this was *news*.

Maybe A1 news! Okay, fine, whatever. He'd pitch Rita Romano in Features and go from there.

As he always did on nights when he didn't have a meeting to cover, Jordan left the office at 7 p.m. exactly, picked up a medium green-pepper pizza at Famous Gino's, and walked home to the apartment he shared off Dupont Circle. He took the stairs to the fourth floor by twos, and got inside to turn on the TV just as the first bar of the *Simpsons* theme sounded. Pleased by his perfect timing, he settled into the caved-in brown couch and opened the pizza box.

Pepperoni.

Damnit. They got his order wrong. Grimacing, he looked around. His mother, of course, would throw it in the trash and call Famous Gino's, demanding a refund—"Of course we can't pick it off; we're *kosher*," she'd say, and her righteous sense of grievance would probably get them a free order of breadsticks too. But Jordan was an adult! He could eat pork if he felt like it. God wasn't going to smite him. Still, the smell as he picked off the pepperoni one by one gave him a sour, itchy feeling of wrongness.

When *The Simpsons* ended, Jordan turned the TV off. He didn't bother to turn the lights on; the room was bathed, as always, in the overbright false moonlight of the streetlight outside the window. His roommate's dirty laundry basket sat next to the TV, abandoned halfway to the washing machine, giving off the damp, mushroomy odor of a locker room. John-Paul, a staffer for an Ohio congressman, was hardly ever home before midnight.

There's something underneath the Greenbrier Resort. It's time for people to know.

All that blood.

He moved to the small desk by the kitchen door, where the squat yellow telephone sat. Its receiver was greasy; John-Paul often ate late-night McDonald's while fighting long distance with his fiancée back in Cleveland.

His mother picked up at the first ring. "Doreen Barber speaking," she said, in her snooty, expecting-a-telemarketer voice. When she realized it was Jordan, her tone transformed. "Hi, sweetheart!" she cried. Then, in a muffled shout as she held the receiver away from her face: "Honey, it's Jordan! Do you want to get on the other phone?"

Jordan was filled with a familiar combination of comfort and irritation. He pictured his mother on the blue floral couch in the rec room, a basket of half-folded laundry beside her, a few squares of her fancy Swiss chocolate on a little plate on the table. *Breaking News Baltimore* would be on, and she'd be clucking at the headlines.

"Jordan, I'm just asking your father if he wants to get on the other line. *What's that? Okay.* He's watching basketball, Jordan. He says to fill him in later. How are you, sweetheart? What's new?"

"Not too much."

"How's work? What are you writing about this week?"

"Just local town council stuff. They want to build a new mall in Fairfax County. Nothing exciting."

"Everybody's got to start at the bottom, sweetheart. Oh, I ran into Mrs. Strauss—you remember her? Your first-grade teacher. She was so thrilled to hear you're at the *Post.* She said she always figured you'd be a meteorologist—you were so into weather the year she had you, always 'tornados this, tornados that.' She said to say mazel tov."

"Thanks."

There was a pause. Then, in a studiously neutral voice: "You haven't heard from your sister, have you?"

"Not since she called from Seattle last month."

"Seattle, my goodness. I hope she's staying dry!" His mother's tone was intently cheerful. "Well, let us know when she calls again. Did you want to come over for Shabbos dinner Friday? Dad could probably leave work early and drive out to pick you up. You could stay the weekend?"

"I can't this weekend, Mom," he said, winding and unwinding the phone's thick yellow cord around his left thumb, and taking a deep breath. "Actually, Mom, can I ask you something? About the Greenbrier?"

"The resort?" His mother's voice was tinged with surprise. "Sure, sweetheart. Why? Are you thinking of going? It's a little out of your price range. It's probably a little out of my and Daddy's price range, if you want the truth. Is there a girl? Are you thinking of taking a girl? Is this a Valentine's Day thing?"

"Mom, chill, no."

"Okay. A mother can ask!"

"It's about . . . there's something there, right? Something under there?"

"What do you mean?" His mother's voice was suddenly tighter, more controlled.

"You've kind of mentioned it over the years. I mean, I've heard you talking to Uncle Pete. The thing that happened to your other brother. And your mom. I know you don't like to talk about it, but I got a letter about it."

"A letter about Alan?" His mother's voice was still controlled. Too controlled.

"No, no, about the resort. It was anonymous. The writer said there was something under the Greenbrier and that people ought to know about it."

There was another pause. He heard his mother swallow. Then,

after a moment, she spoke. "Jordan, promise me you won't go out there. I'm sure this is just somebody's stupid joke."

"I don't understand why it would be a joke."

"Jordan, promise me."

"It's my job, Mom. I'm almost twenty-four!"

"Jordan, please."

There was a click; his father had picked up the extension in the living room. Jordan could hear tinny televised cheering in the background. "How's my man?"

"Hi, Dad."

"Bad news, buddy: Duke won." Jordan's father still never seemed to notice that Jordan didn't care about college basketball. He wasn't big on noticing things, generally. He was a person who, after every meal, rubbed his stomach and said, "That was delicious, absolutely delicious"—whether or not the brisket was dry or the pasta gluey. Jessica used to joke they could feed him a rubber chicken and he'd say it was delicious, absolutely delicious. *The human golden retriever*, she called him. That seemed a little harsh to Jordan. He was a good dad. He worked in sales— something to do with computers or calculators—and watched sports and went cycling on the weekends in an unbelievably dorky spandex outfit and yelled "bravo" embarrassingly loudly at Jordan's clarinet recitals. Dad stuff.

"Oh, sorry," Jordan said.

"Yeah, bummer. We'll get another chance—we play them again at the end of February."

"I better go, guys, I've got a pizza."

"Okay, buddy," his father said. "Love you."

"I love you too, sweetheart," his mother said, sounding almost normal again. "Have a good weekend. And Jordan—"

"What?"

"Please. I'm your mother, and I'm asking you. Please just leave it alone. It's for your own good, I promise."

A memory came to him then, something he hadn't thought about in years. Jessica at fifteen or so, holding a fistful of papers. She'd been snooping in their parents' room. She had a smirk on her face. *I told you*, she'd said. *Mom's got all kinds of secrets.*

At the time he'd dismissed her. But that had been a mistake, hadn't it? If he ever wanted respect—from his sister, from Kelley, from the guys who wrote for A1—he needed to be willing to stop being such a good boy all the damn time.

CHAPTER 6

❧

Doree

JANUARY 1959

Doree couldn't believe how good her ponytail looked. Almost exactly like Shirley Jones's in *April Love*. Brunette, of course, not blond, but she looked as fresh and wholesome as Shirley Jones too, with a floppy white hair bow and a white-and-pink cashmere cardigan. It didn't quite match her coat, but that was okay. She'd hang the coat in the closet as soon as she got to school, and no one would ever see.

It was the first day of the last semester of high school. Doree's whole childhood was behind her. The future would be clean and white, bright as the snow outside. In half a year she'd be at college. She'd wear a twinset with her boyfriend's fraternity pin and attend football games. She'd drink beer and like it. Her ponytail would be a perfect S. Somewhere further down the line would be a husband and babies and a darling little ranch house like the ones in the magazines, very modern. Where? She didn't know. But not here. Far away from here.

Patty was waiting for her by the wall outside school. "We better not have a duck-and-cover drill today," she said, raising her eyebrows at Doree's pristine outfit.

"If we do, I'll kneel on my satchel. How was your vacation?"

"I wouldn't say it was a vacation," Patty said. "Sitting in my aunt and uncle's living room in Columbus is hardly the Riviera."

"Were there any cute boys at least?"

"You are too boy crazy, Doree Zelner." Patty laughed. "No, I did not see one single cute boy the whole week. All we did was watch television with my cousins while my dad helped my uncle build new cabinets. Then we went to see my cousin Billie's baby get baptized. She married a Catholic, so she's a Catholic now. That means she'll have more babies than a Carper by the time she's thirty."

"Was the baby cute at least?"

"Ha! The baby is horrible. Has a face like Alfred Hitchcock. If I had a baby that ugly, I'd give it to the orphanage in Lewisburg."

"You would not. Anyway, you don't want a baby."

"That's right. I'm only getting married for the lovemaking. I'll get a diaphragm."

Patty was the weekend secretary at Dr. Sydenstricker's office, so she knew everything about everything. Once she smuggled an unclaimed diaphragm home and passed it around after school. It was a flesh-colored disk of rubber, rolled at the edges like a pair of stockings. Doree had refused to touch it.

Doree couldn't imagine not wanting a baby. A tiny baby that smelled good like powder and milk, to hold and cuddle. A little piece of love, all for yourself. Why would you not have one if you could? Pete had been her baby for a while, but now he was twelve and the only way to cuddle him would be to tackle him first.

"It's colder than a witch's tit out here," Patty said. Snow had started to fall again. The girls headed into the school. There'd been a small fire in the basement over the holiday, and a faint smell of char lingered alongside the scent of hair oil and the sweet chemical tang of the duplicator machine.

Doree's first class was mathematics, her favorite. As a little girl she'd loved sitting next to her father in the back room of the store, writing down numbers with a Ticonderoga pencil as he dictated them to her. *Smarter than her old dad*, he'd say, bringing her a Hershey's Kiss from the candy display when they were done. Now she was the only girl in Mr. Phillip's advanced geometry class. It was a little embarrassing; she was proud of being a good student, but being *too* good at a boyish subject like math was dangerous. People might start to think you were one of those sexless, shiny-nosed grinds, and then you'd never get a boyfriend.

Alan was in her class too. Alan was only a sophomore, but he'd been so bored in his own math class he'd taken to sitting in the back making animals out of folded paper. So they moved him to Doree's class in the middle of the fall. When he was finished with advanced geometry, he'd have to begin taking courses by correspondence from WVU.

Alan had left the house early that morning to go digging up roots for his plant collection, but was already in the classroom when Doree arrived. Doree sat down two desks behind him. His glasses were crooked and his hair sticking up in dark tufts. He'd been out the door so early that morning she hadn't had a chance to chase him down with a comb. He had mud on the elbows of his sweater, and it had smeared all over the arm of his desk. He was sitting so close to the radiator that steam was rising from his wet socks.

"Alan, if you're going to go digging in the mud before school, you need to wash up in the boys' restroom after," she whispered.

Alan turned around. "I've got a new one for you," he said, slipping her a folded piece of paper.

"Here, wipe your desk at least." She handed him a handkerchief from her schoolbag.

She unfolded the paper. A new cryptogram. A Baconian cipher, if she had to guess. Despite herself, she began translating the *a*'s and *b*'s into binary, glancing around the room to make sure no one was watching. She wasn't too worried, though—advanced math was only for serious students, not the types of rough boys who'd make jokes at Doree's or Alan's expense.

Suddenly, as if just thinking the words "rough boys" had conjured him up, there was Junior Carper, standing in the open classroom doorway. He stopped, and his eyes locked with Doree's. He leaned in and, in a raspy whisper, called to her. "Meet me in the parking lot at lunch. I got somethin' to tell you."

What on earth could Junior Carper want with her? "Beg your pardon?" she said. She looked around to make sure no one noticed them talking, but everyone else was busy taking out their textbooks and chatting about their Christmas vacations.

"You'll see."

Before she could say anything, he turned and disappeared down the hall, whistling tunelessly.

What in the world?

Perplexed, she scrambled to her feet just as Principal Malone started the Pledge of Allegiance over the tinny PA.

You'll see. There was something ominous in his voice. She shook her head, as if to dislodge the image of Junior's pale face from behind her eyelids. Then she reached up to touch her ponytail. It was still reassuringly smooth, with a bouncy curl at the bottom.

. . .

She told herself she wouldn't go. Junior Carper had no right to demand she meet him, without even telling her why. Yet at lunchtime, she found herself slipping away through the custodian's door. She'd go, show she wasn't intimidated by Junior. If he bothered her again, she'd tell the principal. He wouldn't stand for a Carper bothering Doree, who'd made the honor roll every semester since kindergarten and was probably going to win the Perfect Attendance Award at graduation.

She found Junior in the side lot, squatting on the pavement with a car magazine. He wore a pair of stiff blue work pants, which Doree recognized as the Ranch Hand brand they sold at the Seed n' Feed for $1.99, and a pair of battered high-tops. He had no coat. He looked up at her and licked his chapped lips.

"You came," he said, fixing his pale eyes on her.

"What do you want?" She stood with her hands on her hips, as haughtily as she could. "You better leave me alone, or I'll tell the principal."

"I don't think you will."

"Excuse me?"

"I said, I don't think you'll tell the principal. I don't think you'll tell nobody. I think you'll do what I want."

A cold feeling began to spread across Doree's stomach and chest, like she'd swallowed a glass of ice water too fast. "What do you mean?"

"I know something about your mother."

"My mother?" Why would Junior Carper—a Carper from Mill Hill—be talking about her mother? Carpers didn't even shop at Zelner's.

The Carpers were bad news. *Not a good apple in the barrel*, Patty's father would say. Junior's grandfather Cecil ran a bedraggled motel on Route 60. Everyone said he'd been a moonshiner during Prohibition. He had a face like a catfish, all thick lips and bulging watery eyes and untrimmed whiskers. Cecil's son—Junior's daddy—was a religious maniac with an apple orchard up above Mill Hill. He'd had some kind of convulsion a few years back, and now half his face drooped as if his flesh were melted candle wax. In fall, the Carper kids all missed school to help with the apple harvest. Those Carper kids were as pale skinned and pale eyed as if they'd grown up in a cave. Between Junior and his cousins there were at least twenty of them. Always snot-nosed and scab-kneed, running around in grubby pants and dresses worn by a half-dozen other kids before them. At school, everyone called them "hill trash," which was cruel, but Doree had to admit that the shoe fit.

Once, playing on the sidewalk outside the store, Pete had started to write "wash me" in the dust on the rear window of Cecil Carper's parked pickup truck. Their grandfather Sol had come bounding out of the store with startling and terrifying speed, and dragged Pete inside. "Don't fool around with Carpers," he'd said.

Pete had been so shocked he'd started to cry.

Doree understood being poor wasn't the Carper kids' fault. But why were they so mean? Some of the girls were sweet enough, but the boys to a one seemed to enjoy shooting one another with slingshots and setting fires to anthills.

"Yeah, I know something about your mother," Junior said, smirking.

"What, then?" She tossed her hair in what she hoped was a confident, impatient way, like a film star.

"She's a traitor."

"A *traitor*?"

"A traitor."

"I can't imagine what you mean," she said prissily, her heart beginning to knock wildly in her chest.

"Back when the resort was a prison camp for them Nazis."

Doree knew vaguely that the Greenbrier had been some kind of army detention center for bigwigs when she was a baby, during the war. That was before they'd redesigned and repainted, made everything bright and colorful and terribly modern, and all the celebrities—even royalty!—had come for the grand reopening.

Junior kept talking. The words unspooled like a length of barbed wire. Doree felt her vision constrict. It was as if she and Junior were in a tunnel, staring at each other. He kept talking and talking. *Stop, please stop*, she wanted to say, but she felt frozen, as if the ice water in her stomach had traveled through her veins, turning her into a statue.

"So you get it?" Junior said finally.

Doree tried to speak, but no sound came out.

"Gimme the money by next week. You pay ten dollars every week, I keep my mouth shut."

"I don't have any money," Doree said, her voice sounding rusty and far away. It was true. She'd just handed over her life savings to Patty, who was giving it to her mechanic cousin in Lewisburg to get them a used car to take to college together.

Junior scoffed. "Don't gimme that. My grandpa says y'all people always have plenty of money laying around somewhere."

"I don't!"

"That's your problem, not mine. If I don't get the money, you know what I'll do." He folded his arms over his chest, like a gangster in a film.

Doree turned away. She felt a hot, acid pressure building up in her throat. Staggering away from Junior, she made it as far as the outer gymnasium wall before vomiting steaming yellow gouts into the snow-covered bushes.

Suddenly her clean white future seemed as soiled as the knees of Junior Carper's jeans.

CHAPTER 7

Sylvia

"*N*o," said Sylvia, smacking her hands on the worn wooden sales counter for emphasis. How could anyone ask her that? How could anyone dare?

Hope Walsh's eyes widened in surprise behind her spectacles. "I'm so sorry, Mrs. Zelner. I hope my request didn't offend you."

"Offend? To ask me to help a Nazi!"

"But, Mrs. Zelner—" Hope Walsh was the secretary to the Greenbrier's manager, Mr. Johnston, and clearly used to having her requests met. She could go shit in the ocean!

"Miss Walsh, how are you?" said Louis, appearing behind Sylvia, carrying a stack of shoeboxes. He put them down on a stool. "What brings you all the way down here?"

"Mr. Zelner, I'm well, thank you," said Hope, her long face grown pink.

Louis put his hands on Sylvia's shoulders and smiled. "What can we help you with today?"

"Ah, I was just discussing a matter with your wife, a request from Mr. Johnston."

Louis raised his eyebrows. "Really? We'll be happy to help, whatever it is."

"Louis—" Sylvia hissed, but Louis shushed her by squeezing her shoulders.

"We have a guest at the Greenbrier, an Italian, who needs some outfits sewn for his little daughters back in Italy," Hope said. "Since your wife is by all accounts an accomplished seamstress, Mr. Johnston hoped she could help. You'd be well compensated for your time and effort of course, Mrs. Zelner."

"It is not a problem of money," Sylvia said, but Louis cut her off again.

"Of course she will," he said. "We'd be happy to help out the Greenbrier—happy and proud. Just tell us where and when."

"Perhaps tomorrow morning, if that's convenient," Hope said, relaxing visibly.

"Wonderful," Louis said. "Can I offer you a soft drink before you go?"

"Oh, no thank you, I'm watching my figure!" said Hope. "I'll see you tomorrow, Mrs. Zelner."

As she left the store, a pack of schoolboys pressed in and crowded around the candy table. Louis went to stand near them to make sure no grubby fingers made their way into the jars. The boys were followed by a young wife with a carriage, looking to buy a new set of tea towels. On her heels were a pair of Greenbrier laundry workers, their heads pressed together, sharing the tail end of a joke. The afternoon rush had begun. It was like a tide. Sylvia, seething, went under.

"*H*ow could you dare!" Sylvia's anger was an unbearable itch, her body aflame with it. She'd come flying down the stairs in her nightgown the moment she heard Louis on the porch.

It was late, after nine, so late Sylvia suspected Louis had lingered in the stockroom precisely to avoid this confrontation.

"Please, Sylvia, I'm very tired."

"I don't care!"

"Look, it's an honor. Forget who the guest is for a moment. It's the *Greenbrier*. What if—I don't know—what if they liked your work so much they asked you to open a dress shop there when this is all over? Or what if we could open another Zelner's in the Greenbrier Shops? That could change everything for us!"

"*Forget who the guest is*? FORGET?"

Louis rubbed the side of his head. "It's not as if you're being asked to sew for a Nazi general. This is just an Italian, and he could be anyone—he could be the embassy shoe shiner for all we know."

"Oh yes, the embassy shoe shiner. The poor little embassy shoe shiner who knows nothing of fascism yet has plenty of money for handmade dresses for his daughters."

"See, it's not even for the Italian himself—it's for his little daughters."

Sylvia felt as if her lungs were filled with fire. As if she could open her mouth and burn down the house. "I don't sew for Nazis. I don't sew for the friends of Nazis. I don't sew for the little daughters of the friends of Nazis."

"Fine," said Louis, hanging his hat on the hook and walking upstairs with infuriating calm. "Don't go. I'll tell them you're ill."

"*Shtik drek!*" Sylvia screamed after him. "You won't fight the Nazis, you coward, but I should sew for them?"

She heard a tiny gasp from behind the hallway door. Pauline was listening, as usual. She pretended not to understand Yiddish, just to show how American she was. But hearing Sylvia call Louis a piece of shit gave lie to that.

. . .

*L*ouis *had* wanted to serve. He'd brought it up one night, back at the end of December. They were sitting in bed. Sylvia was in her nightgown, brushing her hair. Louis sat next to her in his striped pajamas. She still felt stiff and embarrassed at nighttime, lying next to a man in pajamas. Yes, he was her husband. But it still felt too intimate.

"How would you feel about handling the store, if I signed up?" he asked. "My father would help too, though he can't carry anything heavy on account of his back, of course."

"What does your mother think?" Sylvia asked in a carefully neutral tone.

Louis grimaced. "She says I'll be rejected because of my heart condition."

"Dr. Sydenstricker says your heart is fine."

"Yes, well, that doesn't convince Mother."

Dr. Sydenstricker had passingly mentioned a heart murmur when Louis was seven, and even though he'd never heard it again—it was probably just a gummy old stethoscope, he'd said later, many times—Pauline treated Louis as a confirmed invalid. She wouldn't let him go out for sports, or even run a mile in physical education class. When the Boy Scouts went on their annual camping trip, she kept him home.

"You could visit the recruiter and see."

"You wouldn't mind?" Louis turned to look at her, his eyes owlishly large behind his wire-rimmed glasses, which he only took off to sleep.

"If it's what you want."

"I'll talk to Mother, then. The line for the army sign-up was so long that Nelson Curry and Billy Burdette ended up going marines. But I'd rather the army." Louis kissed Sylvia on the cheek, set his glasses on the night table, and turned out his lamp. He fell asleep immediately, as he always did, sleeping the childlike sleep of a real American.

"You must be joking," Pauline said the next morning at breakfast. She was wearing her flannel nightgown, her hair in metal curlers, a look on her face like someone had passed gas. "A man with a baby and two elderly parents and a store to run wants to go to war? A man with a heart condition."

"I don't have a heart condition," said Louis, frowning over his toast.

That was the end of that. It wasn't mentioned again, though Louis would get a longing look in his eyes when he heard another one of his high school classmates had joined up.

Johnny Burdette got blood poisoning in boot camp and lost his right leg. Now he walked with a heavy, swinging gait on a wood-and-metal one.

"Imagine," Pauline said. "His life is ruined. His poor wife will have to look after him now. Are you glad I kept Louis from joining now? If you'd had your way, that could be our Louis with his leg gone."

"Better someone else's son should fight the Nazis," Sylvia said.

Either Pauline didn't recognize her sarcasm or pretended not to. "Exactly."

Sylvia awoke in the moonlight with an idea, fully formed.

She'd take the job. She'd take the money. She'd simply lie to Louis about how much she was being paid, and hide the extra for herself. It would be hers and hers alone.

Then, when she had enough, when the time was right, she would leave this place.

She imagined herself standing on the platform at the White Sulphur Springs Station, counting bills off a fat roll. She'd hoist Doree onto her hip, step onto the train, and this cold, narrow blue house would be like a bad dream.

Coming to America had been a mistake in the first place. But she could fix it! Like unpicking the stitches on a badly sewn seam, she'd back up and start again from the beginning, do it right this time. From the train, she'd take a boat, another journey across the Atlantic, going east this time. She couldn't return to Poland, of course, but she could go to Palestine, where her mother and younger brothers were.

She could almost feel the sway of the waves beneath her.

Why had she not thought of this before? Perhaps a real American would have. Americans thought happiness was their right. If they didn't have it, they were allowed—encouraged!—to tear their lives apart looking for it. Carole Lombard had been married before she met Clark Gable, to another actor. Sylvia had heard this actor talking on the radio after Carole Lombard died. They'd been the best of friends, he said, but their marriage hadn't succeeded because they were "too different."

Too different! That was no reason at all. If Americans could divorce because they were "too different," then surely Sylvia had no reason to feel guilty for unraveling this life the way you'd unravel a poorly knitted scarf.

*I*t had all started with a scarf, in fact. If Louis hadn't been wearing it on that March evening in Baltimore two years ago,

Sylvia wouldn't be in this place. These cold, dripping, lightless mountains.

It was a thin red scarf with a jaunty, vaguely scoutish air about it. It had reminded Sylvia of the way her brothers' handsome Bundist friends had dressed as they marched down Piotrkowska Street, their arms thrown around each other, drinking beer and singing socialist anthems at the tops of their voices. It had made the young man in the bookstore that evening feel familiar, endearing.

Sylvia had been in America only a few months, and she and her workmate Fruma would go to the Jewish bookstore right next to the union hall in downtown Baltimore sometimes after their shifts at the dress factory to hear lectures and improve their English. There were always Jewish boys there, both American-born and immigrants like themselves. Sometimes afterwards they'd all go to a café and smoke cigarettes and drink strange watery American coffee.

On that evening, the seats were all taken, so Sylvia and Fruma stood in the back. It was a sleety March night outside, but inside it was nearly tropical with humidity rising from dozens of bodies in damp wool coats. The air smelled like camphor from all the girls who worked in the Noxzema factory.

For Sylvia, these evenings were some of the only times she felt like she was actually inside her body. The rest of the week she was watching herself from the outside, the way a stranger would see her. A girl in a boardinghouse, splashing her face with cold water in the morning. A girl walking alone to work with an onion sandwich in a paper sack. A girl bent over the sewing machine in the back of the dress factory, a pincushion strapped to her wrist like a watch.

But tonight, Sylvia was inside her eyes, inside her healthy young body. Fruma was telling Sylvia a long-winded story when

Sylvia spotted him: the boy in the red scarf. He was tall and slender, with sandy side-parted hair and round glasses atop an elegant Roman nose. The way the scarf hung loosely over his shoulders gave him a look of rakish confidence. She could imagine him laughing with friends during a theatrical performance at the Hazomir Society of Lodz, or marching with the Bundists on May Day, cigarette dangling from his lower lip. He'd be doing it to annoy his parents more than anything—he wouldn't be a terribly committed socialist; they were bores. Perhaps he'd be a footballer like Moriz Mostowski.

When the boy in the red scarf finally looked at her from across the room, his gaze felt *haimish*—familiar, reassuring. Like home.

By the time Sylvia realized her mistake, it was too late. She was on a train to West Virginia with a wedding ring on her finger and a complete stranger by her side.

*B*ut she could fix it! She could leave. When she got to Palestine, she'd figure out how to arrange for her older brothers to leave Poland—whether or not Mr. Johnston helped. Suddenly calmer than she'd been in months, Sylvia rolled over and fell back asleep, not even bothered by the sticky rumble of Louis's adenoidal breathing. The next morning, she combed out her hair and parted it severely. She powdered her face but didn't bother with lipstick. She dressed while Doree rolled around on the rag rug on the bedroom floor. Then she carried the baby downstairs and handed her to Pauline.

"I'll be back before lunch."

Pauline raised her eyebrows, but Sylvia ignored her. She had a plan now.

CHAPTER 8

❧

Jordan

Please. I'm your mother, and I'm asking you. Please just leave it alone.

Yet here he was, driving west down I-65 in John-Paul's secondhand Buick, headed to the Greenbrier on assignment. *On assignment!* Just the words were thrilling. The Features editor, Rita Romano, had given him twenty-two hundred words. Twenty-two hundred words! That was front-page stuff. He imagined Rick Lowell turning to him in the break room, saying, "Nice one, man."

Beneath his excitement, though, Jordan felt the acid bite of guilt at the back of his throat. Disobeying their mother had always been his sister's specialty, not his.

He desperately wanted to tell Jessica about his assignment, about his ignoring their mother's wishes like Jessica always wanted, but Jessica was tooling around the country with her latest band, Lunatic Kitten—or was it Crash Riot now? He would have to wait for her to call. If she felt like it. And who could know, Jordan thought as he cranked down the window, when or why Jessica ever felt like doing anything?

. . .

Jessica was the older twin by two minutes, so when Jordan emerged, the world he entered was already filled with her fire truck wails.

"She just came out that way," their mother always said. "A live wire."

Jessica's crackling force field of electricity had always been wide enough to protect Jordan. When Robbie Cohen called Jordan "fatty fatty two by four" in kindergarten, Jessica had smacked Robbie so hard his lip bled and he blubbered for an hour. Jessica had insisted on delaying her bat mitzvah until she was thirteen, though girls were meant to celebrate at twelve, so she could have it together with Jordan. She knew he'd never survive standing on the bimah and reading from the Torah all by himself. In high school, Jessica's don't-give-a-shit attitude had made Jordan cooler by association: girls who would never have talked to him on his own merits (being a Math Olympian wasn't much of a selling point, apparently) thought befriending the brother of Jessica-with-the-shaved-head-and-Doc-Martens was a form of rebellion by proxy.

And Jordan's goodness—his perfect grades and SAT scores, his Mitzvah Awards at Hebrew school—protected Jessica too. He helped her with her homework (he did it himself half the time, honestly). He covered for her when she sneaked out of the Jewish Community Center screening of the Anne Frank movie to smoke cigarettes (*more Holocaust guilt, bo-ring*). He covered for her when she skipped school to see Black Flag at the 9:30 Club in DC. He covered for her when she came home obviously stoned.

He couldn't cover for her when she came home with a tattoo

on her wrist, too heavy and black to be disguised by the longest shirts. Not that Jessica tried to hide it.

What on earth were you thinking? their father had said. *Pierce your ears twice, fine, but Jews don't tattoo themselves!*

Their mother had cried for hours. Jessica could never be buried in a Jewish cemetery now, she said. For some reason, this seemed incredibly important to her.

Who cares? Jessica had said. *I'll be dead.*

At least we have one kid who listens, their father had muttered, as he often did, before calling his dermatologist cousin to ask about tattoo removal.

Yeah, Jordan listened. Jordan didn't get a tattoo. Jordan didn't go to concerts on school nights. Jordan never smoked a cigarette, not even when Nina Goldberg offered to teach him to blow smoke rings.

But Jordan wasn't a kid anymore. He was almost twenty-four. He was a reporter for the *Washington Post* (just saying that still felt unreal). He couldn't ignore a tip—a tip that, no matter what anyone said, felt genuine—just because it scared his mother. He was going to get a page 1 story. He was going to get off the eye-crossingly boring town council beat. And he was going to remind Jessica he was someone too, more than just a reminder of her boring, hideously suburban past.

*T*he DC suburbs fell away, and the landscape turned to shorn winter fields dotted with mournful-looking cows. Jordan passed a barn with the roof caved in, as if it had been hit by a small meteor. At a lonely crossroads he spotted a low narrow cinder block building with a neon sign on the roof reading OUR PLACE

LOUNGE and Confederate flag bunting drooping from the eaves. He thought of the anti-Semites of his childhood imagination. He pictured them inside Our Place, drinking whiskey in their shiny black ant carapaces.

He opened a bag of Doritos and turned on the radio. A crackle of static, then Rush Limbaugh was bellowing in his ears about immigration: "They want amnesty for illegals . . . flooding into our country for handouts . . ." *Barf, no thanks.* Jordan snapped the radio off and pushed a mix tape—he'd made it specially for the trip—into the deck. The Red Hot Chili Peppers' "Give It Away" blasted from the speakers.

Jordan felt his thoughts synchronizing with the hypnotic tempo of the drumming. The next thing he knew, he'd crossed nearly all of Virginia, the Appalachian Mountains rising before him like the swell of a wave. The sun was setting, and the mountains were silhouetted against a pale orange winter sky. He'd be in West Virginia within the hour.

By the time Jordan crossed the state line, the sky was black, and a jagged little smile of a moon hung just over the horizon. The highway cut a trough through the mountains, and the hillsides rose steep and dark on either side. Every so often he could see a sign of life flash by—a church steeple, the leering face of Joe Camel on a billboard. But in between was nothing but deep, soft, inky rural night.

Jordan only realized he had dropped well below the speed limit when a logging truck began to ride his bumper. Its headlights lit the interior of the Buick with an eerie, bluish glow. Foot hard on the gas, Jordan imagined the truck forcing him off the road. The driver would sidle up to Jordan's window like a cop. He'd have an accent like on *The Dukes of Hazzard*: *What the heck you doing, boy, driving that slow in these parts?* He'd have a gun—of course he'd have a gun.

Jordan was so busy imagining this scenario, he almost missed the exit sign: WHITE SULPHUR SPRINGS. He pulled onto the off-ramp so quickly the car skidded for a moment—*oh, shit, John-Paul's car*—then quickly righted itself.

Now on a two-lane road, Jordan found himself amid an even thicker darkness than before. The sliver of moon had disappeared, and there were no buildings, no artificial lights. Jordan felt like he was driving through the forest itself. Eventually he passed a small lumberyard, then a gas station. A few minutes later he began to see houses lit with sulphurously yellow street lamps. Most of them were old and wooden, with steeply pitched metal roofs in varying stages of rusting, mixed with a handful of mobile homes. Then the houses gave way to a downtown of sorts. Clusters of one- and two-story brick shop buildings were interspersed with vacant lots, like missing teeth. He wondered which one had been Grandpa Louis's store, or if the building was even still standing. He'd go look tomorrow.

He knew from the map that the resort's main entrance would be past downtown on the right, yet he decided to turn early, at a road marked EAST ENTRANCE: DELIVERIES.

Hector Espinoza, the adviser at Jordan's college paper, *The Diamondback*, had once remarked that a reporter should "always go in the back way." At the time Jordan had no idea what he'd meant; Espinoza was big on cryptic pronouncements. But Espinoza had won two Pulitzers: When he talked, you listened. A few years later, when Jordan was working his first job—the civic beat at the local paper in Frederick County—he'd begun to understand. The back way into town was always more colorful and interesting than the interstate, for example. And the back way into a building took you past all sorts of things people didn't want you to see. While reporting a profile of a small-town mayor who ran a Roy Rogers fast-food franchise, Jordan had walked in the restaurant's back entrance to find himself amid a knot of disgruntled fry cooks grumbling about unpaid wages. Jordan's story—"Local Mayor Stiffs Minimum Wage Restaurant Employees"—got the mayor fired. It got Jordan in at the *Washington Post*.

Driving in the Greenbrier's back entrance, feeling the bite of gravel beneath his wheels, Jordan found himself on a thickly wooded hillside. The swing of his headlights revealed a row of small cottages, each exactly alike, with American flags hung at the same stiff angle from each porch. The windows were dark empty squares, no signs of people—these must be the resort's summer rentals. Beyond the houses, his headlights caught something white amid the trees: a statue of some sort?

At the base of the hill, the forest suddenly opened into the flat, exposed planes of a golf course, with water traps like yawning black mouths. From this angle, Jordan could see the flank of the hill he'd just descended. A driveway branched off the road and sloped back towards the hillside; at the bottom was a retaining wall with a vast metal door built directly into the hill itself, big enough to drive an eighteen-wheeler through. HIGH VOLTAGE read a sign over the door. EXTREME DANGER. AUTHORIZED PERSONNEL ONLY.

Hmm, Jordan thought. There was a faint scratching from somewhere deep inside his brain, like a cat asking to be let out. He didn't believe in anything so New Agey as intuition. But that feeling meant something.

He drove on. The dark fringe of trees fell away.

And there it was.

It rose from the center of an enormous lawn, its perimeter lit with hundreds of tiny ground lights. The resort. The Greenbrier.

He rolled to a slow stop, just gazing at it. It looked less like a castle than he had imagined and more like the US Capitol, minus the dome—all white columns and windows like eyes.

Thump. The sound made Jordan jerk back in his seat. A deer? He turned to his left and saw a pale oval shape outside his steamed-up window. His heart thudded. It was a man.

CHAPTER 9

❧

Doree

JANUARY 1959

*A*fter school, her temples thudding with the beginnings of a sick headache, Doree walked down Main Street until she came to the green awning of Zelner's Low Price Store. It was so quiet inside that at first she thought no one was there. Then she heard a rustling and saw her father standing at the top of the wheeled ladder, stacking folded linens in the open storage shelves above the sales floor.

"Hiya," he said, glancing down at Doree. "Your mother ordered some of these new 'king' and 'queen' sheets—if anyone wants some, they're up here."

Doree inhaled the warm store air—sweet tobacco and bubble gum and the waxy coating of new blue jeans—and tried to settle herself. Being in here always made her feel calmer.

When Doree's grandfather Sol opened Zelner's in 1911, it sold everything. Ladies' clothes, children's shoes, bolts of gingham and canvas, washtubs, sewing notions, penny candy, dime novels, loose cigarettes, nails and screws, alarm clocks, watches, checker- and chessboards, beeswax candles, Ivory soap, newspapers from Charleston and Baltimore. If you asked, Sol would special order you a bicycle or a china doll or a phonograph. It was the only store in town back then, besides the fancy boutiques at the Greenbrier. Now there were a dozen other retail stores on Main Street, plus the Seed n' Feed on Route 60.

"But we have the best quality," her father would say. "And the best service."

They were also the only shop on Main that served Negroes. Some of the councilmen put in a complaint a few years back, but Sol said he'd sooner close than put up a WHITES ONLY sign.

These days, Zelner's mostly sold home goods and ladies' fashions, though they still had a table of candy and an ice chest of soft drinks. If a customer bought a drink, Louis would pop the top on a cast-iron bottle opener mounted to the side of the cash register. Doree always loved to hear the hiss of the bubbles and the plink of the bottle cap landing on the counter.

"How was school, sweetheart?" Louis asked, climbing down the ladder.

"Fine." An image of Junior Carper's fish-white face floated up behind her eyelids, and she shook her head to get rid of it.

"Good. I won't keep you busy all afternoon; you can work on your applications in the back after inventory."

"College applications? They're done, Dad. I just need some stamps to mail them."

Louis looked at Doree and pushed his round glasses further up his nose, as if to see her better. "Done? Really? Mazel tov. I thought it would take longer." She noticed how the skin around his eyes pleated with tiny wrinkles as he smiled. He looked tired, as usual. He worked so hard. She felt a stab of guilt.

Louis had told her he'd wanted to go to college. But he'd turned eighteen in the middle of the Depression, and the store had been struggling. So he stayed. His younger brother, Doree's uncle Vincent, had studied chemistry at WVU and now worked at Dow Chemical in Michigan. Her father said Doree would be living his dream for him, which made her feel proud but also a bit guilty.

Doree was applying to two schools: WVU and Fairmont State. Fairmont had the better teachers' course, but WVU had more Jewish boys. It didn't really matter where she went anyway—there were plenty of jobs for schoolteachers, and it wasn't as if she'd be teaching for more than a few years before she was married and ready to start a family. Still, it was nice to imagine her father beaming from the crowd at her graduation.

Doree followed Louis into the small stockroom at the back of the store. Crates and boxes of new inventory lined the same wooden shelves Sol had built nearly fifty years before. In the corner was a desk with a green-shaded banker's lamp. The store's Christmas decorations—a plastic wreath and several plastic swags covered in lurid red holly berries—lay on a tarp in the corner. Louis would roll them up and carry them home after closing, where they would live in the attic until next December.

Louis handed Doree a clipboard. "Black is for markdowns, blue is for dead stock. You take Ladies, I'll do the rest."

Doree squinted at the chart. "Why are we marking down the new nighties? They could go for Valentine's Day."

"Ecch, they sold so badly for Christmas. I think the price point is just too high."

"Mama shouldn't have ordered something so fancy. This isn't Baltimore. Anyone who can afford fancy walks up to the Greenbrier shops."

Ever since Doree's grandmother got sick, Sylvia had been doing the biannual Ladies buying trip to Baltimore by herself. As a result, the clothing inventory had become distinctly more glamorous.

"Your mother has good taste," said Louis.

Your mama's a traitor.

Doree said nothing. Silently she took the clipboard and the price labels.

An hour later, Doree carried her box of dead stock to the stockroom. Carefully looking to make sure her father was occupied, she flipped open the inventory log sitting on the desk. She scanned the page to find a number that would work. There. An entry of $30 for the sale of three boys' suits. She'd made that sale herself—the Hoffners' grandfather had died, and they'd needed something for the boys to wear to the funeral. Quickly, she changed the "$30" to "$20." Now she'd freed up ten dollars. She opened the old tobacco tin on the desk and quickly counted out ten one-dollar bills. She shoved them in the waistband of her skirt just as her father rounded the sales counter.

"All finished?"

"Yes, just refolding the dead stock."

"You don't have to do that," he said. "Go on home, relax. You'll work hard enough the rest of your life."

The guilt combined with her growing headache made her feel poisoned. A roiling stomach, a pressure behind her eyes, the taste of hot vinegary bile in her mouth.

It's for the family, she told herself. *It's for the family.*

But that didn't take away the nausea.

The cold outside helped. It was dark now, and a chilly wind was blowing old newspapers and Coke bottle caps into little eddies on the sidewalk. Sparse wet snowflakes felt good on Doree's overheated forehead.

She was halfway down Main Street when the fleet of trucks appeared. Rounding the bend from the east, they moved almost silently, their headlights hazy in the newly falling snow. At least a dozen, they were large and white and very square, like oversized mail vans. On their sides, they said FORSYTHE ASSOCIATES: AUDIO-VISUAL TECHNICIANS. As they receded into the distance, Doree could see their headlights slash arcs in the darkness as they turned into the Greenbrier's side entrance.

How strange.

CHAPTER 10

❧

Sylvia

JANUARY 1942

*N*ormally the only person at the Greenbrier entrance was Mr. Sammy, the Negro guard whose job was mostly to smile at guests as they drove up in their big automobiles. But ever since the detained diplomats arrived, there'd been three or four uniformed men stationed at the main gate night and day. Some of them were West Virginia state troopers. Some were border patrol agents, scraped up from Canadian posts and bused down south. The rest were locals, hired at five dollars a day. Sol said he figured they'd hired up the biggest troublemakers in town, to quiet down the rumblings about Nazis eating nicer than red-blooded Americans.

Sylvia walked up to the first guard shack and told the man on duty she had a meeting with Mr. Johnston. He was a stranger— one of the border patrol agents—with a walrus mustache and a fat belly straining the seams of his brand-new uniform. He looked her up and down, his eyes lingering at her breasts and hips, then waved her through.

Then she came to the second guard shack, on the edge of the lawn; the immaculate grass, somehow maintained through the long winter, was already beginning to die around its edges. Like the first shack, this one was so new she could still smell the cut edges of the wood. It was painted the same green as the Rolls-Royces. Inside was Carl Carper, the moonshiner's son.

Carl Carper stared at her with eyes the pale gray of fish scales, his hand stroking the butt of a rifle. His face was blighted by a scabby pink rash that spread across the bridge of his nose and onto his upper cheeks like the wings of a malevolent butterfly. "Who let you in?"

"I have a meeting with Mr. Johnston."

"What for?"

"A guest matter."

Carl Carper was even younger than Sylvia—barely eighteen, she figured—but was already father to a little boy the same age as Doree. His wife, Addelle, had once come into Zelner's looking for a job. She seemed like a sweet thing. But as soon as she'd left, Pauline had grimaced and wiped the counter down with a rag. "Hire a Carper and no one with class will ever shop here again," she'd said.

The Greenbrier must have been desperate, to hire Carl.

"How do I know you're not a spy?" Carper said.

"Excuse me?"

"I'm pledged to guard this property against spies and traitors bringin' information to the enemy. They ain't even allowed to read the newspaper in there."

"I am not a spy."

"I'm just sayin.' Those Germans and Italians keep comin' up to me and askin' me if they can please have a newspaper, even jest the racing pages. And I say, 'Uh-uh, no. You ain't plannin' another Pearl Harbor on my watch.'"

"I will be late to my appointment with Mr. Johnston."

"All right," Carper said, shrugging his skinny shoulders. "I did my duty."

"Yes," Sylvia said. How stupid was this man?

He waved at her amiably as she continued on towards the resort.

Sylvia'd been in the Greenbrier only a handful of times since moving to White Sulphur Springs. Once was for her wedding luncheon, if you could call it that. She and Louis had married in front of a rabbi in Louis's uncle's house in Baltimore, with tea and cake afterwards. Pauline came, but Sol had to stay behind to mind the store, since they were between clerks at the time. Sylvia's friend Fruma had been the only guest on her side. To make up for missing the wedding, Sol took Sylvia, Louis, and Pauline to luncheon at the Greenbrier the following Sunday. Pauline had thought it extravagant, but Sol had insisted. Sylvia still remembered the menu: a clear consommé with flecks of peppers like paper confetti, grilled fresh mackerel with anchovies, asparagus in butter. She'd thought the hotel elegant, but cold and dull compared to the gilded Grand Hotel in Lodz.

Now, with most of the guests gone and the nicer furniture put in storage, the Greenbrier felt even colder, its lobby echoey and overlarge, all done in marble with Grecian pillars, like a mausoleum. She barely had a moment to look around before a tall white-haired man swept towards her.

"Mrs. Zelner! Thank you so much for coming. I'm Loren Johnston, the general manager here at the Greenbrier. I can't tell you how much we appreciate your service."

She knew who he was, of course. Loren Johnston made every decision at the Greenbrier, from the thickness of the resort stationery to which china should be used for the C&O annual dinner. Anyone who came to work at the Greenbrier had to be vetted by Johnston first. And if someone was fired, he handed them their walking papers. If an especially important guest came in on the train, Johnston would be there to greet them personally at the station. If a senator didn't want to golf alone, Johnston would join him.

Sylvia's friend Aggie said all the employees loved him. "He's like their father, plus Jesus," is what she'd said.

Yet he was also the one who let in the Nazis. He was the one who had said yes to turning his elegant hotel into a snake pit. Sylvia resolved to be suspicious of him.

With his enormous baseball mitt of a hand at her lower back, Johnston guided Sylvia into a small room off the back of the lobby. He held open the door, then closed it behind her.

"We call this the Victorian Writing Room," he said. "Back when the Greenbrier was called the Old White, guests used to sit at this desk here to write their postcards. I sometimes like to use it as my unofficial office."

The room was smaller than the lobby, but it was still enormous, old-fashioned, and strangely proportioned—the ceiling was higher than the room was wide. At one end was a leather settee; against the windows was a large mahogany desk with two high-backed, uncomfortable-looking mahogany chairs. A portrait of one of the American presidents—Sylvia wasn't sure which—hung above the desk. The walls were the same cold bone white.

"Please, do sit down," said Mr. Johnston, pulling out one of the desk chairs.

He settled himself into the chair opposite, the hint of a suppressed grimace on his lips as he bent his legs. He must be well over sixty; he probably had bad knees. His white hair was combed and parted as neatly as a little boy's, and his face had a little boy's look of friendly expectation. He'd probably had a life as smooth and sweet as fresh cream, Sylvia decided.

"So, Mrs. Zelner," he said, "Miss Walsh said she chatted with you yesterday? She said you were uncomfortable with the request, and I just wanted to let you know right away: I understand completely."

"You do?" Sylvia said. But what she meant was *Do* you?

"I do. Our guests are powerful members of enemy governments. No two ways about it. Some of them are no doubt true believing Nazis. I know this is especially hateful for you, Mrs. Zelner, as a member of the Jewish faith. But what I want to tell you is this: By treating these guests with dignity, by honoring their requests, this is an act of patriotism just as surely as fighting in the war is an act of patriotism. And our government honors acts of patriotism." He leaned forward, obviously expecting a response.

Sylvia felt suddenly very young and very stupid. There was clearly another layer to what he was saying, but she wasn't sure what it was.

"I understand you have family members still in Poland?" he said.

"My two older brothers, and my uncle and cousins," Sylvia said. "My mother and younger brothers are in Palestine."

"Now, listen, I'm not able to say anything definitively—I'm a hotel manager, not a politician. But the secretary of state is a regular here, and he's assured me that anyone who helps with the government's efforts will have their patriotism noted on their records."

"Their records?"

"So to speak."

"This is Secretary Hull?"

"Yes, Cordell Hull. He's been coming here for decades. He's even more of an old-timer than me." Mr. Johnston chuckled.

Sylvia frowned. "Secretary Hull who did not let in the ship? The ship of Jews?"

Mr. Johnston's laugh dissolved seamlessly into a look of sympathy, like a film actor practicing different expressions. "You mean the SS *St. Louis*, I take it? That was very unfortunate. I'm sure Secretary Hull finds it unfortunate now, in retrospect."

"Unfortunate, yes, you might say that," said Sylvia. She was feeling the heat at the base of her throat that meant her feelings were about to run away from her. *Anger will cause even a sage to lose his wisdom*, her father used to say. Well, she wasn't a sage. "There were one thousand Jews on that ship," she continued. "Within sight of Florida. But Mr. Hull, he said no, go away."

Mr. Johnston gave an inscrutable head gesture, somewhere between a nod and a shake. "You're admirably well-informed, Mrs. Zelner. You must read the papers. I'm not nearly as informed. But I do know this: I have it on good authority that anyone who helps out during these difficult days will not be forgotten."

Sylvia nodded. Maybe he was lying. Maybe he was telling the truth. Maybe he was just saying what he needed to say to get her to help him. She had no way to know. In any case, she had already settled on getting that money. In her mind it was already hidden in her underwear drawer, a wedge of bills as smooth and heavy and comforting as a river stone. If her work here could help get her brothers out of Poland? She didn't dare to hope. She took the thought and folded it carefully like a letter, then tucked it into a back corner of her mind. She would go along with Mr. Johnston, but she wouldn't trust him.

"What must I do?"

"Sew some dresses for some little girls," Mr. Johnston said. "Nothing else. If you're ready, I can take you to meet the guest. He can explain more about the job."

❧

Sol

BALTIMORE
1909

"For this job, you must be a good walker," Jacob Epstein said in Yiddish. "Are you a good walker?"

"Yes, sir?" Sol said, puzzled.

"Good," said Epstein.

Jacob Epstein was a fellow Lithuanian, from Tauroggen, near the Baltic Sea, he told Sol. He was in his forties, and had a gentle, genteel face, with a soft graying mustache and round glasses. He wore shirtsleeves like the rest of the men in the building. Only later would Sol learn Epstein was one of the richest Jews in Baltimore.

"Open your mouth," Epstein said.

Sol complied, and Epstein peered inside and tapped Sol's teeth like he was a horse.

"Good," Epstein said. "We don't want you getting ill with toothaches on your route."

"My route?"

Baltimore Bargain House supplied peddlers, Epstein explained. His men carried goods to towns all over the southern United

States, places too small or remote to have proper stores. He would set Sol up with his first pack of goods on credit.

"How does that sound?" he asked.

"Great," Sol said. "But, sir . . . I don't speak English."

"Not a worry, my boy," Epstein said, clapping Sol on the back. "You only need to know one phrase to start: 'It good. You buy?' You'll pick up the rest in a few months—you're a clever lad, I can tell. Oh, and one other thing."

"Yes?"

"There are ruffians out there, as there are everywhere on earth," he said. "They know peddlers carry cash. Being robbed is part of the job. Never fight back. Just give them what they want. Fighting back is how you get killed. Just return to Baltimore and resupply."

"Yes, sir," Sol said.

Talking softly to himself, Jacob Epstein sat down at his desk and drew up a map of Sol's route: the coalfields of southern West Virginia.

West Virginia, Sol whispered to himself. It wasn't one of the parts of Amerika he'd heard of. But it had a nice sound to it.

*T*he pack was bigger than he was, Sol would later say, and it was almost true. He wobbled off to Camden Station laden with seventy pounds of silverware; soaps and powders; shoe repair materials; assorted buttons, ribbons, and trim; tablecloths; eyeglasses; hairbrushes; pencils; suspenders; picture frames; tobacco and pipes; sewing patterns; candles; letter openers; children's tin toys; costume jewelry; sheets and pillowcases; and pots of rouge. As the train pulled out of the station, he practiced his two English sentences to himself in a low whisper: "It good. You buy? It good. You buy?"

The brick and bustle of Baltimore disappeared in a blink. Sol ate an onion sandwich and an apple, then fell asleep with the morning sun on his cheeks. When he awoke, it was late afternoon. There were mountains on the horizon. He had never seen mountains before. They were green and gold and rose and fell in endless overlapping waves. Was anything ever so beautiful? What luck he had, to be seeing mountains from the window of a train, rather than sitting in school or (God forbid) carrying a rifle in the tsar's army. He'd have to write a letter to his mother and sisters, telling them of all the marvels he'd seen so far.

Sol quickly got clever to the rhythms of a peddler's life. When he'd arrive in a new town he'd go directly to the largest house— the foreman's house—and knock on the door. The foreman's wife was always delighted to see a peddler. She missed the small luxuries—the hair combs, the perfumes, the pocket mirrors— she'd left behind when she'd followed her husband to these raw coalfield towns. Once Sol was in her good graces, he was safe. Then he could sell to the miners' wives too.

He spent weeks on the road between restocking trips. Miles of trudging through red mud whipped to a slimy froth by horse hooves. Wagon rides so bumpy his teeth knocked against each other hard enough to chip. Town after town with names alien on his tongue: Algoma, Jenkinjones, Cucumber, Anawalt, Elkhorn. All of them looked the same: rows of narrow houses of unpainted wood, mud streets all leading to the squat company store. The newer camps still smelled like the pine tar used to waterproof the roofs. There were few women in those places. Few women meant few sales. Sol learned to assess a town from a distance: If he could see laundry on a line or the wooden cross of a church, that was good, since that meant women, families, customers.

Almost always someone would invite him to stay the night. While the wife cooked supper, he'd teach the children checkers from one of the game sets he carried in his pack. He'd eat with the families at their tables—if they had tables. He ate cornbread and apple cake and hot, floury biscuits smeared with apple butter. He had hot lettuce dressed in grease, wild onions gathered from the mountainside, and something called shucky beans that looked like shriveled shoelace but tasted marvelously smoky and rich. Sometimes the wives could celebrate having a guest by frying up a chicken from the backyard flock or making a pie from a deer the miners shot after church on Sundays. Sol tasted tomatoes for the first time at a home shared by six Italian miners from the same hometown. He ate chitterlings—pig intestines—with colored families from Virginia and North Carolina. The first time he had pork he stayed up half the night worrying that something bad would happen. (What? His stomach would explode? The Lord God would reach down from the bituminous black West Virginia sky and smite him?) But he figured it was better to be polite and fed than rude and hungry. The Lord God would understand.

When his pack began to lighten enough that he no longer ended the day with spasming shoulders, he knew it was time to return to Baltimore. He'd stagger from Camden Station to the Widow Lieb's boardinghouse and fall into a deep black lake of sleep. When he'd emerge the next day, he'd go to the Baltimore Bargain House to see Jacob Epstein.

Switching freely between Yiddish and English, Epstein would pepper Sol with questions: How did the new jewelry sell? Were miners' wives still using tin plates? Did Sol's shoes fit well? Was his digestion regular? Then he'd clap Sol on the back and send him into the warehouse to restock.

(No, Sol's shoes didn't fit—his feet were still growing. Epstein gave him a new pair of boots, on credit. When, on his next visit to Baltimore, Sol went to pay up, Epstein pretended he already had.)

And after he'd seen Mr. Epstein and had a haircut, it was time to visit Pauline Reich.

Sol had met Pauline's brother Hy at a pinochle game one autumn day, and Hy had invited him to lunch. He'd been sitting in the front parlor making chitchat with Hy's mother, when a girl came in the front door. In her arms was a joint of meat the size of a baby, wrapped in brown butcher paper.

"She walked in carrying a brisket, and I knew right then that was the girl I was going to marry," Sol would later tell his sons and grandchildren.

It wasn't her looks—though she *was* lovely, with a long pale oval face and apricot hair that fell in waves. It was that she embodied a real solid American life: a parlor with lace curtains, wedding photos in silver frames, a heavy platter to serve brisket on, a little ceramic bird figurine on a side table, with no purpose other than to look charming. When he looked at Pauline, Sol could see with dizzying clarity down the long tunnel of his future: children, a house, naturalization papers, old age in a comfortable bed.

After that first lunch, every time he came to Baltimore, Sol would visit Pauline at her family's house in Butchers Hill. He'd spend hours beforehand thinking of the perfect gift to bring. All the trinkets from his pack seemed tawdry: the hair combs of false tortoiseshell, the "Czech crystal" brooches. So usually he'd bring food: fruit or nuts or the small boxes of chocolate that cost a day's commission. Pauline was polite, but unimpressed, offering only languid smiles and conversations filled with long pauses as she stared out the window, as if there were something more interesting outside.

Pauline's father liked him, though. He thought Sol had a good *yiddishe kop*—a good head for business. The two of them would sit and drink tea or thimble-sized glasses of slivovitz, and Pauline's father would talk about his own journey from Lithuania, back during the worst of the famines. *Men like us, we know how to adapt*, he told Sol. *We do what we must to succeed in this country. But we don't forget where we came from.*

We don't forget where we came from, Sol agreed. But in his mind he was thinking, *What good to remember the muddy shtetl of his childhood, when there were so many marvels in Amerika?*

CHAPTER 12

Sylvia

Sylvia and Mr. Johnston walked down a long, hushed white corridor that seemed to have no end. When they finally reached a turn, they came upon a middle-aged woman in an armchair, reading a book. She wore her dark hair in marcelled waves in the style of a decade back. Her lipstick was a deep purple red, almost black, far too dark for morning.

"Good morning, madam," said Mr. Johnston, in his full, buttery baritone.

The woman raised her eyes and gave a wan half smile, then went back to reading.

They turned and walked halfway down the next corridor. They were so deep in the resort there was no exterior light anymore. It could have been any time of day, any season.

But when Mr. Johnston knocked on door 151 and it opened, the hallway flooded with daylight.

"Good morning, Mr. Cattaneo," Mr. Johnston said.

The man stood in the doorway in rolled-up shirtsleeves. No tie, no shoes. His socks, Sylvia noticed, were red silk.

"Good morning." He smiled, but looked confused, as if waiting for an explanation.

"This is Mrs. Zelner. The dressmaker. I hope now is a convenient time?"

"Ah, yes, of course, the dressmaker. I'm sorry. I've been writing letters all night and I completely lost track of the time." He held out his hand. "Pleased to meet you, Mrs. Zelner. I'm Giacomo Cattaneo."

Sylvia paused for a moment and took him in. He was rather short, with dark green eyes and curly dark hair that, despite his claims of sleeplessness, was neatly combed. Finally, she held out her hand. "Sylvia Zelner."

"I was telling Mrs. Zelner about your daughters," Mr. Johnston said, as the Italian led them into the suite. "How old are they, again?"

"Giulia is eight; we call her Gigi," he said, striding through the room picking up papers and tidying the pillows on the settee. "Vittoria is ten. They'll be so pleased to have new dresses from America. And, if you don't mind, I'd like a few shirts to match—it's a bit of a family tradition."

"I'm sure Mrs. Zelner can do that," said Mr. Johnston, looking around. "Your secretary? She'll be joining us?"

"Yes, of course, I apologize," said the Italian. "Allow me to find her." He disappeared into the hallway, and Sylvia could hear him knocking on a nearby door and shouting something in Italian. Then he reappeared. "She'll be here momentarily."

Not thirty seconds later, a young woman in a tailored suit appeared. "Ciao," she said, offering the Italian her cheek to kiss.

"This is Miss Bianchi, my secretary," he said; more handshakes all around.

As soon as Mr. Johnston left, the Italian excused himself to the bedroom to change. While he was gone, Sylvia took a look around the sitting area. Oriental carpets. There were two portraits of sneering men on horseback, the paintings hung on opposite corners, facing each other. Were they meant to be the same man? Was he sneering at himself, then? The walls themselves were covered in unfashionable chinoiserie paper with a pattern of peach blossoms, their pink edges so delicate you could almost see them trembling. Below a fussy, old-fashioned wooden desk with intricately carved scrollwork, Sylvia spotted a pair of brown velvet slippers with a monogram embroidered in red on the toe: *GCV.*

"Coffee?" said the Italian, entering. He was now wearing a red tie and a pair of black shoes so shiny they looked wet.

It took Sylvia a moment to realize he was asking her, not requesting from her. "No thank you," she said.

"Ah," he said. "Your accent. You are not American?"

"No."

"Where do you come from, might I ask?"

"Poland."

"Really? I've spent time in Warsaw. Terribly charming city. Where are you from?"

"Lodz."

"Ah," he said again, and smiled.

Foreigners rarely visited Lodz, unless they were in the garment trade.

Sylvia wasn't good with accents in English, but the man's speech sounded quite British to her. She wouldn't have known he was Italian at all.

"You are a diplomat?" she asked. She couldn't help herself. It was her curiosity getting in the way of her judgment.

"Oh, hardly, hardly," he said. "I'm a cultural attaché, you

might say. My background is art." He went to the desk and began rummaging around a box of loose papers. "Apologies again for the state of the place. Let me find the picture of the dresses to show you."

Sylvia stood waiting. A minute passed.

"Mother always said I can barely keep my head on my shoulders," he said, still rifling through the papers. "Please give me a moment." He said something in rapid Italian to the secretary, who was sitting on the settee. She stood up and left the room. "Signorina Bianchi will go find it. It may be with her papers. Are you sure I can't offer you a coffee?"

Because she didn't want to stand there like a fool, Sylvia said yes. And so she found herself sitting on the settee with a cup and saucer as the Italian sat at the desk. He smiled at her. His teeth were very white, and she noticed there was a tiny gap between the front two. Her grandmother Chaja had once said a gap between the front teeth was a lucky thing. Or was it an unlucky thing? She realized she was staring at the Italian's mouth and turned her head quickly, blushing.

"How long have you been in America, Mrs. Zelner?" he asked, holding her gaze as he lifted his coffee cup to his lips. "This really is a beautiful country."

*H*er mother and younger brothers left Poland for Palestine in 1938, but Sylvia wouldn't go. She wanted to stay with Papa and finish school and take her pony to the jumping competition in May. Mama said no, but Sylvia fought tooth and nail—she even called Mama a *klafte*—bitch—and got the hardest slap of her life. But she was her father's favorite—his little princess, even at seventeen—and she got what she wanted, as she usually did.

In the end, Mama and the twins sailed off for Tel Aviv in November, and Sylvia stayed with Papa and Leon and Alfred in the house off Piotrkowska Street. Once Papa sold the factory and Sylvia graduated, they would leave too.

In truth, the real reason she wanted to stay was Moriz Mostowski, star runner at the boys' school. His legs, in their maroon running shorts, had such definition of muscle they looked like they were carved from marble. They'd never even kissed, but Sylvia had ideas.

For this, she stayed. Little fool.

For this boy in maroon running shorts with white piping down the sides, she stayed in Poland even when the Jewish quotas made it clear her brothers couldn't go to university. She stayed even though the government put guards outside the Jewish stores to make sure gentiles didn't enter. She stayed even though her father's cousin, who was religious and wore a full beard and side curls, had been set upon in the street by a gang of boys and had his beard sawed off with a pocketknife.

The white piping on Moriz Mostowski's running shorts came from Sylvia's father's ribbon and trim factory, which supplied the piping for all the Jewish schools in Lodz and many mixed schools too. It was just a small factory, with fewer than fifty employees. Her father wanted to sell it and use the money to settle properly in Palestine, but who could buy? A few gentiles had offered insulting prices, but her father was holding out.

Sylvia sewed at her uncle's dress shop after school. This was part of the agreement between her and her parents. She could stay in Lodz if she would work at the dress shop every day—*no running wild*, her mother had said. But still, during the evenings she would stroll down Piotrkowska Street with her girlfriends, or attend piano recitals at the society, or drink schnapps in the bleachers at the track while the boys ran. Life was almost like normal, she thought. Why did everyone need to make such dramatics out of everything?

Little fool.

Then, in May of 1939, Britain declared no more Jews could immigrate to Palestine. Sylvia's father was sure this didn't mean them—the rest of their family was already there! But he was wrong. For a while they thought they'd go to Palestine illegally, but Sylvia's father was frightened by the stories of ships being intercepted at sea and the passengers sent to detention. In the end, he sold the factory to a gentile for a fraction of what it was worth and used the money to buy their passage to America—first to Rumania, then on to France, then Britain, then New York, then Baltimore, where a distant cousin had arranged a job for him.

Leon and Alfred wouldn't go. They were going to stay and fight for socialism with their friends from the Jewish Labor Bund.

"This is our country too," is the last thing Leon said to Sylvia and her father as they left the house off Piotrkowska Street with just one suitcase each. It was August 1939.

Leon was nineteen. Alfred was twenty. Fools.

Now Lodz was called Litzmannstadt, after the German general who invaded in the last war. Leon and Alfred wrote that they had been forced into a walled-off area of the Baluty quarter along with the other Jews—a third of the city! Sylvia had been sending them money to buy extra food. But then the United States banned remittances to Poland, so there was nothing to do. She got letters for a while longer, illustrated by Leon with cartoons of things he saw on the streets—a cat in a bonnet, a baby with the serious face of an old man. But she hadn't heard anything in nearly five months. Sylvia's mother hadn't gotten a letter since then either. Perhaps the Nazis had stopped the mail. Perhaps they'd been moved. The other possibilities didn't bear thinking about. When those thoughts entered her mind, she would block them off by humming. There: gone.

As for Sylvia's father, he had a heart attack and died in the street in East Baltimore two days after they arrived in America. Two days! Could a merciful God not have waited two months—two weeks, even!—before leaving Sylvia utterly alone? But she had no one but herself to blame, did she? Moriz Mostowski and his long legs in their running shorts. They'd never even gotten a chance to kiss. Instead, her first kiss had been with Louis, a dry peck on the lips when she agreed to marry him. That should have been a sign.

"*I* came in 1939," Sylvia told the Italian.

"I see," he said, and an unreadable look flickered across his face. "It must have been frightening, moving countries?"

You have no idea, Sylvia thought. And then, *What gives him the right to ask about my feelings? The cheek!*

She shrugged her shoulders to make it clear that she wouldn't be answering those kinds of questions.

"Have you been in West Virginia long?" he went on.

"Two years."

"Have you spent much time at the Greenbrier?"

"No."

"It's quite pleasant," he went on, sipping his coffee and crossing one leg over the other. "I'd have loved to come here under different circumstances. Perhaps one day."

Sylvia sipped her own coffee. It was thick and bitter, almost like the Turkish coffee she and her friends used to drink after school, not like the Maxwell House bathwater Pauline made.

"Are you familiar with the Zander apparatus?" he asked.

"Excuse me?"

"The Bath Wing here is extraordinary," he went on. "It has an enormous swimming pool with a mosaic bottom, surrounded by hothouse plants—palms, ferns, so on. The ceiling is a glass dome. It's like being at Baden-Baden. On the second floor they have the men's department, where they do hydrotherapy. Mud baths. Then there's a small gymnasium, with kettlebells and so forth. That's where they have the Zander apparatus. How do I explain?" He looked at Sylvia with a mischievous smile, as if he were about to relate a joke. "It looks something like a ship's wheel, attached to a pully. One end of the pully rope has a wide leather strap, which you slip behind your back underneath your arms." He gestured to demonstrate. "Then someone cranks the wheel and your entire body vibrates as if you'd had an electric shock. It's called mecha-notherapy, apparently. The Germans are wild for it. They'll stand there for hours, vibrating quite merrily."

Sylvia just stared at him.

"May I show you a picture of my girls?" he asked.

Sylvia nodded—what else could she do? The Italian picked a silver frame off the desk and handed it to her. The photograph showed two girls in sailor dresses, their long braids tied with ribbons. One had a mournful expression; the other was laughing so hard her lower face was slightly blurred.

"That's Vittoria with the big eyes, and that's Gigi, giggling. She's just said something very naughty to her mother, if I recall."

"Where are they now?"

"In Rome. I haven't seen them in a year. This is the longest I've gone without them. I miss them terribly. I used to call them after my lunch in Washington, to sing them a song before they went to sleep. But now they don't allow us to use the telephones, which is understandable, of course, but to go without the sound of your children's voices . . ." He sighed. "Do you have children, Mrs. Zelner?"

"A baby."

"How wonderful. A girl or a boy?" He beamed at Sylvia, as if there could be nothing more delightful than sitting here, in this hotel room, chattering about babies with a stranger. It was difficult, she had to admit, to maintain her stiffness in the face of his friendly inquisition. When was the last time anyone had asked her so many questions about herself?

"A girl."

"What's her name?"

Sylvia felt any warmth instantly disappear. This was going too far. She wouldn't say the name of her baby to this man, this stranger, this *Italian*. It would feel like handing Doree to a coal miner encrusted in black dust and watching him caress her white baby feet with his filthy hands.

"Pauline," she said.

Pauline, the real Pauline, would be at home starting lunch, probably opening a fresh jar of those horrible beet pickles she was so fond of. The Litvaks put beet pickle in everything—soup, stew, even kugel. They even drank the salty, mouth-puckering beet pickle juice as if it were a cordial. Vile!

The Italian was talking again.

"It's rather like being at boarding school again, in a strange way," he was saying. "I was sent up to Eton when I was eight—my mother is English—so I spent years living in close quarters with many other boys. This situation here at the hotel reminds me of that. Factions. Rumors. The Italian and German children are having fistfights, which is frankly more adult than the way the adults are behaving."

"Why should the Italian and German children fight when their parents are such good allies?" Sylvia said, unable to suppress a sarcastic tone.

The Italian chuckled ruefully. "Allies, officially, yes," he said. "But let me tell you a story. Our military attaché, Mr. Infante, and the German military attaché, Mr. von Boetticher, might appear cordial—even friendly—to an outsider. They sat for hours in the dining room just last week, discussing policies. Yet yesterday, when Mr. Infante purchased a pipe at the tobacco counter, his wife made him return it immediately. It made him look too Germanic, she said!"

Sylvia's lips curled. What was the point of this story? Did he simply want her to know that Italians were different from Germans? Was he trying to tell her he wasn't a Nazi sympathizer? Or did he just like to hear the sound of his own voice?

"I try to stay out of it," he continued. "I observe. Mostly I've just been writing letters to my girls. Being away from them is like missing my arm or my leg. You're a mother, you understand."

Sylvia had woken up three weeks after her wedding and vomited so hard her nose bled. She'd assumed she was ill—perhaps dying. But Pauline knew better. "That was quick," she said, raising her eyebrows.

As Sylvia's stomach grew, she found herself so eager to meet the baby it was like a sickness. She couldn't think about anything else. She imagined looking into the baby's eyes and feeling her loneliness dissolve like salt into water.

It didn't happen like that. When she'd first looked into Doree's puffy slits of eyes, a stranger had looked back. She'd been carrying a total stranger in her belly for nine months.

It wasn't that she didn't love her. Oh, she loved her with a fierceness that felt animal. If someone had tried to hurt Doree, Sylvia would have leapt on them and gouged their face until it looked like raw brisket. She would have snapped their necks. She wouldn't have needed to think about it, not even for a second.

Yet the baby was still a stranger. A stranger whose bright, clever eyes seemed to see right through her.

Being away from the baby *was* like missing her arm. Her body felt wrong, too light. But being with the baby didn't make her feel right either. When Sylvia tried to cuddle her, Doree would kick and wriggle and pound Sylvia's neck with her dumpling fists. She always seemed to want something, and Sylvia never knew what. Perhaps all Americans were born with this endless need.

She's her own person, Pauline would say with approval. Sylvia always felt Pauline was mocking her, saying that. Sylvia didn't want the baby to be her own person; Sylvia wanted the baby to be *hers*.

The only time Sylvia felt totally at peace with Doree was when she was nursing. Then they were like two gears in a clock, fitting perfectly into each other's grooves. When her milk let down, her entire body would relax. Her shoulders would lower, her hands unclench, even her toes soften and spread. She'd rock in the chair listening to the baby's rhythmic suck and swallow, her mind a perfect blank.

Pauline—born-in-America Pauline—thought nursing was common. She'd wanted to give Sylvia cabbage leaves to dry up her milk and feed Doree on Carnation instead. Sylvia had refused. *Have it your way*, Pauline had said, raising her eyebrows.

The crying had started the day Doree was born. Sylvia knew it was normal for a woman to feel emotional after a birth. This was different. She'd been wretched since she left Poland. But she never used to cry—never! Now she couldn't stop. It was as if child-birth had opened a channel to a hidden river of tears, and now they were streaming out to sea. She'd wake up in the morning, feel the sun warming her face, and begin to weep. It felt like leaking more than crying, an analogue to the milk that sprang from her breasts, wetting the front of her shirtwaist. The crying changed the very shape of her face—her cheeks looked fuller, and her always narrow eyes were further hooded by her swollen upper lids.

When Louis noticed the crying and asked about it—and he did ask, once or twice—she'd told him she was having her monthly. In truth, she hadn't had her monthly since Doree was born, but Louis didn't know that. Her answer seemed to satisfy him, and he never asked again.

Which was why it was especially shocking when the Italian—a man she'd met not fifteen minutes earlier—looked at her and said, "I hope you don't take offense at my noticing, Mrs. Zelner, but you look very sad."

She opened her mouth to answer, then closed it again. What could she say to this man? How dare he ask her such a question! Before she could formulate her next thought, the secretary bounced into the room, breathless, and launched into a stream of Italian.

The Italian listened, then explained. "I'm so sorry, Mrs. Zelner, but Miss Bianchi can't find the photographs. I'm certain they're here. I'll have to look myself, but it may take some time. Let me pay you for your service today, and I'll have Mr. Johnston schedule another meeting once I'm less . . . disorganized."

Before she could respond, he slid a heavy cream envelope into her hand. Without opening it, she could tell that it was more money than Mr. Johnston had promised her. Much more. She had an image of handing money to a railroad agent, of stepping onto a train with Doree, the mountains disappearing behind them.

She stood and gave a tight little nod to the Italian and the secretary, then stepped into the silent corridor. Walking back towards the lobby, she passed the woman with the marcelled hair, still seated in the armchair hiding her face behind her book. As Sylvia passed, she could have sworn the woman whispered something. But she couldn't hear what.

CHAPTER 13

❧

Jordan

The man was bent forward, peering in Jordan's window, saying something Jordan couldn't hear.

Jordan rolled down the window. "Uh, hi."

"Just making sure you didn't need any help," the man said pleasantly, in a syrup-thick accent. He was middle-aged, with a big square head and flat cheeks pocked with old acne scars. He wore a dark windbreaker and held a large, official-looking flashlight on a holster, like a gun. He must be a groundskeeper or a security guard.

"I drove in the wrong entrance, I guess," Jordan said.

"Easy to do. This is a big place. You're lookin' for reception?"

"Yes."

"Up there." He pointed straight ahead. "Under the awning. The valet'll park you."

"Thanks."

"My pleasure," said the man, raising his hand to his forehead as if to tip his hat, only he wasn't wearing one. "You have a good stay at the Greenbrier."

Jordan nervously handed John-Paul's car keys to a valet—he'd never used a valet before; was he supposed to tip before or after?— and walked into the Lower Lobby carrying his University of Maryland duffel bag. As the door swung shut behind him, he stopped and looked up.

Under lights that were harsher than Jordan would have expected, the lobby was a mutiny of colors—blood reds, tarry black greens, lurid baby blues like the ocean in magazine ads for tropical getaways. Every surface seemed to have a different pattern: The floor was a black-and-white checkerboard, topped with a carpet in a pattern of enormous green jungle leaves; some of the walls were painted with thick vertical stripes like beach awnings, while others were covered with faux grape trellises, like an Italian restaurant. The air smelled cloyingly floral, as if a heavily perfumed woman had just walked by.

He tried to imagine the lobby full of people in their traveling clothes, the way his mother had described (*Everyone dressed nicely for the train back then! Hats and gloves and the whole nine yards*). The enormous space was completely empty. Even the doorman had disappeared back into the inky night. Jordan was completely alone. Alone at the Greenbrier.

After a moment, a woman appeared from a side door behind the check-in counter and gave Jordan a slightly harried smile, as if she'd been pulled from the middle of a different job. "Welcome to the Greenbrier, sir," she said, smoothing down the front of her shirt. "Do you have a reservation?"

. . .

When Jordan woke up the next morning, for a moment he couldn't feel his body. The bed was so fluffy and encompassing there wasn't a single point of pressure. He wondered if this was what a sensory deprivation tank was like. Or being in outer space.

The bed itself was a mahogany four-poster fitted with a ruffly skirt in an oversized yellow floral pattern. The same floral pattern was repeated in the wallpaper—fluffy yellow roses the size of Jordan's head. Everything else was a bright, Crayola crayon green: green carpet, green armchairs, and a mahogany desk with a green-shaded lamp. All the greens and florals made Jordan feel like he was inside one of those Easter baskets with the fake grass they sold at Rite Aid every spring, which he'd coveted desperately as a kid.

This was definitely the weirdest hotel he'd ever stayed in, and he'd stayed in plenty. Growing up, his family always did a winter trip to get away from the grim Baltimore weather. Nothing super fancy, but nice—hotels with HBO and good buffet breakfasts with make-your-own waffles. They'd done Disney and Miami and Montego Bay. Then they'd all gone to Hawaii when Jordan and Jessica were sixteen. Jessica had disappeared one night to "take a walk" and had not reappeared until the next morning, climbing out of a Jeep full of surfers in a cloud of pot smoke. Their father had been furious, their mother white-faced with fear. As punishment, Jessica got sent to be a counselor in training at a Jewish girls' summer camp in Michigan, while Jordan was left at home to coach chess for kindergarteners at the JCC. That turned out to be the last family trip they ever had.

See, Jordan wanted to say to Jessica, *we had a nice childhood. Until you started messing it up.*

He stood and pulled open the curtains. The landscape outside was startlingly bright, causing Jordan to squint and shade his eyes. It took him a moment to realize it had snowed overnight. The lawn glittered alarmingly in the harsh morning sun. From the window he could see the edge of what must be the West Virginia Wing, perched on top of a swell of land like a ship on a wave.

He dressed for breakfast, tucking a small reporter's notebook and a pen in his back pocket. The hallway was silent and seemed endlessly long, as if it had stretched overnight. There was no sign of other guests. The *Post* travel agent who'd booked the trip had said January was the slowest season. From the dim corridor, it was a shock to enter the dining room. The space was enormous, with high ceilings held up with gleaming marble columns like something out of Versailles, winter sunlight flooding through oversized windows and glinting off a series of chandeliers. Only two or three of the round banquet tables were occupied. A woman in a vaguely military-looking green jacket led Jordan to a table and handed him a menu so large he had to hold it with both hands.

"Quiet season?" he forced himself to say. You never knew where a little bit of small talk would get you.

But all the waitress said was "Yes, sir."

While he waited for the food to come, he took notes. *Green stone columns. Three chandeliers—9 feet high? Mirrors everywhere. Elderly couple sharing a plate of peaches and whipped cream (I think). Waiters standing the same way—hands behind back, shoulders straight. Almost spooky.*

By the time his waffle arrived, he'd filled three pages with notes.

Sometimes Jordan wondered why he'd felt so drawn to becoming a reporter in the first place. It wasn't the most obvious path for someone who'd been too shy as a kid to call the movie theater for showtimes. *Maybe*, Jessica had once said, *it's because it's the only way for a good little boy to ask questions.*

CHAPTER 14

Doree

"*E*nough with the questions," their father said to Alan, taking a sip of coffee. "Whatever the hotel is building down there, I'm sure it's for a good purpose."

Alan ignored him. "Maybe it's a bomb shelter," he said, cramming toast in his mouth while balancing a book called *Ferns of the Appalachians* on the rim of his breakfast plate. "So we don't have to go underneath our desks when we see the flash."

"Tommy says it's a secret underground safe for the Rockefellers, for them to hide their gold," Pete said. "But Tommy's dad said if he caught him talking about it, he'd slap the snot out of him. Says it ain't our business."

"*Isn't* our business," corrected Louis. "And Mr. Curry is right."

Doree rolled her eyes. This was breakfast these days; listening to her brothers speculate about the hole behind the Greenbrier. It was, she had to admit, an impressively large hole. By now, the excavators had produced enough wet red mud to give the Catholic church a new dirt and gravel parking lot. The rest went towards building out the resort's airstrip, where the bigwigs with private planes touched down. Trucks lumbered in and out of the service road entrance continuously, their dumpers laden with heavy red soil.

Alan had been observing the dig nearly every day after school, sitting on the edge of Copeland Hill with his birding binoculars, taking notes in one of his little yellow notebooks.

A thump and a shriek came from upstairs, then the sound of Sylvia muttering in Yiddish.

"Grandma's having a hard morning," Louis said.

Every morning was a hard morning with their grandmother these days.

Doree poured herself another cup of coffee. She and Patty were on a reducing plan, and breakfast was black coffee and a banana. She didn't need to reduce—she was slim as always—but Patty was trying to lose ten pounds for graduation, so Doree was doing it too, for support. She was starving, though.

As if he'd read her mind, Sol pushed a bag into Doree's hands. "Hey, *shaina maidel*, take this," he whispered. Inside was a slice of leftover apple cake wrapped in a napkin. "I don't want to hear about you fainting in school. I won't tell Patty."

"Thanks, Grandpa." She gave him a peck on his wrinkled cheek, just to the side of his scar-gnarled left ear.

Pete and Alan flung their plates in the sink with a clatter, grabbed their satchels, and followed Doree to the door. Outside, the sky sagged with heavy, wet clouds. The snows of January had melted and refrozen and melted again so many times the sidewalk was covered in a skin of chocolate milk–colored slush. On the radio yesterday they'd said the groundhog in Pennsylvania had seen his shadow, so there would be six more weeks of winter. Doree shivered and cast her mind into the future, the summer, college. She'd be moving into the dormitories with Patty, in their new car. She'd be wearing Bermuda shorts and a crisp white shirt unbuttoned at the neck. A boy would see her struggling with a heavy box and offer to help. He'd have a letterman jacket and a pair of white bucks like Pat Boone.

Splosh! Something wet hit her in the chest. She looked down to see a dark blotch of mud on the front of her coat. "Alan!" she screamed.

"Oh, sorry," said her brother. In his hand was a clump of dripping green foliage. "I just wanted to have a better look at these hellebores. They're really early this year! I didn't mean to splash you."

Doree scowled. But Alan didn't notice; he'd already turned back to his plants.

School felt never-ending, the way it always did on Tuesdays now. Doree sat through her classes in dread, wishing she could twirl the clock's hands ahead and be home eating dinner. Tuesdays were her days to pay Junior. When band practice was done, she would meet him behind his grandfather's Travel Paradise motel, to hand him the money he'd demanded, the money that would keep her family safe.

Today a sharp wind was blowing as she picked her way through the snow on the shoulder of the road, her feet punching holes in the crust with every step. Icy water began seeping through her shoes.

The Travel Paradise was a cluster of decaying fisherman's cottages on Route 60. Nobody ever seemed to stay there. The kids at school whispered stories that old Cecil Carper used the trashy field behind the Travel Paradise to bury his moonshining money.

That theory never made a lot of sense to Doree. If Cecil Carper wanted to hide money, wouldn't it be safer buried under his house on Mill Hill? If Cecil Carper *had* money, why would all his grandkids run around shoeless?

If Cecil Carper had money, why would his grandson blackmail Doree?

Doree skirted the office building and walked around to the back side of the cottages, where the trash cans sat in a row. It was dark behind the building except for a small patch of light from a single lit window. Even in the cold, she could smell the rotting garbage. She wished she were anywhere else.

Junior was already there. He leaned against the cinder block wall in the shadows, smoking a cigarette. His denim jacket not nearly warm enough for the weather—he was shivering like a skinny hound.

"Hey there," he said, fixing his colorless eyes on Doree.

She strode forward with her arm outstretched, ten dollars in her hand. She wanted to keep as much distance between her body and his as possible.

"See you next week," he called.

She didn't answer.

She had to give him the money. But she didn't need to speak to him.

Doree crept silently into the front hallway and hid her wet shoes behind a pair of old galoshes. Smoothing her hair, she headed, as she knew she must, towards the kitchen.

Sylvia straightened her back when she heard Doree enter, but did not turn around. Pauline was propped in a chair, a graying towel draped over her chest like a bib. Her mouth was slack as Sylvia spooned in chicken noodle soup. When she spotted Doree, Pauline sat up and, with sudden vigor, spat out a mouthful of soup. Flecks of chewed carrot and celery spattered the towel, lurid orange and green under the fluorescent kitchen light.

"There she is, Miss High-and-Mighty!" Pauline cried.

"*Alte makhsheyfe*," Sylvia swore. "Look at the mess you've made!"

"She thinks her shit smells like roses," Pauline said, her eyes gleaming with a childlike malice. She turned to the wall and said in a confidential tone, "But she's nothing but a greenhorn, you know. Just off the boat from Poland."

"Hi, Grandma," Doree said, feeling the same familiar sadness at seeing her grandmother this way. "It's me. Doree."

Pauline continued to gaze at the wall.

"Set the table," Sylvia said, swiping at Pauline's mouth with a napkin.

Even now, standing in the kitchen with a soup spoon in her hand, Sylvia looked glamorous. She wore a navy blue boatneck blouse with buttons on each shoulder, tucked into a full skirt, covered with an immaculate white apron. She'd sewn it all herself, of course. The blouse was tight over her bust, which looked like the noses of two B-52 bombers. Doree wished she had her mother's figure. But no matter how many exercises she did—lying on her back lifting a dictionary over and over, like *Seventeen* magazine suggested—she was still what Lee Burdette and them called a "carpenter's dream." The only way Doree resembled Sylvia was in her brown hair and her finely sculpted straight nose.

Still, Pauline mistook Doree for Sylvia more often than not now.

Sylvia's feet, standing on the worn linoleum floor, were in shiny black pumps. There was nowhere in White Sulphur Springs those pumps would fit in, Doree thought. Except the Greenbrier. And Sylvia wouldn't set foot there.

Doree began setting the table with the blue violet-patterned plates, the ones they used for meat dinners. Back when her grandmother used to cook, they'd rarely bothered with separate plates for meat and dairy. But Sylvia followed the kosher laws more strictly. She wouldn't even eat out; when the rest of the family was invited to lunch at a neighbor's house, she stayed home. *I won't eat tref,* she would say. *You can just eat bread,* Louis would tell her. But Sylvia wouldn't relent. Doree figured that, for her mother, keeping kosher so exactingly was just another way of telling the people of White Sulphur Springs that she wasn't like them, that she wanted nothing to do with them.

"You'll cook dinner tomorrow," Sylvia announced. "I'll be doing the windows."

Sylvia still arranged the shop window displays for holidays—Christmas, Valentine's Day, the Fourth of July. It was one of the few times she went to the store these days.

"Yes, Mama."

"Oh, and I decided." Sylvia turned to her daughter. "No to the Valentine's Day dance."

"Mama!"

"Nothing but trouble, such things." Sylvia dried her hands on her apron.

"Mama, I'm almost eighteen!" She could feel tears of anger and humiliation pricking her eyelashes. But she couldn't cry in front of her mother—it would only encourage her. Doree thought, not for the first time: *If only she knew what I was doing for her. Then maybe she'd be sorry.*

Sylvia shrugged. "When you move out, you do as you like. Go to a dance. Get in trouble with hillbilly boys. Go to *college.*" She said the word "college" with contempt, as if it were in the same category as Valentine's dances and other American foolishness. "But until this time, you follow my rules." She turned back to Pauline. Doree was dismissed.

No wonder her mother had no friends. She was the most miserable person Doree had ever met.

CHAPTER 15

Sylvia

"*C*hocolates?" Sylvia grinned. "You stole these from the maid's cart?"

Aggie fluttered her eyelashes with comic innocence and shrugged her shoulders. "I figured it would be quiet in the store after lunchtime, and we could eat sweets and gossip like the rich ladies back home."

Agnieszka Jankowski was a masseuse at the Greenbrier. She had immigrated from Warsaw to New York at twenty with her new husband. The husband had promptly run off, so Aggie got herself a scholarship to the Swedish Institute for Massage, then a job at the Greenbrier. She was resourceful. Sylvia admired that.

When Aggie had first heard there was a new Polish woman in White Sulphur Springs, she'd used her day off to march into town and inspect Sylvia. It didn't bother her that Sylvia was a Jew, not a Pole.

"We all eat pierogi, no?" Aggie had shrugged.

"Yes, but are your mother's pierogi fried in lard?" Sylvia had responded.

"Of course. But they would be delicious fried in butter too."

After that, they were friends. At thirty, Aggie was nine years older than Sylvia, and she enjoyed acting the part of the older sister. Sylvia found she didn't mind: She liked it, actually. To be able to relax into the part of being the petted younger girl, to be fussed over and laughed at. To speak Polish again. It was a relief.

"How's the spying?" Sylvia asked teasingly.

"I'm not a spy!" Aggie responded, with a face of mock protest. "I'm just a good citizen being paid for services rendered."

Several FBI agents had recently come to speak discreetly with certain Greenbrier employees. The agents told them they could earn twenty dollars a week for keeping their eyes and ears open for anything "of national security interest." They told Aggie that she was an especially valuable asset.

"Anyway, even if I was a spy, there'd be nothing to report," Aggie said. "Every day is the same. The Germans swim laps in the morning. The Italians swim later, before lunch, though not for half as long. The ladies have their beauty parlor appointments. If it's nice out, they stroll on the lawn. And they play so much bridge—Italians and Germans separately, of course. It's incredibly dull. The biggest excitement is when somebody tries to bribe a bellboy for a newspaper and gets reported to Mr. Johnston."

"Truly, you've got a resort full of Nazis and you've seen *nothing*?"

"Well, something a bit strange did happen yesterday," Aggie said, popping a chocolate in her mouth. "I had that client again, the one I told you about, the German ambassador's wife. Bebe Thomsen. Such an odd woman—pretty for her age, but does her hair like it's still 1933."

Sylvia thought of the woman she'd seen reading in the Greenbrier corridor, with the marcelled waves and dark lipstick.

"She spent the whole massage blabbing about how she's no

Nazi supporter, that her husband's not even really the ambassador, just the chargé d'affaires. That she wants to stay in the US after the war."

"Maybe she's hoping you'll put in a good word?" Sylvia said.

"As if anyone would listen to me. Me a spy, imagine! Anyhow, I better be going. Oh, but wait!" Aggie's round eyes became even rounder. "Tell me about the Italian! The dresses! What happened?"

"Nothing happened," Sylvia said. "I went all the way to the resort, and he couldn't even find the picture to show me the design. I'll go back tomorrow, if he's found it."

"That's it? You went and he didn't have the picture, so you left?"

"We talked."

"About what?"

"Just . . . our children. That sort of thing."

It was true. They'd talked about these things. He'd talked about them, at least. How could Sylvia explain to Aggie that it had felt like more? That somehow, in less than an hour, the Italian seemed interested in her—in who she was—in a way Louis never had been.

*L*ouis wasn't a bad husband. There were men who'd talk sweetly before the wedding, then knock your teeth out on your honeymoon, Sylvia knew this. He wasn't that, not at all.

The problem was that, to Louis, Sylvia could have been anyone. His mother had sent him to Baltimore to find a wife and he'd found one. He'd picked Sylvia like a shopkeeper stocking a shelf. She had the right shape, the right qualities—young, pretty, Jewish. But did he notice any of her particulars? Did he care that she loved the poetry of Adam Mickiewicz, that she hated beets, that her favorite color was blue, that her father had called her "princess"? If he'd set eyes on Fruma first, would he be married to Fruma instead, and equally indifferent?

Sylvia's grandmother Chaja had a story about a woman who made a golem out of clay to do the housework. The golem cooked, the golem cleaned, the golem wiped the children's bottoms. The only difference between the woman and the golem was that the golem had red eyes. If Sylvia made a golem of herself, would Louis be able to tell?

Were all men like this? It had seemed possible. But then she'd met the Italian. He'd noticed she was sad. He'd understood that she didn't belong here.

Sylvia figured she'd need two hundred dollars for her plan.

The Italian had paid her five dollars for her time, more than she could have dreamed. The detainees wouldn't be allowed to take American dollars back to Europe with them when they left, so perhaps he was merely dropping ballast. She told Louis she was earning two dollars an hour, which was enough to make him whistle. The rest she'd stuffed into a pair of socks and crammed in the back corner of the drawer.

Still, she'd need to work forty hours at the Italian's rate to earn enough, and that wasn't likely. She'd have to make up the difference somehow.

So she'd begun skimming a dime or two from the register whenever she was in the store, then making a hair comb or a few sewing notions disappear from the books. It wasn't much, but it would add up eventually. She felt a faint whisper of guilt, but she was only doing what she had to.

At night, rocking Doree in the nursery, she'd stare at the

postcard. She'd spent so many hours holding it between her thumb and index finger that its bottom right corner was soft as felt.

In the foreground of the postcard was an orange tree. In the background was the skyline of a white city. On the back, in her mother's faint, sloping handwriting, it read:

Tel Aviv is so sunny you wouldn't believe. The twins and I miss you terribly. Any news of Leon and Alfred? I pray all day.
  Love,
  Mama

Tel Aviv. Tel Aviv. The words vibrated on her tongue with the tang of oranges. When she had the money, when the war was over, she would go. Train to Baltimore. Train to New York. Ocean liner to London, then Haifa. She had to hope there would be ocean liners again, once the war was over. She had to hope the British would allow her in.

The twins would be fifteen now. The last time she'd seen them, in that awful spring of 1939, they'd been cowlicked twelve-year-olds. Asher and Oscar. She imagined them growing tall and brown under the Palestine sun. *So sunny you wouldn't believe.*

She longed for that sunshine like a delicacy she'd read about in a cookbook but had never tasted. The Greenbrier Valley was meant to be paradise—it said so right on the resort brochure—but it seemed to Sylvia it rained more here than in Poland. Slushy snow. Garish orange mud. Mountains trailing clouds like winding sheets.

She longed for her mother too, though she'd spent most of her girlhood irritated at her for one thing or another. For making her help in the kitchen while her brothers ran around outside. For being plump, but vain of her delicate ankles. For leaving her children's cheeks moist with spittle when she kissed them—disgusting. It had always been her mother standing between Sylvia and what she desired: a new frock, a free Saturday afternoon, staying in Poland.

Now she dreamed of sitting on a balcony with her mother, Doree playing calmly between them. Doree would grow up speaking Yiddish, not wrinkling her nose at it the way Pauline did.

Would it be wrong, taking the baby from her father? She supposed so. But sometimes you did things for survival, even when they were wrong. Would Louis understand that this was for survival, for Sylvia's survival? And Doree's too—babies needed their mothers, right? She hoped he would. That's all she could do: hope.

*T*he Italian looked so pleased to see her that Sylvia almost began to cry right on the spot.

"Mrs. Zelner! Thank you for coming again! I've found the picture of the dresses. It was in one of the suitcases that hadn't been unpacked, if you can believe it."

Sylvia and the Italian sat down at the desk. The young assistant was sitting on the settee, writing on a pad of paper, her mouth twisted into a knot of concentration.

The Italian handed Sylvia the picture. It was a sort of postcard, actually, like a souvenir photo you'd get at a funfair. It showed his daughters in old-fashioned outfits—costumes, really: gowns with contrasting bodices and full petticoats, floral kerchiefs tied around their shoulders. They both wore frilled white mobcaps and expressions of suppressed amusement. Behind them was the Italian himself, in a frock coat, breeches, and a three-cornered hat. A woman—his wife, presumably—stood beside him, in a gown similar to her daughters', though instead of a mobcap she wore a wide flat straw disk of a hat trimmed in ribbon. She was pretty, the wife, paler and plumper than Sylvia had imagined (She'd imagined? She supposed she had). Despite the ridiculous outfit, her expression was as gracious and dignified as if she were greeting an ambassador at a dinner party.

Sylvia looked up at the Italian, eyebrow raised but unsure about whether to smile. Was this a joke?

He laughed. "I know. It's quite silly. The last time my girls were here, we visited the colonial settlement of Williamsburg, in Virginia. The Rockefellers have been restoring the buildings there. They have a few costumed playactors demonstrating old-fashioned skills—blacksmithing and so on. My girls were enchanted. Mr. Rockefeller arranged for us to try on the costumes. I was hoping to bring them similar dresses, and perhaps a shirt and breeches for myself, as a souvenir of America. They'd love it." His expression darkened. "It was such a nice day."

Such a nice day. A day before everything changed. A day when you thought all the days in front of you would be nice ones, an unbroken chain of nice days stretching luxuriously towards the horizon. Sitting on the bleachers watching the boys' track team under the stadium lights. A nip of brandy that Ewa had filched from her father's cabinet. Chicken for dinner with the whole family there. Then, suddenly, a wave picks you up and deposits you on the other side of the world, and you realize your last nice day was years ago and ten thousand miles away.

Though it wasn't really sudden, was it? She could have seen the clouds massing overhead, if only she'd been paying attention. Little fool.

"It's possible?" The Italian was looking at her, his greenish eyes keen and bright.

"The dresses? I suppose. I've never made anything in that

style, but it should be possible. I will need measurements, naturally. You will not be too particular about the materials?"

"No, no, just something that resembles the picture in its basics. Will you do a sketch?"

"A sketch?"

"Isn't that how dressmakers start, sketching? I have pencils here. Charcoals as well."

Sylvia could hardly suppress a snort. What did he think she was, some kind of Parisian couturier? She took in alternations for Zelner's customers—dungarees, flannel nightdresses. Sometimes she made a dress, but hardly the type of fine gown she'd once stitched for her uncle's dress shop. She didn't do *sketches*. Before she could say as much, she had a thought: If she worked slowly, she would make more money.

The boat to Haifa. Oranges. Sunshine.

"Yes, a sketch," she said.

The Italian stood up and made a sweeping gesture at the desk. He pulled out a chair for her to sit down. "Your studio, if you please. I'm so eager to see your handiwork. Based on what Miss Walsh has told me, I'm quite prepared to be amazed. It's an art, sewing, isn't it?" He smiled, the gap in his front teeth showing, and once again his eagerness made Sylvia feel like weeping.

*B*ack outside, Sylvia walked back past the guard box. More of the grass had died, and a wide brown border of mud oozed around the base. As she passed, a head jutted out, like a turtle sticking out of its shell. Carl Carper.

"Hello, Mrs. Zelner. Can I ask you a few questions?" Carper's downy upper lip trembled as he tried to keep it stiff, in imitation of a military man in a film, surely.

The rumor in town was that Carl Carper was rejected by the army for feeble-mindedness. But how smart did you need to be to point a gun at a Nazi?

"What is it, Carl?" Sylvia sighed. She'd been out all day, and her breasts were heavy with milk. If she waited much longer, she'd have wet patches on the front of her dress.

"Did you see anything strange?"

"Everything is strange, Carl," she said, and turned to leave.

She heard it before she felt it.

A whistling sound, then a thick squelching thud. Then a voice, male but falsetto high with emotion, screaming, "Eat dirt, Jew!"

Then she was on her back looking up at the sky, the branches of a tree black in silhouette. What? A cold stinging on her left cheekbone and something in her eye, wet and gritty. The ground was ice hard against her back. Carl Carper's face came into view. His pale eyes were wide and his wet mouth hung open.

"Mrs. Zelner? Are you all right?"

She sat up. As she did, something unpeeled from her face and tumbled into her lap. Mud. She'd been hit by a ball of icy mud. She saw something flash past the corner of her eye, and heard a man yell, "Got him!"

A pair of uniformed policemen were kneeling over a figure sprawled in the grass, its legs kicking like a beetle's.

"My Lord in heaven," said Carl Carper. "That's Wagner, from the laundry."

Before she could get a good look, two guards ran down from the main gatehouse and picked her up by the arms. "I can walk," she told them, but they insisted on holding her elbows and steering her back into the lobby, then down a series of corridors until they came to a heavy door with a sign that said GENERAL MANAGER in gold letters.

Hope Walsh looked up from her typewriter in surprise. "Mrs. Zelner! Oh dear, did you have a fall?"

"It was Wagner, ma'am," said one of the guards. "He got loose during the raid. Hit this lady with a mud ball. They got him pinned down on the lawn now."

Hope Walsh stood up, frowning, and began issuing rapid instructions. Sylvia was laid down on the office settee. A house-keeper appeared with a washbasin and a pile of white hand towels. Sylvia recognized her: Evangeline Curry, the mechanic's wife, the one with the baby girl Doree's age. She had a kind, round face with ruddy cheeks and yellow hair scraped back in a bun. Evangeline began dabbing at Sylvia's face with the towels, clucking and murmuring the whole time, as if Sylvia were a baby. The towels, dipped in warm water from the basin, were as soft as anything Sylvia had ever felt against her skin. When they came away, they were streaked brown and red. Blood. She was bleeding?

"Just a few scratches, I reckon," said Evangeline.

It was warm and dim in the office. Sylvia let her eyes flutter halfway closed.

The interior door flew open, and Mr. Johnston strode in, his elderly baby face flushed. "Mrs. Zelner, I'm so sorry for this incident," he said. "Hope, have you called the doctor?"

"No doctor," said Sylvia, rousing herself and struggling to sit up.

"It's no trouble," said Mr. Johnston. "We have an on-call physician. He can be here in less than five minutes."

"No, no," she said. She straightened her dress, then reached up to smooth her hair. The top of her head was crusted with mud. What would she say to Pauline?

"I should explain," said Mr. Johnston. "The police were conducting a raid in the staff quarters this afternoon—I'm afraid several of our waiters and kitchen staff have been caught passing out German American Federation pamphlets. It was a minority— a small minority—and they've been arrested for collaboration. Wagner, the one who attacked you, managed to get away briefly. He's under arrest now."

Sylvia was suddenly overwhelmed with the urge to get out of the resort. She stood and nodded stiffly at Mr. Johnston.

"I will be fine," she said. "I will come back tomorrow with fabric samples for Mr. Cattaneo."

Before Mr. Johnston or anyone else could respond, she had pushed open the heavy wood door and was striding down the corridor as fast as she could. But it was already too late. The milk had overflowed and was trickling warmly down her stomach.

❧

CHAPTER 16

Jordan

Jordan blinked in the snow-spangled light as he stepped out of the North Lobby. There was no one around, not even a doorman. *Weird*, Jordan thought again. The way his mom had described it, the Greenbrier was like a constant New Year's Eve party—always stuffed to the gills with movie stars and millionaires, champagne bottles popping like arcade gunfire. Times changed, he guessed.

Jordan was headed into town. He carried a backpack with his notebook and a small silver Olympus point-and-shoot camera he'd gotten from his uncle Pete for his twenty-first birthday. He also had an apple and a banana he'd taken from the breakfast buffet; even though he knew it was included, taking food from the dining room still felt like stealing.

The road between the resort and downtown was a two-lane stretch of Highway 60, with no sidewalk and a steeply sloping shoulder. Jordan figured not too many guests would bother to walk to town. The dead winter grass was wet from the melting snow, and he felt cold water trickling into his shoes. A truck with rusted fenders rumbled by, and the driver tossed a paper cup out the window. It hit the road on the dotted white line, brown liquid splashing up in a ragged arc.

Once off the resort's grounds, the woods had a threadbare look. The trees were skinny and anemic, with damp drooping branches and brown needles like worn-out brooms. Through the skimpy winter underbrush Jordan saw the shape of a house, then another. They had been half consumed by vegetation and rot, like the corpses of enormous animals.

As he walked, he started to see the sparse rows of buildings he'd passed the night he drove in. The first several looked abandoned. A ground-level shop had lost most of the gold letters from its sign. Only the *o* and *r* remained. In the window beneath the eaves, a purple curtain seemed to move, though that must have been Jordan's imagination.

Jordan tried to picture his mother as a girl growing up here, but he couldn't. She was too ordinary. People from grim little Appalachian towns like White Sulphur Springs ought to be odd in either charming or sinister ways, like something out of a Faulkner novel. His mother was so normal, so suburban, such a *mom*. Like every other Jewish mom in the northwest suburbs of Baltimore, more or less. Worked a job, volunteered at the synagogue, shuttled her kids to soccer in the Volvo, got her hair done before Sabbath dinner every Friday. Was it really possible she'd grown up in one of the sad-looking houses clinging to the hillside across the road?

He kept walking, passing a café whose sign was in an old-fashioned font that reminded him of vintage car ads. THE STARLING. He peered in the half-open blinds and saw all the tables and bar stools had been removed, leaving rusty bolt holes in the tiled floor. Creepy.

All he knew about his grandfather's store was that it had been on Main Street, which wasn't much help; Main Street seemed to be the only street with anything at all on it. He supposed he could have called his grandfather, but somehow that hadn't occurred to him until now.

Jordan's grandpa Louis wasn't much for conversations. When Jordan and his family would visit him at his house in Huntington, West Virginia, Louis would ask normal, grandfatherly questions—How's school? What's your favorite subject?—but he never quite seemed to listen to the answers, always nodding a beat too late. He'd stand up and start washing dishes while the rest of the family was still eating breakfast. It was like his mind was always in some other room. He seemed happiest in the jewelry shop where he worked, polishing watches and rearranging displays.

Now that he thought about it, Jordan wasn't sure he'd ever had a proper sit-down conversation with his grandfather, just the two of them. More talkative was Nana, Jordan's step-grandmother— the only grandmother he'd ever known—always on hand with a plate of banana bread or a story about their latest vacation to Puerto Rico. There was a single photo of Alan in their house, a black-and-white of a gangly kid in a fisherman's vest looking away from the camera. Jordan had never asked about Alan. If it was too painful for his mother to talk about, it must be doubly painful for his grandfather.

He stopped and looked up. There, in front of him, was a brick shop building with a tattered green and yellow awning. It stood alone between the street corner and a vacant lot. On the bricks of the side wall, in white paint that was surprisingly intact for being more than thirty years old, were the words ZELNER'S LOW PRICE STORE: WE HAVE EVERYTHING YOU NEED AND MORE!

Jordan walked around to the front and pressed his face against the cold glass of the window. The shadowed interior was almost completely empty. He could make out high shelves and a counter, with a bleached square where a cash register must have once sat. There was a lone object lying on the floor next to the counter—a shoe? Jordan was squinting, trying to make sense of it, when he heard a scraping sound behind him.

He turned to see a tiny old woman dragging herself along the sidewalk with a cane. She was dressed entirely in purple: a purple coat buttoned down the front, purple pants sticking out beneath, even a pair of lavender sneakers with Velcro straps, like a child would wear.

"You there, son," she rasped. "Whatcha doin' lookin' in the old Jew store?"

CHAPTER 17

Doree

FEBRUARY 1959

Doree was working alone in the store after school—her father was doing a pickup in Lewisburg—sitting behind the counter half-heartedly working on a cryptogram for Alan, tapping her pencil in time to the Everly Brothers on the radio. "Dreeeeeam, dream, dream, dreeeeeam."

Then something made her look up. Later, she would wonder if it was a feeling, a rearrangement of air molecules. She saw the man through the store window before he opened the door. There was something about the way he walked that said he was handsome. Shoulders a bit back, hips a bit forward, a graceful pivot as he turned to enter the store. He stopped. He looked around. He smiled at Doree—an easy, happy smile, as if Doree were an old friend.

Doree had never seen a man so good-looking. He had full lips that turned up at the corners, round dark eyes, and shoe polish-black hair with the wave of a matinee idol. Was he a film star? It wasn't impossible. He could have wandered down from the resort, bored of golf, looking for trouble. But she didn't recognize him, and she saw all the films that came to the Greenbrier theater.

"Good afternoon," she said, feeling like she was speaking underwater. "Welcome to Zelner's. Can I help you find something?"

"A frying pan," he said. "Do you sell those?"

A frying pan. A frying pan. For a moment she couldn't remember. Her face felt hot and her body seemed to move in slow motion as she stood up. She took a deep breath. "Yes, right over here." She smiled at him, and he smiled back again, and wow, she suddenly felt as dizzy as she had when she'd fainted after the flu.

She floated to the kitchen shelf, and he followed her. He picked up a frying pan and she stared at his hands—large and olive-skinned, a stainless-steel watch with a khaki band around his left wrist. No wedding ring.

No wedding ring. She shook her head as if to shake the thought out. What was wrong with her? This was a stranger.

And yet.

He held up a bar of kitchen soap, and when she reached to take it from him and put it on the counter, it felt like he'd given her a gift.

Then he said he needed bedsheets.

"Single or . . . full-size?" Doree asked, feeling her scalp prickling with embarrassment.

"Single." That smile. Those lips. His round eyes were large, in a way that made him look friendly and slightly comic, like he was about to tell a joke. He looked a few years older than her—perhaps twenty-one or twenty-two, enough to make him seem fully adult, somehow solid and finished in a way that the boys at school were not.

"Looks like you're setting up housekeeping." She was shocked at her boldness; it almost felt like someone else was speaking through her mouth.

"I guess so!" he said. "I'm moving in on Laurel Drive. I must seem like a terrible bachelor, moving in without even my own bedsheets."

He had an interesting accent, like a tough city kid in a film, his speech quick, vowels slightly nasal. "Bachelor" came out "bache-lah."

"What brings you to town?"

"Just work. I'm with a company doing audiovisual work for the Greenbrier. Fixing televisions and that sort of thing."

Doree thought of the vans she'd seen driving through the dark. "Forsythe Associates?" she asked.

He tilted his head and gave her a curious look, reassessing her. "Yeah," he said. "Forsythe. You know it?"

"I saw the vans."

He must be at least a little bit important to get his own house—and on Laurel Drive too, where the houses were new brick ranches with fences and yards. Usually Greenbrier workers lived in the employee boardinghouses on Copeland Hill.

"This is a swell little town," he said, his eyes roaming around the store. "I thought it would be like Dogpatch in *Li'l Abner* or something. You know, all log cabins and turnip fields." He grinned at Doree. "Sorry, that was rude, I didn't mean it like that. It's just I've never been to West Virginia."

Doree smiled. "Where are you from?"

"Newark."

"New York, wow," she said, then immediately regretted the "wow"—she didn't want him to figure her for a hick who'd never been anywhere. Even if she *had* never been anywhere but Baltimore.

"*Newark*, actually," he said, grinning a loose, easy grin. "It's in New Jersey. Only about ten miles from New York, but it sure felt like a million when I was growing up there." He picked up a pack of playing cards and a chocolate bar and laid them on the counter with his sheets and pan.

As Doree rang up his purchases, he leaned on the counter on one arm. All of a sudden, he gave a low whistle. "A cipher!" he said.

Doree felt herself blush from her chest in a slow humiliating wave all the way to her face. The cryptogram she'd been working on was sitting right there in the open. Now the handsome stranger would think she was some sort of geeky, unfeminine girl.

She nodded—what else could she do? "It's a game I play with my brother sometimes," she explained. "He loves math."

"Neat," he said. Then he grinned. "Ciphers. You could be a spy."

Doree gave a small laugh, not sure if he was making fun of her.

"Sorry, my manners, I haven't even introduced myself," he said, holding out his hand. "I'm Antonio, but everyone calls me Tony." His face was so friendly and open.

He wasn't making fun of her. She held out her own hand. "Doree."

"Pleased to meet you, Doree. Hope I'll be seeing you again soon."

This was where a girl was meant to simper or giggle or stare coyly at the floor, Doree knew. But instead she channeled her mother's fearless gaze, looked him right in the eyes, and said exactly what she was thinking: "I hope so too."

He was almost out the door when he turned around. "I had a thought, Doree," he said. "Maybe you could take a drive with me sometime? Show me a sight or two? I just got to town, and I haven't had a chance to see anything yet. Maybe Saturday?"

Seventeen magazine said a girl should never accept a date for Saturday any later than Tuesday. It was Thursday.

But maybe *Seventeen* magazine hadn't seen a man as good-looking as Tony.

"Sure," she said. "I'd love to."

*A*ntonio. Tony. Antonio. Tony. She walked home to the bouncy rhythm of his name, her tongue curling around the syllables, almost tasting them. Antonio. Tony.

Her insides felt as if they'd been scooped out and replaced in a slightly different position. She thought of a field mouse, snatched up by a hawk and dropped in another county, one with different weather, brighter sun. Even the colors of the houses on her walk home—winter-beaten grays, dull blues, and peeling whites—seemed clearer, more alive. Every sight on her walk seemed to have a slight force field around it, an energy.

Often, when he had a receptive—or merely captive—audience, Sol would tell the story of when he first saw Pauline. *She walked through the door carrying a brisket wrapped in brown paper,* he'd say, pausing for drama, *and I knew this was the woman I would marry. My* beshert—*my destiny.*

Was today the day Doree would tell her grandchildren about, decades in the future? *I saw him through the window, and I knew. He was my* beshert.

She shook her head again. Was she losing her mind?

It was dark when she got home. Stepping inside, she found her grandmother sitting on the chair in the front hall, next to the side table with the bird statue. The bird's head had been knocked off at some point in the distant past and glued on slightly crookedly, such that its eyes seemed to see you no matter where you were.

"Grandma?"

"Hello, sweetheart."

Doree bent down to kiss her grandmother's wrinkled walnut of a face. It was almost as if Pauline really recognized her. How long had it been since her grandmother had said her name? Two years? Three? How desperately Doree still missed her childhood afternoons of sitting in the kitchen together, eating Pauline's applesauce cookies, listening to stories about Baltimore, sun slanting through the curtains.

"There's terrible trouble in the parlor," Pauline said. "Has Hy returned?"

Hy was Pauline's brother, who'd died of mustard gas during the first World War. He was buried in the cemetery in Baltimore with Pauline's parents. They went there most years for his yahrzeit, lighting a candle inside the little bronze box attached to his gravestone and reciting the mourner's kaddish. Before they'd leave, they'd all place a small pebble on the stone as a show of remembrance. ("But I *don't* remember him," Alan, rock in his left hand, would say. "I never met him!")

"I don't know, Grandma, maybe," Doree said. "I'll go check."

There was indeed noise coming from the parlor. She caught the sound of her father's low, even voice. Why was he here? He should be at the shop, unloading the inventory from Lewisburg. Then came her mother's high, serrated voice, slashing at the air like a knife. Sobbing too. That was Alan. *Oh no.*

Doree crept up the stairs, careful not to make the old pine floorboards creak. If she sat halfway up the staircase, she could see into the parlor through the transom window above the door.

Through the pebbled glass Doree could see a distorted image of Alan curled on the sofa with his hands over his ears the way he did when he was extremely angry or upset. His face was red and shiny with tears. Doree's father sat in the easy chair. Grandpa was there too, on the piano bench. Her mother stood in front of Louis, hands on hips, her head jutted forward like a bird of prey.

"Just explain it again, Alan," Louis said. "If the principal has the wrong idea, just explain it again so I understand."

"I explained it!" wailed Alan. "I explained it!"

"Why should he explain himself again?" shrieked Sylvia, jabbing the air with one red-painted fingernail. "He told you. If that *khnyok* principal has a problem, he can go jump in the lake."

"Sylvia, Alan needs to get along in school. Alan, if you want us to help you, you need to explain what happened again."

Alan sniffed and wiped his nose on his sleeve. The words came out in a rush. "Rodney Level said Jews would burn in hell because we don't take Jesus into our hearts, and I said there was no such thing as hell, and Rodney Level said the Bible says so, and I said the people who wrote the Bible didn't know what they were talking about, and Rodney Level said God wrote the Bible, and I said there's no such thing as God, it's just a story. Then Mrs. Dickson said I had to go to the principal."

"Oh, Alan," said Louis.

"What?" Sylvia shrieked again. "You explain to me exactly what he did wrong!"

"You can't go around telling people at school there's no such thing as God."

"That's his opinion! What, he's not allowed his opinion? In freedom of speech America?"

Grandpa Sol reached out to pat Alan's arm. "A Jew is allowed to question," he said.

"The questioning is not the problem," Louis said. "The problem is talking about it in school."

"The goyim can say Alan will burn up in hell, but Alan cannot say, 'No, I don't believe you.'" Sylvia bent down so close to Louis their noses were nearly touching.

"He didn't simply say, 'No, I don't believe you.' He went and told him God's just a story."

"I just told the truth!" Alan said. "You told me to always tell the truth, and now you're mad because I told the truth."

"This is not so much about truth or not truth," Sol said to Alan. "No person wants to hear another person say bad things about his God."

"I didn't say bad things," Alan said. "That's what I'm telling you. I just said the truth. There's no way God is real. It's just a story. The world wasn't made in six days. It's scientifically impossible. Rabbi Lieb agrees."

"That's not exactly what Rabbi Lieb said." Louis sighed.

Rabbi Lieb was the elderly circuit rabbi who traveled around southern West Virginia and southwest Virginia in his paneled station wagon. After incessant questioning from Alan about the details of Noah's Ark (Didn't the lions eat the gazelles? How did Noah travel all the way to Australia to get kangaroos?), Rabbi Lieb had told him not to take all the Old Testament stories literally but to consider their moral lessons.

"Look," Louis went on, "we're not here to debate about God. We're here to talk about how to smooth things over at school. Principal Patton wants you to help wax the gymnasium floor this weekend, to make up for what happened. Just do it, then stay clear of the Level boy."

"He will not!" hissed Sylvia, looming over Louis. "He will not clean a gymnasium like a janitor for saying what he believes."

"Sylvia, please," said Louis, taking off his glasses and rubbing the bridge of his nose. "It's not always bad to cooperate. It doesn't mean you agree. It doesn't mean any of us agrees. But should Alan's life be harder? It's hard enough, isn't it?"

"Cooperation? Who gets the benefit of *cooperation*? Them. Always them." Sylvia snorted and strode out of the parlor.

Doree barely had time to dash up the stairs and into her bedroom before her mother spotted her. From her bed she could hear Sylvia angrily opening and slamming kitchen cabinets, preparing Pauline's dinner.

The stairs creaked, and Doree saw Alan heading towards his bedroom.

"You all right, Alan?" she asked.

"Did you hear?" he asked, poking his head through her half-closed door. He was smiling and his greenish eyes were clear again, though still puffy from crying. "I'm going to get to use the floor buffer to wax the gymnasium at school this weekend!"

"That's great, Alan," Doree said.

He walked away, and she lay down and closed her eyes. She imagined her family's problems—Alan, Junior Carper, her mother—being bricked up behind a tall wall. Just for now. Just for now, she didn't want to think about them. Just for now, she wanted to concentrate on the small, glowing pleasure of the afternoon she'd just had. She conjured up Tony's face, his round dark eyes, his grin. *Pleased to meet you, Doree,* he'd said. *Hope I'll be seeing you again soon.*

CHAPTER 18

Sylvia

FEBRUARY 1942

"*L*ovely to see you again, Mrs. Zelner," said the Italian. Then he looked up from his desk and, seeing Sylvia's face, gasped in a way that was so dramatic—almost womanly—that Sylvia couldn't help laughing.

"Mrs. Zelner! What happened?" He stood up, his green eyes as wide as a scandalized *bubbe*'s.

The mudball had left a plummy bruise on Sylvia's cheekbone and forehead, and the scratches had crusted over into a spiderweb of scabs. She didn't even try to hide it with cosmetics. There was no point.

"One of your associates threw mud at me as I was leaving the other day," she said.

"My associate? I don't understand. Who?"

Sylvia gave a snort. "Mr. Wagner. The head of laundry. A fascist, it seems. He'd like to see America become like Europe."

The Italian nodded. "I heard about that. Please, sit. And let me take the bag."

Sylvia was carrying a laundry sack filled with fabric samples.

She ignored him, upending the bag on the desk. There were five different calicos, which ladies normally bought for quilting, not dresses. Then there was the deep green rayon taffeta, which Sylvia thought might work for the breeches, and a white muslin that imitated the look of the linen shirt in the picture.

She arranged the calicos in a fan. "You can choose."

The Italian sat down at the desk. "Does it hurt?"

"It's fine."

"Why would the man from the laundry throw mud at you?" The Italian was gazing at her very keenly.

"I think you know why." She began unfolding the other fabrics and arranging them on the table.

"Because you're Jewish?"

Sylvia looked up. So he did know.

"I hope you don't think I'm being too direct." He kept gazing at her. "I'm making an assumption, of course. Your surname and your family's profession. As well as you coming from Poland when you did."

"Yes, because I'm Jewish," she said stiffly. "We're everywhere, as Mr. Hitler is so fond of saying."

"Is it difficult, being a Jew in this area? There can't be many of you."

"Not as difficult as being a Jew in Italy."

"I imagine not." He stood up and said something in Italian to Miss Bianchi, who was sitting on the settee as usual, making notes. What could she possibly be writing? "Miss Bianchi is going to the dining room to bring some tea and cakes." He was shoeless again, with the same red socks, bright as a cardinal's feathers.

There was something brazen about a man in stocking feet,

Sylvia thought. Louis always wore slippers at home, up until the very moment he got in bed.

"I feel the need to say this," the Italian said, looking at her, one toe making circles on the carpet like a schoolboy. "I'm not a Hitler supporter, and I never have been. So if the idea that I was a Nazi sympathizer was making you feel ill at ease, please put it out of your mind."

With a rush of irritation, Sylvia understood what was happening. The Italian was doing with her the same thing the German ambassador's wife was doing with Aggie. Trying to make a pet of her so she would smuggle him forbidden newspapers or pass on a good word about him to the FBI.

She slapped the table, harder than she'd meant to. The lamps rattled. "Listen, Mr. Catanneo. I'm here to sew your—your *costumes*, and this is all. I will not pass messages about how you're not really a Nazi." Sylvia felt her face grow hot. Did he look at her and see nothing but a poor seamstress, accented and uneducated, biddable? "You can stop trying to fool me. I am not stupid."

"Of course not."

"I had a pony, you know!"

"A pony?" He raised his brows and his green eyes sparkled with—what? Amusement?

Sylvia paused, suddenly embarrassed. Bragging about her pony like a child! But it felt important, urgent, that this Italian see she'd been someone, once—a sister to four brothers, her father's little princess, a champion jumper. She pulled her shoulders back and went on. "Yes, a pony. I had a pony, back in Poland. Everyone envied me. I won prizes for jumping."

"How lovely," the Italian said with apparent sincerity. "My daughter Gigi loves horses. She would be envious, I'm sure." For a moment he was quiet, studying the fabrics. "I like the one with the small blue flowers," he said. "They're smaller than the ones in the photograph, but if memory serves, the fabric is a similar color to what Gigi is wearing." Then, a moment later, he rubbed his head and said, "I'm not trying to fool you about anything. To be honest, I'm rather lonely here and I'm terribly worried about my family. I talk too much when I'm anxious. I don't expect you to say or do anything. I just didn't want you to feel uneasy around me."

Sylvia looked at him through narrowed eyes. Rubbing his head had caused a curl of thick black hair to flop over his forehead. It made him look like a little boy who'd just woken up.

"If you're so lonely, why do you not talk to everyone else who's already here?" she said. "There are hundreds of you."

"Oh, I talk to them. We chat at breakfast, we swim together. In the evenings there are card games. Bridge, mostly. Cocktails."

"How terribly difficult."

"I didn't mean it like that," he said. "It's wonderful. Your government has been incredibly generous. Mr. Johnston is doing his best to treat us like any other guests. Everyone's been honorable, all around. But the atmosphere among the rest of the Italians and the Germans is strange and unpleasant. Paranoid. Everyone's trying to figure out their next move on the chessboard. I've never been good at that."

"If this is true, then why are you a diplomat? Is this not precisely what a diplomat must do?"

The Italian laughed and sat back down. There was something about the line of his jaw, the curl of his hair that reminded Sylvia suddenly of Moriz Mostowski.

"I'll tell you the story, if you like," he said. "But I'll warn you: It all makes me look rather silly.

"First of all, my Christian name is Giacomo, but I'm always 'Jack' in English. So please, call me Jack."

Sylvia nodded noncommittally.

"My mother, as I've mentioned, is English," he went on. "She met my father at Lake Geneva during her Grand Tour. Converted to Catholicism to marry him, which was a terrible scandal for her family—her second cousin was the Archbishop of York. My father is from an extremely old Roman family—the earliest wing of our house is from the thirteenth century. Rather gloomy place. Technically a palazzo, though if I told the boys at Eton I'd grown up in a 'palace,' they'd have laughed till they died. The cellars were excellent for playing hide-and-seek amongst us children. Do you have brothers or sisters, Mrs. Zelner?"

"Two older brothers, two younger brothers."

"Ah, how nice. We were four, us Cattaneo boys. It would have been lovely to have a sister. We spent a lot of time on our own—my parents weren't very fond of each other, as it turned out, and did their best to stay out of the house. My father, who fancied himself an artist, took 'painting trips,' and my mother became very involved—obsessed, really—with the Church. Charity events, pilgrimages, and so on. Converts are always the most devout."

"Why did they have so many children if they disliked each other?" Sylvia asked. Her own father had adored her mother, had called her his "little sheep" and brought her enough earrings and necklaces to fill two jewelry boxes.

"I asked myself that question every day of my childhood," Jack said, laughing. "In any case, it was not the happiest home, and my two eldest brothers ran away as soon as they could to join the British Navy. My mother sent me up to Eton at eight, probably to annoy my father. Then it was just Marco at home."

"He didn't go to school with you?"

Jack smiled, but it was a melancholy smile. "Marco wasn't made for school. He was different. He was born two months early, and they didn't think he would live. But he turned out the smartest of all of us. Smart, but different. He had no use for teachers; no use for most people, really. He taught himself mathematics from old copies of Euclid and Descartes in the family library. He could identify all the birds in the Orto Botanico before he was five." He chuckled. "My mother had to pray rosaries for the sin of pride."

Sylvia found herself picturing a little boy, dark haired like Jack, staring pensively at a bird on a branch.

"If I'd had a fraction of Marco's intelligence, I wouldn't have gone into diplomacy," Jack went on. "But I graduated from Oxford with third-class honors."

"Third-class honors is good?" Sylvia asked.

"It's bad, quite bad," Jack laughed. "So bad, in fact, no one would hire me; my father had to get me a job at a small auction house back home. I was dismissed after a few months, for tardiness, which is a true feat in Italy. By this point, my father had gambled away most of our assets and lost most of his influence in Rome. So my mother stepped in. A church friend's husband was a retired ambassador, and he managed to produce a job as a cultural attaché to the embassy in Bucharest. My mother gave me a choice: take the job or find your own place to live. An Italian mother would never have done such a thing, but the British are hard-hearted." He laughed again.

"A Jewish mother wouldn't do that either," said Sylvia. "Not to a son."

"So that's it," Jack said, holding his hands palms up. "I joined the diplomatic corps because my mother made me. Like I said, pathetic." He held her gaze, bringing her into the joke.

Sylvia laughed. It had been a long time since she had laughed. "Are you a better diplomat than an auction man?"

"Barely," Jack said. "When I'm giving a reading about Tintoretto, I'm like a fish in water. But as soon as I'm asked to do anything strategic, I might as well be a lamppost. That's what Miss Bianchi is for."

Miss Bianchi, Sylvia suddenly noticed, had not come back.

"What happened to Marco?" Sylvia asked, leaning forward. "Is he now a mathematician?"

She could see Jack's face readjust itself ever so slightly. The jolly air cast by the telling of the story evaporated.

"Marco died of the Spanish flu, sadly," he said after a minute. "And my elder brothers in the Spanish Civil War, fighting with the socialists."

"I'm very sorry."

"Yes, well. I suppose anything 'Spanish' is bad luck for our family."

"Your poor mother." Sylvia thought of her own mother, sitting on a balcony in the gleaming Tel Aviv sun, her mind as gray as a West Virginia winter, wondering where her older sons were.

Jack sighed and rubbed his eyes. "My mother faithfully anticipates her reward in heaven," he said. "She spends most of her time in the chapel, praying for their souls. In fact, she hardly leaves. Sometimes they have to bring her supper to the pew, on a tray."

"How sad."

"Yes. But enough about sad things. I should choose these fabrics, shouldn't I?"

Sylvia nodded. Jack nodded back. He didn't move.

His lips were soft and dry when Sylvia kissed him. She could smell his soap and some kind of cologne underneath, spicy orange and the green scent of crushed leaves. He put his hand on the hollow of her lower back and drew her closer. His palm was warm through her dress. She reached up and ran her fingers through the curls at the nape of his neck. Sparks of desire flickered through her chest, her belly, her thighs.

CHAPTER 19

❧

Jordan

Whatcha doin' lookin' in the old Jew store?

Jordan opened his mouth and closed it again.

"I don't mean it like that," the old woman said to Jordan, waving her hand as if to dismiss his shock. "That's just what we called it back when."

Back when. Jordan looked at the old woman's face. She was as wrinkled as a shar-pei, slivers of dull blue eyes peering from beneath drooping folds of skin. She had to be eighty at least; about his grandfather's age.

"This was my grandfather's store."

"Sol?" The woman responded with a quickness that belied her age. "You're Sol's grandboy?"

"Sol?" For a moment he was baffled, grasping. Then the name clicked into place. "Oh, no, that was my great-grandfather. I never knew him. His son Louis is my grandfather."

The woman seemed to consider this information. Then she took a step closer to Jordan and tilted her wrinkled face. "You're Louis's boy's son." She shook her head. "Your daddy was a strange one." She coughed a wet, leisurely cough.

Jordan couldn't imagine anyone thinking his uncle Pete was

strange. Pete was a bank manager who golfed on the weekend and voted for Reagan. "I'm Doreen's son," he said. "Louis's daughter, Doreen."

"Oh." The woman looked disappointed. "Of course you are. How's your mama? She was a clever little thing. She wind up working on the spaceships?"

Spaceships? The old woman must be demented. "She's good," Jordan said. "She lives in Baltimore and works in an office. I'm sorry, I didn't catch your name."

"It's Cricket. Cricket O'Malley. My real name's Christine, but everyone's called me Cricket since I was knee-high to a grass-hopper."

"I'm Jordan Barber."

"Whatcha doing here in White Sulphur Springs, Jordan Barber?"

"I'm a reporter, actually. I'm working on a story about the Greenbrier."

"You don't say!" She edged closer. "I used to work there, you know. Near about fifty years. I ran the little Doll House shop, sold the sweetest little French baby dolls you ever saw. I 'retired' about ten years back, but just between you and me, they put me out to pasture. Brought in some young thing from Virginia to run the place. She started selling those dolls that do real pee-pee. This is what the little girls want these days, they say—real pee-pee! Imagine!"

Jordan didn't know what to say, so he just smiled apologet-ically.

Cricket O'Malley stood gazing off in the distance for a moment, as if thinking of those ridiculous little girls. Then she shook herself back to attention with a surprisingly youthful little shimmy of her shoulders, and asked, "So what's your story about?"

"Well . . ." Jordan hesitated. He imagined Cricket O'Malley shuffling up to the manager at the Greenbrier and croaking, "What's this about Doreen Zelner's boy up here asking questions?" The manager would call the *Post*. Rita Romano would call Jordan back to DC. There'd be a sit-down in the office, Romano and Kelley standing on either side of the desk, Kelley saying what a mistake it had been to hire someone who wasn't an Ivy guy.

But something about the irreverent gleam in Cricket O'Malley's eyes made him feel like it might—it just might—be all right to tell her the truth.

"I've learned—well, I have reason to believe—that there's something underneath the Greenbrier. Something important. Something in . . . in the national interest."

Cricket O'Malley went still. She looked long and hard at Jordan. Then she shook her head. "Boy, I didn't live to be ninety-four years old by sticking my nose where it didn't belong. Your uncle Alan sure learned that the hard way."

He couldn't leave it alone. All that blood.

"Do you know . . . do you know what exactly happened to Alan? And to my grandmother Sylvia? I know there was an accident—an incident—but I don't have any details."

Cricket O'Malley had already begun shuffling away down the sidewalk. She turned slowly, leaning on her cane. She gave Jordan another long look, her eyes the milky blue of glacier ice. "Y'all Zelners love your secrets, don't y'all? I have no idea what became of that woman, but I tell you what—everyone in this town felt sorry for your grandpa, her running off like that."

"What do you mean, running off?"

Cricket O'Malley snorted. "What a world," she said, almost to herself. "Everyone in White Sulphur Springs knew Sylvia Zelner's business, but her own grandbaby has no idea. What a world."

She turned and continued to shuffle away. Jordan called after her, but she just raised one hand as if to dismiss him. Then she turned the corner and was gone.

*B*ack at the hotel to change clothes before his meeting with the manager, Jordan's mind was whirring. His grandmother *running off like that*. What did that mean? His grandmother was dead. She and his uncle Alan had died in the *incident*. It was *terribly sad*.

Right?

In seventh grade, Jordan and Jessica's class made family trees. Jordan had carefully cut out a photocopied picture of Grandpa Louis for his mother's side. In the space next to his grandfather, he drew a picture of a smiling woman with her hair in a bun ("Why is she wearing a turban?" Jessica asked scornfully. Jordan wasn't very good at drawing). Jessica drew her own picture for the grandmother spot: a blank outline of a face with a question mark inside. "SYLVIA ZELNER: MURDERED BY THE MAFIA 19??" she wrote.

"That's untrue and unacceptable," their father had said, and forced Jessica to Wite-Out the whole thing and start over.

"Nothing makes any fucking sense in this family," Jessica had yelled, and gotten grounded for cursing.

Jordan never pried. He certainly never cursed. But he did wonder. Why wouldn't their parents tell them what *was* true?

Why would you pester your mother for details about something so unpleasant? their father would say. *We'll talk about it more when you're grown-ups, if you really want.*

But by the time they were grown up, Jessica was gone. New York, Seattle, San Francisco. Screaming into a microphone. Leaving Jordan behind to take the bus back to Baltimore for Passover and give their parents something to brag about. *Our son, Jordan, the reporter for the* Washington Post!

Jordan pulled his day planner from the side pocket of his suitcase. He'd bought it for work, thinking it seemed like something a *Post* reporter should have. But Rick Lowell on the National desk told him it looked like something an accountant would carry. So now Jordan only used it for nonwork things. Things like his sister's tour schedule. He flipped to January and thumbed down the page. Saturday: The Rathskeller, Boston.

Jordan picked up the hotel room phone and dialed Information. Then he placed a long-distance call (he hoped he wouldn't get in trouble for using the paper's per diem for a personal call).

"The Rat," answered a surprisingly perky-sounding woman.

"Yeah, hi, uh, I need to leave a message for Jessica Barber. Her band's playing tonight," he said. He'd never tried this before. Would it work?

"You're not a stalkah, are you?" Jordan could hear chewing gum snapping.

"A what? A *stalker*? No!"

"Cool. Cuz we had Kentucky Fried Barbie playing last week and some creepazoid stalkah followed the bassist home. She smashed his balls in with her boot. What's your message?"

"Uh, well, tell her her brother called. Tell her I'm at the Greenbrier." He gave the number.

"That's it?"

"That's it." With the magic words—the Greenbrier—he knew she'd call.

CHAPTER 20

※

Doree

FEBRUARY 1959

*P*atty's bedroom had yellow walls and a high iron sleigh bed covered in a pink chenille blanket. Next to the bed was a dresser that Patty had turned into a vanity, with a mirror from Zelner's that Louis hadn't been able to sell because of a chip. Behind the dresser, Doree knew, the wall was covered in crayon scribbles. When she and Patty were little they'd written the naughtiest words they could think of on the wall, then pushed the dresser in front to hide their handiwork. Patty's word had been "damn." Doree's was "schmuck."

The girls flung their satchels and clarinet cases on the carpet and lay down together on the bed. Then Patty hopped up and put on a record—James Brown and the Famous Flames. They only listened to that kind of record when Patty's father wasn't home—he didn't like Negro music. He'd been so angry when the school integrated, he'd wanted to send Patty and Tommy to live in Ohio with their cousins and go to private school. But Mrs. Curry talked him out of it.

Patty began to dance.

Patty always complained that she had her mother's body. And

it was true, she had Evangeline's stocky legs and round rear and her big soft bosom. But Doree thought she was beautiful, and never so much as when she was dancing—narrow waist twisting, breasts swinging. Boys thought so too. Patty never seemed interested, though. She was waiting for a college boy, someone "with quality."

Doree was waiting for the right moment to tell Patty about Tony. She'd been saving the news, caressing it in her mind like a lucky pebble. She wasn't sure what words to use. How could she convey what had passed between her and Tony without making it sound cheap and childish, another dumb schoolgirl crush? She didn't want Patty to tease her about Tony, the way she teased her about Lee Burdette. This was something else. Something different.

"Ugh, my bust is so sore—my period must be coming," Patty said, flopping onto her bed. "Maybe that's why I've been so disagreeable."

"What does your diary say?"

Dr. Sydenstricker had a book in his office called *Voluntary Parenthood*, which Patty had smuggled home for the weekend more than once. She and Doree had read it from cover to cover by the time they were sixteen, giggling over words like "womb" and "semen." It had a chapter on how to keep track of your cycle to know which days were safe for intercourse and which weren't. Doree and Patty had begun recording their cycles in their diaries; that way, if they ever decided to go all the way with a boy, they wouldn't get knocked up.

Patty picked up the pink diary from her bedside table and flipped through it. "Not until next week. Guess I'm just a disagreeable person!"

Doree laughed.

Patty was never agreeable. Yet everyone liked her anyway, because she was pretty, plucky Patty Curry whose dad owned the garage and had a Purple Heart. Pretty, plucky Patty Curry whose mother was deputy head housekeeper at the Greenbrier. A mother who laughed when Patty was fresh and called her a fireball. Pretty, plucky Patty Curry with her apple-cheeked little brother and her cousin Keith in the army in Korea. She could do what she wanted because she belonged no matter what.

If Doree was bossy like Patty, all the boys at school would have called her a pushy Jew. If she'd have thrown hissy fits when boys pulled her hair, the way Patty used to, they'd have said she was crazy like her brother. Her father didn't have a Purple Heart—he had a bad heart, which was why he hadn't even gone to war like everyone else's father. Her mother who, well, if the things Junior Carper said were true . . .

Doree thought of what she was about to do. She must have shuddered, because Patty stopped dancing for a moment.

"What, a goose walk on your grave?"

"I'm just hungry."

"Me too." Patty sighed. "I have to reduce, though. They say college girls all get fat their first year. So I can't already be fat at the start."

"You're not fat," Doree said. "And who says that about college girls, anyway—who here even knows any college girls?"

Patty paused, considering. "Wendy Sydenstricker went to college."

Dr. Sydenstricker's granddaughter Wendy was a legend in White Sulphur Springs the same way ghosts and train robbers were legends. She'd been the first-ever girl valedictorian at White Sulphur Springs High. She went to college at Radcliffe and studied art, which was so bizarre people in town didn't even say it was odd, they just said, "She's studying *art*," and stared at each other all pop-eyed. Then she moved to Europe. Some people said she was dancing in a cancan bar there. Other people said she was just working in a museum. Then she married a man who Dr. Sydenstricker said was a Spaniard, but other people had heard was actually an Indian from India.

"Did she get fat?"

"I don't know. She's never come back."

"We'll be the only college girls anyone in town knows," Doree said, "so they'll have to start saying, 'Oh, look, when girls go off to college they get extra-beautiful!'"

"Pshaw! All right, I'm starving. I'm going to get some crackers. Crackers are dietetic, right?"

As soon as Patty walked out the door, Doree hopped up and opened the top dresser drawer. *I don't have a choice*, she told herself. *It's for the family.* She knew the Japanese puzzle box—a gift from Keith—would be at the back of the drawer, behind the bra and panties. She knew which panels to slide to unlock the box's secret compartment and that there would be a wad of dollar bills inside. She knew that Patty—messy, detail-hating Patty—wouldn't have counted the money.

She peeled five dollars off the wad and began to slide the thin wooden panels back together. But something wouldn't go. She'd forgotten a step. She pushed, but instead of gentle clicking, there was resistance. Panic setting in, she pushed harder. Just then, she heard footsteps. She pushed the panel even harder, and then it happened—the wood cracked, and a rectangular piece of the beautiful mother-of-pearl inlay popped loose and fell to the ground. Doree froze.

"Okay, I know I said crackers, but Mama went and made

preacher cookies," Patty exclaimed, bursting into the room holding a plate. "I'll just have one, but you can have three." She looked up and saw Doree holding the puzzle box. Her face flattened. "Doree, what are you doing?"

Doree opened her mouth, but no words came out.

"What the heck, Doree?" Patty put the plate on the bed and strode forward. "Did you break it?"

"I'm sorry." Her voice was tiny.

"Hell's bells. Why were you messing with it, anyway?"

Doree looked into her friend's round blue eyes. She heard Junior Carper's voice hissing in her ear. *Your mama's a traitor.* She felt the vinegar rise in her throat. "I'm sorry," she said again, "I was just looking at it. I've got to get home." She grabbed her satchel and clarinet case and flew out the bedroom door.

*F*at spring raindrops began falling as Doree left the Carper's Travel Paradise parking lot, and by the time she got to the resort gate to fetch Alan, her clothes were pasted against her skin. Miss Cricket, the old bat who ran the Greenbrier doll shop, peered suspiciously at her from beneath her purple umbrella as Doree hurried up the path to Copeland Hill.

But when she got to Alan's usual spot at the edge of the woods, all she found was a sodden picnic blanket and an empty box of Lorna Doones. Huh. It wasn't like Alan to leave before she came to get him; he'd have happily stayed in the woods all night, sketching diggers and making calculations. She scanned Copeland Hill, but saw no one but a pair of laundry workers pushing a cart of dirty sheets towards the cinder block laundry house, which was hidden from guests in the trees by the creek. Alan couldn't have gone inside the resort to look at stamps at the tobacco stand—the doormen, seeing his wet school clothes, would have gently steered him away, telling him to come back another time when he was dressed proper.

A strange, low crackling sound like television static made Doree look up. The sky was the sodden gray of wet cement, pierced by a single ray of orange light on the western horizon. The crackling grew louder, filling the air. Suddenly, the trees on the opposite side of Copeland Hill began to shiver and thousands of black spots rose from the branches, like raindrops in reverse, coalescing into a cloud.

Starlings. A murmuration of starlings.

Alan had taught her that word. Doree called his name, but the hiss and screech of the starlings drowned her out. She called it again, and again. Cold fingers of panic gripped her. She had a vision of Alan lying at the bottom of the creek, his face gray. She quickly blocked the image from her mind and called his name again, louder, on the verge of screaming.

Then, a voice came from somewhere above. "Coming!"

Doree wheeled around in time to see Alan in his khaki army vest, shimmying down a tree trunk like a monkey.

"Alan! What were you doing?"

"Shoot, my notebook." Alan began poking around in the underbrush at the base of the tree. "Aha, there it is."

"Alan!"

Her brother looked up, startled. "What?"

"Why on earth were you in a tree? You could have fallen and gotten hurt."

"Nah. I was very stable."

"But why were you up there?"

Alan mumbled something.

"What?"

"I said, some of those basketball boys were bothering me. Interrupting my research. So I made the tree my office."

Doree sighed. She'd been defending Alan from other kids since elementary school. They called him names, tied his shoelaces together. She used to report them to the teacher, until the boys in her grade started calling her a snitch and drawing pictures of her with a long, ratlike nose on the chalkboard when no one was looking. She didn't think she'd still have to be defending Alan at sixteen. He needed to learn to take care of himself. Soon she'd been up at college, and what would happen then? She thought of what had happened to her grandfather and shivered. Getting called some silly name was really nothing compared to that. Nothing at all.

CHAPTER 21

Sol

AUGUST 1910

Sol had been on the road nearly a year and a half. In that time he'd gone from a scrawny, soft-skinned boy to a young man with ropy muscles and feet calloused from walking miles across ridges and hollows. He'd also learned English, enough of it at least to chat with anyone he met. He learned that people bought more if you chatted—asked about their hometowns, their dogs, their favorite foods. Plus, he loved to talk. Always had.

It was late summer, Sol's favorite time of year in southern West Virginia. The dirt roads were mostly dry, there were ripe blackberries to nosh, and the sky was a particularly marvelous shade of blue, deep yet luminous, a shade Sol had never seen in Lithuania, never knew existed. He'd been on the road for two weeks, and his pack was nearly empty, which made walking a delight rather than a burden. He was singing the song about the little bird on the branch, the one Freya remembered their father singing. He only knew one line, so he sang it over and over again as he crested the ridge just past Kimball.

Everything had gone well on this trip. He'd started this run on a Friday afternoon in Pocahontas on the Virginia border, which was a stop on the Norfolk and Western. Pocahontas was also the biggest Jew-town on his route, bigger even than Keystone. As soon as Sol got off the train, he'd gone to the Kwass family's home. The Kwasses came from Telz, a half-day's train ride northwest of Vilna. Samuel, the father, was a jeweler with a shop in town. The Kwass sons, Norman and Solomon, ran a saloon and an ice factory. They all lived together in a house on Center Street with gingerbread trim.

Sarah, Samuel's wife, opened the door. "Sol the peddler!" she cried, gathering him into a hug. Before he could even say hello, she had him sitting at the kitchen table with a fat slice of bread and butter. He played checkers with their daughter, Ida, while Sarah cooked supper, then Norman and Solomon came home from work.

"Sol the peddler!" they exclaimed.

Samuel arrived home a few minutes later. In a town like Pocahontas, a Jew could close his store early on a Friday; the gentiles expected it. Everyone ate supper, then walked in the summer evening sunlight to the stout brick synagogue, where a Russian rabbi filled Sol's ears with the sounds of home.

Afterwards Sol sat on the porch with Norman and Solomon, drinking bourbon. Usually liquor made Sol flushed and queasy, but tonight it just seemed to put an extra gleam on the deep blue summer evening. He'd even told Norman and Solomon about his hopes to marry Pauline, and they both clapped him on the back and promised to get him the best price on a ring at their father's store.

He set out again on Sunday morning, walking east along the Bluestone River to Bramwell. It was only an hour's walk, but his pack was so heavy he stopped at a grassy clearing to eat the sandwich Sarah had packed for him. The river was the yellow-green of a cat's eyes; later Sol would learn the color was waste pouring downriver from the mine. Trees grew close on the banks, throwing shadows over the water. As he munched his sandwich—tongue with mustard—he saw a snake slipping across the water, its body writhing in a frantic S shape.

Maybe that should have been a sign?

But why would it be? He saw snakes every week when the weather was warm.

He skirted around Bramwell itself—the town was full of rich coal bosses and had plenty of shops, no need for peddlers—and headed north. He knocked on the door of a tar paper shack a mile outside town and sold a comb to a woman with thin lips whose eyes seemed fixed on a point somewhere above Sol's shoulder. Her children stood in the shadows at the back of the room until finally the biggest boy stepped forward and asked, in a blustery voice he must have learned from watching his father, if he could see Sol's horns.

"Why, of course," Sol said, as he always did when asked this question. Then he took off his hat and held two fingers up behind his head like bunny ears.

The children just stared, bug-eyed and confused. The boy opened his mouth as if to say something, then closed it again. Eventually one of the little girls smiled.

"I'll tell you a secret," Sol said, crouching down so he could look the boy in the eye. "Jews don't have horns. We look the same as any other person. Except we're all very, very handsome and extremely tall, as you can see."

Finally, the boy smiled as well.

Day after day, Sol climbed up the ridges and down into the valleys. When he was tired, he lay against his pack on hillsides foamy with blooming angelica. Coaldale, Maybeury, Switchback,

Ennis, Upland, Powhatan. Patchy encampments with naked wood houses built so close to the railroad tracks you could reach out from the front porch and stroke the hot steel side of a hopper as it chugged by. Scraped-bare hillsides were dotted with soot-smeared coke ovens, their dark mouths yawning. Chimneys and coal tipples cast shadows across entire settlements, at least when the sun wasn't hidden behind the mountains.

Sol sold both tablecloths to a foreman's wife in Algoma, which was a relief because they were the heaviest things he carried. His new stock of mother-of-pearl buttons sold quickly; the "Spanish Ladies Toilet Water" did not. He slept on floors and ate at tables made from old coal carts. Biscuits, fried chicken, dried ham so salty it sucked all the saliva out of his mouth (*Forgive me, Lord God*). The men who knew how to read sometimes wanted to talk about the Bible—how big was the whale that swallowed Jonah? Did God drop frogs from the sky like hail balls, or just release them into the Egyptian streets like what happened after a hard rain? They reckoned Sol was as close to an authority as they'd meet, being a son of Israel and all. After a while Sol began to think he was an authority too, not a *pisher* of an eighteen-year-old who'd been kicked out of *cheder* for talking during Talmud lessons.

He was outside Kimball, coming up on the homestretch. In a day or two he'd be in Welch, where he'd spend the night with Meyer Visner, who ran a dry goods shop, then get on the train back to Baltimore. The morning was especially warm, and Sol had taken off his jacket and tucked it, neatly folded, into the top of his pack. He was humming, then singing, then humming again. It was a Sunday.

There they were. Still as deer; so still Sol almost didn't see them. Two young men sitting in the grass on the side of the road. He recognized them immediately; they'd been drinking outside the company store in Kimball the day before. One tall, one short. Both with the whey-colored skin that came from working underground since childhood. Sol tipped his hat as he passed, as was his custom.

In a second, they were on top of him. The world flipped on its side as Sol was shoved forward onto his stomach. A knee in his back and a hand pressing his face into the dust.

"Gimme your money, Jew," said one.

Just give them what they want, Jacob Epstein had said. *Fighting back is how you get killed.*

"In the pack," Sol said. "In the bottom."

They tore the pack from his back and turned it upside down. The remnants of his stock tumbled into the road. A bottle of Spanish Ladies Toilet Water shattered, and rivulets streamed through the dust towards Sol's downturned face. The stench of artificial rose filled his nose.

The short man kicked Sol in the ribs. "Turn over. What's in your pockets?"

Obediently, Sol rolled over and turned his pockets inside out. They were empty but for a handful of hawthorn fruits he'd picked on his way out of town.

"All right," said the tall man, looking at the short one, as if asking permission to be finished.

Sol had a moment of relief. So that was it. That was being robbed. He would survive that. And Epstein had some kind of insurance to pay for the loss.

Then the short man knelt down, close enough for Sol to smell the rotten fruit odor of last night's digesting liquor on his breath. "Whass that under your shirt?"

Back in Lithuania, Sol had once seen a badger attacked by a pair of dogs on the road to Rudamina. The badger had bucked and thrashed so ferociously its body became a blur of gray, a tiny tornado driving up clouds of dust.

When the short man slipped his hand under Sol's shirt and closed his fingers around the leather pouch, Sol fought like that badger. He thrashed, he clawed, he hocked long ropes of foamy saliva at the men's faces. He scratched until he felt skin split open under his fingers like ripe peaches.

In the end, the badger had lain dead, its pointy head cocked at an odd angle.

In the end, Sol got up from the road alive, blood pouring from his nose, ribs throbbing, a ringing and stinging in his left ear. He touched his neck, afire with rope burn from where they'd wrenched the pouch away.

Then he dissolved. Every moment of homesickness and loneliness and fear that he'd pushed to the pit of his stomach for the past year and a half sprang from his eyes as tears. He saw his mother's face, bent over the leather pouch by candlelight. He saw a man with honey-colored eyes—his father?—squinting at the pocket watch. He saw Dina, standing by the wagon. *See you soon.* He cried until he felt as if he'd used up every bit of water in his body, the tears stinging as they coursed down his injured face. Then he stood up, throbbing and bleeding, and began to walk again.

CHAPTER 22

Jordan

*T*he staircase in the Upper Lobby made Jordan think of *The Shining*. It was vast and curved, with a red carpet like a spill of blood. Snow-reflected sunlight poured through high windows and made the black-and-white-checkered marble floors at the bottom of the staircase gleam. Each square was at least three feet across; walking through the room made Jordan feel like a chess piece in a human-size chess game. A fire crackled in a broad fireplace flanked by two green velvet couches. Above the mantel was a portrait of George Washington, dressed all in black. In his hand he held a scroll. Jordan got closer to read the words: *Beware of Foreign Influence.*

Jordan heard the click of heels behind him, their sound magnified by the largeness and emptiness of the room. He turned to see a woman in a business suit approaching him.

"Mr. Barber?"

Jordan nodded.

The woman extended her arm. She was young, perhaps just a few years older than he was, with blond hair pulled back in the kind of fluffy high ponytail favored by UM sorority girls. "Hi, I'm Melanie, I'm the assistant to the manager, Mr. Lawler."

Jordan shook her hand. It was soft and warm. He suddenly wondered if he'd remembered to comb his hair. "Nice to meet you."

"I'll just take you back to meet Mr. Lawler." She gestured towards the far side of the room.

As they walked through the lobby, two employees entered, silent as deer, and began rearranging chairs. "It's a quiet time of year," Melanie explained. "We have the Christmas and New Year's crowds, then it's pretty slow until Valentine's Day. It's too bad you didn't get to see the Christmas decorations; we only took them down a few weeks ago. They're just amazing."

They passed through an arched doorway into a room that at once felt darker and more intimate, with forest-green walls and its own fireplace. Above the fireplace was a convex mirror in a heavy gilded frame topped with an eagle. The eagle was midflight, the sharp tips of its gold wings extended.

Jordan almost didn't notice the man standing in a pool of shadows beside the curtains, his black suit blending with the dark wall. The man stepped into the light. He was middle-aged, with sandy hair smoothed back from his temples. He smiled, showing all his very white teeth. "Mr. Barber, welcome to the Greenbrier. I'm Truman Lawler."

Jordan shook his hand. "Nice to meet you."

"Thanks so much for coming. We love the *Washington Post* here," Lawler said, still smiling. "We get fresh copies every morning for the newsstand."

"Thanks," said Jordan, unsure of what else to say.

"Shall we walk and talk?" Lawler asked. "I'll give you the full tour and answer any questions you've got. Or would you like to sit and have a coffee first? Or a tea?"

"I'm okay, thanks. Let's walk."

"Terrific." Lawler extended his arms in an "after you" gesture. A smell of cologne radiated off him—Drakkar Noir, Jordan guessed; John-Paul left the bathroom polluted with the stuff whenever his fiancée was in town. "Right now we're in the Victorian Writing Room, which we call 'the most photographed room in America.'"

Yeah, right. Jordan thought of the empty lobby, the vacant grounds. But he smiled encouragingly and flipped open his notebook. People liked a chance to brag.

"You've seen our main lobby, of course," Lawler continued, as they walked under the arch. "It's a good example of how the resort was Draperized after World War II. You're familiar with the interior designer Dorothy Draper?"

Jordan nodded. He'd read something about her in the batch of Greenbrier articles the *Post*'s librarian had pulled from the archives for him. Draper had redecorated the place in the 1940s to much publicity. Jordan could hardly think of anything less interesting than decorating.

"Before the war, the lobby would have been very traditional— a huge rectangular room with carpet and white walls. Rather dreary. Draper broke the space into an enfilade of smaller rooms. She tore out the carpet and put in this checkerboard, which is bold even now, but was *very* bold at the time. And the paint color she chose"—Lawler gestured towards the aqua walls—"was so daring, the general manager at the time threatened to resign if she went through with it." He chuckled. "She did, and he didn't, of course."

Jordan chuckled back. Turquoise. Daring. Okay, sure. He wrote it all down.

"This is where our largest indoor Christmas tree goes." Lawler gestured towards a semicircular alcove flanked by columns. "We have seventy-five trees throughout the property, each decorated with a different theme. I'm sorry you missed them; Christmas is such a special time at the Greenbrier."

Jordan followed Lawler through a series of rooms, each brighter and stranger than the next. A lobby bar with blood-red walls and green club chairs that blended into the green floor. The Trellis Lobby, with carpet covered in basketball-sized roses and walls the color of Jell-O pistachio pudding. All the bright colors and weird proportions reminded Jordan of *Pee-wee's Playhouse*, which surely was not the intention.

"The Cameo Ballroom," Lawler said with satisfaction, as they entered the most bizarre room yet. It had walls the lurid pink of Pepto-Bismol and a ceiling the grayish pink of the cold poached salmon Jordan's mother sometimes served for Sabbath dinner. In the center of the ceiling was an enormous round chandelier, like a birthday cake for a giant. "Nine feet wide, that chandelier," Lawler said, with the pride of a new father announcing his baby's birth weight. "Draper had it designed after a picture she'd seen of one in a Russian palace."

"Wow," Jordan said, with what he hoped was appropriate enthusiasm, scribbling down notes, unsure how to spell half the words that came out of Lawler's mouth: *colonnades, coromandel screen, Aubusson rug.*

They saw the Crystal Room, the Chesapeake Room, the Colonial Hall. At the end of the corridor, they stopped in front of a table flanked by two overstuffed green velvet armchairs. A vase of flowers on the table smelled overwhelmingly of tropical sunscreen. A small sign with gilded lettering said WEST VIRGINIA WING ➡.

"That's the newest wing of the resort, with our Exhibit Hall and the clinic, built in the late 1950s and early 1960s," Lawler said. "Are you interested in seeing that, or shall we head down-stairs now and see the shops?"

Jordan thought of the view of the West Virginia Wing from his window, the way it perched atop the hill.

There's something underneath the Greenbrier.

Your uncle Alan sure learned that the hard way, the old lady, Cricket, had said.

The late 1950s—that's when his mother was a teenager, right? Around when Alan had died.

Huh.

"Yes, I'd like to see that, please."

Lawler smiled with all his teeth. "Right this way."

CHAPTER 23

※

Doree

*T*ony was waiting in his car behind the school gym, just like he said he'd be. Looking at the car, Doree understood why he hadn't parked in the main lot. This was no regular car. It was tiny and rounded and snub-nosed, like the baby version of a real car. If any boys from school had seen it while walking down Main Street, they'd have been gathered around, tapping its round headlights and cracking wise about its size.

"Hey," Tony said, his smile unfolding in slow motion. "Good to see you again."

"Nice car," said Doree, feeling her entire body vibrate with a mixture of nerves and excitement.

"You ever seen a Beetle?"

"I don't think so? Who makes it?"

"Volkswagen."

A German car. Her parents wouldn't buy a German car. They wouldn't even buy a German toaster oven. It was ridiculous, as if the war never ended.

"It's goofy looking, I know," he said. "But they're cheap and they don't break down. My cousin Marco—he's a mechanic—thinks they're gonna be big. Anyways, hop in. You can show me how to find a decent radio station. I can't manage to get anything but fuzz."

Tony steered the car out of the parking lot and went the back way down Surber Road, parallel to the train tracks. Doree slid back in her seat until they were out of downtown, nervous of being spotted. She'd told her mother she was studying at Patty's today.

"Take a left," she told him. "We can drive up Kate's Mountain and get a good view of the Greenbrier Valley."

Doree had agonized over where to take Tony for this drive. It was March, still dim and muddy. Organ Cave was still closed for the season. What else was there to see?

"Did you want to hear the story about Kate's Mountain?" Doree asked, hoping to make the mountain seem a little more interesting, a little more like a *sight*. "It's sad."

"For sure," said Tony, leaning back in his seat with one arm resting on the window, his fingers drumming against the inner console. His forearm was covered in neat dark hair. She felt the strangest urge to reach out and stroke it.

"Well, just about exactly two hundred years ago, there was a pioneer family, Nicholas and Kate and their baby girl, who lived on the land where the resort is now. One day Indians raided the valley and Nicholas and Kate knew they were sure to be scalped. Nicholas ran to Fort Dinwiddie to get help—that's about fifty miles yonder"—she gestured backwards, towards the north. "But Kate couldn't run fast enough carrying the baby, so she headed for the highest mountain she could find. She and the baby hid in a hollow log up here for two days and two nights, waiting for Nicholas. Thing is, Nicholas had gotten killed by the Indians, right outside the gates of Fort Dinwiddie. When Kate realized he wasn't coming, she tied the baby to her back and walked all the way to Staunton. Their daughter inherited the land, and then she grew up and married one of Thomas Jefferson's friends."

"Wow," said Tony. "She must have been a tough lady, Kate. Reminds me of my mom."

Doree hesitated, unsure if he was making a joke. "Really?"

"Well, sure—all right, my mother never carried a baby on her back across the mountains. But she did raise me and my sisters on her own after my dad died. Worked the night shift at Saint Michael's Hospital, got home every day to make breakfast. Made sure we kept our ears clean and our school uniforms ironed—I learned how to iron before I could read."

"She's a nurse?"

"Yep. Maternity. Delivered half the babies in Newark's First Ward, probably. Delivered Frankie Valli and his brothers—their real name is 'Castelluccio,' same as my mom's maiden name. Probably all came over from the same village in Italy, back in the day. You see him on *Ed Sullivan*?"

"I'm not sure," she answered, not wanting to admit she didn't know who Frankie Valley was.

"How about you? Does your mom work in the family store too?"

Doree thought about how to answer. What *did* her mother do? She didn't work in the store anymore except to make the twice-annual buying trips to Baltimore. She didn't belong to the Ladies Auxiliary like Evangeline Curry, or play bridge like Annette and Wanda's mother. She didn't raise money for the fire department or bake Congo bars for the school bake sale. She didn't organize winter coat drives like the ladies at the Methodist Church or collect pennies for the Indian orphans like the Catholics.

"She takes in sewing," she said finally, thinking of the angry clicking of Sylvia's sewing machine through the walls.

The beginning of Kate's Mountain Road was paved, but as they drove on, the trail turned to dirt. The snow had only recently melted, and it was muddy going at first. Doree wondered if Tony would be upset at his car being splattered. It was a mild afternoon, but as they climbed higher, the muddy furrows and ridges created by other cars were still partially frozen, and the Beetle bounced up and down as it went, making Doree's tailbone numb.

Abruptly, the road ended. They'd reached the summit. Tony pulled the car into the mud-crusted half circle that served as a parking lot. They got out, picking their way through the icy brown mush.

"Wow, the hotel looks even bigger from up here," Tony said, putting his hand over his eyes like a sailor scanning for land.

Below them, the Greenbrier Valley was a wide trough rimmed by waves of mountains. Ragged gray clouds hung below the peaks like chimney smoke, and fog blanketed most of the town. But they had a perfectly clear view of the resort. It sat surrounded by its smooth expanse of grass and golf course like a lady in white enjoying a picnic on a lawn. The hole was hidden on the far side of the Virginia Wing; Doree could just make out the tip of the dirt mountain spat out by the diggers.

"What's it like, growing up near that?" Tony asked, gesturing at the resort. "It's a pretty swell place, huh? I hear Bob Hope was just here?"

"The Greenbrier? We all feel proud of it, I guess. Like it belongs to us in a way, even if it doesn't."

They stood together, looking. "What's Newark like?" Doree asked. There was no image in her mind of 'New Jersey,' no movie or television show she could conjure up to create a setting.

"Well, when I was little it was fantastic," said Tony, leaning against the wooden railing. "Everybody in the neighborhood knew everyone. I mean, we were practically all related anyway. I had fifteen cousins—no, sixteen—within about two blocks of my house. Italian Catholics, y'know. There was always something going on—church processions, feast days. Oh man, you've never had such good zeppole like at the Feast of Saint Gerard. We had the best restaurants too, seriously—Joe DiMaggio used to bring the Yankees down to eat clams at Vesuvius. But the neighborhood's gone now. They knocked it all down for the highway." He sighed and held his hands up. "I guess it worked out for me, because if the First Ward was still there, I'd be working in my cousin's auto-body shop. And, believe me, I'm no mechanic. Instead I joined the army."

"Where did you get sent?"

"Nowhere." He laughed. His laugh was big, loud, loose. "I was too late for Korea. So I just wound up doing a bunch of different trainings here and there. Got to go to Europe a couple of times. My cousins don't let me hear the end of it—call me the Duke of Newark, that sort of thing, like I'm up on myself. That's the thing about leaving home—you never really fit back in again."

The thought of Tony in an army uniform made Doree's neck tingle. She was on top of Kate's Mountain with a man who'd been in the army. A grown man from *New Jersey*. An Italian! She'd never met an Italian before.

"How about you guys?" he asked. "Have you always lived here?"

"My family's been here since 1911. My grandfather was the one who opened the store."

"What made him set up shop here? There isn't much, besides the hotel, is there?"

Doree couldn't remember ever being asked so many questions about her life. Everyone in town already knew her. Not that they cared so much anyway.

"He was a peddler, before, and he always says, 'This is where the horse died,'" she told him. "It was a joke; he didn't have a horse—" She hesitated. But she might as well tell him now, because surely he'd figure it out—everyone in town called Zelner's 'the Jew store.' And something about Tony's warmness and ease made her sure he wouldn't look at her differently if she told him the truth. So she continued. "His boss told him this would be a good place for a Jewish family, because of the resort. People here would be used to seeing foreigners, different races, that sort of thing."

Tony didn't miss a beat. "Is it? A good place?"

Doree saw Junior Carper's grub-white face loom up in her mind's eye.

Before she could answer, a thunderclap detonated overhead, the crack reverberating through the valley. Tony looked up, startled. The echoes were still sounding when a sheet of rain dropped from the sky like a fishing net thrown on a lake. In the ten seconds it took for Doree and Tony to run for the Beetle and dive inside, they were both completely soaked. They sat there, breathing, in the muffled quiet of the car, the windshield foaming white with furious rain.

"Yowza," Tony said.

"Yeah."

Tony turned back towards the window. "I guess that's our signal to split!"

He put the car in reverse and they shot backwards on the slippery mud, then came to an abrupt but soft stop, as if the car had been caught in an enormous catcher's mitt. Tony revved the engine, but they didn't move.

Doree's heart pulsed in her throat. They were stuck. They were stuck. Her mind leapt forward. They'd have to walk down the mountain. It would take hours. They'd be covered in mud. Everyone would see them. Her parents would know where she'd been.

Tony got out of the car. "Well, shoot," he said, whistling through his teeth.

Doree went rigid. She realized she had no idea what kind of person Tony was, and therefore no idea how to make everything better. Was he like her father, proud of his cool in an emergency? If so, she could play fearful so he'd grow even calmer, showing off. Or was he like her mother, stretching like an overwound violin string before snapping in a rage? If that was the case, she would keep up the light chatter, hoping to distract him.

Tony slid back behind the wheel, his face slick with rain. He tapped the gas again, and for a moment it seemed the car would move. But there was nothing but an awful grinding noise.

"Cripes," he said.

Doree sat stiffly.

But then Tony grinned that easy grin. "I didn't do all that emergency training for nothing." He got out again and rummaged under the bench seat in the back. He withdrew, holding a plaid blanket, which he laid behind the back wheels. "Added some friction!" he said, sliding back into the driver's seat. He stepped on the gas.

Again, the car moved for a moment, and Doree's heart leapt. But then it settled back into its rut, wheels spinning uselessly.

"No dice," Tony said, staring out the front windshield, a drop of rain suspended on the tip of his nose. "I've got a rope. It's too bad we don't have another car to hitch to. Don't suppose anyone else comes up here often?"

"No," Doree admitted. As she said it, she had a sudden thought. It was a good thought; it might even work. Yet she hesitated. If she told Tony, he might think she was a grind. Or worse. Men didn't like it when girls acted too clever—*Seventeen* magazine was clear about that.

But if they didn't get unstuck, they'd have to get out and walk.

"We could try something," she said carefully. "I don't know if it would work—it's just an idea."

Tony nodded, eyes on her.

Doree continued. "We could try tying one end of the rope to the bumper, and the other end to that tree." She turned and pointed to a sturdy trunk about ten yards past the rear windshield.

"Righto," Tony said, leaning in. "But what then?"

"You'll get out and stand about halfway between the car and the tree. I'll rev the engine, and you'll pull the rope perpendicularly."

Ugh. She shouldn't have said "perpendicularly." She could hear Edisto Level hissing "brain" at her, like he had when she'd won the eighth-grade spelling bee.

But Tony's round eyes widened, and his whole frame seemed to lighten. "A force multiplier!"

Doree couldn't help herself. "Exactly! The perpendicular displacement of the rope will multiply the tension."

"Fantastic," Tony said, with a burst of enthusiasm that reminded Doree of a little boy with a new toy. "Let me grab the rope. If it's springy, we'll have to start with a higher level of tension, of course."

He leapt out of the car. Doree could feel her heart pounding through her shirt. She'd never talked about math or physics with anyone but Alan. Even the physics teacher, Dr. Bell, rolled his eyes slightly when she raised her hand with a correct answer. But Tony had known exactly what she was talking about, and not only that, *he'd liked it*. She turned to watch him through the back windshield.

"Okay!" he called, his voice muffled by the rain. "That's as tight as I can get it. I'm gonna pull now."

"Great." Her heart began to race again. What if it didn't work? What if she'd messed up? What if disappointment and anger flickered across Tony's beautiful face and she never got the chance to touch his beautiful forearms?

"Here we go!" Tony cried. He pulled the rope towards him with both hands, bracing himself on his back leg like a tug-of-war player.

With an enormous sucking sound, the car moved. Not much—perhaps no more than six inches—but it moved.

Tony retied the rope more tightly. Then he pulled again. This time, the car slid left as lightly as an ice-skater.

"Ha!" Tony yelled, jogging forward to slap the car roof in triumph. After he untied the rope, he slid back into the driver's seat and tried the gas. Sure enough, the car leapt forward.

"Wow, Doree!" he said, turning to her and grinning an enormous open grin. "You're a genius!"

Doree felt her muscles unclench. It had worked! Even better, Tony didn't think she was a grind!

Tony drove on down the mountain, one arm lightly on the steering wheel. The sight of his biceps, swollen with exertion beneath his wet shirt, gave her a flutter of electricity in her thighs.

Doree had only kissed two boys before: Vance Calwell at the

homecoming dance, and Ricky McDowell during seven minutes in heaven at his brother's graduation party. Vance's kiss was barely a peck—he'd been dared. Ricky had missed her mouth in the dark of the coat closet and kissed her jawline, leaving a trail of saliva she'd had to wipe away with the cuff of her cardigan.

Neither kiss had made her want to do it again. But now, looking at Tony's rain-slicked face, his cheeks flushed, his pulse flickering at the base of his throat, she felt that if he didn't kiss her she'd evaporate into the air and disappear in a million tiny particles.

But he didn't. He just drove down the mountain, talking about force F and tension T. She got out of the car by Carper's Travel Paradise, her body feeling like an overripe peach, skin tight with hot, frustrated energy.

"Thanks for showing me around, Doree," he said, before he drove off. "And that tension trick was pretty genius. If you hadn't been so smart, we'd still be stuck up there."

Doree smiled.

What else was *Seventeen* magazine wrong about?

CHAPTER 24

Sylvia

FEBRUARY 1942

Sylvia tried to concentrate on the ladies' magazine. "Create a Charming Breakfast Nook." "Beauty Recipes for Three Complexion Types." What stupidity. What nonsense. Pauline's, of course. Sylvia would never read such a thing if she hadn't been trying to avoid the letter that had arrived in the post that afternoon.

The letter was pretty. A snowy white with a red striped airmail border, like the peppermint candies American children ate at Christmas.

So pretty, and yet it could contain nothing but bad news. If it didn't, Sylvia's mother would have sent a regular letter and saved the money on the airmail stamp.

Sylvia leaned the letter against her vanity mirror. She would open it later. Another time.

Still, she couldn't stop glancing at it from over the top of her (stupid!) magazine, Louis snoring beside her.

Eventually she got up and took the letter downstairs. She put it on the coffee table while she fussed with the ruching on the shift for Jack's older daughter. She stared at it as she sorted through her button jar, looking for the right horn button for the sleeve.

When she couldn't think of anything else to do, she went to the kitchen, took a butter knife from the drawer, and opened the letter. She held her breath as she read, her heart thudding in her throat:

> *Dear Sylvia,*
>
> *I pray you and the baby are well. Mr. Kowalczyk has seen your brother Alfred. He was getting on a train at Radogoszcz Station. They are sending the Jews they say are criminals somewhere north called Kulmhof. Perhaps in America you know more. The twins are well. They feel very much at home here. They have joined a Zionist defense group, but they don't tell me anything about it.*
>
> *Love,*
> *Mama*

So Alfred was still in Lodz. Or at least he had been, until recently. Was that good?

As members of the Jewish Labour Bund, Alfred and Leon were against Zionism. Bundists thought moving to Palestine—Eretz Israel—was cowardly. *If the Jews always flee—from the tsars, from the Cossacks, now from the Nazis—they'll never have a home*, they said. That's why Alfred and Leon refused to go to Palestine with Mama and the twins. Now Alfred was on a train with criminals, heading God only knows where. Everyone in her family was stubborn to the point of utter idiocy, it seemed.

Mr. Kowalczyk was a gentile neighbor. He lived two houses away in the alley off Piotrkowska Street (it was called Adolf-Hitlerstrasse now, Sylvia had read). Sylvia had always suspected he was besotted with Mama. Her mother was pretty, dimpled, and blue-eyed, though thick waisted after five children (six, if you counted the baby born without breath). Mr. Kowalczyk always smiled when she walked past.

What if Sylvia had demanded they all leave Poland together when they'd had the chance? What if, instead of begging to stay in Lodz, she'd insisted they all go to Palestine? Would Papa have agreed? Would Alfred and Leon have agreed? Unlikely. Papa would have still needed to sell the factory. And Alfred and Leon only cared about the opinions of the Bundist friends they spent hours drinking beer and singing songs and marching with, not the opinion of their little sister. But what if? What if?

Perhaps in America you know more. Sylvia read all the papers. The *Post*, the *Star*, the *Baltimore Sun*. The Charleston *Gazette* and *Daily Mail*. The *Post-Herald* and the *Register* from Beckley. The *Times-Dispatch* and the *News Leader* out of Richmond. They got the New York papers on Sundays.

Every few weeks she'd find a crumb of news, one or two paragraphs tucked between ads for furs and the war stories that didn't make the front page. *Nazi efforts are now concentrated on the Germanization of Lodz.* "Final Sale! Terrific reductions!" *The property of Poles and Jews has been confiscated.* "Robes styled by men, for men." *Jews threatened with death for trading in textiles.* "British Get More Sugar." *Piotrkowska Street barred to Jews.* "He'll like this handsome pipe rack in saddle-sewn pigskin." *Any Jew leaving his house between 5 p.m. and 5 a.m. without a special permit may be punished by death, the German administrator decrees.* "Beauty Is Your Duty. Carry on with a pretty face."

Every time she read about a specific incident—two men hung and left dangling in Lodz's Baluty quarter, a "Jewish bandit" shot by Nazi officers, corpses of spotted typhus victims rotting on ghetto streets—it was impossible not to imagine the bodies with Alfred's and Leon's faces.

Alfred, like Sylvia, looked like their father. Dark hair and narrow eyes that made people think they were angry even when they weren't (though they often were, weren't they?). Alfred had a scar on his chin from falling off the roof of the ribbon and trim workshop as a little boy. He'd been trying to fly. Leon took after their mother, with wheat-colored hair and a pudgy chin. Leon was Alfred's loyal lieutenant. He also had a scar on his face, from the time he and Alfred were playing blind beggars and Alfred led him into the path of a pushcart.

The twins both looked like Sylvia's mother as well, with soft faces and blue eyes and pushed-in *goyische* noses. Maybe they were actually Mr. Kowalczyk's children—ha ha! It wasn't as if twins ran in the family.

Sylvia pulled the Rand McNally *World Atlas* off the shelf and laid it in her lap. Kulmhof. Kulmhof. It wasn't a Polish name, but the Germans had been renaming everything. Maybe it was on the coast? In any case, what could she do?

Our government honors acts of patriotism, Mr. Johnston had said, leaning forward, locking his big blue trusting elderly-baby eyes on hers.

Maybe, just maybe, it was true. Maybe, just maybe, she could do something to get her brothers out of Poland.

She crept back upstairs and fell asleep thinking of the seashore at Sopot, where as a child she'd once stood at the end of the pier, the Baltic smooth and gray as flagstone below. Just before she drifted off, she felt a man press against her from behind, wrapping his arms around her waist. She smelled oranges and salt. Together, she and Jack watched the sea.

. . .

*T*his time, Sylvia could feel the excitement in her body growing as she walked down the hallway towards room 151. She knocked on the door, hoping Miss Bianchi wouldn't be there.

She wasn't. Just Jack, standing in his stocking feet, smiling his gap-toothed smile. As soon as the hotel room door shut behind them, Sylvia dropped the bag of fabric samples on the carpet and she and Jack fell into each other's arms.

Jack laid her on the big bed with the emerald bedspread. The sheets were cool and silken on her bare arms as they lay tangled, kissing deeply. The hollows of Jack's neck smelled of his cologne, spicy and sweet and green. His lips were soft, so soft compared to Louis's perpetually chapped ones. Heat radiated from his body to hers as he pressed against her, his arms slipping up to her nape to unzip her dress.

"Is this all right?" whispered Jack, as he slipped her dress off.

In a world where her father could drop dead on their second day in America, where her brothers could be shot for leaving home without a permit, why should she not take this pleasure? Would the Lord God punish her for it? Ha. A year of sleeping on a narrow bed in a Baltimore boardinghouse, listening through the thin walls as Catholics and Protestants and Jews prayed sobbingly to their Gods in the dark and woke in the blue dawn to the same lives, was enough to make her doubt the Lord God cared about anything so small as the human heart.

"Yes. Yes." She wore a pale peach brassiere and matching panties. She'd filched them from the new arrivals in the store's stockroom. She couldn't wear her usual underthings, fuzzy and graying from dozens of trips through the wringer. Her breasts, double their pre-baby size, spilled over the top of the satiny bra cups like risen cake.

Jack reached behind her and with one quick movement the bra was off, and her breasts swung freely as he kissed her collarbone and made his way down towards her belly button. His breath was hot on her bare stomach, the kisses light and dry. Down. Down. He kissed the white swell of her lower belly. He kissed the skin at the waistband of her underwear. Then, gently, he tugged her underwear downward. The satiny fabric slid over her thighs, her calves, her ankles, her feet, and Jack's kisses followed. Leaning back on her elbows, she watched the wavy black top of his head descend. Then, it began to rise again, and she expected him to stretch out against her and kiss her on the mouth.

Instead, he rose only halfway. Suddenly, his firm wet tongue was pressing between her legs.

Oh my God.

Was this allowed?

Was this something people did?

Time slowed. Her eyelids fluttered shut. The room went silent. She heard no sound but her own heartbeat. She saw colors behind her eyelids, constellations of blue and purple forming and rearranging in the blackness. Then a flickering like a butterfly, and her body shattered into a thousand pieces.

When she opened her eyes—how long had it been?—she was shocked to find herself still in the same position. A second heartbeat was pulsing in her lower belly. Her whole body felt heavy, the way her breasts did when they were full of milk.

She must have looked bewildered, because Jack looked up at her and laughed.

"What can I say?" he said. "Pleasure was invented in Italy."

CHAPTER 25

Doree

MARCH 1959

"*D*ear," Cricket O'Malley called, as Doree walked past the Doll House on her way to meet Tony. "Dear. Come over here."

Doree stopped, sighing internally, then smiled at Miss Cricket.

Cricket O'Malley's Doll House was a miniature shingled cottage at the edge of the Greenbrier property that looked like a home for one of the Seven Dwarfs. It sold dolls and miniatures— French *bébés* with ringlets surrounding dry bisque faces that looked warm to the touch; Madame Alexander ballerina dolls in pink tutus; Hummel figurines of little boys fishing or bashfully singing Christmas carols; terrier statuettes; garden gnomes. One of Doree's earliest memories was asking if she could have a French doll for her birthday. It was so beautiful, with soft straw-colored hair and a petticoat foaming with lace. Her mother had laughed bitterly and said, "These dolls are for resort people. Not for us."

Miss Cricket herself was a tiny woman of an indeterminate old age, with a creased face and a perpetually impatient expression. She smoked thin cigarettes at the end of an ivory holder and dressed only in purple. People said she'd been engaged to a soldier who was killed in the war (which war?), and after that she'd made a vow never to marry. She lived above the flower shop with a half dozen dachshunds, which she dressed in doll's clothes and brought to work.

"I saw you driving," Miss Cricket said. "With one of those men." A dachshund in an argyle sweater vest lifted its stub of a leg to urinate on the pavement, giving a small growl of satisfaction as beads of urine rolled down a crack and puddled under Miss Cricket's purple heel.

"Pardon?"

Miss Cricket tapped ash from her long cigarette. "That *was* you in that silly little car the other day, wasn't it?"

"I'm not sure what you mean."

"Sure," said Miss Cricket witheringly. "Whatever they're doing down there, that hole they're digging, I keep out of it. It's not my business. But that doesn't mean I don't see." She fixed her glittering blue eyes on Doree.

Doree wasn't sure what Miss Cricket was getting at—Tony was an A/V technician, not a construction worker—but she just nodded. "It was nice seeing you, Miss Cricket," she said in a bright voice. "I ought to be going."

Miss Cricket gave Doree a long look. "Be careful, that's all I'm saying," she said. "When town people get involved with resort people, it's trouble, always trouble."

Why is everyone always trying to ruin things for me? Doree thought, as she gave Miss Cricket a wide fake smile and turned away. It was bad enough what was happening with Junior, what had happened with Patty. She wasn't going to let anyone—let alone cuckoo Miss Cricket—spoil the first really wonderful thing that she'd had all to herself, this electric feeling between her and Tony.

Tony was standing by the GREENBRIER ART COLONY sign wearing his work uniform—a gray jumpsuit with the words "Forsythe Associates" printed on the back. What looked to be a tool bag was slung over his shoulder. When he saw her, he grinned and gave her a little jokey salute. She felt a shimmer of power, and the incident with Miss Cricket melted away. The resort itself shone like a palace in the background, too far away for anyone inside to see them.

"Hey," he said.

"Hey yourself." She hoped she sounded like she felt—sophisticated, up for anything. She wore a black scoop-neck top with a full ballerina skirt, and felt very chic and bohemian and daring.

The Greenbrier Art Colony, in the cottages on Alabama Row, had just opened for the season, and Tony had suggested taking a walk to see the art during his lunch break. The artists who summered there were all out-of-towners, so nobody would know Doree or start any gossip.

They walked up the steps of the first cottage, which had a freshly hung sign on the eaves reading NORA TUCK: SCULPTURE. As they entered, Doree became aware of Tony's scent—spicy, like the Rexell's bay rum aftershave they sold at the store, with an undercurrent of soapy musk. They walked through the doorway at the same time, and she could feel the heat of his body radiating through his jumpsuit.

"Heya, Nora," Tony said as they entered, grinning at an older woman sitting behind a table in the middle of the room, a block of clay before her.

The woman looked up. Though seated, she was clearly tall, with severely cut gray-streaked hair and a strange feathered pendant hanging around her neck. "Tony," she said. "Good to see you again."

"Doree, this is Nora," Tony said. "We met at the employee

canteen the other night. Her work is amazing. Nora, this is Doree. Doree's a physics genius."

Doree felt herself go red from the base of her throat up towards her scalp. "I'm not, really," she said.

"Don't underestimate yourself, darling," said Nora, in a low, velvety voice with a surprising mountain drawl. "The world will do enough of that for you."

Doree wasn't sure what she was supposed to say to that, so she just smiled what she hoped was a sophisticated smile. She looked around. Low white tables ran around the perimeter of the room, with sculptures displayed every few feet. The first sculpture she saw was recognizably a human woman, but just barely. Its neck was as long as its torso, twisted such that the woman's long oval of a head was looking up at the sky in a beseeching posture. Her fingerless hands, curled into C shapes, scrabbled helplessly at the air. Her ceramic breasts were bare, with long cork-shaped nipples pointing in different directions. The white paper placard in front of the sculpture read *Coal Miner's Wife Number 1*. Doree swung her head away, embarrassed.

Doree had met plenty of coal miners and coal miners' wives. She used to help her grandmother and the other Hebrew Sisterhood ladies from Beckley take Thanksgiving turkeys to the mining camps around Fire Creek. The coal miner's wives looked like ordinary hill people. They certainly weren't naked like something from a *National Geographic*.

The other sculptures were similarly baffling. There was a horse with wings, its front hooves raised as if it were about to take flight, but a chain around its back leg tethered it to a rusty spike. That was called *Boissevain 38*. Another was an arch formed from two arms, each rising from a pebbly base to hold hands in the middle. It looked less like they were shaking hello than they were desperately trying to pull the other one up. The arms had a heavy, mottled texture, almost like orange peel. It was disturbing in a way that Doree couldn't quite define.

"These are so interesting," she finally said, disliking the silence.

"Thank you," said Nora. "They're all inspired by the coal mining history of the Appalachians. Some of it's quite grim." She gestured towards the horse with wings. "Thirty-eight men were killed at Boissevain mine back in the early thirties. I wonder if this won't be too much for the clientele here."

"The Greenbrier gets all sorts," Doree said. "There are Hollywood people, Europeans."

People that might like strange, un-pretty statues, she thought.

"Is it true you studied with Brâncuși?" Tony asked, scrutinizing a small sculpture of what seemed to be a dead bird.

"Studied would be an exaggeration," Nora said. "I did meet him, about ten years ago, when I was working in Europe. He was very elderly by then, but a lovely man."

"You know Brâncuși?" Tony turned to Doree. "The sculptures that look like outer space aliens? Wild stuff. French guy."

"Romanian, actually," Nora said.

"You got me," Tony said, laughing. "What do I know about art?"

"No, what would a simple *audiovisual technician* know about art?" Nora replied, with what seemed to be an ironic smile on her lips.

Doree turned to Tony to see if his face gave any clues to Nora's strange tone, but he'd already turned away and was looking intently at another sculpture.

Doree stood back and watched Nora work. She sat behind her potter's table, legs spread, the head of what appeared to be a horse emerging from a block of wet-looking gray-brown clay. Holding a loop tool, she scooped and smoothed with unbroken confidence, as if there were already a horse under the clay and she were simply cleaning it off.

"Do you work for the Greenbrier too, Doree?" Nora asked, not looking up from the clay.

"No, ma'am," Doree said, immediately wishing she hadn't said "ma'am," as if Nora were a schoolteacher. "Most people around here do work at the resort, but my family has a store in town, so we work there."

"What kind of store?"

"A little bit of everything. Ladies' and children's clothing, work wear, home furnishings, notions. Toys and gifts, at the holidays."

"She sold me a frying pan!" Tony interjected.

Nora ignored Tony. "Interesting," she said to Doree, in a way that sounded like she really meant it. She looked up. Her eyes were the same gray-brown as the clay in front of her. "A general store. A company store, you might say. For a company town."

"Company town?"

"I grew up in the Pocahontas Coalfield down in McDowell County," Nora said. "We moved from camp to camp following the seams. Every camp had a company store, for the miners and their families to shop at. They sold a little bit of everything—they had to, there was nowhere else to shop. It strikes me that White Sulphur Springs is a bit of a company town, in the sense that there's really just one main employer, the Greenbrier."

"I guess so," Doree said.

Nora went back to her horse. Doree continued looking around at the sculptures, thinking. Nora was from West Virginia just like her. And now she was a real artist, an artist who'd lived in Europe.

Huh. In her mind, she tried out a vision of herself at college—not wearing a twinset and a fraternity pin this time, but dressed in slacks and a large, interesting pendant like Nora's. She was reading in the library, looking beautiful and serious. A physics genius.

With the click of heels on the porch, two resort guests—cocktail-flushed women with Mamie bangs and pearls—came through the door. They'd buy something for sure. Tony and Doree waved goodbye to Nora, who nodded back.

As they walked down the steps, Tony suddenly reached out and enveloped Doree's hand in his own. "I brought sandwiches," he said. "Wanna have a picnic?"

Doree just nodded, her hand suddenly feeling like the center of her entire body, every inch alive to Tony's warm, dry skin. She allowed herself to be led towards the far end of the south lawn, feeling the friction of palm against palm. The midday sky was a pale, delicate china cup blue as she and Tony strolled along the brick path. The trees were just beginning to show their first tentative leaves, and daffodils were unfurling in wet patches of new grass where the snow had only recently melted. She was close enough to Tony to see the pulse flicker at the base of his throat, where the top button of his jumpsuit was unbuttoned. She wanted to stand on her tiptoes and kiss it.

Louise Level's whiny little voice rang in her mind. *Doesn't Doree have to marry a Jew?* She felt a stab of annoyance. She'd marry whoever she wanted! Anyway, she wasn't marrying anyone. She was just having a picnic.

They sat down on a marble bench beneath a glossy magnolia, its drooping branches hiding them mostly from view. Tony put down his bag and handed Doree a sandwich and a small half-circular object wrapped in waxed paper.

"I snagged the sandwiches from the employee canteen. I hope you're okay with sorry-looking tuna salad. My ma would definitely say, 'That's not a proper lunch, Tonio!,' but it was either these or chipped beef, and that doesn't travel. These things here in the wax paper are 'hand pies,' apparently—I bought them from the lady with the fruit and vegetable stand down by the main road."

He must mean Leota Carper. Junior's grandmother, or maybe his great-aunt—she never knew quite how the Carpers were related.

It was a bit cool in the shade, and the chill of the marble bench seeped through Doree's skirt. Tony was quiet, and she racked her mind for something to say. She didn't want Tony to think she was dull, especially compared to someone as cultivated as Nora. "Do you like working here?" she finally said. *Seventeen* magazine said men loved to talk about their work.

"It's kinda boring, to be perfectly honest," Tony said, chewing. "Mostly just servicing TVs."

"They must have a lot of broken TVs?"

"Well, they've got a lot of TVs period. Radios too. There are hundreds of rooms. So it's always something."

"How did you go from the army to doing TV repair?" Doree wondered if Tony still had his army uniform. She'd like to see him in it. She thought also of something he'd said when they were on Kate's Mountain: *Believe me, I'm no mechanic.* Was being a mechanic and being a TV repairman really so different?

"Whoa, what's that?"

Doree turned quickly, expecting to see something surprising— a deer or even a fox on the lawn. But it was just a flock of ducks flying in V formation just above the employee dormitories on Copeland Hill.

"What, are there no ducks in New Jersey?" she teased.

"I guess not like here," he said, laughing.

Doree laughed too. But she also had the distinct feeling that Tony had not wanted to talk about his job. *Seventeen* magazine, wrong again.

Tony unwrapped his hand pie and took a big bite, flakes shearing off and landing on the front of his uniform. He made an appreciative noise. "These are amazing," he said. "Have you tried them before?"

Doree hadn't. Her family didn't buy from the Carpers. But she could hardly tell Tony that. It would make it sound like they were snobs, or—worse—weird feuding hillbillies, Hatfields and McCoys. So she just took a bite.

It *was* delicious, with a tender sweet-salty crust and warm chunks of cinnamon apples. She nodded and smiled at Tony, her mouth full.

"Good, right? The pie lady says the secret's the lard crust." He put on a mock Southern accent. "'Some ladies use butter, but it ain't as tender that way,' she says."

Doree froze, an unchewed wad of pie in her mouth. *Lard.*

Tony noticed, and his eyes widened. "Oh shoot, lard's pig, right? Does that mean you can't eat it?"

Still frozen, Doree asked herself: *Who cares?* Was God going to strike her dead? Of course not. Her grandfather had eaten pork all the time when he was a peddler in the coalfields. And she'd once spied her father eating a country ham biscuit at the fire department carnival. The only person who'd really care was her mother. The thought of eating tref with an Italian man from New Jersey while her mother was probably at home koshering brisket for dinner was strangely pleasing. She was an adult now, really and truly.

"No, it's fine," she said, swallowing. "I don't follow those rules."

As she said it, it suddenly felt true. She didn't. She wouldn't. She could live whatever life she wanted. Her mother was the only person who really cared about the rules, about lighting the Shabbos candles before sunset and separating the milk and meat. And where had following the rules gotten her mother? What did that stuff matter anyway? This was 1959. A new world.

CHAPTER 26

Sol

AUGUST 1910

*E*ars ringing and watch gone, Sol cried as he limped down the slope towards the camp at Big Four. He would have to walk straight to Welch, eight miles west, to Meyer Visner's house. There was no point in stopping at the camps along the way: Who wanted to buy shattered perfume bottles from a bleeding peddler?

But as he crossed the wagon-ridged track that cut between the Big Four company store and the mine, he heard someone yelling.

"Eh! Eh! You!"

He looked up, his vision fogged with tears, and saw a black figure standing in front of him. Blinking to clear his eyes, he could see it was a miner, his entire face sooty with coal dust except for an oval of clean pink lips. A bulge in his cheek and a half-eaten sausage roll in his hand suggested he'd been in the middle of eating his lunch.

"You a . . . what . . . a owww?" the miner said, his English splintered and singsongy. Tiny plumes of dust rose from his mustache as he spoke. His liquid brown eyes, shining against the dull gray of his face, studied Sol.

"I'm all right," said Sol. "Just heading on to Welch."

The miner glanced over his shoulder at several other men sitting in a line on a stone retaining wall. They also had sausage rolls in hand and flasks of coffee.

The miner said something to them in a language Sol thought was Italian, and in a blink, the men had put down their food and were surrounding Sol. Just in time, as the moment their strong hands gripped his upper arms, Sol felt the world shimmer, then melt, then go completely black.

Sol woke up some hours later, a rectangle of late afternoon sunlight having stretched far enough through the window to reach his face. He was in a bed. He hadn't been in a proper bed in weeks. He sat up, careful not to hit his head on the sloping ceiling. The attic room had the raw green stink of fresh cut pine boards. There was another bed across from his, with a pair of long underwear neatly folded on the pillow and a steamer trunk at the foot. On the wall between the beds was tacked a picture of the Virgin Mary in a blue cloak, her hands clasped at her heart as she gazed up at a circle of thorns.

Sol stood. As he did, he felt a rush of nausea. He sat back down, chilled by a sudden cold sweat. Someone had taken off his boots. His pack was gone too. He breathed deeply and deliberately for a few minutes, then stood again and walked slowly downstairs in his stocking feet. The front room held two more beds and a pine table that looked like it had been cobbled from scrap lumber. On the table, an enameled tin bowl held a small mountain of knobbly yellow-flecked green squash. Some type of dried plant hung upside down on a string from a nail in the wall. He was alone.

Sol limped into the kitchen. There, thank God, was his pack, leaning against a Hoosier cabinet. Like the table, the cabinet looked to have been homemade. Its metal work surface was a tin Coca-Cola sign, the kind that hung from the wall of every company store: DRINK COCA-COLA IN BOTTLES 5¢. A tea towel was laid across the sign. Someone had rinsed the perfume and dust off the few remaining items in Sol's pack—several pairs of glasses, a thimble set, enameled coffee flasks and cups, a brooch—and set them to dry on the towel.

Peering through the back door, Sol saw a yard, most of which had been planted as a garden. He stepped outside. Rows of dusty green tomato vines drooped with bulbous red fruits. Pole beans hung like long skinny fingers on a trellis. Melons lolled in the half shade of their vines. More green squash—what could you possibly do with so much squash? Next to those was a plant Sol had never seen before. Teardrop shaped and nearly the length of his forearm, it was a shocking purple, nearly black, with skin as shiny as burnished leather.

Next to the garden was a clothesline hung with pants and socks. At the far end was Sol's jacket, swinging gently in the breeze and secured by stout wooden pins.

Sol sat down on the back step. The sun was still high in the sky, though its rays were just beginning to touch the top of the mountain, spreading golden over the summit like butter on a mound of potatoes. The air smelled of sun-warmed dirt and the spicy greenness of the tomato plants. He closed his eyes and began to cry again.

Your father wasn't sentimental.

Maybe if he'd grown up with his father, he wouldn't be sentimental either. But he hadn't. What else did he have, besides that watch? His mother couldn't write, so she'd never send him a letter. He'd received a few notes from Freya, care of Mr. Epstein, but they were so light they might as well have been air: The children are well, Mama sends her regards, etc. etc. Reading them always made him feel more homesick than before.

"'Ello?"

Sol hadn't heard the footsteps behind him. The miner was standing in the doorway in his stocking feet. He'd wiped the dust off the center of his face, leaving a ring of gray behind. It made him look like he was peering at Sol through a cutout oval in a board, like the ones at Electric Park in Baltimore, where you could pose as a strongman beside the carousel.

"Hello," Sol said back. "Thank you for cleaning my things. Thank you for everything."

"Welcome," said the man. "No English." He motioned for Sol to come inside and pointed at a chair.

Sol sat down carefully on the wooden chair next to the Hoosier cabinet. In the kitchen, three other miners were busy stripping off their dust-clotted clothes. A pot of water was heating on the stove. Sol assumed the hot water would be used for them to bathe, but instead the first man knelt on the floor and leaned over the zinc washtub while the man behind him poured cold water from a bucket over his head and began to vigorously scrub his back with a rag he'd rubbed over a cake of hard brown soap. The second man sluiced the gray lather off his friend's skin with more cold water. The first man washed his own face and neck and underarms, then went to stand on the back steps to dry. The others repeated the process—the first kneeling over the tub while the one behind washed his back.

The first miner smiled at Sol before kneeling over the tub himself. "Very dirt," he said.

When the miners had all rinsed, they went upstairs and came back down wearing clean clothes.

The first miner returned holding a bottle of liquor and a handful of clean rags. "This," he said, pointing to his own ear.

Sol reached up to touch his ear. Where normally he'd expect to feel a smooth firm curve of cartilage, his fingers instead touched a sticky crust, like leftover bread with jam. The pain made him shiver.

The miner dipped the rag in an enamel cup of water. Then, with the calmness of a nurse, he began dabbing at Sol's ear. He rewet the rag in the water, which immediately turned a sickly pink. When he was done dabbing, the water was rusty red, spidery black scabs floating on its surface.

Another miner had begun cooking, chopping onions and cabbage on the Coca-Cola sign and adding salt to the water on the stove. He looked at Sol, grinned, and snapped his teeth together with a mock snarl.

Sol understood. The top of his ear had been bitten off. In the heat and the swirl of the fight, he hadn't noticed what happened.

Now the first miner poured some of the liquor onto the rag and wiggled the bottle in front of Sol's face. "Eh?" he said.

Sol squinted at him, confused.

"Take?" the man said, miming drinking from the bottle.

"Oh, no thank you," Sol said. He didn't want to feel more flushed and nauseated than he already did.

The miner shrugged. Then he leaned forward and pressed the liquor-soaked rag against Sol's ear.

Sol screwed up his face against the stinging.

The miner who was cooking laughed. "*Ayaaa.*"

The cook had taken down an enormous black cast-iron pot from the cabinet and poured in some oil. Now he was cooking the onions, and the greasy-sweet smell of them awoke a small growl of hunger deep in Sol's stomach. The cook added the cabbage and ladled some hot water over it, then covered the pot.

He couldn't be much older than Sol himself, Sol reckoned. Unlike the other three, who had mustaches as black and heavy as shoeshine brushes, the cook barely had a squiggle of reddish-brown fur on his upper lip. As he worked, he whistled a tune that Sol vaguely recognized. It was bright yet sad, like a soldier walking jauntily off to war.

Through the open door, Sol could see the other three miners had begun to play cards at the front room table. He didn't recognize the game, nor the cards, which featured brightly colored swords and goblets and men on horseback. Whatever it was, it was clearly great fun—the miners were chattering like canaries, slapping the table and rocking back and forth with laughter until they nearly fell out of their chairs.

Sol thought, with longing, of the games of pinochle with Hy and his pals in the room above the deli in Fell's Point in Baltimore.

And he thought, of course, of Pauline.

Pauline. Pauline. Pauline, with the cool slender white hands. Pauline, with the impassive oval face. Pauline, with the heavy-lidded eyes—the sleepy, uncurious eyes of a real American, someone with nothing to prove. Pauline, peering through the lace curtains of her parlor. *Parlor!* What a word. Sol imagined trotting up to her door with his pathetic box of chocolates and watching her recoil in disgust at his ragged half of an ear.

The cook had poured a flurry of rice on top of the cabbage in the pot and was slowly stirring in more water. He added slivers of hard, waxy-looking cheese, so thin they were translucent. After a while, he tossed in another small handful of salt from a paper bag, gave it a last stir, and ladled it into enameled tin bowls. He shooed Sol into the front room, then pulled the kitchen chair Sol had been sitting on up to the table. The other miners pushed their cards to the side and fell upon the food.

Sol raised the tin spoon to his lips. The rice was hot and salty, with a deep, almost meaty flavor from the cheese, the cabbage turned to slippery shreds of silk. It looked like nothing so much as porridge, but it tasted as good as anything he could remember eating in his life. He ate another spoonful, then another, and soon his spoon was scraping the last bits of velvety sauce from the bottom of the bowl.

"Delicious, thank you," he said to the chef, who was sitting on the floor eating his own dinner out of the cast-iron pot. They must have only had four chairs and four bowls.

"*Cose 'e niente,*" the chef said, grinning so wide Sol could see the black rot on his back teeth.

The miner who'd cleaned Sol's ear tried to encourage him to join in the after-dinner card game, but Sol's head was beginning to pulsate, a sickly sloshing feeling growing behind his right eye. So he just smiled no and sat on the floor, watching, as the men whooped and slapped the table for hours. Later, the same miner insisted that Sol sleep in the bed, which clearly belonged to him. When Sol protested, the miner flapped his lips like a horse and gave Sol a mock-scornful look as he gathered his nightclothes and went downstairs.

Sol woke in the dark. Instinct told him it was a few minutes before dawn; the sun hadn't yet begun to dilute the blackness of the sky, but there was a sense of energy gathering. Silently he slipped downstairs, sliding past the two sleeping miners, and gathered his boots from next to the kitchen stove.

Before he tiptoed out the back door to get his jacket from the clothesline, he left something on the Coca-Cola sign on the cabinet. It was the one thing the robbers hadn't managed to find, hadn't managed because it was hidden in a slit he'd cut in the waistband of his trousers and sewed shut again. It was the gold eagle coin he'd been saving to buy Pauline's ring with.

*W*hen he returned to Baltimore, his ear still scabbed and swollen, Sol went directly to the Bargain House to tell Jacob Epstein he was quitting. He'd sell cabbages from a pushcart or paint drays at the docks, anything. But Epstein shook his head and handed him a piece of paper. "I've got something better for you," he said.

On the paper were written three words: *White Sulphur Springs*.

Sol looked at the paper. His old delight at new words and new places felt dim and far in the past. But he thought of what Pauline's father had said: *Men like us . . . We do what we must to succeed in this country.*

If he was ever to have what he'd seen in his vision—the house with lace curtains and silver-framed wedding pictures, the naturalization papers, Pauline's cool white hand in his—then he'd have to do what he must.

"When does the train leave?" he asked Jacob Epstein.

CHAPTER 27

❧

Jordan

JANUARY 1992

"Welcome to the Exhibit Hall," said Truman Lawler, flicking a switch. Hundreds of fluorescent bulbs sizzled to life at once.

At first Jordan thought he was standing in a house of mirrors, in a single small room reflected over and over to infinity. Then he realized it was actually a single vast room broken up with parallel rows of support columns. Acoustic ceiling tiles and a speckled linoleum floor gave it the look of a warehouse. From the ceiling hung rows of industrial track lighting. There were no windows.

"It doesn't look like much at the moment, but when we have a convention here, this room holds more than fifteen hundred people," Lawler said. "Trucks can back up right through the vehicular entrance"—he pointed to a garage-style metal door against one wall—"and unload equipment and displays. When we had GM here about ten years ago, they rolled in twenty brand-new Cadillacs."

"Why aren't there any windows?" The buzzing fluorescent lights made Jordan want to close his eyes.

"Ahh." Lawler raised his eyebrows and leaned in as if he were going to let Jordan in on a particularly delicious secret. "You can't tell, but we're actually partially underground right now, right beneath Copeland Hill. When they started to build the West Virginia Wing, back in 1958, the architects took advantage of the natural contours of the landscape to put the lower levels underground. The lack of windows is actually an advantage for some of our convention clients—it gives them privacy. Take GM—they got to show off their prototypes without worrying that some reporter might snap a photo through the window. We also hosted a wedding"—here Lawson's voice grew low and confidential—"for the daughter of a very prominent Latin American president, one who requires quite a security detail. The president was driven right into the Exhibit Hall in his armored vehicle, then driven out again after the party." He chuckled. "You don't get *that* at the Plaza."

Jordan imagined fifteen hundred people waltzing around the ugly square columns of the Exhibit Hall in tuxedos and ball gowns, their faces jaundiced under the industrial lights.

On the far side of the wall, Jordan noticed an enormous door, like the entrance to a walk-in restaurant refrigerator, only three times larger. It was secured with four metal bolts. Two of the bolts locked into the floor and the other two into the ceiling; each was padlocked.

"What's down there?" Jordan asked.

"That's just an equipment area," Lawler said. "Nothing exciting to see, I'm afraid."

"Can I see it anyway?" Jordan blurted out.

A strange look momentarily darkened Lawler's face, like a shadow crossing the moon. Almost instantly Lawler's features rearranged themselves back into a look of professional politeness.

"I'm sorry. It's actually a high-voltage area, so it would be a health and safety violation to let you back there."

"No problem," Jordan said. He took a mental picture of the

door and filed it away for later. In his head, he heard Hector Espinoza holding court in the *Diamondback* newsroom: *When they say there's nothing to see, that's when you keep digging.*

Jordan took off his shoes and lay back down on the bed. It was 4 p.m., plenty of time before dinner. His brain felt overheated. He put on his Walkman and pressed Play. The Smiths began to pour into his ears, dark and orchestral. The bed was so damn soft that he struggled to keep his eyes open as he picked up his notes and began to read through them.

The next thing he knew, the phone was ringing. He tore off his headphones. The ring was surprisingly harsh and metallic; a room this comfortable should have a phone that rang like a cat purring. He rolled off the bed and lunged towards the desk, barking his shin against the mahogany desk chair in the process.

"Hello."

"Holy shit, you *were* telling the truth," Jessica said.

Jordan's body snapped to attention. "What do you mean, telling the truth?"

"The message you left. That you were actually at the Greenbrier. I kind of thought you were fucking with me. But I called the front desk, and here you are!" With no background noise, Jessica's voice sounded amplified, almost like she was speaking through a microphone. Jordan could hear a wheeze at the end of her sentences. He wondered if she were smoking. She really shouldn't. She had allergies.

"Why would I do that?"

"I don't know. Sometimes I think you tell me stories to keep me on the phone longer."

"Well, maybe, but why are you always in such a hurry to get

off? I've said you can call collect. If you give me the number for where you are now, I'll call you back. The *Post* gave me a per diem—ninety dollars."

The tiny brag just slipped out. He braced himself for Jessica's teasing. But instead she said, "I don't need to; I'm at someone's house and they have free long distance."

"They?"

"He. Jimmy. The drummer for Naked with Socks On. We're all crashing at his place in Allston this weekend before we head to Philly. Or maybe it's Pittsburgh."

"Oh. Cool." It was Philadelphia. How could she not know her own damn schedule?

"So what are you doing at the legendary resort, anyway?" Jessica said. "I wasn't even sure it was real—Mom might have made it up, like the kingdom of Florin in *The Princess Bride*."

"Mom's not that creative."

"Ha ha, true."

When Jessica laughed, it reminded Jordan of Sunday night family dinners of moo shu chicken at Dynasty Palace. Watching *Jeopardy* together. Jordan and Jessica driving to Dairy Queen the day they got their driver's licenses—Jessica driving there, Jordan driving home.

"Are you there with Mom and Dad?" Jessica asked.

"No. It's for work."

"I thought you were covering PTA meetings in the burbs."

"Town council meetings. But they're letting me do a travel story on the Greenbrier for the Features section."

There was silence on the other end of the line, and Jordan wondered if Jessica had hung up. But finally she spoke: "Bullshit."

"What?"

"That's some bullshit, I said. You're going to go all the way to

Mom's, like, semi-legendary hometown to write a puff piece? How about finding out about *Mom*, about all the stuff that happened to her family. The 'incident.' *That* would be a real story."

Jordan held the phone receiver to his ear so tightly it was beginning to hurt. He wanted to tell Jessica the truth. That he— *he*, Jordan Barber—had gotten an anonymous letter with a big tip. That *he* was going undercover, basically, to investigate the mystery. That he had learned something—maybe?—about their grandmother already. He wanted to tell Jessica all this, to hear her say, *Wow, Jordan, that's actually really cool.*

But now he saw he couldn't. Not until he had more. Because what if he was wrong after all? What if Kelley was right, that the whole anonymous letter thing was just some stupid prank—*Hey, let's haze that dorky new guy!* What if that old lady was just demented? Jessica would laugh. *I thought you were covering PTA meetings in the burbs.* He gritted his teeth. Sorry, Jessica, not everyone can be an awesome rule-breaking punk rocker who doesn't give a shit about what anyone else wants!

"I'll let you know if I happen upon anything exciting," he said, knowing how bland and stupid and square he must sound to his sister.

"Do that," she said.

There was a long silence over the phone. Then a click.

"Bye," Jordan finally said, to no one.

※

CHAPTER 28

Sylvia

*O*utside, it was a grim, lightless February afternoon, but inside the Greenbrier, Sylvia and Jack lay in bed with the lamps on, eating marzipan from a small green box tied with a golden ribbon.

"My mother used to send me boxes of amaretti—sort of a marzipan cookie—when I was up at Eton," Jack said. He reclined against the pillows, one arm bent casually behind his head. "They were my favorite. I think it was her way of making up for never sending letters."

"Why didn't she write?"

"I don't know," said Jack, sighing. "Perhaps it had to do with being English. She figured I was settled and sorted, no need to bother with the sentimentality of letter writing. And she knew that boys who received too many letters from home got teased— 'mummy's boy' and that sort of thing."

"Were you happy to be away at school?" The idea of sending a small child alone to another country seemed impossibly cruel to Sylvia. Even the Americans didn't do that.

"Yes and no," Jack said. His moss-colored eyes studied the ceiling, and his wavy hair looked very black against the crisp white of the pillows. "It's awful at first. The youngest boys are subject to all sorts of initiations. They call it 'fagging'—every junior boy is assigned a senior one to 'fag' for. Sometimes it's just a laugh—making tea and sharpening pencils. But if your fag master was a bad apple, well . . ."

"A bad apple?"

"A bad lad. A bad sort. Cruel. He might ask you to do things that were humiliating, like washing his underwear or warming the toilet seat. If you didn't do it right, he might beat you or make you sit on the open windowsill in a wet shirt until you turned blue. Or worse."

"The teachers allow this?" She felt a flood of tenderness at the thought of young Jack, bullied and alone in a foreign country. It was such an unexpected pleasure to speak with a man like this, so intimately. She'd never even dreamed of talking to Louis this way—it would be bizarre, unthinkable. He couldn't even sit still long enough to listen; he'd be too busy thinking about the account books, the overstock.

"Oh yes. It's tradition—the English value nothing more highly than tradition. Even terrible traditions."

"Did you ask to go home?"

"Certainly not. Fetching coffee and being whacked with a cricket bat every now and again was better than being home, especially after Marco died. And my mother would never have allowed me to come home anyway. Plus, I knew if I endured, I'd become a senior myself, then I'd rule the roost."

"Were you a, a *bad apple*?"

Jack laughed and reached over to run one finger down Sylvia's bare thigh. "I like to think I was fair. I've always been a bit soft-hearted." He picked up the box of marzipan. There was one left, a delicate cream-colored oval spangled with sugar. "Have it, please."

Sylvia popped the marzipan into her mouth. "This is like the cake we would eat at the café near my school," she said. "It was almond sponge with a very white frosting. It was so sweet you would only eat it in between sips of very black coffee."

"Sounds decadent," Jack said. "Your family was quite well-to-do?"

"Well-to-do?"

"Wealthy. Rich."

"*Well-to-do.* Yes, we were well-to-do. We had enough money for nice things. Yet my brothers still became socialists."

"Ah yes," said Jack. "That's something we have in common. Socialist brothers. Well, in my experience, wealth has never stopped anyone from becoming a socialist."

"I suppose not." Then she brought forward the question that had been itching at her mind all day. "Have you heard of a place called Kulmhof? Near Lodz?"

"No, I don't think so," said Jack, frowning. "But I'm no expert on Polish geography, despite my time in the consulate. That sounds German—they've renamed everything, you know."

"I know."

"Why do you ask?"

"I had a letter from my mother. A neighbor saw my brother at the train station. They were sending him to some place called Kulmhof. Perhaps it's one of these 'concentration camps'?"

"It could be," Jack agreed. "Would you like me to ask around? There are still a few members of the German faction that will speak with me."

"Would you please?"

"Of course." He leaned over and kissed the curve of her neck.

"But, Jack?"

"Yes?"

"If it *is* a concentration camp, is that better than the ghetto? Or is it worse?"

"Better, I should think. They'll need good strong workers in the camps, so I imagine they feed them well. But I will ask all about it tomorrow after breakfast."

"Thank you."

*I*t was late afternoon by the time Sylvia left, and the mausoleum-like lobby was full of detainees dressed for dinner, milling around with cigarettes and cocktail glasses as if they were celebrities being feted before an awards dinner, not enemies of America. Sylvia wanted to hiss at them. Instead she held her chin in the air, straightened her back, and strode purposefully towards the main doors.

Matthew Portnoff, the organist, slipped into the room. He and Sylvia caught each other's eyes. He nodded. She nodded back. Matthew was the only other Jew besides the Zelners in White Sulphur Springs. Matthew—his real name was Nathan—had been born in Russia and his father was a rabbi. Matthew sat down and began to play "How High the Moon."

Across the room Sylvia spotted the woman with the marcelled hair: Bebe Thomsen, the German ambassador's wife. The one who had tried to tell Aggie she wasn't really a Nazi. She wore a wine-red evening dress with a slinky V-shaped back line that exposed her bony shoulder blades. She held a wineglass in her white-gloved hand, tipping its contents straight down her throat. Her husband stood nearby. Hans Thomsen, the ambassador. Or, no, not the ambassador, the "chargé d'affaires," whatever that meant. He had pale ginger hair that looked like it belonged to another person entirely; it didn't match with his gloomy eyes, ringed in purple circles like the goggle marks on an old-fashioned aviator. His lips were thick and dark and meaty, like uncooked liver. On his jacket he wore a variety of military ribbons and medals. Medals! These people had no shame.

Reaching over to place her empty wineglass on the tray of a passing waiter, Bebe Thomsen saw Sylvia looking at her. She stared back with a curious look of recognition, the corners of her lips curling up.

Sylvia turned and pushed open the heavy bronze door.

Outside, it was dark already, and a fine, sleety rain was falling. Johnny Burdette, who was working as the groundskeeper's assistant now, knelt at the edge of the lawn tenderly patting mud into the roots of a box hedge.

Carl Carper stood erect in his little pine guardhouse, like a toy soldier. "Mrs. Zelner," he called, as Sylvia walked across the Greenbrier lawn towards the exit.

"Yes?"

"Be careful."

"What?"

"Be careful." Carl's red-ruined face was serious. "The enemy is wily. They can confuse you into doing things you shouldn't be doing."

"I do not know what that means," Sylvia said. But as she walked away, her heart was pounding.

*A*s she approached the narrow blue house on Spring Street, she could hear Doree crying before she opened the front door. Taking a deep breath, she strode into the kitchen and plucked the baby from the high chair, then spun on her heels and hurried upstairs.

She couldn't bear to hear about Carnation and syrup and how many times the baby had made a bowel movement.

"Excuse me," Pauline called after her. "I was about to give her applesauce!"

Sylvia ignored her. She carried Doree into the nursery and sat down in the rocker. Unbuttoning her dress, she could see the baby's face relax with the anticipation of warm milk, her pink bud of a mouth falling open. As Doree began to suck, Sylvia sang:

> *Somewhere there's music*
> *How faint the tune*
> *Somewhere there's heaven*
> *How high the moon*

She imagined herself and the Italian on the steps of a villa, surrounded by orange trees. He took her hand and spun her around and— *Stop it!* she told herself sternly. You're a grown woman, a mother. He's a grown man, with a wife and two daughters. This thing—whatever this thing is—is an island. A floating world, separate from her life and his life, from her past, from her future. She would enjoy the island while she could. But that was all.

MARCH 1959

Doree was doing homework in the kitchen with the radio on when the phone rang.

"Mrs. Zelner?"

"This is her daughter speaking."

"Hi, Doree, this is Sheriff Badgett."

Immediately Doree's body went cold. There were no good reasons for the sheriff to call. An image reared up before her: Pete's bike pinned beneath a pickup truck, wheel spinning, blood glinting on the spokes.

But it wasn't Pete. It was Alan. And he wasn't hurt.

He'd been arrested. For trespassing. Trespassing at the Greenbrier.

Doree dropped the receiver in its cradle and called for her mother. But there was no answer. She must have taken her grandmother shopping or for a walk. Forgetting her coat, Doree flew out of the house and ran down Spring Street, the cold burning the inside of her nostrils. She arrived at Zelner's breathless, shoving the door open so hard the chimes crashed against the glass.

"Alan's in the jailhouse," she heaved.

"What?" Her father's long face remained placid, as if he hadn't really understood the news. "He's where?"

"In the jailhouse. He's been arrested for trespassing at the Greenbrier. The sheriff called. You have to get him."

"Watch the store," her father said, then grabbed his hat and went flying down Main Street.

His heart, Doree thought, pierced by the same fear she always felt when watching her father exert himself. She took a seat behind the counter and tried to calm her own breathing.

It wouldn't be the first time her brother had gotten in trouble, but *arrested*?

Alan had spent nearly every other day in the principal's office during elementary school. He'd refuse to do craft projects because he didn't like the feel of the glue on his fingers. He'd read books when he was supposed to be practicing addition. *But I already know how to do addition*, he'd say.

Doree would collect him from the office and walk home with him at the end of the day, carrying a note for Sylvia, explaining whatever had happened this time. Doree felt sorry for Alan, though he never seemed to feel sorry for himself. He liked the principal's office, he said. He could just sit there and read. But Doree also felt an itch of embarrassment as they'd walk down the hall from the office to the front door. *It's not because he's Jewish, it's because he's* Alan, she wanted to say when she saw boys sniggering and mouthing "kike."

Last year, Sheriff Badgett had brought Alan home one day; he'd been caught climbing the water tower. He'd needed a higher perspective to draw a map, he'd said. He hadn't been in trouble, though. The sheriff knew him, and had just given Sylvia a firm warning about keeping him off the tower.

How could they arrest Alan?

It wasn't until nearly closing time that Louis came back, alone. His eyes were glassy with fatigue.

"It's fine," he said, before Doree could ask any questions. "It's all fine. A misunderstanding. Your brother's back home."

"But what happened?"

Alan had been in his usual spot in the edge of forest by Copeland Hill, her father explained, watching the construction equipment and taking notes. A man from the audiovisual company—the same one Tony worked for—had spotted him and asked him to leave. Alan had responded that he wasn't on resort property, he was just in the woods. He wasn't trespassing. The man had gone away, but a while later he'd come back with the sheriff's deputy.

Doree was bewildered. The sheriff's deputy, Bill Frogmore, was a friendly, slow-moving man who liked to come into Zelner's for a Coke and a chat. "Why would Bill Frogmore arrest Alan?" she asked. "There's no law against watching construction."

"It was a misunderstanding," her father repeated. "Come on, let's go home."

Back home, Doree found Alan lying in the parlor with his head on their mother's lap. She was stroking his hair in the special swirling pattern she used. Doing that had calmed Alan down ever since he was a baby.

Sylvia looked up. Her eyes were black as engine oil. "We're going to take them to court," she said.

"Take who to court?" said Louis, still in the hall hanging his hat and coat on the rack.

"The sheriff. The Greenbrier. The town. The whole *farkakte* state."

"Sylvia. Stop. It's fine. He's fine."

"He's *fine*? My fifteen-year-old son is taken to prison for *playing in the woods*? This is *fine*?" Sylvia rose and began walking towards Louis slowly, deliberately, eyes unblinking.

"He's sixteen," Louis said, glancing over his shoulder, almost as if he was looking for a rescuer. "Has my mother had her supper?"

"It's bad enough," hissed Sylvia, "that I should have to live with you in this drek town full of goyim. But to have my children be treated like, like *foreigners*, like they don't have the right to play in the woods like any other child. As if they're less than some Carper with holes in their shoes. Because why? Because we're Jews."

"You know what, Sylvia?" said Louis. "Our family's been here since 1911, and people have always treated us all right. That's not the problem."

"All right? All right? All right to you is they don't throw rocks at us or lock us in camps. But you think we're equal? You think they treat our children as equal?" Sylvia's voice had taken on a high-pitched, trembling edge.

"Doree and Pete are just fine," said Louis, speaking slowly and deliberately. "They have friends. They're on the honor roll. Nobody treats them differently."

Doree thought of Edisto Level hissing "Heil Hitler" and laughing like a goon. Of the boys who wrote "kike" in chalk on Pete's backpack. But those were just goofs. Everyone got teased for something or other.

"The only one who has trouble is Alan," Louis went on. "Everyone else in town is trying their best to ignore whatever's going on behind the Greenbrier because they understand it's none of our business. Except for Alan. Why can't he understand that? What can't he just act like a normal boy?"

"If they're building a missile base down there, they should tell us the truth!" Alan shrieked, leaping off the couch. "I won't tell the Russians. I just want to know."

Sylvia grabbed Alan and clutched him to her side. She was vibrating now. Her hands clenched and unclenched like a cat's claws.

"A normal boy?" Sylvia said, her voice suddenly deeper and abnormally slow. "A normal boy?"

Doree felt the out-of-her-own-body sensation she got when Sylvia went over the edge, like she was watching a film with the sound turned down. She was there but not there. Nothing she could do but stand and see it all unspool in horrible slow motion. From deep in the water of her mind, a thought floated up, unbidden:

It's true. What Junior Carper says about Mama is true.

*Y*our mother scares people, her grandfather once told Doree, chuckling. *It's too bad. If only they could see the sweet girl inside.*

The sweet girl inside. Doree would sometimes stare at the wedding photograph on the parlor mantel, the phrase "sweet girl" running through her head, trying to see it. In the picture Sylvia was wearing a calf-length dress with a narrow skirt and short puffed sleeves. She held a bouquet of flowers to her chest so tightly it looked like she was afraid someone would take them away. One of the flower stems had bent, so the flower jutted out at a crooked angle, like a broken arm. Her expression was flat and cloudy. Louis grinned at her side in a crisp black suit.

If Doree's parents had ever been happy together, Doree had never seen it. One of her earliest memories was of her mother sweeping her arm across the green-and-white enameled kitchen table, knocking a pitcher of orange juice onto the floor, then staring at Doree's father with fierce, daring eyes. It must have been breakfast time, with the orange juice. What could make a person so angry already at breakfast?

Doree only knew a few things about her mother's life. She'd left Poland before the war. She'd worked in a dress factory in Baltimore. Even these broad details were only mentioned grudgingly; it seemed like Sylvia would prefer everyone to think she hatched fully formed from an egg.

Doree knew her grandmother and uncle lived in Israel, though she'd never met them. Occasionally her grandmother would send a letter, which would come in an envelope with a red dashed border and an airmail stamp. Alan would steam the stamps off and add them to his album. Sylvia never shared the letters.

Doree did know, from Sol, that her mother had once had four brothers, and now only one was alive. Two died in Poland, during the war, and one died in Israel, something to do with a bombing. She was always afraid to ask for more. She'd seen the pictures of the thin men in striped pajamas in the camps, their eyes like Halloween skeletons. She'd been to a lecture at the synagogue in Beckley where a man showed slides. He called it "a holocaust." She was thirteen then, and she'd stared at the floor and hummed to herself. Still, she sometimes dreamed of pits and dirt mounds and woke with a sense of fathomless dread.

Your mother has had a hard life, her grandfather would say.

Doree understood it was awful, what had happened. But her mother could have a nice life now, if she wanted. Instead, she seemed to insist on making everything worse and more miserable.

If that were true, then Junior's story would make sense.

After all, Sol had had a hard life too, but Doree had never seen him knock a pitcher of orange juice onto the kitchen floor.

At dinner the next night, Sylvia told Louis she'd contacted a lawyer in Beckley. He was willing to take the case. He thought they could sue for false arrest, and perhaps even what was called "mental anguish." His retainer was $150. She said all this as matter-of-factly as if she were describing her latest sewing project.

"Sylvia," Louis began, in a soothing voice.

"It's already done," she said. "I took the money from the savings account."

Louis stopped chewing. Sol blinked. Pete put down his fork and slunk lower in his chair. Only Alan kept right on eating.

"You did what?" Louis's chin had begun to tremble. "Sylvia, that's my bank account. You can't just walk in there and take money without discussing it."

Sylvia shrugged and took a prim bite of brisket. "Mr. Darnell didn't stop me."

Doree noticed her mother was wearing her best blue dress, the one that flattered her narrow waist and full bosom more generously than the rest. She imagined the bank manager's eyes sliding up and down her curves.

"We can't afford to pay a lawyer just because you're angry. Do you know how bad sales were last quarter? Doree's college tuition is only a few months away. And *suing the sheriff*? Sylvia, we have to live here! Do you think anyone is going to shop at Zelner's if they think we don't respect law and order?"

Sylvia looked at her husband, black eyes glittering in an otherwise placid face, and picked up Pauline's gravy boat. "I really don't care."

Not for the first time—and not for the last—Doree felt a curious twinge of envy. What would it feel like not to care? What would it feel like to pick up your mother-in-law's gravy boat and hurl it across the kitchen so hard it took a chunk out of the plaster before falling, whole, to the floor and shattering?

CHAPTER 30

❧

Sylvia

MARCH 1942

Pauline, barely five feet tall, drove perched at the edge of the seat, her nose nearly touching the steering wheel, which she gripped in clawed hands. Sylvia and Pauline were taking the baby across the mountains to Beckley to help the Sisterhood ladies with the Purim fundraiser. It took two hours to get to Beckley on the best of days, and with Pauline at the wheel it was more than three.

"You could learn how to drive," Pauline said, as they rattled over Sewell Mountain, pumping the brakes so hard on the downslope Doree's bassinet nearly slid off the back seat. It sounded more like an accusation than an invitation.

"I could," Sylvia agreed mildly, knowing this would inflame Pauline more than outright disagreement.

Temple Beth-El in Beckley was a stolid white rectangle planted such that its short end faced the street like a snout. The front door was atop a flight of bare concrete steps. A Star of David above the awning was the only thing that distinguished it from the rest of the houses on the block.

Doree was awake when Sylvia went to pick her up from the

bassinet. She gave a wet burble and raised her arms towards her mother. Sylvia put her on a hip, and they waded through the grass to the back door of the synagogue, where a bevy of Buicks and Studebakers were already parked in the gravel lot.

"Pauline!" cried a tall woman with a lumpy blond beehive, who was carrying a tray covered in tinfoil. "You came!"

"Bella," said Pauline. "How are you? Your hair looks stunning."

Sylvia had seen this before. With the Beckley Sisterhood ladies, Pauline was a different woman. Gone was the pursed mouth and the sideways looks. Here, she was Pauline from Baltimore, the sophisticated city girl, gracious enough to help the backwoods Jews with their little projects and compliment their terrible hair.

Perhaps if Sylvia had been a shtetl girl—a simple homely thing in a sack dress, desperate for her mother-in-law's advice—maybe then Pauline would have welcomed her, treated her as a companion instead of a rival? Feh!

Inside, the cinder block Sunday school classroom was thrumming with energy. Women sat at the crayon-scuffed table, drinking tea and eating coffee cake as they cut out letters for poster boards. The child-sized plastic chairs pushed against the perimeter of the room were laden with coats and pocketbooks. The air smelled like paste and chalk dust and Lysol, with a faint undercurrent of mildew.

"Oh, hello there, sweetheart," said a woman in a yellow shirt-dress to Doree, gently thumping the baby's cheeks with her index finger. She looked up at Sylvia. "Edith Sitkowitz is doing a nursery in the blue room, if you want to drop her."

"Thank you," Sylvia said stiffly.

If the Purim fundraiser had been for the Beckley TB hospital, like it usually was, Sylvia wouldn't have come at all. But this year they were raising money for the United Jewish Appeal for

Refugees and Overseas Needs. The president of the Sisterhood had called a month before and asked Sylvia to make a speech at the precarnival ladies' luncheon.

"I am not a refugee," Sylvia had said at dinner that evening.

"Are you not?" Pauline responded.

"What they call you doesn't matter," Sol said. "You talk a bit about Poland, about your family in Palestine, they give some money. Someone gets some help. How could this be a bad thing?"

So she was doing it for Sol. She hated the thought of losing his sly, conspiratorial looks, his friendly jokes, his comforting shoulder squeezes.

She hid in the stairwell to give Doree a quick feed, then carried her down the hall to the blue room, where a smiley teenage girl was playing with a half dozen small children on the rug. The girl reached out to take Doree, who smiled and cooed in return, snuggling into her lap.

Would it be so bad if Doree cried just a little? Just so Sylvia would know she missed her? She thought of Jack, being sent away to a foreign country at eight and glad to go, so unhappy was his life at home. Was Doree already a real American girl, eager to get away from her greenhorn mother? Would she want to leave her as soon as she had the chance?

When Sylvia returned to the main Sunday school classroom, yet another woman thrust a stack of paper into her arms.

"Can you make the mitzvah money?"

"What?" (*Don't say "what," say "pardon,"* Pauline would scold.)

"The mitzvah money the children earn at the carnival games. They can redeem them for candy at the end."

"How do I do this?"

"Just cut the paper into dollar shapes and write 'mitzvah

money' on it. Maybe draw a picture of the pyramid thing or the eagle thing, if you're good at drawing. If not, get Elise to do it— she's the one in the green sweater."

Sylvia sat down. Had she always hated being around groups of women? It couldn't have been so. Back in Poland she'd had plenty of girlfriends. They used to go to the café she'd told Jack about nearly every afternoon after school. The Astoria. It was meant to resemble a Parisian café, with its black-and-white tiled floor and its yellow walls hung with mirrors. In the evenings all the players from the Jewish theater would pack onto the red velvet banquettes, drinking wine and dripping cigarette ash every- where. But in the afternoon, it was mostly just high schoolers and young Bundists and the occasional artist drinking slivovitz at 4 p.m.

Sylvia and her friends would eat almond cake and drink coffee and gossip about boys (Herman Warshofsky would be handsome if he were taller. Moriz Mostowski had such beautiful legs it was honestly unfair; they ought to belong to a girl).

A few months after she'd come to America, she'd read in a Jewish news bulletin that the Gestapo had arrested thirty Jews in the Astoria and shot fifteen. *The survivors were ordered to bury the victims and then were taken away to an unknown destination*, read the story, only four lines long.

Today the sound of women's chatter was like crows squawking.

So Sylvia sat by herself at the end of the children's table, cutting paper into rectangles and writing "mitsvah money" on them with a marking pen. She'd done nearly a hundred when Pauline crept up and leaned over her shoulder.

"We spell 'mitzvah' with a 'z' in America," she said, her voice full of the sugar she used with the Sisterhood women. "You should probably do those again. You wouldn't want to confuse the children."

"You know, it's actually spelled with an '*s*' in the Torah," said a voice from the other side of the table. The woman in the green sweater. Elise. "I think it's nice that the children should learn the original spelling, personally."

"Oh," said Pauline airily. She turned and wandered back to the other side of the room.

Sylvia looked at the woman in green. The woman smiled at her. She had a small face and was slightly bucktoothed, like a cartoon mouse.

"The Torah's written in Hebrew, no?" said Sylvia.

The woman shrugged her thin shoulders and smiled. "It sounded true, didn't it?"

Sylvia smiled back.

*T*he ladies' luncheon was not at the synagogue but in the much-larger Presbyterian church. Sylvia wore a dark blue dress she'd made, with extra pads sewn into the armpits of the puffed sleeves, since she knew she'd sweat. She hadn't given a speech since school.

In the church basement, a painting of Jesus cast a watchful eye over a buffet table laid with food: tuna salad, egg sandwiches, a ring of tomato gelatin. A dozen or so Sisterhood ladies milled around, drinking punch.

"Oh, Sylvia," called Honey Greenberg, the Sisterhood president, the one who'd invited Sylvia to speak. She was heavily pregnant, wearing a white sailor dress with a yoke. It made her look like a giant baby.

"Thank you again for giving this little speech," Honey said, clasping Sylvia's hands in her own. "Hearing the story of someone who's experienced these hardships herself will just add that extra touch. The ladies can go home and tell your story to their husbands, and maybe it will make them feel a tad more generous."

"Of course," Sylvia murmured.

Sylvia sat at a table between Honey and Pauline, picking at her tuna salad and listening to the women chatter. A son almost ready to be bar mitzvahed. A brother shipping out. Plans to open a pharmacy in town, with a soda fountain.

I lie naked on white sheets with an enemy diplomat, Sylvia thought. *When the war is over and I have enough money I will take my baby and sail to Palestine and never see a mountain again in my life.*

After a dessert of whipped prunes, Honey stood up and tapped the side of her glass with a teaspoon.

"Ladies," she said, "as you know, this year's Purim carnival and dinner dance is raising money for the United Jewish Appeal for Refugees and Overseas Needs. Though the Beckley Sisterhood is small, we are so proud to be able to help our brothers and sisters in Europe. And we are very lucky today, because we have a true European refugee here to tell us about the unspeakable horrors faced by our brothers and sisters overseas. Please allow me to introduce Sylvia Zelner of White Sulphur Springs."

Sylvia stood, unnerved by the applause. Was she supposed to stand right here, by her chair?

"Why don't you come over here, Sylvia," whispered Honey, leading Sylvia to a spot at the front of the room, directly in front of the portrait of Jesus.

"Thank you," Sylvia said, suddenly aware of her accent. "I am very glad to be here today. Please excuse my English. I am from Poland, from the city of Lodz. It is a large city, famous for the manufacture of fabrics. There were many Jews. My father owned a factory that made ribbon and trim. We had a very ordinary life. Then, before the Nazis came, we had to leave. My mother and two younger brothers went to Palestine. I came to America with my father. My two older brothers stayed behind. Now one is living in the ghetto, where there is very little food and many outbreaks of spotted typhus. The other has been sent away; we do not know where. If you donate money to help the Jews of Europe, I am very grateful."

She gave a sharp nod and hurried back to her seat as the ladies clapped.

"Thank you so much, Sylvia," Honey said, patting her on the shoulder.

Later, as Sylvia helped tidy up the buffet table, she overheard two of the other women talking.

"I thought she was going to talk about the horrors," one said.

"I know, everything she said I could have read in the newspaper," said the other.

Sylvia felt her eyes narrow. Then she felt a dry hand slide down her forearm. It was Pauline. She'd heard everything too.

"I do think they were expecting a little more than that, dear," she said. "That's all right. I'm sure the Beckley families will be generous anyhow."

Ha, so they'd wanted someone who would cry and moan and create a *drama*? A little afternoon weepie for the ladies, so they could pull out their handkerchiefs and dab their eyes, thinking of the poor Jews in Europe. So they could go home and tell their husbands they felt so lucky compared to Sylvia. So blessed to live in America, land of the free.

To hell with all of them. Stones on their bones.

Sylvia put down the platter of sandwiches she'd been about to carry back to the kitchen and strode towards the church door. As she walked away, she heard someone calling her name. She turned and saw Elise, the woman who'd told Pauline "mitzvah" was spelled with an *S* in the Torah.

Elise waved for her to come over, a look of friendly expectation on her face.

Sylvia thought of her friend Ewa in Lodz, of sitting for hours in the Astoria café, laughing so loudly over nothing the barman gave them stern looks and they were forced to buy more cake to make peace. She ached for that. But remembering the women whispering at the buffet table, their eyes gleaming with condescending pity, she turned away from Elise, opened the door, and escaped.

CHAPTER 31

※

Sol

*B*y the time Sol's ear healed, leaving a corrugated ridge of scar tissue that he took to running his fingers across when he was thinking deeply, he was back in West Virginia.

Jacob Epstein had loaned him fifty dollars and given him a pallet of supplies on credit. Sol used some of the money to rent a brick building on the single paved street of White Sulphur Springs, and spent the rest on lumber for shelves, a cash register, and a new suit. At night he hung the suit from a nail and slept behind the counter beneath a burlap sack that once held coffee beans.

Though the town wasn't a coal camp, it reminded Sol of one. Everyone served a single master: the new resort they were building on the ridge to the west. There was an old summer hotel on the site already, with a golf course and rows of white cottages. But the new resort would be bigger than all that, much bigger; the brand-new railway station would receive guests by the hundreds year-round. Every man in town was working on it. In the morning, a steam whistle summoned workers from the clapboard houses on Mill Hill to the resort grounds. Sol would watch from the window of the shop as the men and boys marched down the street in ragged pants and too-small shoes, then watch again as they headed home in the evening, grimy from clearing brush and digging basements but buoyant from a day's work behind them, jabbering and poking each other. Behind the shop window, Sol felt as lonely as a ghost.

Sol's landlord, a stout, whiskery man named Cecil Carper, seemed to be the only person in town who didn't work at the resort. Though he couldn't have been more than thirty, he had half a dozen children. The youngest few would tag along when Carper came to collect the rent, as their mother was said to be laid up in bed with some kind of sickness. Carper treated the children like a pack of dogs—caressing this one's head, giving that one a backhanded smack for no reason at all.

Carper liked to talk, and whenever Sol saw him trundling down the road, he knew he needed to set aside building shelves or marking inventory. Carper had big plans. He was going to build his own hotel, he said. The new resort on the ridge would make White Sulphur Springs even more famous than the old summer cottage colony had, and people would want to visit who couldn't afford to stay there. So they'd come to Carper's place instead— real nice little cottages, Carper said, with toilets and everything.

"What will they do when they visit, these guests?" Sol asked Carper carefully.

"Take the air," Carper said, confidently. "City folks love country air."

The Greenbrier Valley *was* stunningly beautiful, a sea of forest cradled by the green-black Allegheny Mountains. But Sol doubted city folks were all that interested in fresh air for the sake of fresh air. The resort, which was steadily growing over on the ridge, was said to include several ballrooms, a swimming pool, and a theater—some whispered they would even show "moving pictures" there. Sol figured the main attraction of the new hotel would be for rich people to look at one another and have themselves looked at in return.

Every Sunday, Sol would sit down and write a long letter to Pauline. He tried to make the townspeople into funny characters—Cecil Carper became a comical blowhard; the toothless old woman selling manure from a truck turned into a babushka from a folktale. He wrote about his walks along the Greenbrier River—the moss so thick it felt like a feather mattress, the greenbrier vines with their vile-smelling flowers. He wrote about the three baby squirrels he found fallen from their nest, as pink and smooth and translucent as Turkish delight. He carried them back to the shop nestled in the tails of his shirt, and made them a home in a cigar box, feeding them sugar water with a dropper from an old bottle of Murine Eye Remedy. He did not tell Pauline about how the baby squirrels died overnight.

He did not tell Pauline that he'd stopped wearing his yarmulke. Nothing bad had happened, just the usual stares and questions about his horns, and whether it was true that Jews killed Jesus. But, while a bit of an ear was a small price to pay, Sol wasn't keen to lose more. Taking off his yarmulke seemed a reasonable safety measure, just for now. He still prayed. He still kept his milk from his meat (unless he was a guest at a neighbor's). If Pauline came, he figured he'd be able to live a regular Jewish life again.

When the money began coming in, Sol would be able to supply the shop with everything, even that very day's newspapers. Until then, he had to hitch a ride across the state line every week to collect bushels of goods shipped down by Jacob Epstein. He started off selling clothes, mostly ladies', since the men in town seemed to wear nothing but work trousers and oft-mended home-spun shirts.

Cecil Carper, watching Sol unbox a package of ladies' under-garments, gave him a sideways look. "Shouldn't a lady be the one touching ladies' things?" he asked.

"A lady will be here soon," Sol said. It was thrilling to say the words out loud, even if they weren't quite true. But if he was a shopkeeper—a man with his own business!—surely he could make it true.

He wrote to Pauline about the beauty of the stars on cold October nights—so clear you wouldn't believe! He told her about the theater they were building at the hotel, repeating the rumor about moving pictures as if it were fact. He said he was planning to buy a house.

Pauline's responses were short and languid, when they came at all. At least until March that next year, when one frost-furred morning Sol opened a letter that said simply:

My father has died. Please come.

*T*hey'd found Pauline's father collapsed behind the counter of his butcher shop one evening, his body still warm. He was buried the next day in the Baltimore Hebrew Cemetery on Belair Road. By the time Sol arrived, they were already done sitting shiva, though Pauline and her mother and brothers still wore torn black ribbons pinned to their clothes.

Pauline guided Sol into the parlor with the lace curtains and served him a cup of tea. She'd remembered that he preferred it in the Russian style, with a sugar cube. He was surprised by this, and touched.

Sol hadn't finished his tea when Pauline set down her own cup hard enough to rattle the saucer. "Do you still want to get married?" she asked.

"What?" Sol nearly spit out his sugar cube.

"You did before, though you never actually asked. Do you still?" Pauline's face was a calm oval.

"Well, yes, of course. But . . . I wasn't sure that you . . ." For once in his life, he was at a loss for words.

"I do. We should. I—" She looked away, and Sol could see tears had formed in her eyes but she was too proud to let them fall. "Father's gone. Mother's selling the house and moving in with Hy and Dottie. I just want . . . I just want somewhere to go. I just want a home of my own, and someone to take care of me."

The afternoon sun poured through the lace curtains like honey, and Pauline's pale red hair glowed like a halo. Sol reached to take her cool white hand in his. He knew she didn't love him. That was all right, love—affection, children, comfort—would come later.

"I will always take care of you," he said. "Always. Always."

*T*hey married the following month, after the thirty-day *sheloshim* mourning period was over, in the old red-brick synagogue near the Baltimore harbor. Jacob Epstein, in the place of Sol's father, led Sol to the chuppah. As Pauline, her face hidden beneath a white lace veil, walked the seven circuits around Sol, the rabbi spoke: "Dearly beloved, look. Behind this blessed bride walk her children. And behind them, her children's children. And so on and so on, an unbreakable chain linking our past and our future."

Pauline circled Sol again, and again, and again. *A son*, Sol thought. A son with the same gold-brown eyes of Sol's own father. He could see the boy, clear as a picture, walking behind Pauline as she circled. The chain connecting Sol to his family hadn't been broken, it had simply been stretched—across an ocean, across the veil between life and death.

Afterwards they had a reception at Pauline's aunt's house, everyone eating roast chicken and borscht and honey cake on card tables carried up from the social hall. Jacob Epstein had to go back to the warehouse, so Sol's only guests were Benny and Lenny Mirvish, Litvak brothers who worked in Epstein's stockroom. They both inhaled two full plates of food, then sat eyeing the half-plucked chicken carcass on its greasy serving platter. Before they left, Sol slipped them each a napkin-wrapped chicken sandwich spread thickly with schmaltz. He thought it was what Jacob Epstein would have done.

After kissing his bride goodbye, Sol left on the train for White Sulphur Springs the next morning. Pauline would join him in a week, once he finished furnishing the small room above the shop. It was an attic, really. But it would be only temporary. Once Sol saved enough money, he'd put a down payment on one of the new wooden houses on the hill north of Main Street, just like he'd promised Pauline.

He bought some boards from a cousin of Cecil Carper, who had a scrapyard behind his house on Mill Hill, and built a bedstead. He varnished the wood, growing so woozy from the fumes he nearly fell down the steep attic stairs. When the varnish was dry, he laid down a real mattress and two plump pillows he'd ordered from the Sears catalog. On the floor, he placed a pretty little round rag rug. A girl by the unlikely name of Cricket had brought it by when Sol first rented the shop.

"It's a welcome-to-White-Sulphur-Springs present," she'd said, standing in the doorway in pigtails and bare feet. "Braided it myself. Ma don't want me talking to no foreigners, she says. But you know what? I'm gonna live in a big city one day. And I reckon big cities are jest full of foreigners."

Sol looked at her bare feet and her worn plaid dress and smiled. "It's true," he said. "You'll like it in the city."

Now that the little apartment was ready, all Sol had to do was stock the store and wait for Pauline's train. He sat down and ate his dinner—boiled potatoes out of the cooking pot—and dreamed of sitting down to a real meal with Pauline: roast chicken maybe, an oven-warm challah to bless on the Sabbath. How nice it would be, he thought, to spend his evenings reading while Pauline sat by his side, needlepointing (though he had to admit he didn't know if Pauline did needlepoint). He'd be a real American family man, like in the adverts. He sipped from his tin cup of reheated coffee and smiled to himself.

CHAPTER 32

Jordan

JANUARY 1992

Jordan shivered as he walked outside for his tour of the grounds. The morning sky was a gunmetal gray and small, hard snowflakes were blowing sideways, stinging his cheeks.

The groundskeeper stood still as a statue beside the golf cart, as if he didn't notice the snow at all. He wore a quilted green jacket with a *G* embroidered on the breast pocket. Seeing Jordan approach, he raised his hand in a short sharp wave almost like a salute. "You gonna be all right, out in this?" he asked with no preamble. "We can do it later, if it's too cold for you."

"No, I'm fine, thanks."

The groundskeeper gave him an appraising look. *City boy*, his squint seemed to say.

Stop it, Jordan told himself. He imagined Jessica laughing at him.

"Hop in," the groundskeeper said, wedging himself behind the wheel of the golf cart. "Name's Wesley."

"Jordan."

"We'll do the quick tour, what with the snow. Golf course,

cottage rows, old employee dorms. Not so much to see in the winter." The groundskeeper had a narrow head with a slash of a mouth and a nose that looked like it had been broken a time or two. He stepped on the gas, and the golf cart lurched to follow the path down the curve of the lawn.

The hedges were trimmed into unnatural geometric angles, their glossy green-black leaves quickly accumulating a frosting of snow.

"Just took down the big tree," the groundskeeper said, gesturing towards the apex of the lawn. "We take down the decorations the day after Christmas, but the big tree stays up till January sixth."

Enough with the damn Christmas trees, Jordan thought.

The groundskeeper turned right as the path entered the woods. Now they were on the same road Jordan had driven down on the first night. Even though it was 10 a.m., the wintery sky and the thick-needled trees made it feel like dusk, shadowy and blue. Everything was silent except for the thrum of the golf cart's motor. Then the landscape opened up again, and they were bumping across an expanse of snow-scrimmed golf course.

"We got three courses here," the groundskeeper said. "We're on the Old White now, built at the start of the First World War. That was the resort's nickname then. The Old White. Before the railroad bought the place, decided to build something big, like in Europe."

"There's a lot of history here," Jordan said.

The groundskeeper didn't reply.

"Did you grow up around here?" Jordan went on.

Warm them up with some small talk, Hector Espinoza always said. *Make them feel like it's a conversation between friends.*

"Yes, sir," the groundskeeper said, with a firmness that invited no further questions.

They rode in silence up and down the small mounds of the golf course, the cart slicing neat tracks in the snow. The course was fringed with thick, deep woods, the kind of woods you could imagine yellow eyes peering out of, unblinking. It was so overcast, Jordan almost didn't spot the statue of an angel behind an iron fence, its milk-white wings catching a sliver of grayish daylight.

A cemetery. That's what he'd seen the first night.

"Who's buried over there?"

"Calwells. Copelands. They used to own this hill."

"Do they still bury people there?"

"Yes, sir."

Jordan thought of his mother's mother and brother. Where were they buried? There must be a Jewish cemetery somewhere in West Virginia. Why had they never visited their graves to say the mourner's kaddish and leave pebbles on the gravestones, the way they did every year for his paternal grandparents? Why had he never asked this before?

As the golf cart started up again, he asked, though he knew the answer perfectly well, "Which one is the West Virginia Wing?"

"Over yonder." The groundskeeper pointed at the looming left flank of the resort. "We'll go round back there to see the skating rink."

"It's sort of new, right? The West Virginia Wing, I mean."

The groundskeeper shrugged. "Newer than the other wings. They broke ground when I was in high school, so 1958, 1959, thereabouts."

The late 1950s . . . so the groundskeeper must have gone to school with his mother!

"Did you know a girl named Doreen Zelner—Doree, they called her back then? She grew up here around that time."

The groundskeeper made a sudden, lurching turn, and Jordan slid so quickly he had to grab the side of the cart.

"Sorry," the groundskeeper said. "What was that?"

"Doree Zelner," Jordan repeated. "Did you know her?"

"Can't say I remember the name. It was a big school. Gone now. My own kids had to take the bus clear to Lewisburg for high school."

Small blades of wind sliced through the loose collar of Jordan's peacoat, making the hair on the back of his neck stand up. As the cart turned, Jordan saw the huge door in the retaining wall, the same one he'd seen on his drive in. Now he put it together: That door went into the underground area of the West Virginia Wing. It was almost disguised, painted the same green as the surrounding fence, which itself blended in with the tall bushes planted around the resort's foundation. Just outside the door was a white utility van with the words FORSYTHE ASSOCIATES on the side.

Again, Jordan felt that same faint scratching deep within his brain. There was something he needed to put together here. The West Virginia Wing had been built when his mother was a teenager. His uncle Alan had learned *the hard way* not to stick his nose where it didn't belong. There was *nothing exciting to see back there*, down there.

"What's underneath there, besides the Exhibit Hall, do you know? It's built really deep into that hillside."

The groundskeeper stopped the cart. His face was a granite block. "Electric stuff, I reckon. You interested in electronics?"

"Just curious. Do people ever talk about anything else down there?"

"Anything else like what?"

"Rumors, anything at all." He felt his heart pulse in his throat. But smoothing over discomfort didn't get you a front-page story. Smoothing it over didn't earn you anyone's respect at all.

"People around here don't talk about what's none of their business," the groundskeeper said curtly, starting the cart so abruptly Jordan's head jerked backwards.

Jordan felt a small firework of satisfaction light up in his chest. He was on the right track.

CHAPTER 33

❦

Sylvia

MARCH 1942

"*I* wish the world outside this bed would disappear," Sylvia said. She lay nude on her stomach on the Greenbrier sheets—oh, such soft sheets. She had never been naked this way with Louis; when they made love—which they'd only done a few times since Doree was born—he simply pushed her nightgown around her hips.

"What would we eat?" said Jack, laughing. He was lounging against the pillow, reading one of the few books from the resort library permitted to the detainees—a history of the Greeks. He looked like a Greek statue himself, his beautiful shoulders white against the dark green pillow shams.

"I don't care about eating."

"That's because you just had lunch."

Jack had ordered a room service spread before Sylvia had arrived. Fillet of beef in a glossy, herb-flecked sauce, scalloped potatoes, cups of new green peas so perfect and smooth they could have been tiny marbles. For dessert, coupe glasses of peach mousse with whipped cream. After two years of Pauline's sour beet soups, the rich, unkosher hotel food tasted like a luxurious gift. They ate sitting across from each other at the desk. Sylvia's limbs felt heavy with anticipation.

"Yes, all right, the world can go away, but someone can continue to bring lunch."

"Sounds delightful," said Jack. "Do you enjoy cooking at home? Or is it a chore?"

"I don't do the cooking. My mother-in-law does. She says my food is too heavy for my father-in-law's stomach. And I sugar my gefilte fish."

"What's that?"

"Gefilte fish?"

"Yes—is that a Jewish dish?"

Sylvia laughed. "Yes, quite. It is fish meat chopped fine and made into balls. Every housewife has her recipe, which her own mother has taught her."

"And you put sugar on this?"

"Only a small bit. It makes the gefilte fish more mild. I believed all gefilte fish had sugar, but Pauline says no, only Polish Jews do this. Litvaks—Lithuanians like my mother- and father-in-law—eat gefilte fish with only salt and pepper, no sugar."

"So you don't have to cook. And you only work in the store occasionally?"

"Yes. My husband has a clerk—though he's leaving soon for the war—and my father-in-law helps when he can. He has a bad back. I work only some days; I'm learning. When my baby is older, I'll be needed more."

"And your mother-in-law minds the baby?" Jack was looking at her with a lazy smile on his lips.

"Yes. Why?"

"You say you never want to leave this bed? Well, I have an idea."

. . .

*F*or a week before the rendezvous, Sylvia wore cabbage leaves in her brassiere. Big stinking flabby greenish-white cabbage leaves, slick and shivery against the flesh of her breasts each morning. By evening they'd be wilted to half their size, and Sylvia's brassiere would smell like farts in a musty closet. But it had to be done. The milk had to be dried up.

Pauline was pleased that Sylvia was weaning Doree. "She was really getting too big for that, wasn't she?" she said, pursing her little cat bottom of a mouth.

Of course, Pauline didn't know why Sylvia was actually weaning the baby. Didn't know that Sylvia planned to spend the entire night with Jack at the Greenbrier, and she didn't want to leak milk all over those smooth cool white sheets.

She told Louis that she was going to Lexington with Aggie and her boyfriend to see the boyfriend's brother at the Virginia Military Institute. It seemed unnecessarily complicated, but she couldn't think of anything better.

Louis, of course, just nodded and said, "That sounds nice," as he took a bite of soft-boiled egg.

"It does sound nice, taking a holiday," Pauline said, looking sharply at Sylvia. Pauline never sat at breakfast. She stood by the counter, tense as an arrow, waiting to slide another piece of toast onto Sol's or Louis's plate the moment they finished.

"I'm not having a holiday," Sylvia said. "I'll be a chaperone for Aggie."

"A divorced lady of Aggie's age with a chaperone," Sol said, his face buried in the paper. "She can do what she pleases, no?"

Sylvia shrugged. Sol was the only person she felt guilty lying to.

The lie about Lexington meant Sylvia had to tell Aggie about Jack. But Aggie, as it turned out, already knew.

"Well, I didn't *know*," she said, when Sylvia came to visit her in the employee dormitory. "But I'd heard things. I figured it was your business and you'd tell me when you were ready."

"You must think I'm a fool," Sylvia said.

"Never." Aggie put her arm around Sylvia's shoulder and pulled her close. "I think you're brave, taking your little piece of happiness. But, Sylvia?"

"Yes?" Sylvia looked into her friend's round blue eyes.

"Be careful. People here talk. They've got nothing to do but talk."

The next morning, Sylvia packed a small bag with clothes and cosmetics, kissed baby Doree, and walked up Main Street. She passed the Greenbrier gate guards, and Carl Carper in his silly box. He saluted like always. She just rolled her eyes.

As soon as Jack opened the door, she could smell his cologne, as if he'd sprayed it into the air. He'd drawn the curtains, so despite the bright March morning, the room was dim and still.

"For today, the outside world has disappeared," he said, pressing Sylvia against the door and kissing her so hard she felt their teeth clink.

She laughed and they pushed each other into the bedroom, tumbling like animals onto the bed. A feral energy coursed through Sylvia's body as she unbuttoned Jack's trousers and pushed up his shirt, kissing his flat ivory stomach along the trail of black hairs that led from his naval to the band of his silk undershorts. She wanted to bite him, to suck out his marrow, to have him do the same to her. He seemed to understand, and he pulled her dress over her head in one smooth motion. As they made love, he held her arms above her head with force enough to bruise, and she was glad.

Afterwards, they took a bath together in the white tub twice the size of the one she had at home. He soaped her back with a seashell-shaped soap, then they each lay against opposite ends of the tub, legs akimbo, staring at each other. It was the gap between his teeth when he smiled that made Jack's beauty, Sylvia decided. Without it he would be too handsome, too slick, like one of those matinee idols with a fake name.

"Were you a virgin when you married?" Jack asked, with a cheeky look.

"Really?" she exclaimed, splashing water at him.

Laughing, he raised his arm to shield his face. "All right, fine. Don't tell me. But is there really any reason to be shy about such things?"

"I never even kissed a man until my husband," she said truthfully.

"On account of your religion?" Jack asked, suddenly more serious.

Sylvia made a raspberry sound. "No. We weren't like those black hat people. We were modern. Modern for Galitzianers anyhow. I never kissed anyone because I never had a chance. I was a girl when we left Poland, and then I was married. Did *you* make love with a woman before you married? You're a Catholic—you believe in hell for this sort of sin, no?"

"Catholicism was my mother's hobby, not mine," Jack said. "In any event, every faithful Italian Catholic manages to live with contradiction: the holiness of pleasure on one side, a pleasure-hating God on the other."

"Contradiction." Sylvia had learned this word only recently, and it had sat in her mind ever since, like a little bird on a branch.

America was the land of immigrants, yet Sylvia, an immigrant, would always be a foreigner. Jack was both an enemy diplomat and the lover of a Jew. Contradiction.

After the bath, Jack put on a robe and called for lunch, while Sylvia remained nude, wrapped in a bedsheet like an ancient Greek woman. They ate on the bed—sandwiches and dishes of vanilla ice cream, spooned up with tiny silver spoons fit for dolls—then tumbled nearly immediately into deep sleep, neither bothering to pull up the blankets.

"*I* asked Mr. von Boetticher, the German military attaché, your question about those concentration camps," Jack said in the morning, as Sylvia was dressing to leave.

Sylvia dropped her hairbrush. "What did he say?"

"He said there's some hard labor in those camps, to be sure, but nothing a strong young man can't handle."

Sylvia felt relief. Alfred had always been the most athletic of her brothers. He'd competed in the shot put at the Bar Kochba club. "And the food?"

"Von Boetticher says he's certain they feed the men just as well as they feed the guards."

Thank God, she thought. At least Alfred wasn't going hungry while she was filling herself on steak and mousse. That would have been too much to bear.

CHAPTER 34

❧

Doree

APRIL 1959

"Shhh." Tony put his finger in front of his lips, like a comic book cat burglar.

Doree giggled, then clapped her hand over her mouth.

It was just after dusk on a Saturday, and Doree and Tony were at the employees' entrance to the Greenbrier. Tony had a surprise for her, he'd said.

Tony poked his head through the doorway and looked both ways. "All clear! C'mon."

Doree followed him. She wore a navy dress with a sweetheart neckline she'd sneaked from her mother's closet. She didn't fill out the bust, but it still suited her; her arms and neck looked white and elegant against the dark fabric. It was sophisticated and adult in a way none of her own clothes were.

Tony gripped Doree's hand and pulled her along through an endless maze of gray staff-only corridors before they emerged, blinking, into the robin's-egg-blue hallway just outside the Chesapeake Room, like Dorothy landing in a Technicolor Oz. Small knots of guests stood here and there, waiting to enter the dining room. The women wore evening dresses and fur stoles, their freshly styled hair gleaming almost as brightly as their jewelry. The men wore suits with sharply pressed creases and silk pocket squares. One man had a raspberry-colored ascot knotted loosely at his throat. Guests greeted each other with exclamations and back pats, like animals performing some kind of herd ritual.

Doree looked around anxiously. What if someone she knew was here, one of the girls at school who worked as a night maid, or—worse—Mrs. Curry? Doree still hadn't told Patty about Tony. In fact, they'd barely spoken since the puzzle box incident. When they did talk, at lunch or during band practice, Patty kept a strange, quizzical expression on her face, like she was just about to solve a cryptogram.

As if reading her mind, Tony said, "Just over here," and pulled her along past the main dining room entrance and down the col-onnaded passageway overlooking the porch. The passageway was thick with guests—men smoking cigars in front of the yellow silk curtains framing the floor-to-ceiling windows; women seated in brocade armchairs, legs crossed, leaning forward to hear one an-other amid the hubbub. A small girl sat solemnly in a cushioned window seat holding a doll with perfect corkscrew curls matching her own. The air smelled of smoke and perfume and the heady scent of the lilies in vases at every console table.

Tony opened a door with a bronze plaque reading WASHINGTON ROOM and guided Doree inside by the small of her back. The skin beneath her dress glowed at his touch. Tony pulled the door shut behind them.

Immediately, the noise disappeared. Doree found herself standing in a dark narrow room with a fireplace at one end and a china cabinet at the other. The stiff chintz curtains over the only window were drawn against the cold night. A table in the middle of the room was set for two, though it could easily have accommodated twelve. A fire crackled in the fireplace, its glow reflected on walls the dark glossy green of magnolia leaves.

Doree looked questioningly at Tony. He gave her an arch smile, raising his dark eyebrows. "My new friend Richard, who works in the kitchen, told me there was a cancellation of a private dinner in the Washington Room," he said. "Apparently a 'Mr. and Mrs. Birtwistle' were supposed to be celebrating their first anniversary, but Mrs. Birtwistle is not feeling well. But the meal was already half ready, and Richard doesn't like good food to go to waste. And neither do I! So, tonight we are Mr. and Mrs. Birtwistle, enjoying our five-course dinner." He pulled out a chair and made an exaggerated "sit down" motion, like a fussy French waiter in a comedy film.

Doree sat. She stared at the place setting in front of her. She had never in her life seen so many different pieces of tableware, not even at Passover. Above the plate, three wineglasses stood together, like women gossiping. Doree gave them a nervous glance. She'd never had more than a half glass of wine at the holidays.

Tony sat down opposite her and unfolded his napkin. She did the same.

"Yowza," he said, casting a glance at the place settings and giving Doree a grin. "This is really the whole shebang. I feel like Frank Sinatra."

Doree wondered what Mrs. Birtwistle looked like. She imagined an icy blonde with an updo as smooth as a submarine. Like Kim Novak, maybe. She'd have a silver stole and a collar necklace. She'd know how to use all the forks.

Just then, the door opened and a waiter strode in holding a silver tray. Doree was relieved to see it wasn't anyone she knew.

The waiter stopped beside Doree and bowed, then lifted the lid on the tray with a smooth quick motion. "Good evening. To start, artichoke à la vinaigrette."

Doree stared down at the object the waiter deposited on her plate. It was an enormous green flower with thick, almost rubbery-looking leaves. Its center was hollowed out, and inside was a small ceramic cup of oily yellow liquid.

The waiter was filling one of Doree's glasses with a pale bubbly wine—was this champagne? Manischewitz Kosher Concord Grape was as purple and thick as cough syrup.

She looked across the table at Tony, hoping for a clue.

"Cheers, Mrs. Birtwistle," Tony said, holding up his own glass.

Doree clinked her glass against his, then took a sip. It exploded into her nose, like Coca-Cola but bubblier. Its taste made her think of moonlight, of shooting stars, of icy winter air at midnight.

"These things can be tricky," Tony said, plucking a leaf off the flower on his plate and dipping it in the yellow liquid. "Only part is edible—you scrape the bottom against your teeth like this."

"Where did you learn that?"

"In France, actually," Tony said. "The army had us outside Paris for some training. Boy, was the food there something else— I ate a whole loaf of bread every day, just plain with butter."

France. The only person Doree knew of who'd been to Europe—besides her mother and grandfather, of course, but they didn't count—was Dr. Sydenstricker's granddaughter Wendy, the one who danced the cancan in Paris and married a foreigner.

Tony had been to France. He knew how to eat these strange flowers, and was doing so with gusto, scraping the green meat with his teeth and placing the spent petals in a crystal dish in the center of the table. It was funny, she thought, trying to square Tony's rough, city boy accent and puppyish grin with the idea of him eating artichokes in France.

Tentatively, she plucked a leaf off her own flower and carefully pulled it between her teeth. Oh. It didn't taste like a flower at all, but tender and nutty, like a potato reduced down to its earthiest essence. The dipping liquid was sharp and bright. "Wow," she exclaimed unconsciously.

Tony laughed. "Good, huh?"

"Yes," said Doree, feeling suddenly bold and saucy. "It's delicious, Mr. Birtwistle."

Tony looked at her with his dancing dark eyes, and she felt the center of herself tingle.

They ate for what felt like hours. Maryland oysters on ice, Doree's first shellfish. (Doree thought again of her grandfather, eating pork chitterlings in coal camps and wondering if God would strike him down. But He didn't, and He didn't strike her down either.) A pâté as silky as pudding, topped with a wiggling layer of cognac aspic. Crisp-skinned duck with sweet roasted oranges. A plate of something called asparagus, which looked like thick green pencils and tasted like grass.

With every new dish the waiter poured another glass of wine. Cold golden wine that smelled like the inside of an icebox. Pale red wine like the juice of ripe summer berries. Purple wine that tasted of chocolate and campfire smoke. With dessert—peach mousse—came a thimble-sized glass of something dark as blood and sweet as marzipan.

"So what do you think of the Greenbrier?" Tony said, laying down his fork and stretching contentedly in his chair, having finished his peach mousse.

"Well, I've been here before, but not like this," Doree said. "I come here for movies sometimes and for the Christmas party. My mother hates this place." She immediately wished she hadn't mentioned her mother—she wanted her family to exist in another world from Tony, another universe.

"My ma would hate it too," Tony said thoughtfully.

"How come?"

"She'd say, 'This isn't for us, Tonio—it's for the merigans.'"

"Merigans?"

"It means 'not Italians,' basically. But more like 'not like us.' You guys have a word too, right? 'Goyim'?"

Doree giggled, hearing her mother's word on Tony's tongue. "Where did you learn that?"

"There's plenty of Jews in Newark. My uncle's body shop was right next to Abe's Deli. Their chopped chicken liver was something else."

Doree's mother made excellent chopped liver. Everyone said so. For once, Doree wished she knew how to cook.

"My ma would also say this place was haunted for sure," Tony went on. "All the old parts, all the long creepy hallways. You ever seen a ghost here?"

"Mrs. Curry, my friend Patty's mom, says she feels the hair on the back of her neck stand up whenever she walks through the ballroom at night when it's empty. They used to do operations there, back when the resort was an army hospital. Mrs. Curry says there are still bloodstains under the parquet floor."

"If my ma was here, she'd make me wear a Saint Benedict Medal on a chain around my neck," Tony said, grinning.

"What's a Saint Benedict Medal?" The tone of easy, teasing affection Tony used to speak about his mother fascinated Doree. There were no light, teasing words to use about Sylvia. Only heavy, dark, angry ones.

"It's a medallion with Saint Benedict on the front and a prayer against the devil on the back. My mom used to hide them in me and my sister's sock drawers. You know, in case Satan wanted a pair of argyles. Catholics and superstition go together like cheese and crackers."

Doree laughed.

"Anyway, I don't believe in ghosts, personally. And this place being just for the merigans and the goyim—I don't believe that either. The world's changing, right? They say that fellow Kennedy might run for president next year, and that he'll have a good chance too, even though he's a Catholic. All that 'us' and 'them' stuff, I think it's old news."

Doree thought of her mother at Miss Cricket's Doll House, bitterly snapping that the dolls were *for resort people.*

"Sorry, I'm rambling on about myself," Tony said, breaking her thoughts. "Let's talk about you. What's your dream?"

"My dream?"

"Your dream for your life. What do you want to do?" He was looking at her, his dark eyes earnest.

Her dream? No one had ever asked her that. She had never asked herself that. Wasn't going to college enough of a dream?

"I'm going to go to college in the fall."

"I remember. What are you going to study?"

"Teaching."

Tony nodded slowly. "Why?"

Why? What kind of question was that? "Well, I'm good at math. So I figured I could be a math teacher."

"A math teacher, huh? Okay, I've got a problem for you."

"A problem?"

"A math problem. It goes like this: Two missiles are speeding towards each other. One's traveling at nine thousand miles per hour, the other at twenty-one thousand miles per hour. They start twelve hundred and forty-eight miles apart. How far apart will they be one minute before they crash?"

Doree put down her own fork. She closed her eyes. All she could hear was the crackling of the fire. "Simple trick question," she said, after a minute. "It doesn't matter how far apart they started. All you need to know is that they're traveling at a combined speed of thirty thousand miles an hour. You just multiply that speed by the time—one minute, one-sixtieth of an hour—to get the distance: five hundred miles. The missiles will be five hundred miles apart a minute before they crash."

She opened her eyes and looked at Tony. He was grinning at her.

"Nice," he said. "I had to answer that one for an interview, and it took me twice as long to figure it out. You could be a mathematician, you know. The government hires lots of lady mathematicians. You could work at Los Alamos, or even NASA, where they're building the spaceships."

"You think so?" she said.

"Why not?" Tony picked up his fork again. The waiter had just placed a platter of cheese in the center of the table, along with a small bowl of candied walnuts and a cluster of grapes as tiny as blueberries.

"Why not?" Doree repeated. *Why not?* A window opened up in her mind. Through it, she could see herself sitting behind a desk in a large office in a high tower. She had her hair pinned up in a practical but elegant way, and she held a slide rule. A mathematician.

Tony got up to stoke the fire, crouching on the Oriental rug with his back to Doree. She studied the back of his head. *Why would an audiovisual technician need to solve math problems for a job interview?*

Miss Cricket's voice chirped in her ear: *I saw you with one of those men.* And Nora the sculptor's sardonic words: *What would a simple* audiovisual technician *know about art?*

But before she could think too long, Tony straightened up again and picked up his tiny glass. He raised it to her. "Here's to us, Mrs. Birtwistle. To a long and fruitful union."

The wine was streaming through Doree's veins, exploding in her skull like tiny sparklers. "To us," she said, raising her own glass.

A few minutes later, when he pressed her against the wall by the fireplace and gave her a firm, slow kiss, those same tiny sparklers exploded all over her body.

*T*ony walked Doree to the edge of the Greenbrier property and kissed her good night under a magnolia. She floated down Main Street, too dazzled to think of going home. This was it. Her real life was beginning. It would be bigger and brighter than she'd ever imagined. College and WVU and a boy from the Jewish fraternity weren't her only choices, her only path out of White Sulphur Springs. Tony knew she was a brain, and he liked her anyway! He thought she could work on spaceships! What else could be possible?

Without consciously intending to, she found herself in Patty's front yard. She had to tell someone about her evening, to let the bubbles of joy spill over, to see that thrill reflected back on their face.

It was a church barbecue night, so Mr. and Mrs. Curry would

be out. A light in the upper window showed Patty was home. Probably listening to records with Annette or one of the girls from cheerleading.

A shadow of an unpleasant thought crossed her mind. What if Patty *wasn't* happy for her? Maybe she'd still be too sore about the puzzle box. Maybe she'd be mad that Doree hadn't told her about Tony earlier.

Blinking hard to push the thought away, she went inside—unlike the Zelners, the Currys never locked their door—and walked up the stairs, skipping the creaky fifth stair out of long habit. She pushed open Patty's bedroom door.

Patty was lying on her wrought iron bed with the pink chenille cover. But she wasn't with Annette or one of the cheerleaders. And she wasn't with a boy either.

She was with a girl—a woman—who was lying on top of her, and they were . . . well, Doree didn't quite know what they were doing.

Patty's dress was unbuttoned and one of her round pink breasts was exposed. It jiggled gently like a Jell-O mold, its strawberry nipple pointing towards the ceiling. The woman bobbed downward and closed her mouth around the nipple. Her arm, which Doree could now see was up underneath Patty's skirt, worked back and forth slowly. Patty moaned.

The woman had long black hair as shiny as patent leather and wore nothing but a camisole and a pair of plain white panties. Even from the doorway, Doree could see the gooseflesh risen on the backs of her thighs where her panties met her buttocks. She was thin, so thin her shoulder blades poked at the sheer cotton of her camisole like sprouting wings as she moved her arm back and forth, back and forth, back and forth.

Doree felt a rush of brackish saliva in her mouth. As she

turned away, the floorboards squeaked. The woman didn't break her rhythm. But Patty did. She raised her head slightly from the pillow and, just for a moment, she and Doree locked eyes.

Doree flew down the stairs, five or six at a time, landing on the first floor so hard she felt an electric shock in both ankles. She tore through the front yard, trampling a patch of Mrs. Curry's violets. She turned, walking backwards, to see if Patty was watching from the window, and smacked the back of her head against a branch of the Kearns' dogwood tree so hard she tasted metal.

She stood, rubbing her head, staring up at the light in Patty's window.

What in the world? Her mind spun, trying to grasp something that would anchor what she'd just seen to reality.

Then she remembered something: When she was thirteen, Sylvia had taken her on a buying trip to Baltimore. They'd gone to the shop of a man Sylvia called a decorator. They'd sat in slipper chairs in the back of the shop, paging through books of fabric samples. The decorator had soft gray hair and a thin mustache that reminded Doree of a pirate in a film. He gave Sylvia tea and opened a tin of Danish butter cookies for Doree. At some point, another man came from the back of the shop and laid a hand briefly on the decorator's shoulder before putting on his jacket and leaving by the front door.

In that casual touch, Doree recognized love. The same kind of love she'd seen in the movies or between her own grandparents.

As they were walking back to the car, Sylvia said, "The decorator is a nice man. Some people are like that, and it's nobody's business."

So women could be like that too? Was this something everyone else knew? Was Doree really as stupid as a hard-boiled egg?

She must be, if she'd not known that her friend—her best

friend from kindergarten—was doing such things. And who was that woman? Doree could recognize every girl at White Sulphur Springs High by her hair alone. But the gleaming black curtain on the woman bent over Patty was a stranger. Clearly Doree wasn't the only one keeping secrets.

CHAPTER 35

Doree

APRIL 1959

On Sunday morning, Doree awoke with a sick headache. She always got one before her monthly—a vile, nauseating throb behind her right eye, pulsing in time to her heartbeat. This one was worse than normal—maybe it was the wine? Or maybe it was her skull trying to hold two enormous thoughts inside.

She was curled on her side on her yellow tufted coverlet when she noticed Alan hovering in the doorway. He was wearing his striped pajama bottoms and his favorite house shirt, an old white undershirt of Louis's that he claimed was the only shirt that didn't itch him. The hem was tattered nearly to lace from constant wear. He clutched a sheet of yellow notebook paper.

"What is it, Alan?" She barely raised her head off the pillow. It felt like the mercury of a broken thermometer was rolling poisonously in her eye socket.

"I've got a new cryptogram."

"Neat." The last thing she felt like doing was a puzzle.

"Want to look at it together? You might need hints."

"I'm not feeling well."

"Okay."

"You can put it on my desk."

"Okay." He remained in the doorway, shifting from foot to foot. "They brought a hundred and ten urinals yesterday. I counted."

"What?"

"The Greenbrier. The hole. Three semi trucks came yesterday, from Locklear Plumbing. Virginia plates. They carried out a hundred and ten urinals and left them under the tarp with the equipment. I counted. What kind of place would need more than a hundred urinals?"

"It's a big hotel," Doree said.

"I guess so?" Alan said.

"Alan, I'm feeling sick." Doree wanted to lie under her bed-spread with her eyes closed. "I might be catching."

Alan didn't move, but instead started chattering away about plants. "The greenbrier is blooming in the woods now. Smells so bad. Like dead rats or something. Kind of funny the resort's named after something that smells like dead rats."

Her brother never in his life took a hint.

"Alan, I really need to rest."

"Its Latin name is *Smilax herbacea.*"

"Alan!"

"Yes? Yes, all right, I'm leaving. But will you please ask Tony about the urinals?"

"What?" Doree stiffened.

"Tony. He's in charge down there at the dig site. Or maybe second in charge?"

"Do I know him?" she asked cautiously.

"I saw you guys together a few times. You went into the em-ployees' entrance together."

Doree felt her face go red.

"I don't know any Tony," she told her brother. "It was probably just a coincidence we were walking near each other. Anyway, you're supposed to stay away from the resort—you know that." She turned towards the wall and fake coughed. Eventually she heard Alan walk away.

After breakfast, Alan, Pete, and Louis left, and the house went quiet, as if breathing out a sigh. A few minutes later, the whirr and click of the Singer started up, familiar to Doree as her own heartbeat. Her mother would be sitting at the sewing table in her bedroom, hemming pants or putting pleated panels in dresses for ladies who were expecting.

Doree turned towards the wall and fell asleep. When she woke up, the house was silent. The sewing machine was off. Sunlight was streaming through the window like melted butter. Her head felt a bit better, but her stomach was still sour and churning.

A sudden knock on the door made her sit up quickly. Before she could say "Come in," the door opened and her mother emerged, holding a tray.

"Alan says you're ill. I brought your lunch," Sylvia said. She set the tray on Doree's desk. On it was a plate of plain toast and a bowl of tomato soup.

"Thanks," Doree said hesitantly. She couldn't remember her mother ever bringing her a meal in her room.

Sylvia looked around, as though seeing the bedroom for the first time. Her eyes landed on a book—*The Prairie*, with a nubbly blue library cover and an engraving of Natty Bumppo in his fringed jacket and coonskin cap.

"This is for school?"

"Yes. Mrs. Brooks is making us read all the Leatherstocking Tales."

"They are interesting?" Sylvia's eyes didn't meet Doree's; she was still peering around the room, like she was searching for something to tidy.

"Not really. But Mrs. Brooks loves James Fenimore Cooper."

"Who?"

"The writer."

Sylvia nodded. Doree felt suddenly shy, like she was chatting with a stranger at a party.

"Patty does not come over anymore?" Sylvia asked.

"Not as much, I guess."

"You are no longer friends?"

Doree paused. She could hardly explain the truth to her mother. "We're both just busy," she said finally.

"I used to have a friend," said Sylvia, fixing her eyes on a spot somewhere above Doree's head. The sunlight from the window behind her illuminated her profile; her dark hair glowed orange at the edges. "In Poland I had many friends, of course. But here, only one."

Doree nodded. She hardly dared take a breath, lest she break the spell and Sylvia dart away like a deer. She couldn't remember her mother ever speaking to her like this.

"Her name was Aggie—Agnieszka. She was Polish, like me, but a Christian. She did massages at the Greenbrier. We would eat pierogis together, talk in Polish. But then she married her boyfriend—he is a teacher of golf at the Greenbrier, a 'golf pro'— and moved away to work at a different resort. The Camelback Inn. In Arizona. It does not allow Jews. Aggie says don't worry, this will change soon. And anyhow, it is not her choice, it is her husband's choice. I said, 'The day the Camelback allows Jews, I'll eat a pork chop.' Then I told Aggie I never wish to speak to her again. Now fifteen years have gone past, and the Camelback still does not allow Jews."

Sylvia fell silent, still staring at the wall above Doree's head. Her eyes glowed like black coals.

Doree opened her mouth to ask a question, to keep her mother talking. Who were your friends in Poland? What happened to them? But her tongue was tangled in her mouth, so shocked was she by her mother's rare chattiness. It was almost as if Sylvia was another person entirely. A mother like Evangeline Curry, who sat on the edge of Patty's bed and told stories about her youth like it was perfectly natural, like her daughter was a friend.

But before Doree could think of what to ask, her mother spoke. "Women are foolish," she pronounced, and for a moment, her posture sagged. Then it straightened again, like a rubber band snapping back into place. "Eat," she said, shoving the tray towards Doree

Then she was gone.

CHAPTER 36

❧

Jordan

JANUARY 1992

"*I* need more time," Jordan said, holding the phone receiver between his ear and shoulder as he scrawled notes.

"You're covering the zoning board meeting in Fairfax County tomorrow night," Jim Kelley replied, sounding irritable and distracted.

"Give it to someone else." His voice sounded bold, even to himself.

"Why? Did you find the buried treasure?" Kelley laughed before it turned into a cough.

"I just need more time. Trust me."

"Kid, this isn't a paid vacation. You give me a story, or get back to town before that meeting."

"I'll have something."

"You'd better."

Jordan hung up the phone. His knees were shaking so hard they were hitting the underside of the desk. *Holy shit!* He stood up, exhilarated, and pushed open the curtains. Snow was falling again, and the white West Virginia Wing blended in with the hillside below, white on white.

I'll have something.

He'd never said anything in his life with such confidence. It sounded as if he wasn't scared at all.

*Y*ou're scared of what you might find out, Jessica had hissed, on that day she found the letters.

They were fifteen or so, standing in the empty rec room. "I told you," Jessica said, a note of triumph in her voice. "Mom's got all kinds of secrets."

"What do you have?" Jordan asked, warily eyeing the papers in his sister's hands.

"Mom's papers. The ones she keeps in that box."

Jordan immediately pictured the pale wood jewelry box that sat on their mother's dresser, next to the little bird figurine with the glued-on head. It had a big old-fashioned lock at the front, the kind you opened with a key, the keyhole so big you could put your eye to it and see inside just a little.

"Did she give them to you?"

"No, Jordan, she didn't *give them* to me," Jessica said disdainfully.

"You stole them?"

"I popped the jewelry box lock with a bobby pin, like we used to do with the basement door. You got a problem with that?"

What was he supposed to say? "No. What did you find?"

Jessica paused, then in a low voice, said, "It was a bunch of letters, but in code."

"In code? What kind of code?"

"I don't know, I'm not a code breaker, Jordan."

"Didn't you and Lisa Cohen used to have a secret code?

When we were like nine. You wouldn't tell me what it was. You said it was girls only."

Jessica smiled. "That was Ubbi Dubbi. You know, from that show, *Zoom*. You just add an *ub* before every syllable. Kind of like pig Latin."

Jordan's heart leapt. Could he steer the conversation to something happy? Get Jessica laughing, go get some ice cream? Put the papers back later.

But in a split second Jessica's face was twisted into a scowl again. "This was some kind of numbers code, not Ubbi Dubbi. Something *advanced*. Mom's way smart, you know that, right? She could have been, like, a math professor."

"She says she likes her job," he said carefully, wondering where Jessica was going.

"And you believe that?"

"Why not? If she'd wanted a different job, she would get one."

Jessica let out an exaggerated sigh of disgust. "If you say so. I just feel like this proves something about Mom. Like it's part of this whole thing in our family—push down your true self, lock it up in a little box, never talk about it."

"Are you gonna at least ask Mom about the papers, now that you've broken into her jewelry box?"

Jessica laughed bitterly. "Seriously? Like she'd tell me anything. When has Mom *ever* told us anything?"

That wasn't literally true, of course. Their mother talked about plenty of things from the past. The Greenbrier Christmas parties. Uncle Pete as a kid patrolling the yard with a slingshot. Meeting their father. But, yeah, of course Jordan knew what Jessica meant. The abrupt silences. The shadows falling on their mother's face. The feeling of a conversation suddenly hitting a stone wall. The shame of having stepped past a boundary you hadn't known was there. The anxiety of what lurked underneath in that unspoken blackness.

But what was the alternative? Pushing and pushing and making their mother cry, or worse?

"Look, can't you just leave Mom alone? We shouldn't try to make her talk about stuff she doesn't want to talk about."

"You're scared of what you might find out, aren't you?" Jessica said, thinning her mouth into a straight line. And that was the end of that.

Later, Jordan sneaked into Jessica's room and looked at the papers himself. Some of them were seemingly random chains of numbers. Some of them were letters in formations that looked like words but weren't.

It was weird for sure, he had to admit that. But if his mom kept them private, then there must be a good reason. Right?

%

CHAPTER 37

Doree

MAY 1959

*D*oree hummed along with the radio as she washed herself carefully at the sink. She put on her favorite kilt and brushed her hair till it shone, then tied it with a yellow ribbon. She sprayed a cloud of Blue Waltz in the air and walked through the mist. Because today was a special occasion, she applied a subtle flick of eyeliner to the corner of her eyes, just like she'd seen her mother do.

She'd checked her diary that morning, the one she used to track her cycle. Her period had just ended, which made this week safe.

She felt a twinge thinking about herself and Patty not so long ago, giggling over Patty's smuggled copy of *Voluntary Parenthood*. They had both agreed they wouldn't go all the way until they were in college. No White Sulphur Springs boy was worth it, Patty had declared. At the time, Doree had privately felt Lee Burdette might be worth it, but the chances of him being interested in her seemed so low, she'd nodded and pinkie swore with Patty anyway. Now the idea of going all the way with a child like Lee made her physically cringe.

What was more childish than a pinkie swear anyway? Obviously Patty hadn't really meant it. So why should Doree? School was nearly over, she was eighteen. She was ready. Ready to step over the invisible threshold and into whatever new life was waiting for her. Magazines always talked about virginity as a precious flower, but she imagined it as a dress—a childish pink party dress, outgrown. She couldn't wait to step out of it.

Tony met her at the employees' entrance. "Quick," he said, "Your friend's mom just went that way."

Doree dashed behind him, feeling giddy and light on her feet. The door at the end of the corridor opened onto a guest hallway. Tony poked his head out, then, seeing the coast was clear, motioned Doree to follow. He took her hand, and they both straightened up and walked down the hallway at a normal pace; if anyone spotted them from behind, they'd look like normal guests. *Normal guests.* A thrilling idea. But why not? Maybe one day. When she was a famous mathematician, perhaps.

When they reached the room, Tony pulled a long silver key from his pocket and unlocked the door with one twist. They rushed across the threshold together, giggling.

The Greenbrier guest rooms never failed to make Doree feel like Alice in Wonderland. Everything was bright and strangely sized—the blowsy peonies on the carpet were as big as watermelons, the curtains as glossy and yellow as buttercups.

Doree sat down on the bed, and Tony kneeled in front of her. They kissed lightly at first, then deeply. When Tony put his hand on Doree's quivering thigh, she placed her own hand on top of it and moved it higher.

"Are you okay?" he asked. His speech was slow, his breathing heavy. "Is this okay?"

"Yes," she said. "Yes." She touched his chest, and he began to unbutton his shirt. Then he unbuttoned hers, staring into her eyes the whole time, his mouth slightly agape.

Tony slid off her skirt in one smooth motion, then her panties, and then she lay back and pulled him on top of her. The weight of his body felt so good. She ran her hands over his lean muscled arms, the hard planes of his back. He leaned to one side, and she heard a soft snapping sound as he pulled the rubber on. Then she closed her eyes, gasping at the sudden, stinging fullness.

It didn't really hurt. That must just be a lie they told to make girls stay virgins. Doree drew Tony closer to her, feeling his heart beating so hard against her breasts she could hardly tell it from her own.

And then it felt good. Why hadn't anyone told her it would feel so good? Did every woman know this?

Was this what doing exactly what you wanted to felt like?

*A*fterwards they lay on top of the sheets, Tony on his side, one leg thrown over Doree's. Every part of her skin felt alive and new, like she was a fresh spring plant feeling the air for the first time.

After a few minutes Tony got up and, nude, rummaged through his tool bag, which sat on the carpet. "You gotta try this," he said, climbing back in bed holding a small red rectangle.

"Chocolate?"

"Yeah, but you've never tasted chocolate like this. It's Swiss. Nora shared it with me. She stocks up whenever she's overseas, she said. Once you've had the European stuff, American chocolate tastes like baby food." He unwrapped a corner of the bar and snapped off a piece, handing it to Doree.

She slipped the dark, glossy square into her mouth. Oh. It was dark and deep, with a bitter edge, like coffee. It melted as smoothly as butter. "I will never, ever eat a Hershey's Kiss again," she declared, laughing, and they curled up together and ate the rest of the bar, square by square.

They were still lying there, in a pleasant daze, when Tony said, "So will I get to meet your family one day? Or is this a secret forever?"

Doree was stunned, and her face must have shown it, because Tony laughed. "It's all right," he said. "I'm just kidding. I mean, not really. I'd like to meet your family, but I get that this"—he gestured towards himself—"is probably not what they had in mind for you. Still"—he gave her a sly look—"parents usually like me."

Doree laughed. "They'd like you." Her father would. He'd admire Tony's cleverness and how hard he worked—Tony had been at the resort till midnight lately, setting up audiovisual wiring for the new wing. He and his team had been up on Kate's Mountain too, building an enormous TV antennae, despite the heavy spring rains. Her father would also respect that Tony had been in the army; he still carried the disappointment of not being able to join up himself, during the war.

Doree's mother would hate Tony, but no more than she hated everyone.

"What about your mother?" she asked. "What would she think of . . . this?"

Tony grinned. "Ma would cry for a month if I married a merigan. But she'd get over it. I'm her baby boy, you know."

If I married a merigan. Married! Doree had certainly not expected him to bring up that word. She felt an electric thrill, then told herself to stop being silly. He was making a point, not proposing.

"She's very religious, your mother?" she asked, thinking of Tony's talk of Saint Benedict medals and church feasts.

"Average, I guess. She only goes to mass on Sundays, not every day."

"What about you?"

"Am I religious? I guess I'm what you'd call a 'two-timer'—church on Christmas and Easter only. And really just for my ma." He dropped his voice to a faux whisper: "Don't tell her that, please."

Doree laughed.

"But seriously, God must care more about the spirit of the law than the letter, you know?" he went on. "Like, love and family and being a good person matters. But those rules about rosaries and confessions and no meat on a Friday? Nah. I just can't believe He would care." He rolled over and stroked Doree's bare shoulder. "What about you? Would your God be mad about this?"

How could she explain?

It wasn't God that would be mad. At least she didn't think so. The Jewish God wasn't there in your house, looming over the hallway in his flowing robes like the picture of Jesus in the Currys' house. When Doree imagined him—if she imagined him at all—he was an outline of a bearded old man amongst the stars, like a constellation. He didn't talk to you. He didn't peer inside the bloody chambers of your heart.

It wasn't God she imagined when she thought about telling her family about Tony. It was Hal.

Hal, Doree's second cousin, had married a gentile. Their wedding was at a steak house in Baltimore. Doree had been a flower girl, six years old in a pink velvet dress with a scratchy lace collar her mother sewed from a doily. Hal's new wife was an Irish girl with a wide, happy, freckled face. She'd hugged everyone in the receiving line and taken off her shoes to dance barefoot, pulling Doree and Alan onto the dance floor with her. Still,

Doree remembered the wedding as sad. Hal's mother had sat stone-faced through the ceremony, and her smile in the receiving line made her look like a puppet whose lips were being drawn back on strings. Sol and Pauline didn't dance; they just stood against the wall whispering to each other.

Later, Sol had told Doree that Hal had "broken the chain." "We still love him, of course," Sol had said, his normally merry face strangely mournful. "But we're no longer connected the same way."

Yet, Hal and his wife seemed so happy—happier, certainly, than Doree's parents. Their big brick house in Baltimore was always noisy with laughter and the wild yipping of their four freckled children.

Shouldn't that be what Doree's family wanted for her? A life of love and a house full of laughter?

But, Doree thought, *who cared what they wanted?* Doree was eighteen. Her life—her real life—was beginning, no longer bounded by the Allegheny Mountains, or her mother's grim looks. She could go anywhere. She could be anything. It was her life. *Hers.*

She pulled Tony back on top of her.

Doree left by the back employees' entrance and walked the grounds in the spring dusk. She felt like she had after drinking the wine, her body effervescent, her head like a balloon on a string. She strolled lightly down the brick path, watching the old-fashioned gaslights go on one by one. The air held the balmy green scent of early spring flowers. It was chilly, but the air felt good against her overheated skin. A man in tennis whites smiled at her and tipped his visor. One day she would be a guest here, or somewhere like here. She'd learn tennis. She'd eat only European chocolate.

She felt so free, she completely forgot about Junior Carper. She'd been meant to meet him at 5 p.m., to give him that week's money. It was almost 6 p.m. now. But Junior hadn't forgotten about her. She'd just crossed the bridge over Howard's Creek when he appeared from behind and fell in beside her, his breath stinking wetly of tobacco.

"You're goin' the wrong way, Doree," he said.

How she hated the sound of her own name in his mouth.

"That's a pretty outfit." He rolled his bulging eyes up and down her body.

Was he going to try to touch her?

Your mother is a traitor, he'd said, on that first day in the school parking lot. And then he'd added: *A traitor slut.* The word "slut" was so ugly, slithering off his tongue like a wad of chaw and landing on the sidewalk with a splat.

Now he stood in front of her, with that same leer on his face.

Full of sudden confidence, she swung to face him. "When is this going to end, Junior?"

Junior smirked. "It'll end when you want the whole town to know your mama's secret. But you don't want that, do you? You reckon Alan needs any more shit than he already takes at school?"

"Leave Alan alone!" Doree was surprised by the vehemence in her voice.

Junior put up his hands in a faux conciliatory gesture. "I ain't gonna do nothing to Alan. I'm just sayin'. People've been sayin' he's a—what do they say?—*a threat to the nation's security.* Some-body's gonna teach him a lesson sooner or later if he don't shut up about the construction at the resort."

"That's a lie and you know it. Alan's not a threat to anyone. You leave him alone."

"I *am* leaving him alone. I'm just telling you."

If Doree were Patty, or Wanda or Annette, or even Louise Level—someone whose mother raised money for the fire department and didn't smash gravy boats against the wall—she would have just laughed when Junior first approached her.

Your mother's a traitor.

A traitor slut.

Your daddy ain't Alan's daddy.

It was unbelievable. And yet the instant he said it, she knew it was true. Junior's words resonated somewhere deep down in her body. It was as if she'd known without knowing. Known in her soul, if not her brain.

All mothers favored their firstborn sons, Doree knew. But the way her mother favored Alan had always felt different. If, as small children, Doree or Pete scraped a knee, Sylvia would dab at the cut with some Mercurochrome and wave them out of the kitchen. If Alan scraped a knee, it was like someone punched Sylvia in her own face. If other children teased Doree or Pete, Sylvia would say, "You let those *pishers* get the best of you? Feh." If anyone teased Alan, Sylvia would practically have to be restrained by Louis or Sol to keep her from running to the other kid's house and cursing his mother up and down.

It was as if Doree and Pete belonged to their father, and therefore to the life that made Sylvia so unhappy. But Alan was *Sylvia's*, hers as if he'd been carried with her from another, happier existence. There was something different about the way she looked at him, the way her face arranged itself in his presence. He was different, and she was different with him.

It was like Doree's brain had been working a cryptogram her whole life, only she hadn't known it. So even though Junior's accusation was nauseating, she had felt a strange relief to have the pieces of the puzzle suddenly fit together.

It was the second part of Junior's claims that hadn't fit.

She went to bed with one of them Nazis. That's right, your mother was a Nazi lover. Put that in your pipe and smoke on it!

How could it be possible? Her mother, who wouldn't even buy a German coffee maker, had made love with a Nazi? That part felt so ugly, so frightening, so threatening, Doree had immediately wanted to bury it deep in a field like one of Cecil Carper's jars of money.

But now she thought, why was it her job to keep the ugly parts of her mother's life hidden? If it was true, then her mother had made her bed. And she could lie in it. It wasn't Doree's problem anymore. She could already see over the horizon of the Allegheny Mountains. She was on her way out.

"Go to hell, Junior," she heard herself say, in a voice that was deeper and louder than her own. "You're not getting any more money from me. I'm done. I've got my own life. I don't care anymore."

CHAPTER 38

Sol

"What do you mean, 'fee'?" asked Sol. "I pay you rent already."

Cecil Carper leaned his bulk against the shop counter, leisurely combing his whiskers with his stubby fingers. "This ain't rent. I reckon you could call it 'insurance.'"

"Five dollars a month for 'insurance'? But for what should I need insurance?"

"Y'all Jews are clever, I reckon you can work it out," Cecil Carper said.

And then Sol understood. This happened in Lithuania. The gentile peasants would sometimes single out a Jewish merchant and plunder his shop. It was a way of saying, "This is our town, we can do what we please." It was a way of making the Jews feel not quite at home in their own home.

"No," he said.

Cecil Carper's face showed no emotion. "No? I'm just tryin' to help you, Sol. I don't want nothing bad to happen here."

"I cannot accept this, Cecil. If we start this now, where will it end? I will not be treated as an outsider here. I'll have a family soon. I won't have them treated as outsiders."

Cecil Carper nodded, then paused to slap the back of his son's head as the little boy galloped by, using Sol's broom as a hobby horse. "Quit it, Verne," he grumbled. "You're gonna break something." He turned back to Sol. "Listen, this ain't even for me. Everybody knows I got enough money hidden away to last till judgment day."

Nonsense, Sol thought, looking at little Verne's battered shoes.

"No siree, this ain't for me," Cecil Carper went on. "It's more of a . . . community donation, you could say. Since we've been so nice about lettin' you set up shop here, you know. You want everyone to keep bein' nice, don't you, Sol?"

"I cannot pay more," Sol said again. He stood, his hands flat on the counter, unsure what to say next.

But Cecil Carper simply changed the subject. "Dandelions'll be up soon," he said, settling into the chair Sol had bought for customers to sit in while they tried on shoes. "You ever had dandelion wine?"

Sol shook his head.

Carper laced his fingers over his belly and leaned back in the chair. Little Verne crashed into the counter and began to bawl, but Carper didn't notice now that he was deep into a story about all the things his sister Leota could do with dandelions and their roots. Sol gritted his teeth and forced himself to nod along with his ramblings, adding an "oh" or an "I see" when it seemed necessary.

It felt like hours passed before Carper finally stood up to leave. He was almost out the door before he turned around and said, "Think on what I said, Sol. It's for your own good."

"Goodbye, Cecil," was all Sol said.

. . .

$\mathcal{T}$he apartment was as clean and cozy as Sol could make it. Cricket's rag rug was set neatly by the side of the bed. There was a new cushion on the rocking chair. The small round wooden table was set with Sol's only two plates and glasses; Pauline would be bringing more when she arrived—they'd received an entire dining set as a wedding gift from her aunt and uncle. Sol hung a 1912 calendar from the Coca-Cola Company on the wall over the table and circled Monday, May 13, in pencil.

Pauline's train arrived at noon. Sol would close early, then he figured they'd stroll the short distance from the station down Main Street to the shop and have lunch. Later, he'd take Pauline to the resort and point out the sights—the golf course, the new bathing wing, the old cemetery with the angel statue. The dogwoods were still blooming, and the grounds were a froth of white flowers.

Sol stood on the train platform, twisting his wedding ring. As the train pulled in, blowing a fine mist of dust against his cheeks, he searched the windows for a glimpse of Pauline's apricot hair. When he finally spotted her, she was being helped down the steps by a porter. Another porter followed, carrying her trunk. She was crying.

Only later—years later—would Pauline admit she'd been crying because she was frightened. She'd never been outside Baltimore. Now here she was, in the middle of the Allegheny Mountains, about to step off a train and start a life with a man she hardly knew.

But on the day she arrived in White Sulphur Springs, all she told Sol was that she didn't feel well. So a bewildered Sol, his sobbing new bride on his arm, tossed a nickel to a pair of boys to carry the trunk and headed down Main Street. As they walked, he was already seeing the apartment through Pauline's swollen eyes and finding it lacking. He hadn't even put up curtains. Why hadn't he put up curtains!

They were almost to the shop door before he noticed the smoke.

*T*he damage to the building itself was mostly on the surface. It seemed to have started in the stockroom at the back of the shop, but hadn't spread as far as the counter, thank God. Sol and the boys who'd been carrying Pauline's trunk smothered it easily with a rug snatched from a shelf. One of the boys scorched his hand slightly, little more than a sunburn. Sol gave him a dollar and a new shirt for his trouble.

But much of Sol's inventory, still sitting in the stockroom waiting to be priced and shelved, was ruined—some burned, some spoiled by the thick, greasy smoke. Sol spent the afternoon scrubbing the blackened ceiling and throwing away bundle after bundle of smoke-stained bedsheets and nightgowns. Pauline sat atop her trunk, holding her little ceramic bird statue, staring straight ahead. Everything smelled of fire.

That evening, Sol lay next to Pauline in their smoke-smelling bed in their curtainless attic, listening to his bride weep quietly. He thought of Lithuania, and of what happened when the agent of the tsar's army knocked on your door. Jewish boys had two choices: They could run, or they could cut off their own trigger fingers. Running meant keeping your body whole, but leaving everything else behind. Cutting off your finger meant spoiling the body created in God's image. But then you could stay.

(You could join the tsar's army, of course. But you might as well tie rocks to your feet and walk into a lake. Not really a choice.)

Sol had thought coming to America meant the end of such choices. In America, he thought, you could be both safe and whole. Yet here he was. Pay Cecil Carper and live with the shame. Refuse and live with the fear. Or leave.

Sol wasn't leaving this time. He knew what it felt like to run, to cross the sea with nothing but a pocket full of stale mandelbrot and a handful of rubles.

He was staying. He would make his home here. His children would be born here. His bride—when she stopped crying—would gossip by the post office with the other women or stroll to the resort to see the dogwoods on a fine spring afternoon. There would be no glancing over her shoulder, no worrying about rocks crashing through windows and tumbling at her feet as she sat with her needlepoint (did she know needlepoint?).

Sol would cut off his own finger, so to speak. He'd do it for Pauline, and for his children, and for his children's children. They would have a place to be safe and call home.

The next time he saw Cecil Carper, he handed him five dollars. Cecil pocketed it with barely a nod and went on yammering about turkey hunting season.

No one touched the store again.

CHAPTER 39

Sylvia

APRIL 1942

*P*assover stretched grimly ahead of Sylvia. Being trapped in the kitchen as Pauline's assistant was always dreadful. But this year would be particularly so, as Sylvia would have no chance to return to the Greenbrier until at least the third day, when the seders would be over and the men had gone back to work. No cool white sheets. No Jack. No escape.

She woke on the morning of the first day with a hot little headache pulsating behind her right eye and a sense of agitation that mounted with each hour as she and Pauline swept the floors and took the carpets out to beat in the backyard. She and Pauline ate an early lunch of apples and cheese standing up in the kitchen. Outside, the sky was a swollen and shimmering gray, as if you could pierce it with a fork and diamonds would come tumbling out.

Passover was Pauline's annual triumph. This year, for the first night's seder they'd be hosting the Epsteins from Beckley and—a coup!—Rabbi Lieb, who drove a circuit around the small towns of western Virginia and southern West Virginia.

Normally Rabbi Lieb would have gone to Beckley, Pauline explained, but Beckley had just gotten its own full-time rabbi.

"So he's coming here!" she crowed, standing in the kitchen with a knife raised like a victory flag.

Pauline also showed off her beneficence by inviting the friendless—this year's guest of pity would be a peddler's widow named Bella Linsky who lived in a boardinghouse in Covington. Louis would be dispatched in the afternoon to collect Mrs. Linsky in the car and bring her to the house, where she would spend the night on the spare bed in Sylvia's sewing room.

"The Freemans don't invite her," Pauline told Sylvia in a tone of hushed disapproval, referring to the only Jewish family in Covington.

"Maybe because she's a *makhasheyfe*?" Sylvia said, just for the spiteful pleasure of watching Pauline's mouth draw closed as though by a purse string.

"I've asked you not to use vulgarity in the house, please. God forbid Doree grows up to talk like that."

"It only means 'witch.' This is not a . . . vulgarity." Sylvia played dumb.

"Well, it's not polite. Ladies should be polite." Pauline began to chop an onion, and Sylvia's eyes prickled with the pungent sting.

Sylvia shrugged. "I suppose I am not a lady."

Pauline snorted and gave her a sour look. "Where did you put the matzah?"

Pauline had ordered boxes of matzah from Baltimore. They were perfect squares, crossed with even rows of minuscule dots, like the tracks left behind by a sewing machine. They reminded Sylvia of Polish farm fields in the cold weeks after harvest, a shorn and lightless gold with darker patches from the burning of the stalks.

What was the idea of buying matzah anyway? You could make matzah in the time it took the glazed carrots to soften in the pan. In fact, you *had* to make it in eighteen minutes start to finish, or it wouldn't be kosher. Sylvia suggested as much to Pauline, who said modern people didn't need to make matzah when Manischewitz did it for them so nicely.

The Manischewitz company also made the wine, which Sylvia was sent to the cellar to fetch. No one in the Zelner family drank at all, save for thimbles of the syrupy purple Manischewitz on the Sabbath and holidays. They bought it by the case and stored it under the stairs; Sylvia wiped the dust on her apron as she carried the bottle back to the kitchen.

The brisket lay in the pan on a puddle of gravy, shimmering like spilled gasoline. Next to it was a sack of potatoes. It would be Sylvia's job to peel the potatoes for the kugel, chop carrots and onions. Then she would be sent off like a child.

She *was* a good cook. How could she not be—the only girl in a family of hungry boys. She'd been making kugels since she was eleven. She'd spent a decade of summer mornings helping pickle herring and cucumbers. She could stuff pierogis quickly enough to make dinner for eight in an hour. Her plum cake had been considered just as good as her mother's.

But because she put a little sugar in the gefilte fish, she was too low-class for Pauline's kitchen. Bah. What made Pauline think she was so high-and-mighty? Sylvia had traveled all the way across an ocean. What had Pauline ever done but sit in her father's lovely Baltimore row house and wait for a bridegroom?

Pauline was boiling beets for her revolting Litvak beet soup, which would be soured with vinegar and laced with so many herbs it felt like eating a mouthful of grass.

A few more months and Sylvia would never have to smell that soup again.

*I*n the parlor, Doree was stacking books on the coffee table. She gave her mother a wet grin. Still only six teeth.

"So strong, this one," Sol said. "One year old and lifting dictionaries like Charles Atlas!"

Sylvia wiped her wet hands on her apron and knelt down next to Doree. "Time for your nap?" she asked, in Yiddish.

Just as she hoisted Doree onto her hip, Louis came into the room. Passover and the High Holy Days were the only times of year the store was closed. They had to put a notice in the White Sulphur Springs newspaper the week before to remind people: *Zelner's to close Thursday and Friday. Remember your necessities!*

In the gray morning light of the parlor, Louis looked even older than usual. Only twenty-nine, and the flesh under his eyes was already sinking in, as if his face were being slowly dehydrated. His shopkeeper's stoop seemed to get worse by the month. Sylvia tried to imagine Louis under a blue sky on a balcony in Tel Aviv. His milk-pale skin seemed designed for the dark and damp of these West Virginia mountains. In Palestine, he'd dry out like an earthworm in the sun.

She felt a twist of tenderness for her husband. How could he have known that wearing a red scarf on a March night would bring the wrong woman into his life?

He would remarry. Maybe the Epstein cousin, the one with the faint mustache. Or some other cheerful American-born Jew, someone stout with a loud voice who would fit behind the counter of the shop as if she'd been born there. Someone with no accent. Someone who would never think of putting sugar in her gefilte fish. Someone who didn't lie in the bed of an Italian, eating marzipan, her mind already on the other side of the ocean.

"My brother called this morning," Louis said, stooping down to chuck Doree under the chin. "Did Mother tell you? He got a promotion at Dow."

"How nice," said Sylvia.

"He's lucky that his job is so crucial to the war effort," Louis said. "Because people say they might be scrapping the fatherhood deferment."

"Vincent is not a father."

"Not yet," said Louis, smiling.

Sol grinned too.

"Oh?" Sylvia said.

"I guess Mother didn't tell you, then," Louis said. "I'm surprised—she was so excited. Dorothy is expecting. This fall."

"How nice," Sylvia repeated.

Dorothy was the right kind of wife. A plump giggly secretary at the synagogue. She would be the right kind of mother too. She'd read the *Care of Infant and Child* book instead of pushing it under the bed. She'd make her own liver mash and strained peaches. She'd be happy.

Sylvia carried Doree up the stairs and rocked her to sleep, imagining with each back and forth of the rocking chair that she was cresting waves on board a ship, sailing towards the sun.

*S*ylvia took as long as possible getting dressed. She sat at her dressing table, slowly patting rouge into her cheeks, thinking of Jack's sculpted white shoulders. Doree sat at her feet, playing with a stuffed bunny. Through the thin walls, Sylvia could hear Pauline's movements downstairs become noisier as she grew more annoyed. The sharp rattle of silverware told her that Pauline was setting the table with a heavy hand; setting the table was meant to be Sylvia's job. She heard her mother-in-law at the bottom of the stairs clearing her throat strenuously, then slamming the door. She must be sweeping the porch herself. Sylvia smiled at herself in the mirror.

She put on a blue crepe dress with a high neck, which she'd sewn back in Baltimore as part of her meager trousseau. It was roomy enough in the hips, but clung slightly to her bosom, which was still larger than before, despite the cabbage leaves. Finally, she smoothed her hair with pomade and gave herself a leisurely look in the mirror.

Was Jack's wife prettier than her?

Jack's marriage, Sylvia had decided—though they'd never discussed the subject—must be one of convenience, something arranged by his mother the way she'd arranged his job in the diplomatic corps. Still, the idea of him escorting his wife through an elegant dinner party, his hand on the small of her back, gave Sylvia a shiver of jealousy.

When Sylvia finally opened the bedroom door, Pauline stood on the other side, like a jack-in-the-box ready to spring. For all her slamming and throat clearing downstairs, she had crept up the stairs in perfect silence.

"There you are," Pauline said, eyeing Sylvia coldly. "I was worried you'd fallen asleep. The guests will be here any minute."

Sylvia just gave Pauline a chilly half smile and carried Doree downstairs.

Rabbi Lieb, a small man with enormous gray eyebrows, arrived first.

"Please, let me take your coat, Rabbi," Pauline cooed, leading him to the parlor, where Sol already was sitting with the papers. "Sit, sit."

"Hello," said the rabbi, nodding to Sylvia. "What a sweet baby."

"Louis should be here by now," Pauline said. "He went to pick up Mrs. Linsky."

The rabbi settled himself on the chair and turned to Sol. "What's the news?"

"Echh," Sol said, shaking his head and folding up the paper. "Who can tell? The British sink a ship, the Italians sink a ship. The Red Army is doing nicely—Grigorenko says the Nazis will never take Moscow or Stalingrad. But the Pacific?" He shrugged. "And I'm not happy with this Japanese situation."

"Which one do you mean?" the rabbi asked.

"The exclusion." Sol's coffee-colored eyes seemed to darken. "The 'reception centers' where they're putting the Japanese farmers from California. This is so different from what the Nazis are doing to the Jews how?"

"I agree, it's not necessary," the rabbi said. "But we shouldn't make comparisons with the Nazis. It's not as if the American government is killing the Japanese the way the Germans are killing the Jews in the camps. I'm sure the Japanese get rations every bit as good as our enlisted men's. Maybe not quite as nice as the detainees at the Greenbrier! I hear they're feeding them chateaubriand and cognac up there."

Sylvia, who had been gently bouncing Doree on her knee, felt her body turn to rubber, her hands nearly losing their grip on the baby's chubby upper arms. "Killing?" she choked. "The Nazis are killing the Jews in the camps? How do you know this?"

Rabbi Lieb, startled, looked towards Sol. A low rumble of thunder sounded in the distance.

"Sylvia's brother may be in a camp in Poland," Sol explained. "But maybe not! Who can know? So much rumor, so little news."

"That's exactly right," Rabbi Lieb said, turning to Sylvia. "I'm sorry to have upset you, I wasn't thinking. Everything is only rumor; you shouldn't fret. 'Fear not—for it is the Lord your God who is fighting for you.'"

The pain behind Sylvia's eye seemed to leap forward, as if it were trying to jump from her head onto the rabbi, managing only to smash against the inside of her skull. Sylvia was about to open her mouth to respond—though she didn't know what she would say—when she was interrupted by the doorbell. The Epsteins— Lenny and Laura, and their three little girls—stood on the porch shaking droplets off their umbrellas. The moment they crossed the threshold it was as if the house warmed by five degrees. Laura Epstein ducked into the kitchen and could be heard loudly exclaiming over the food, while Lenny came into the parlor to offer big, pumping handshakes to Sol and the rabbi, and a smack of a kiss to Sylvia. His daughters skipped over and formed a half circle around Doree, marveling at her as if she were a toy doll just unwrapped.

"Look at her hair!" cried the oldest, who must have been eight or nine. "It almost curls. Do you think it will curl?"

"Her hands are like dumplings," observed the middle girl, who had the same dark braid and close-set eyes as her sisters.

"Come, sit," Sol called to Mrs. Epstein, patting the sofa. "We're waiting for Louis to return with Mrs. Linsky before we start the seder."

Mrs. Epstein crossed the room and sat down on the side of the couch closest to Sylvia. "How are you, sweetheart?" she said, patting Sylvia's hand warmly.

"Who can say?" Sylvia said, feeling her voice tremble. If she lost control of her emotions now, they'd only keep gathering speed and size, like ocean waves.

"Your baby has such clever eyes," Mrs. Epstein said, squeezing Doree's foot. "You can tell there's really something going on in her little mind."

People said Laura Epstein was clever. She'd even been to university before she was married. Clever women frightened Sylvia a little. A clever man was no problem; he still couldn't see any further than the end of his own nose. But a clever women might look all the way into her soul and see her as the little fool she was.

Yes. Doree did have clever eyes. Sylvia had always thought this. She would be smarter than her mother. This frightened her too.

"I don't know if we should start without Louis or not," said Pauline, standing in the parlor doorway in her apron. "I hope it wasn't raining on the road."

"Eh, maybe he stopped for gasoline?" Sol said. "We wait another ten minutes?"

Ten minutes passed, and Louis did not appear. Then another ten. In her peripheral vision, Sylvia could see Pauline pacing faster and faster between the kitchen and the dining room. It was dark outside now, and the storm was growing closer. Every few moments, the windows lit with the pure electric blue of the stove's flame.

Sol stood up and went in the kitchen. A few minutes later, he and Pauline came out and stood in the parlor doorway. "Let's start," Sol said. "Louis and Mrs. Linsky still aren't here; they probably pulled over because of the rain. But I see some hungry little girls, and we don't want to keep them waiting all night, do we?"

The table was set with Pauline's hideous "company" china,

cream-colored with a pattern of brown leaves. In the center was the seder plate, an enormous copper thing like the breastplate of some ancient warrior. The six seder items rested in their own oval indentations: a wet sprig of parsley; a boiled egg; a scoop of pasty tan charoset; a smaller scoop of slightly paler chopped horseradish; a tangle of cress, and the showpiece, the shank bone, mottled brown and still webbed with bits of desiccated flesh. Next to the seder plate sat a stack of matzah beneath a napkin Pauline had embroidered with the Star of David. A blue Maxwell House Haggadah was laid upon each plate.

Everyone fell into their places, with Sol and Pauline at opposite ends of the table. Sylvia was next to Sol, Doree in her high chair between them and the rabbi opposite. Louis's empty seat was next to Pauline.

"I'm embarrassed, we only have the Maxwell House," Pauline said, in the direction of the rabbi, as she stood to light the candles.

"All Haggadot are equal in my mind," the rabbi said.

The first syrupy cup of wine sat nauseously in Sylvia's stomach. She could barely choke down the parsley dipped in salt water. She hardly needed to swallow symbolic Jewish tears anyway—she'd had enough real tears in her life, hadn't she? When Doree began to squawk midway through the youngest Epstein girl's recital of the Four Questions, Sylvia gratefully picked her up and carried her into the kitchen. She sat down on the linoleum and leaned against the cabinet, the wood blessedly cool against her back.

She thought of the year Alfred refused to attend the seder. He must have been fifteen or so, right when he started reading about socialism and attending the Bundist meetings. This of course meant Leon refused to attend either. Their father, though not especially pious, had been so angry he told their mother not to serve them breakfast the next day. Alfred and Leon had sat at the breakfast table with smug, superior expressions while the rest of the family ate matzah smeared with farmer cheese and dusted with sugar and cinnamon.

L'Shana Haba'ah B'Yerushalayim, they said at every seder. *Next year in Jerusalem. Next year we will all be together again.*

Maybe next year it would be true. Next year in Tel Aviv. The Russians would destroy the Nazis, her brothers would be free.

She looked down at Doree and imagined her as a young girl tanned golden by the Palestinian sun. She'd run barefoot under the orange trees chasing her cousins—there would be cousins, no? Alfred and Leon would meet and marry girls with brawny forearms and hair in braids under kerchiefs. The twins too, when they were old enough. They'd live on one of those communal farms, maybe, where Jews harvested wheat and danced in a circle. On Passover they'd all eat at a long wooden table with no table-cloth, the windows flung open to let in the still-warm night air. They'd have a whole goose stuffed with apples, and gefilte fish sweet with sugar and raisins. Jack would write her letters, perhaps come visit, and they'd make love to the sound of the sea.

Louis would remarry. He'd be fine.

Or—maybe—Louis wasn't fine.

Maybe he was lying in a ditch along I-64, rain leaking through the cracked windshield, his skin as gray as gefilte fish. The image emerged whole in Sylvia's mind, and she examined it without guilt. She didn't wish for it—the thought of Sol's elfin face crumpling in grief made her stomach twist. But would she feel sad? Only in an abstract way, she thought, the way she'd felt when she heard the sweet boy from her primary school class had drowned in the pond in Ludowy Park. What was his name? She could only picture his face—plump and smiling, unaware of his fate. She thought again of her brother, standing on the train platform, and felt as if a lightning bolt had pierced her heart. She whimpered, and Doree looked up at her curiously.

At that moment, a clap of thunder rattled the kitchen cabinets. It was so loud Sylvia didn't hear the door open. It wasn't until a shadow fell across the kitchen floor that she looked up and saw Louis standing in front of her.

"Oh!" she said. "There you are. Your mother was worried. They started the seder."

Louis nodded. He was soaked, his glasses fogged and his shirt pasted to his skin. He leaned down and kissed Sylvia with cold lips, then caressed the back of Doree's head. "I'll go tell them I'm here, then I'll change."

"Where's Mrs. Linsky?" she asked, as he turned to go to the dining room.

"Mrs. Linsky is, well . . ." Louis's eyes had the blank, large-pupiled look of genuine shock. "Mrs. Linsky has unfortunately . . . passed away."

She must have been dead for days, Louis told Sylvia later. He hadn't wanted to tell her the details at first, but once they were in bed the story came tumbling out.

"As soon as I knocked on the door and she didn't answer, I knew," he said.

"But how?" Louis's horror had filled Sylvia with a surprising feeling of tenderness.

"The smell. You could smell it in the hallway. I'd been thinking, 'Oh, she's forgotten to take out the trash—the landlord should do that for her, she's an old lady.' I was thinking I'd do it myself, as soon as she let me in. But then she didn't let me in, and something in my mind, you know, just *knew*."

When the landlord had unlocked the door, they'd found her stretched out on the bedroom floor with her hands folded across her chest, almost as if she'd chosen that spot to lie down and die. Her face was as black as a plum.

"Maybe she saw it coming," Louis said. "Maybe she knew it was her time, and she knew I'd be coming by, so at least she'd be found."

"Why the floor, then? Why not the bed?"

Louis shrugged. "Maybe she didn't want to ruin it."

Sylvia thought of Mrs. Linsky, with her bullfrog neck and her dirty wig. She'd been young once, back in Russia. Then she came to America and ended up in *hotseplots* with a husband who lost all their money on poker and walked into the James River with his pockets full of rocks. Was Mrs. Linsky staring out the window at the bruised mountains as she died, wondering how far away her home village was? Was she wishing she'd never set foot in this country, the Land of the Free? Was she wishing she'd gone home when she'd had the chance?

※

CHAPTER 40

Jordan

JANUARY 1992

*I*n the bowels of the West Virginia Wing at midnight, it was impossible to tell if it was day or night. The hallway of identical doors seemed to narrow towards an infinity point. The green carpet was so plush Jordan's footsteps didn't even make a sound, which suited his purpose. He didn't want anyone to notice him.

Not that there was anyone around. Other than a maid pushing a cart on the second floor, he hadn't seen a soul since he left his room.

How could he square this empty, echoing Greenbrier with the stories his mother used to tell, of lobbies thick with cigar smoke, of lawns covered in picnickers, of waiters flambéing Baked Alaskas tableside in a dining room full of fawning guests?

Maybe that Greenbrier had never existed. After all, his mother had lied about or omitted so many other things—*Running off like that . . . Everyone in White Sulphur Springs knew Sylvia Zelner's business*—so maybe she lied about this too. Maybe the Greenbrier had always been an illusion.

He came to the end of the guest corridor and descended the

stairs to the Exhibit Hall. The doors were unlocked, but when he pushed them open he found himself standing in darkness. The silence in the dark Exhibit Hall was so profound it was like his ears had stopped working. Instinctively, he reached up to tug his earlobes the way he had as a kid when he'd gotten an earful of water at the pool. Feeling along the wall next to the door, he found a large, heavy switch. He pushed it and, high above his head, the fluorescent lights came to life with a reverberation Jordan could feel in the soles of his feet, like heavy machinery turning on.

He crossed the room, aware of the loudness of every footstep. He stood before the enormous white door and stared up. He felt again like Frodo Baggins standing at the gate of Mordor. Tiny and insignificant, but determined nonetheless. Then he noticed: The four bolts were open. The padlocks were gone.

Someone was inside.

If someone was inside, they'd have to come outside sooner or later.

So Jordan sat down on the cold tile floor of the enormous Exhibit Hall, crossed his legs in front of him like a kindergartener, and waited.

*M*aybe running away was genetic, Jordan thought as he sat. Maybe it was imprinted somewhere in Jessica's DNA that she had to leave. To leave him behind.

Jordan had been seventeen—*they* had been seventeen—when Jessica first ran off to start her new, free life. It was a Friday morning. He'd driven to the airport to pick her up from the summer camp where she'd been working—the summer camp where their parents made her work, after the Hawaii incident.

Jessica was one of the last passengers off the plane. When she finally emerged, Jordan could immediately see something was different. She was thinner, for one. And her face was guarded, somehow. Her eyes were narrow and watchful.

He thought the look would go away when she saw it was just him and not their parents, but it didn't. She hugged him politely but didn't make conversation. She didn't joke. She didn't tease him about the copy of *Crime and Punishment* tucked under his arm. When they got in the car, she didn't say anything sardonic about his Smiths tape ("sad boy music," she used to call it) or reach for the radio dial. Her hands stayed perfectly still in her lap, like dead birds.

Jordan felt tears begin to prickle his eyelashes. How stupid he'd been to think he'd get his old sister back, the way she was before the anger had taken over every other aspect of her personality. The goofy sister who demanded blue food-coloring dyed pancakes for their birthday. The sister who read *From the Mixed-Up Files of Mrs. Basil E. Frankweiler* and insisted she was going to live in the Metropolitan Museum of Art one day—Jordan could come too, she said. The sister who choreographed dances to Queen songs and made the whole family watch. That sister was gone.

Back home, Jessica was gracious but reserved with their parents, like a visiting niece. She asked about their father's work. She helped wash the dishes without being asked.

She's really matured, Jordan heard their father whisper to their mother. *This has been good for her.*

Jordan felt the cold water of fear begin to swirl in his stomach.

That afternoon, Jessica went shopping with their mother for Shabbat dinner. They came home with a challah, a roast chicken and chopped liver platter from Edmart, a bottle of the kosher grape juice that left syrupy streaks on the inside of the glass. As they walked in, arms full of groceries, their mother was in the middle of telling Jessica some story about the daughter of one of their family friends, a girl who'd won a prize for an essay about Israel. Jordan thought he spotted the faintest smirk of contempt on Jessica's face. But as soon as he caught her eye it disappeared.

Jessica helped put the chicken on the good crystal platter. She helped set the table. When Jordan made a joke about the liver, which, for as good as it tasted, looked like dog shit on a cracker, she didn't laugh, just gave a closed-lip smile.

He wanted to grab her by the shoulders and shake her.

Everyone went upstairs to change. Jordan put on nice slacks and the Baltimore Orioles tie his father had bought for him, and a matching Orioles yarmulke. He came downstairs. When dinner was ready and Jessica hadn't come down yet, their mother sent Jordan upstairs to get her. If they didn't eat now, they'd be late for synagogue.

He knocked on her bedroom door. He knocked again. And again. The cold feeling began to spread through his limbs. He knocked again. Finally, he tried the doorknob. It was locked. His legs felt like they were underwater, being pulled by a current. He staggered to the bathroom and got a bobby pin. Hands thick and clumsy with fear, he popped the door lock.

She was gone. Of course she was gone. The window was open, curtains flapping.

They tracked her down a week later, staying with a boy she'd met at a punk show in Michigan. She came home, unapologetic and closed-lipped, sulky as a cat. She didn't leave again until after they'd turned eighteen, the following March, to live with some musicians in a squat house in Philadelphia. *Just finish the semester and graduate from high school, for God's sake,* their father had begged, baffled.

But Jessica had already smashed whatever was left of the links that bound her to the rest of them. She was free. Or alone. Or both.

"Jordan Barber?" said a voice.

Jordan heaved himself to his feet, whirling around.

Standing behind him was a man in a dark blue jacket. It was the security guard. The one who'd tapped on Jordan's window the first night.

Jordan and the man stared at each other. The man's flat cheeks were pale under the fluorescents and his pockmarks stood out in sharp relief. For a moment, Jordan thought the man might come at him, even hit him. But then the man's square face broke into a grin. "You found me. Guess it ain't no surprise you're smart. She was the smartest girl I ever knew."

"Who are you?" Jordan said. His heart was pounding hotly in his throat. "What girl? What is this?"

The man beckoned towards the tunnel gaping behind him. "C'mon. I'll show you."

CHAPTER 41

❧

Doree

MAY 1959

"*D*oree!"

Her mother's scream was short, but so sharp it penetrated the floorboards and arrived in Doree's ears loud enough to startle her upright out of bed. A pen clattered to the floor. She must have fallen asleep doing Alan's latest cryptogram.

"Doree!" Her mother's heels beat a frantic tattoo on the stairs. Her mother never ran. Her mother never screamed like that— in fear.

"Doree!" Sylvia burst into her daughter's room. She clutched a piece of paper in her fist. "Have you seen your brother?"

"Which one?"

Sylvia looked at her blankly, as if for a moment she'd forgotten she had two sons. "Alan."

"Not since breakfast. What's wrong?"

"He wrote a note." She thrust the paper at Doree.

Doree smoothed the crinkled paper. It read, in Alan's tall, wavery handwriting:

I may have "cracked the case." I've got to follow some clues,
so I've taken the car. I have also taken two boxes of Lorna
Doones.

She looked up at her mother. Sylvia normally had two faces: angry and impassive. Now the fear in her eyes made her look like an entirely different woman. Younger, less angular.

"He means what, do you think?" Sylvia took the paper back and worried it between her thumb and forefinger.

"It must have something to do with the hole behind the resort, right?"

"Yes, surely. But he would go where?"

"I don't know." Doree flipped through her memory of things Alan had mentioned. The trucks with Virginia plates that delivered the urinals. He wouldn't do something utterly crazy like drive to Washington and demand to talk to someone in the government, would he? She imagined her brother being grabbed by security agents in dark suits.

"We have to find him." Sylvia twisted her hands together. "He cannot drive. He will have an accident, surely."

"Did you call the police?"

"The police?" Sylvia gave a scornful look and once again she seemed like herself. "They would only laugh at my face. They don't care about us, the police. I'll call your father. He'll have to borrow a car and go looking. Where's Pete? He knows something, maybe."

"Probably at the Currys' house."

"Well, go!" In a flash, Sylvia had gathered herself and once again stood as rigid as a marble statue in her blue day dress, her lipsticked mouth set in a line. "For what are you waiting?"

Doree slipped on Pete's old raincoat and ran all the way to the

Currys' house. It wasn't until she rang the doorbell that she even considered whether Patty would be the one who answered the door. Yet there Patty was, standing in the open doorway, wearing her fisherman's sweater over old dungarees. She gave Doree a strange sideways look, a hint of amusement on her lips.

Doree looked down at herself. She had on a child's yellow raincoat over her yellow lounging set. She must look like a demented duckling. "Alan's missing," she blurted out. "He took the car and left a note. We don't know where he's gone. Is Pete here?"

Patty raised her eyebrows and motioned Doree inside. "They're in Tommy's room."

Upstairs, Pete and Tommy were sprawled on the rag rug reading *Superman* comics, an open bag of potato chips between them. Neither so much as looked up when their sisters opened the bedroom door.

Pete didn't know where Alan was, he said; he hadn't seen him since breakfast. He looked worried for a moment, but his hand was already reaching for the potato chip bag as Doree and Patty left the room and walked back downstairs.

"Knowing Alan, I'm sure it's fine," Patty said, as they stood in the dim, Pine-Sol–scented front hallway. "He's probably sitting in the car somewhere, recording license plate numbers on trucks as they go by, or something like that."

"You're probably right." Having avoided direct eye contact with Patty for weeks, Doree found herself shyly studying her friend's face. Somehow she thought Patty would look different to her now. Older, or harder. But her face was exactly the same: the same round cheeks with their flush of freckles, the same snub nose, the same wide-set eyes that gave her a deceptively innocent air.

Patty looked back, holding her gaze. There was no trace of

shame in her expression. Doree wondered if she looked older to Patty. "You saw me and Gwendoline," Patty said, as calmly as if she were giving an answer to the history homework.

Doree didn't know what to say. She'd never imagined Patty would actually bring it up. Finally, she managed, "Who is she?"

"Gwendoline Sydenstricker. Wendy—but nobody calls her that anymore. Dr. Sydenstricker's granddaughter. She came back from Paris. She's staying with Dr. Sydenstricker until she starts at the University of California this fall. She's studying to be an art history professor."

Wendy Sydenstricker. A figure so mythic Doree could not remember if she'd ever actually met her in person or only heard of her. So *she* was the owner of the black silken curtain of hair and the winglike shoulder blades. She was the one dipping her mouth to Patty's breast while her hand moved back and forth like a piston beneath the blanket.

"Oh."

"We're not the only ones like this, Gwendoline and I." Patty's voice remained perfectly calm, perfectly level. "It's called being a homophile. There's a group in San Francisco. Hundreds of people, maybe even thousands. Gwendoline's asked me to go with her there, to California."

"I don't understand," Doree blurted out. "Two women can't have a baby together. How can it be normal?"

"I don't care if it's normal." Patty spoke with the same firm confidence she'd always had. "If I pretend to be what my parents and everyone expect me to be, I'll end up like Miss Cricket."

"Miss Cricket? How?" Desperate to pull the conversation towards the familiar, Doree made a joke: "Purple doesn't suit you."

Patty smiled but didn't laugh. "She was in love with one of the Negro doormen at the Greenbrier, back even before my mother worked there. They got found out, and the doorman ran off before the men in town could catch him. Miss Cricket was going to follow him, but then somebody threw a burning brick through her window and she got scared. Our parents all know about it. Everybody knows about it, they just don't say anything. And Miss Cricket just stays here with her cigarettes and her stupid dogs and her stupid dolls because this is where she grew up and she doesn't know anything else, and it makes me so sad I want to scream. I won't do it. I won't."

"Isn't Wendy Sydenstricker married?"

"Oh, him. Farid. That was just a marriage of convenience so he could move to America to study. He's from Algeria. It's over now."

Oh, him. The way she said it spoke to an entire world of intimacy Doree knew nothing about.

Doree looked at her friend's face and for a moment she saw six-year-old Patty egging her on to write naughty words on the wall behind the dresser. Then there was twelve-year-old Patty, cross-legged on the brass bed, patiently explaining how the period blood came out your down-there, not your bottom hole like Louise Level claimed. Patty only a few months ago, sitting at the desk writing out a budget for the car they'd share when they went to college together.

She thought of the decorator in Baltimore, how tenderly the other man had touched his shoulder. That was love. "I'm glad for you then," she said. "For you and Wendy."

Patty reached over and patted Doree's back, close enough that Doree could smell her familiar scent of Dial soap and baby powder. "Thanks, Doree, that means a lot. I'm sorry I didn't tell you before." She turned to open the front door.

"Patty?"

Patty turned back. "Yes?"

The words came out in a stream. "I've met someone too. His name is Tony. He works for the new audiovisual company at the resort. He fixes televisions. Or at least that's officially what he does. I don't know. I think Alan might be right—there might be something funny going on with the new wing. We went all the way. It didn't hurt!"

Patty's eyebrows shot up.

"I know. Don't worry, I won't get pregnant. I counted my cycle days. And he used a rubber."

"Are you in love?" Patty's blue eyes searched Doree's face.

"I love him—I think I love him—but it's about more than love. He has ideas about me."

"Ideas? What do you mean?"

"He said I could be a mathematician, that's how smart he thinks I am. He said I could work for the government. For Los Alamos. Or NASA, where they make the spaceships, even!"

Patty looked her right in the eye. "Doree, if you want to, you could be the goddamn president."

Doree laughed. It was the most Patty-like thing Patty could have said.

"But right now," Patty said, putting on her coat, "let's go find Alan."

Doree nodded, feeling immensely, overwhelmingly grateful, and followed her friend out the door.

*D*oree and Patty cut through the tall grass behind the fish hatchery and across an empty lot to downtown, peering into every storefront and over the top of every backyard fence. At Main Street, a paneled station wagon came sliding around the corner from Old White Trail, then screeched to stop in front of them. It was Doree's father, in Mrs. Calwell's car. Louis began to roll down the window, but, growing impatient at its halting progress, flung open the door. The bags under his eyes looked like bruises. "Jump in," he called. "Johnny Burdette just called from the resort. He found our car."

Doree's body flooded with cool relief. Of course. Alan was probably just in one of his usual spots, hunched over a yellow notebook.

Doree and Patty jumped in. Louis lurched down Main Street and made a hard turn into the white-brick front gateway of the resort, not pausing to wave to Mr. Sammy. He parked in the lot by the Motor Lobby and all three of them hurried across the lawn.

At the foot of Copeland Hill, its fender gleaming in the late sunlight, was the Zelner's station wagon. Its front two wheels rested atop a bed of crushed tulips. Johnny Burdette crouched next to the open driver's door. When he saw Doree and Louis, he straightened up, leaning against the car to take the weight off his wooden leg.

"No sign of him?" He had a kind, plain, flat face, with none of the sharp wolfishness of his son.

"No, sir," Doree answered.

"I'm just looking here, and, see, I don't want to worry anyone, but . . ." Mr. Burdette looked down at the inside driver's door panel. "I reckon that spot there is, well . . . it's not a lot, but . . ." He took a clean white handkerchief from his pocket and wiped it across the bottom of the panel. He held it up and squinted, and even in the now quickly fading light it was perfectly clear: a thick red-black smear of blood.

CHAPTER 42

✤

Sylvia

APRIL 1942

*L*ooking back, she should have known something was wrong as soon as she left the house and noticed a fringe of smoke dissipating above the treetops. A train had just left White Sulphur Springs Station. But no train was scheduled this time of day.

As she approached the Greenbrier, a green Rolls-Royce was pulling out of the station at a slow, almost funereal pace, heading up the driveway back to the resort. A deep, cold water panic began to build in the pit of Sylvia's stomach. *Something is wrong.* As she reached the main entrance, she saw a knot of bellboys hunkered shoulder to shoulder behind the valet desk. They were counting tips. One glanced over and saw it was only Sylvia, and gave her a little wave and a grin.

The lobby looked like the aftermath of a performance at the Scala Theater in Lodz: trampled papers and sweets wrappers and crushed cigarette butts littering the floor; half-full water glasses sweating rings onto the concierge desk; a velvet glove caught in the leaves of a potted palm. A large number of people had been assembled here, and now they were gone.

A chilly sweat beginning to prickle her underarms, Sylvia spotted Evangeline Curry sweeping on the far side of the room. She rushed up to her so quickly Evangeline startled and dropped her broom.

"Mrs. Zelner! Are you all right?"

"Yes, fine, thank you." The words gummed up in her mouth. She couldn't bring herself to ask the direct question, so instead she said: "Why is the lobby a mess?"

"Did you hear? They sent the Italians away this morning. Not an hour ago. They're going down to the Grove Park Inn in Asheville. But here's the thing of it—they're bringing in Japanese. Isn't that something!"

"Are . . . are they all gone?"

Evangeline's round friendly face furrowed with concern. "Oh no, you didn't get to give him the dresses you sewed? Is that it, honey?"

Sylvia just nodded. Or at least she thought she nodded. Her body felt rubbery and no longer under her control, like a marionette dropped by its puppeteer.

"Don't worry, he left you the money—I've got it!"

"What?" The word came out more violently than she'd intended.

"The money for the sewing work. Here." Evangeline reached into her green uniform pocket, pulled out a thick cream-colored envelope with a *G* embossed in gold on the flap and "Mrs. Zelner" written on it in Jack's hand, and gave it to Sylvia.

Sylvia tried to raise her hand to take it.

A look crossed Evangeline's face, her smile subtly tightening and her eyebrows lifting. But just as quickly, her expression returned to friendly concern. She tucked the envelope into Sylvia's bag and gave it a brisk pat. "I can ask Mr. Johnston if one of the cars can take you home. I'm sure someone meant to call you and say you didn't need to come today, but everything was just a mess all morning."

"No, thank you." Sylvia began to walk away, then, feeling that she owed Evangeline an explanation, at least a feint of one, added, "I'm just going to walk through the corridor and leave by the North Entrance."

"The tulips are so pretty there," Evangeline said, and Sylvia was nearly overwhelmed at the kindness of this small offering of solidarity.

"Yes, the tulips," she said faintly.

As soon as she turned the corner, she tore the envelope open. Out flew a stack of green bills secured with a band. Money. Nothing but money. How could this be? He must have left her something else. His room! She had to get to his room. She started to run, but the carpet was so plush under her soles it was like treading on sand. The upholstered silence of the white hallway added to her sense of panic, her breath rasping in her ears. She turned a corner and nearly bumped into an enormous, lumpen brown laundry sack on a trolley. A maid must have been stripping the beds room by room, as the doors of half the rooms were propped open, naked mattresses visible.

Then she was there, room 151. She slipped inside and closed and locked the door behind her. The curtains had been opened all the way and tied back with thick gold cords. Awash with cool morning light, the room looked exposed and anonymous. Someone had already vacuumed the carpet, leaving symmetrical tracks and a hot, slightly burned smell. Sylvia wheeled around. The mattress, its sheets peeled away, looked puffy, its fabric sagging between the buttons, the color a disturbingly fleshy off-white. The bare pillows were piled carelessly in the bed's center in a way that struck Sylvia as disrespectful, as if the maids knew this room had been special and made a joke of it.

There was nothing here. There was nothing left.

Little fool, she said to herself. *You little fool.*

Still, she ran her hand along the back of the headboard. Still, she opened every drawer in the desk.

Finally, she gathered herself enough to go back in the hallway. She walked with her head down, feeling the eyes of the maids on her as she crossed back past the lobby entrance and into the East Corridor. She was almost to the exit when a figure stepped directly into her path. The carpet was so thick Sylvia hadn't heard her coming: the woman with the marcelled hair. Bebe Thomsen.

Bebe Thomsen's eyes were small and very black beneath eyebrows thin as knife slashes on her pale, overpowdered face. She wore a peach lounging ensemble with a tunic top belted over loose pants, topped incongruously with a black mink capelet. She was gloveless, and her nails were perfect red ovals.

"Is he helping you too?" the woman hissed, in a rusty, accented voice.

"Excuse me?"

"Giacomo. Is he helping you too?"

"I don't understand."

Thomsen's black eyes bored into her. She wore a strange scent, something fruity and vaguely rotten. "Giacomo. 'Jack.'" She said the name "Jack" archly, as if it were a joke. "What did he promise you?"

"I don't know what you're saying." Sylvia's throat began to tighten.

Thomsen gave a short, barking laugh. "Of course not. You're just a seamstress."

Sylvia took several steps backwards. The overripe smell on

Bebe Thomsen was last night's alcohol, half-digested and seeping through her pores. She was drunk. A drunk. Just a crazy drunk.

"The famous Casanova was a 'Giacamo' too, you know," Thomsen said, smirking. "Italians. It must be in the blood."

"Jack is half English." The words were out of Sylvia's mouth before she could think. Her panic had moved to her stomach, where it was beginning to spin in slow, nauseating circles.

Thomsen raised her knife slash eyebrows. "Right. I'm just telling you, whatever he promised you, don't believe it. He told me he would help me leave my husband so I could stay in America. He had friends in high places in the State Department. But now he's gone and *phfffff.*" She waved her wrist loosely at no one in particular.

A drunk. Just a crazy drunk. Sylvia turned around to leave, but before she could move, she felt Bebe Thomsen's hot breath on the back of her head.

"Mussolini's mistress was a Jewess too," Thomsen purred. "They say your women allow men to do unnatural things in the bedroom, and that's why they like you. Is that what you let Giacomo do, hmm?"

"Filthy bitch," Sylvia managed to spit. Then she ran.

*S*ylvia didn't know how she got outside, but suddenly she was standing at the edge of the north lawn, taking huge gulps of cool air.

She began to walk again but found she didn't know what direction to move towards. South towards the train station? East towards the store? Northeast towards the narrow, freezing house and her mother-in-law? The bruised purple mountains loomed in every direction, closing her in. She needed to get high enough to breathe. So she crossed the Midland Trail and picked her way over the train tracks. The Kate's Mountain walking trail, kept clear most of the year by Greenbrier staff, was clogged with a winter's worth of sodden leaves. Spring's new branches grew shaggily on either side, and some kind of thorny vine snagged Sylvia's coat as she plunged into the forest.

The newly lush trees formed a leafy arch overhead, blocking out most of the sunlight. It was like being in a tunnel. When Sylvia was a girl, she and her brothers would play in Łagiewnicki Forest. At least, her brothers would play, while Sylvia minded them, carrying sacks of sandwiches and making sure the twins didn't fall in the creek. She would sit against a tree watching her brothers with half an eye, feeling the cold seep into her bottom and the backs of her legs, daydreaming. Even at twelve or thirteen she was already thinking of boys. Before Moriz Mostowski, there had been Jerzy Mandelbaum, a friend of Alfred and Leon's. He had gray eyes and a limp from when he fell off his bicycle and broke his leg in two places. She imagined that his injury made him kinder, more tender than the other boys.

Even at twelve, she realized now, she was already creating false versions of people. A limp didn't make you soulful. A red scarf thrown over your shoulder didn't make you raffish and gallant. And a brother who died of the Spanish flu doesn't make you a kindred spirit.

Little fool.

Was there even a brother at all? Perhaps not. Perhaps the intricate tale of Marco, the bird-loving mathematician, and the two socialist brothers was plucked from the ether, to make her soften to him.

Or maybe he was telling the truth. Maybe Bebe Thomsen was just drunk, crazy, jealous.

In Łagiewnicki Forest, there was a small wooden chapel dedicated to Saint Anthony. It was a gloomy windowless building, clad in dark, water-stained wood with a steep mossy roof and a stubby steeple. It sat on a spot where Saint Anthony was said to have resurrected a child crushed by a carriage's wheels. Inside was a font of holy water supposed to have healing powers. Factory workers would duck into the forest during their lunch hour to drink a ladleful and make the sign of the cross.

Sylvia was struck with a powerful urge to kneel on the forest floor and pray. But for what? And to whom? Adonai, the Lord Our God, Ruler of the Universe, was for blessing bread and wine, for handing down rules, for smiting. He didn't take prayers from women on the forest floor, did he? The Christian God was the one who went on about welcoming sinners. Did he welcome fools too?

The trail was wet and Sylvia's dove-gray pumps, the nicer of her two pairs of shoes—the ones she wore to see Jack—slid on the hard-packed red mud. So she took them off and dropped them in her bag. The half-finished dresses would be spoiled by mud, but who would wear them now? The ground was cold, but it felt good, tempering the nausea throbbing in her belly. Something smelled awful in the woods, like a small creature had died. Maybe Sylvia could just lie down here in the slick cold mud and die too, add to the stink.

Doree would be fine. Pauline would raise her on Carnation and mashed bread, and she'd grow up to speak English without an accent. Sylvia imagined Pauline murmuring about *Doree's poor mother, she simply couldn't adjust to life in America*. The Beckley Sisterhood women would bring pies and kugels. *Poor Pauline, so brave, so good*. How Pauline would simper!

No. No. Never. She couldn't give her mother-in-law that satisfaction.

She trudged on and the trees thinned out. Eventually she crested a ridge and stood on the bald patch at the edge of the mountain with a view north across the valley. From up here, the Greenbrier seemed to fill the entire valley. The nausea pulsed in her stomach, a small goblin stretching and yawning.

She remembered that this mountain was called Kate's Mountain because of a woman who hid here with her baby. Like lying down in the mud, this idea too seemed pleasant: just her and Doree alone on the mountain, living like elves in a hollow log.

The sun was directly overhead. Why was it only sunny on the worst days of Sylvia's life? Soon her cheeks would begin to burn.

Jack would be on the train, the sun falling on one cheek. Perhaps he was dozing, or writing letters to his wife, or eating marzipan from a green box tied with a silk ribbon. Was he pleased? Was he laughing at her? Would he try it all over again at the new hotel in North Carolina, ordering up a seamstress for some silly project, hoping she'd be young and pretty enough to pull into bed? *Foolish* enough to pull into bed. Maybe she hadn't even been the only one at the Greenbrier. Maybe he'd had other women coming from town to cobble him new shoes and weave him tapestries and trim his hair, a harem dancing for the pleasure of the sultan.

Little fool.

She pulled the torn envelope out of her pocket and counted the money inside. Fifty dollars. That, plus the fifty dollars she'd collected at home, was still only half of what she needed to escape. Half might as well be nothing.

She had no choice now. She would go back to the house on Spring Street. The crooked, shadow-filled house with its creaking stairs and cramped, slope-ceilinged bedrooms. She'd bide her time, slipping money from the till so slowly Louis would never notice.

Then, when the war was over, she'd go. *Palestine. Oranges.* Her mother's plum cake on the balcony overlooking the whitewashed Tel Aviv skyline. Doree, brown as a berry and speaking Yiddish like she'd been born to it. She'd grow up in the fields, strong as any boy, her head filled with folk songs, not fairy tales about love.

With the image of her daughter's little pierogi of a face in her mind, Sylvia picked her way down the trail. She walked slowly up Main Street, her muddy feet sliding on the pavement. Cricket O'Malley, that loon with the purple dresses and the tiny dogs, stood smoking a cigarette on the corner by the flower shop. She stared openly as Sylvia passed. Sylvia gave her a fierce look and she had the good sense to turn away.

Though it was dusk, no lights were on in the house, and Sylvia had a brief moment of relief thinking Pauline had gone out. But no sooner had she stepped inside than Pauline popped out of the kitchen. Disgust creased her narrow fox face as she looked at Sylvia's muddy feet.

"You're filthy—I hope you weren't attacked again," she said, in a way that suggested the first attack was some sort of melodramatic fancy.

Sylvia felt her fingers itch. Without a thought, her hand swung out like a tennis racket and smacked Pauline's china bird statue off the hallway table. For a second, the bird seemed to fly. Then it smashed into the bottom stair. Its head, cleaved neatly from its body, rolled onto the floor and stopped at Sylvia's muddy feet. Its glassy little painted eyes stared up at her.

Pauline's mouth opened and closed like a carp's, but she said nothing.

Sylvia walked upstairs slowly and deliberately. She took a bath, watching the red mud swirl down the drain like blood. Then she went into the nursery and plucked sleeping Doree from her crib, gently so as to not wake her. She carried the soft heavy lump of the baby to the bedroom and lay her in the sagging center of the bed, then curled her own body around her in a C shape.

She didn't feel drowsy at all, but what felt like an instant later she was blinking awake in the blue darkness. Doree still lay next to her, her smell chest rising and falling. Louis wasn't there—he must have gone to sleep on the couch. Sylvia's mouth was dry, so she sat up to go downstairs for some water, but the act of rising made her insides swirl and bubble like a pot of soup. She bolted to the bathroom, but she wasn't quick enough—a lash of hot yellow vomit flew from her mouth and spattered violently on the white penny-tiled floor.

She'd only vomited like that one other time in her life. When she was pregnant.

CHAPTER 43

Doree

MAY 1959

*F*lashlight beams sliced the deepening shadows of the Greenbrier forest. From every direction, Doree could hear men calling Alan's name, branches cracking under their boots as they strode through the underbrush. She heard her father's voice among the others, tight and terrified.

It seemed like everyone in town had come out. Johnny Burdette had gathered the other landscapers, and they'd been joined by several Level men who worked on the Greenbrier grounds. Patty's father, Nelson Curry, had come too, once Patty told him what was going on. Evangeline Curry had gone to Doree's house to sit with Sylvia and Pauline. Despite Sylvia's vehemence, Louis had called the sheriff; he and several deputies were now driving slow loops around town. Mr. O'Toole, the resort's night manager, had come out with hot chocolate and raisin buns for the searchers and had lent them a golf cart. Pete and Tommy were riding their bikes along the Greenbrier's paved walking paths, looking for "clues," as Pete put it. Doree had testily responded that this was not an episode of *Dragnet*, then immediately felt guilty to see Pete's face crumple with shame.

Tony, who'd been alerted to the hubbub by Nora in the Art Colony, was helping too, searching the hotel corridors with the other A/V men. He came out every few minutes to share a look with Doree and give a little shake of his head. Doree wished he could hold her in his arms, just for a moment. Though if he did, she might break down completely.

Doree and Patty were now at the base of Copeland Hill, next to the Zelners' car, sitting in lawn chairs Mr. O'Toole had brought out for them. Someone needs to stay by the car in case Alan comes back for it, Louis had said.

It was an incongruously lovely evening. The crickets were chirping, and the warm air carried the powdery scent of rhodo-dendron blossoms. Three men in Bermuda shorts with heavy, au-thoritative bellies were ambling back from the golf course, their caddies carrying their clubs a respectful few feet behind. A woman strolled by with a tall silver carriage, the baby inside so swaddled in layers of white lace Doree could barely make out its eyes. Inside, guests would be dressing for dinner, the ladies powdering their noses and sliding into gowns of organza or silk, the men slipping on jackets and standing behind their wives to knot their ties in the mirror.

Did they all have secrets? Doree had only ever imagined the guests as background actors in a glamorous movie, all satin and surface. But they were real people, weren't they? Some of the handsome husbands probably loved other men. Some of the wives had never wanted the beautiful babies in their silver carriages. How had she never thought of this before?

Even the hotel had secrets. When the guests glided across the floor of the Cameo Ballroom in their tuxedos and silk gowns, did they know that beneath the gleaming wood there were still red stains on the underfloor from the days when it was an operating theater? And now something really was happening under the new wing, wasn't it? Did Tony know? Was he in on it? Was it really something to do with—what had Junior Carper said?—*the nation's security*?

Junior Carper. His mushroom-white face loomed up in her mind. She jumped to her feet. "Patty," she said. "Can you stay here? I just thought of something."

*A*s little girls, Patty and Doree called the Carper place on Mill Hill "the scrambly house" for its wild mosaic of peeling paint— yellow under blue under white under gray. A chain-link fence enclosed the yard, the peaked silhouette of a doghouse inside. As Doree approached, a skinny streak of a hound exploded from the doghouse, hurtling towards the fence with teeth bared. Seeing her, it abruptly stopped and slunk back into the shadows, unimpressed.

She reached the door. She knocked.

Junior's father opened the door. The tinny voice of a radio preacher blared from an old-fashioned crystal radio set. His good eye blinked in confusion. "Sylvia?"

Huh. Doree had never seen Junior's father talking to her mother, let alone calling her by her first name. "It's Doree, Mr. Carper. Sylvia's daughter. Is Junior home?"

Mr. Carper didn't seem to register his mistake. "Sure, he's in back with Rebecca. I reckon I should call her Mrs. Carper—ha! You heard the good news?" Doree's face must have looked blank, because he carried on. "Junior and Rebecca tied the knot last week. Not much of a weddin', just Pastor Avery from the Holiness church and a few from my side. Rebecca's from Organ Creek and don't have no people. Had cookies and cake afterwards at my pa's house. He woulda liked to of served somethin' harder, but I don't partake in liquor, you know."

Doree nodded. Everyone had always said Mr. Carper was crazy, with his Jesus pamphlets and his angels talk.

"Sorry, I'll talk your ear off, everybody says so." Mr. Carper smiled, but only half his mouth went up. "Junior!"

Junior's pale moon of a face appeared. Behind him was a plump, very young-looking girl with blond hair and roughly cut bangs. She was visibly pregnant, the swell of her stomach pushing out the front of her dress.

"Doree?" Junior's voice was softer than she'd ever heard it, none of the sneering, faux-gangster bluster. "What are you doin' here?"

Doree stepped towards him. "Where's Alan?"

Junior looked away. "I don't know. Why you askin' me?"

"Alan's missing. They found the car. They found blood. You said Alan needed to watch himself. You said if I didn't pay you, he'd get hurt. So what have you done?"

"I didn't do nothin' to him, I swear."

"Pay you?" Junior's father was frowning at his son with half his mouth.

"That's right." Doree felt the heat gathering in her stomach. "Junior's been blackmailing me. Said he'd tell the whole town my mother's business if I didn't pay him. But now Alan's missing, and I don't care what Junior says anymore. I just want to find my brother. Where is he?"

"I don't know. Ask someone else!"

Mr. Carper had fixed his good eye on his son. The pink on his cheeks grew redder. "Set down!" he ordered. "We're gonna get to the bottom of this."

Junior sat down on an old bench and looked at his lap. "Y'all people have plenty of money," he mumbled.

"But how did you know about my mother?" asked Doree. "Who told you?"

Junior fidgeted and looked at the wall till his father reached out and smacked him on the ear, as if he were five. "Out with it, boy," Carl rumbled.

"My grandpa," Junior said softly. "Two, three years ago your mama gave my cousin Gibson a smack, cuz he spit on the floor of y'all's store, and Gibson come whining to Grandpa. Grandpa got mad, he says, 'That Jew store lady don't have no right to be uppity. She's a traitor, you know. Had a baby with a Nazi. Tried to get rid of it too.'"

At this, Mr. Carper pounded his fist on the kitchen table. "That ain't nobody's business," he said with such force it was clear to Doree that he already knew. Which meant the story was true. Did everyone know? She thought of what Patty said about Miss Cricket and the doorman. *Everybody knows about it, they just don't say anything.*

Anyway, he was sorry, Junior said. He'd pay Doree back once he got his job.

"You'll pay her back now!" his father hollered. "And tell her where her brother is!"

"All right!" said Junior, holding his hands up. "But I wasn't the one did nothing to Alan."

"Liar," Doree hissed, her voice as fierce as her mother's. Junior was tough enough to threaten Alan, but not tough enough to admit what he'd done! "Where is he?"

"I dunno." Junior looked at the wall again. "Check the old Calwell Cemetery, maybe."

Doree stood up so quickly she knocked her chair over. She didn't stop to pick it up, and she didn't say thank you.

But as she stepped across the threshold of the front door, a hand grabbed her shoulder. She spun around. Mr. Carper was standing in the doorway, his crooked frame silhouetted against the uncovered kitchen light. He leaned his ruined face close to hers, and she felt certain he was about to spout one of his Bible verses. But instead he whispered, "He was an Italian, not a German. Your mama wouldn't of done what she done with a German. He told her he didn't go in for that Nazi stuff, and she believed him. Your mama's a good person."

"*D*addy," Doree screamed, as she tore along the path across Howard's Creek and spotted Louis amid a group of searchers. She hadn't called her father "Daddy" in years. "Check the cemetery."

Despite the moonlight, the small cemetery surrounded by a dense ring of hickory trees was a pocket of blackness on the far side of the hill. It couldn't have been more than two hundred yards away, but Doree felt like she was running in slow motion. Before she reached the gate, she heard someone yell: "Here! Here! It's him."

"Alan!" she screamed, as she ran towards the darkness.

And then, from Louis, a ragged wail carved the night sky.

Doree closed her eyes and felt the world stop spinning. Alan and his plants and his bugs and his construction equipment. Alan, with his sheaves of lined yellow paper and the pencils he pressed so hard they snapped. Alan with his mildewed botany books. Alan with his crooked smile. Alan, who never ate the crusts of toast. Alan in his ratty undershirt in her doorway.

Alan was dead.

CHAPTER 44

❧

Jordan

JANUARY 1992

The security guard beckoned Jordan to follow him beyond the enormous white door. Inside, Jordan could now see that the door was at least a foot thick and made of solid steel. Beyond, darkness yawned, like the opening of a mine shaft.

With only a glance backwards, Jordan followed the man into the darkness. The heavy white door closed behind them with a deceptively soft click. Then the man flicked a light switch, and Jordan found himself standing in yet another corridor, this one gray, with metal walls like a submarine's. It had the lighting of a submarine too, dim and bluish. It sloped gently downward, deeper into the earth.

The man turned to him. "Welcome to the US Government Relocation Facility."

"The what?"

The man turned and started down the corridor. "This way," he said. "You'll see."

Jordan followed. At the end of the corridor was a submarine-like hatch with a turning mechanism. The man spun the wheel to the left and the door opened with the gasping sound of pressure releasing around a gasket. Jordan followed him through it, and found himself in what appeared to be . . . a cafeteria?

He blinked. It *was* a cafeteria, not all that different looking from the one at Baltimore Jewish Day School. Green-and-white-checkered linoleum tile. A low acoustic-tile ceiling with fluorescent panel lights. Several dozen round tables surrounded by molded plastic cafeteria chairs with skinny metal legs. On one wall was a chalkboard with a picture of a grinning Italian chef and the words "Today's Special." There were no windows of course—they must be 150 feet below ground.

The man surveyed the scene in a leisurely way, like a captain admiring his freshly scrubbed ship. "Can you imagine hundreds and hundreds of Congressmen—and ladies, I guess, these days—eatin' MREs around these tables here?"

"*Congress?*"

"Yep. This was all for Congress. If the Russians had pushed the nuke button, they would've come down here to run the government. We've got room for all of them." He smiled. "C'mon, I'll show you one of the bunk rooms."

Jordan followed the man into an adjacent room, where twenty or so metal bunk beds were evenly spaced against the wall. The bunks were made, with pillows and tightly tucked green wool army blankets. Each bunk had a spot for a removable paper tag at its foot. Jordan leaned over to read one: *Howell Heflin—D-Alabama*, read the tag on the top bunk. *Jesse Helms—R-North Carolina*, read the bottom one.

"They assign the bunks alphabetically—senators and congressmen separate, but Republicans and Democrats all together," the man said. "We change out the tags after every election."

What. The. Hell.

"I've been taking care of it for almost thirty years." The man smiled again, like he was waiting for some kind of praise.

"Taking care of it how?"

"Oh, lots of things. Cycling out the food supply to keep it fresh—we do that every three months. Redecorating. Cleaning. Getting rid of any bugs that get down here—you wouldn't think spiders could get past a blast door, but they do. The only part I don't do is testing the communications—the CIA guys do that. Pretend they're here to repair the TVs. Pretty smart cover. Nobody's never blinked at them all these years." The man looked pleased and proud, the way old people do when you ask about their grandchildren.

What a secret to keep for so long, Jordan realized. "So the idea was that Congress would come all the way from DC to shelter here?" he asked. "That would have taken hours."

The man nodded slowly. "Yeah. Well. Back at the start—the bunker was finished in 'sixty-two—the Commies would've had to fly nukes all the way over the Arctic to get here from Russia. There would've been some warning. Now, not so much."

"And the Cold War is over," Jordan added. He was putting the pieces together quickly, building a 3D puzzle in his mind. He felt a flash of the thrill he always got when the shape of a story started to emerge from the muck.

The man nodded again, the corners of his mouth turning down. "It's over. That's why I can tell you. I reckon it's not a threat to national security anymore."

"Why the Greenbrier? Why not pick somewhere closer to DC?"

"We've always been patriots here at the Greenbrier," said the man, with the same proud look. "The government trusted us, I reckon."

"But why me?" said Jordan. "Why did you pick me to tell? I write town council stories. This is way bigger than that."

The man looked at him blankly. "Because of your mama, of course."

"What do you mean?" Jordan gave the man's face a closer look. His hair was a colorless gray blond, and his eyes were the pale silver of the puddles that appear briefly on the sidewalk after a hard rain. "Did you know my mother?"

The man nodded. "Sit down, son," he said, gesturing towards one of the round tables.

Jordan sat and took out his notebook.

❧

CHAPTER 45

Sylvia

APRIL 1942

She could feel it inside her, bloody red like a beet, burrowing into her flesh with its tentacle roots. She wanted it out with a fierceness that verged on panic.

She could hide the vomiting only for so long. With Doree, she'd been sick from the week after she'd missed her monthly until she was nearly halfway along. She'd vomited every day—eight, nine, ten times a day—waking in the night to gag into the mixing bowl Pauline left on the bedside table ("I don't understand," Pauline would say. "I was never sick a single day with either of my boys!"). Dr. Sydenstricker had to come give her vitamin injections; eventually he ordered her to bed. But, with Doree, the sickness had felt productive, like she was expelling the poison of her old self in order to grow a clean, unblemished baby.

This was different. This time, it felt like the poison was coming from the baby itself. Like Jack had planted a malignant seed inside her and now its vileness was pulsing through her veins. This baby must be unnaturally strong, Sylvia reasoned, as it had managed to put down roots despite her cycle not having returned since Doree's birth. She hadn't even known it was possible to get pregnant without a cycle.

Finally, she confessed to Aggie, sobbing so violently she began to vomit apple-green stomach acid. It was Aggie who suggested she go to Leota Carper.

Leota Carper was a mountain of a woman who sold squash and apples and fried pies at the roadside Carper stand. Sylvia assumed she was Cecil's wife. But she was actually his sister. As squat as her brother, she had the same bulging eyes, with a bullfroggy neck and a hump of flesh tenting the back of her dress above her shoulder blades. She was what the locals called a "granny woman," the person who'd helped birth the babies before Dr. Sydenstricker came along. She still helped many of the women in the hills and hollers, the ones who didn't want an outside doctor—a *man*—at their birthing beds. Leota Carper also helped women who didn't want babies to come. Aggie said she'd helped a Greenbrier masseuse when she got into trouble.

"She gave her some kind of herbs," Aggie said. "She had cramps like a bad monthly—she had to call out sick for two days. But after that she was good as new."

The very next morning, Sylvia wrapped herself in her plaid wool coat and set out for the Carper compound on Mill Hill. A graying wooden fence surrounded the red dirt yard in a sort of crooked rectangle shape. As Sylvia approached, a dog barked so sharply she jumped back a step and half twisted her ankle. She could see the dog's wet black eyes leering at her from the gap in the fence boards. The house itself was scabby with peeling paint, the whole thing fronted by a porch raised off the ground on cinder blocks. Several more dogs lay in the cool hollows of dirt underneath. None seemed very interested in Sylvia.

Cecil Carper's truck was parked in the dirt drive in front of the house, but Sylvia knew Carl would be on his shift at the Greenbrier now. She couldn't possibly let him see her here.

She swallowed, then knocked on the door. She heard creaking inside, and another dog barking. The door opened. Cecil Carper stood there in his undershirt and trousers with suspenders. He looked at Sylvia unblinkingly with his water-pale gibbous eyes. "What do you want?"

"Is Miss Leota in the house?"

"Anybody knows Leo knows she don't wake 'fore noon."

"Please." Sylvia heard her voice break.

"Your funeral." Cecil motioned for Sylvia to come in, then disappeared up the stairs.

The porch blocked most of the morning light from the interior, and Sylvia blinked to adjust her eyes to the sepia darkness. The front room ran the whole width of the house. The raw board walls were dominated by a stone fireplace. The only furniture was a table, some old wooden chairs, and a lumpy daybed covered with a quilt.

Five minutes passed. Then ten. Sylvia noticed a rag doll with glossy blue button eyes peeking out from under the daybed and a battered baby chair next to the table. Carl must live here with his little son. There were rumors that Cecil had buckets of moonshine money hidden somewhere, but, looking around the plain, rough room, Sylvia doubted it.

After another five or so minutes, the stairs creaked again and Leota Carper filled the doorway. "Come in the kitchen. Need to eat 'fore we talk."

Sylvia followed Leota through the doorway and into a small kitchen that was much brighter than the front room. Sylvia sat at a small table beneath the window while Leota warmed a pan of coffee on the enameled woodstove. Cast-iron pans hung from hooks on the ceiling beams and pots of herbs sat in a row on the windowsill.

Leota poured coffee into a dish and took a cold biscuit from beneath a tea towel. She crumbled the biscuit into the coffee and sprinkled it with sugar, scooped straight from a ten-pound sack of Domino sitting on the tabletop. "Soaky bread," she said, pushing the dish towards Sylvia.

Sylvia wanted to refuse, but the sense that Leota Carper was someone to be obeyed was so strong she picked up a spoon and began to eat. The sweet slurry reminded her of being a child sick in bed with a fever, her mother sitting at her bedside spooning bits of challah soaked in milk into her mouth. It was the first thing she'd eaten all week that didn't make her want to vomit.

Leota settled her weight slowly into a chair opposite Sylvia with her own dish of soaky bread. She gave her a long, frank look. "You got a late monthly?"

Sylvia nodded.

"How long?"

"Only a few weeks."

"You sure?"

"Yes."

"Sure-sure? Cuz what I give can bring on your monthly if it's late, but it won't do no more than that. I don't do the other way, and I don't do for ladies more'n a few weeks gone. Ain't safe, ain't decent. You understand?"

Sylvia nodded. In the boardinghouse in Baltimore there was a girl who'd tried with a hatpin. She'd been carted, bleeding and moaning, to the hospital by a pair of visibly disgusted ambulance attendants. She never came back to the boardinghouse.

Leota finished her dish and stood up. She went to the windowsill and trimmed some herbs, then reached into the cabinet for a jar of what looked like wood shavings and another of what looked like dried grass. She poured a measure of each onto a square of brown paper and dropped a handful of herbs on top. Then she twisted the paper into a little bundle. "You take a spoonful in hot water, just like tea. Three times every day till your monthly comes on."

"And if it doesn't?"

"Then the Lord has other plans."

*B*ack home, she waited until Pauline went to the butcher, then she heated a kettle and spooned a small heap of the herbs into one of the pink glass teacups. She sat down with the newspaper, just as if she were having her morning tea, and took a sip.

It tasted of mint, but with a bitter, oily undertone.

She looked at the headlines. *Japan's Fleet Crippled, Driven Back at Midway. A Momentous Victory. Enemy Withdraws.*

She took another sip. It would be better with sugar, but that felt wrong, an indulgence at a time she deserved none.

It would all be over soon.

*B*y the third day, she began to worry. She scanned her lower belly for pinching or tugging, and felt nothing but the same nauseous fullness. Her breasts began to swell and tingle, and one night in the bath she noticed tiny pearls of milk blooming from her nipples. Her body was a traitor, the same way she'd been a traitor to Louis, to America. Harboring the enemy, letting it snuggle in as cozy as can be.

She started eating the spent leaves at the bottom of the tea cup, thinking that might make the potion more effective. Her teeth bristled with tiny twigs.

· · ·

*H*er monthly didn't come on. Not a speck of blood. Not a smudge. The Lord wanted to punish her. But Sylvia had known that for a long time.

*S*ylvia thought about a hatpin, a fall down the stairs. But she couldn't stomach the idea of Pauline raising Doree if she died. So instead she decided: She would have the baby and leave it with Louis. She and Doree would get on the boat together and sail for the land of sun and oranges. It would be better this way, actually. Louis and his parents would get a baby to continue the Zelner line, to make up for the hole Doree would leave.

To make this story possible, she pulled Louis on top of her in the dark one night, much to his surprise. "This was nice," he said afterwards.

She burned with shame. But it was all right, she told herself. After all, religion was handed down from the mother—the child would be a Jew because Sylvia was a Jew. Jack was irrelevant—Jewish law said so. The Zelners would have a Jewish baby to dote over until Louis remarried and had some more Jewish babies.

But of course she still didn't have enough money for their boat passage. And the war wasn't over either. Surely it would be soon, though. Surely.

*O*ne morning, a few days after she'd taken the last of Leota Carper's tea, Sylvia opened the bathroom door after an early morning vomit to find Pauline standing on the other side.

"Did you eat something funny?" Pauline smirked. "Or is an announcement in order?"

Louis was so happy when Sylvia told him that it made her insides twist. He picked her up and laid her gently on the bed. "You should just rest now," he said, smiling down at her, his eyes looking brighter and less exhausted than they had in a long time. "You don't need to come into the store anymore. Mother will take care of you. We can even get you a little bell to ring, like in the movies. And no more taking in sewing—we'll have Mrs. Lamb do the alterations. She's not as good as you, of course, but people here aren't fussy."

Sylvia wanted to protest, but she was like a machine that had run out of steam. So she allowed herself to be tucked into bed.

She hardly stood up for the next three months.

Time grew blurry. She slept, she woke, she vomited, she ate the toast Pauline brought, she dozed. Sleeping all day seemed to only make her more tired. She made a game of it, seeing how long she could go with her eyelids shut. Eight hours, ten, twelve, fourteen. She listened to the radio Louis had brought into the bedroom. Gunboats torpedoed, submarines sunk. Cities with unfathomable names—Myitkyina, Bacolod, Mandalay—falling to the Japanese. She imagined them falling literally, their skylines crumbling into the sea. In the evening, the bells following the CBS eight o'clock news bulletin let her know it was time to sleep again.

One morning—or was it afternoon?—she woke to a soft knock and saw Aggie standing in the doorway. Sylvia struggled to pull herself upright.

Aggie sat on the corner of the bed. She was wearing a pink dress with blue cornflowers and a smart-looking white boater hat with a blue ribbon. "I'm glad you're in bed," she said, in Polish. "If

I'd found you upright, I would have been angry that you haven't come to see me. I've been so worried."

"It didn't work. Nothing happened."

Aggie sighed. "I'm sorry. So that's it, then? Will you tell him?"

"Who?"

Aggie gave her a pointed look. "If you want to send him a message, I can help. Some of my clients manage to keep in touch with the Italians down at the Grove Park Inn. They must have an inside man in the telegraph room. People have been sending letters too. The guards keep trying to catch them, but it's cat and mouse."

"He doesn't exist."

Aggie patted Sylvia's knee with her strong hand. "I wish it worked that way. I really do. Lord knows I have plenty of men I'd like to erase from the world. My little prick ex-husband, for one."

Sylvia managed a small smile. Aggie had so little shame about her past. It was one of the things she most admired about her friend.

The beet pulsed inside her. She swore she could feel it moving its little root legs, though it was far too early. Perhaps it would be born unnatural, monstrous—twice the size of a human baby, its face gnarled.

"They came for the rest of the Germans this morning," Aggie said, picking up a hairbrush and beginning to smooth Sylvia's tangled hair without asking permission. "They're putting them on a ship to Portugal, to be traded for our people. Thomsen's wife— the lady with the marcelled hair—threw a fit. She lay down on the lobby couch and refused to get up. Two G-men had to carry her out to the train like a madwoman."

"She *is* a madwoman," Sylvia said. She thought of Bebe

Thomsen's slurring voice, her face so close Sylvia could see her thickly powdered pores. *Mussolini's mistress was a Jewess too.*

"Good riddance to all of them, I say," Aggie said.

Sylvia mustered the strength to squeeze her hand.

*T*he morning news bulletin had been repeating on the half hour, bits of it penetrating Sylvia's dreams like shrapnel.

> *According to reports published in Britain's* Daily Telegraph, *evidence has emerged of mass extermination of Polish Jews by the Nazis in what may be, quote, "the greatest massacre in history." Extermination began in Eastern Galicia last year. Men and boys from fourteen to sixty are regularly gathered in town squares and forced to dig their own graves before being knifed or machine-gunned. In the Kulmhof district, formerly known as Chelmno, thirty-five thousand Jews from the Lodz ghetto were killed in vans fitted as gas chambers.*

Kulmhof. Chelmno. That letter from her mother all those months ago: *Mr. Kowalczyk has seen your brother Alfred. He was getting on a train at Radogoszcz Station. They are sending the Jews they say are criminals somewhere north called Kulmhof.*

Alfred had been dead all along. Leon too, surely. That "patriotic" duty Mr. Johnston had told her she was doing when she'd agreed to help the Greenbrier with Jack's request had never been for anything.

Her brother. Serious and bossy, his dark eyes flashing at injustice. Punching Meir Wagman for dipping Sylvia's braid in the inkwell. Leaning across his dinner plate to lecture their mother on the perils of Zionism and getting gravy all over his shirt. Marching down Piotrkowska Street with the Bundists, singing revolutionary songs, arm linked with his friends, all so jaunty and handsome in their caps, scarves flapping in the cold Polish wind. She thought of him as a little boy standing on the roof of the workshop, wanting to fly. He turned, he spread his arms like wings, and he was gone.

She felt a wail explode from her body. It was all for nothing. All for nothing.

A minute later the door opened and Pauline entered, wearing her dish-washing apron.

"What's all this noise?"

"My brother is dead," Sylvia said flatly. She waited for Pauline to harrumph, to ask her how she knew such a thing.

But instead Pauline sat down on the bedside chair. Instead, she picked up the stack of magazines Louis had brought from the store for Sylvia. "I imagine reading must provoke the sickness," she said, not looking at Sylvia. "I'll read to you for a while. At least until Doree wakes up from her nap." She opened a magazine and began to read.

"'How to whiten your laundry on a budget. The modern way to cook cabbage.'"

Sylvia lay curled on her side while the words washed over her. It was not a comfort, exactly. But it did allow her to drift back into the blackness of sleep, the only place where she could hide from the pain.

CHAPTER 46

※

Jordan

JANUARY 1992

The man's name was Carl, he said, but everyone called him Junior, on account of his father also being Carl. He was the same age as Jordan's mother. They were even in the same kindergarten class, he said. Carl's family were hill people.

"Your mama was always nice to me when we were little," he said. "And she was so pretty. I wish I hadn't did what I done."

"What did you do?"

The man sighed. "I was eighteen," he began. "Eighteen, angry, and stupid. Got a girl from Organ Creek in the family way, had to get married. That didn't last long, ha." He laughed mirthlessly. "Needed some money first, to prove I was a provider, a man. Not like my own daddy, laughingstock of the whole dang town. Well, my grandpa used to say Jews were so rich they kept jars of money buried in the ground. So I made your mama pay me. I just figured it wasn't nothing to her—her family had all that money, you know. But I guess I was wrong; her daddy's store closed down not too long after."

"What do you mean, you made her pay you. Made her how?"

The man rubbed one of his big, curdy cheeks. "Did you ever meet your grandma Sylvia?"

"No. Why?"

"I knew something about your grandma. A secret, you might say. I figured your mama would pay me to keep the secret. I reckon you'd call that blackmail."

Everyone in this town felt sorry for your grandpa, her running off like that.

"What did you know?"

"It's not my place to say what, it really ain't. Why don't you ask your mama about it?"

"My mother doesn't talk about that stuff."

"Well, look," the man said, "point is, I've spent thirty years feeling sore guilty about making your mama give me that money. But there's something else. Something worse."

"What?"

"Her brother got hurt. Bad."

Jordan felt a sickly throb behind his eyes. He ignored it, and kept taking notes. "Hurt how?" he asked. "Specifically."

Jessica was right. The secrets did matter.

Carl gave Jordan a funny look, and opened his mouth as if to say something, but then closed it again. "Alan was an odd one," he said, starting again. "But he was sweet. Wouldn't of hurt a fly. Nose always in a book. When they started diggin' the hole for the West Virginia Wing, he got curious. He could tell it wasn't no basement. Heck, we could all tell. But the rest of us, we knew to keep our mouths shut or our daddies or granddaddies would of laid into us with a switch. But Alan"—the man wrinkled his forehead and looked upward, like he was trying to think of the right words—"he didn't follow the same rules. He just kept asking questions. People didn't take kindly to that."

"So what happened?" Jordan could feel the tons of dirt and steel on top of him. The buzz of the fluorescent lights was suddenly loud, far too loud.

"The other boys—the basketball team boys, Lee Burdette, Edisto Level, and them—they had it out for Alan since grade school. But they never did nothing, because they liked your mama, didn't want to make her sore. But when Alan started flappin' his lips about the dig—how it wasn't a basement, how it must have been some secret government project—they got real lit up." He paused and looked at the floor. "One day, they decided to teach him a lesson. They wrote him a note pretending to be someone who knew about the dig, tricked him into thinking he was gonna get some kind of clues to follow. Lured him up to the resort."

"And killed him."

The man shook his big square head and continued. "I saw them just after they'd finished. They were coming down the hill from the old Calwell Cemetery carryin' their baseball bats. Lee Burdette, he had a two-by-four. I knew what must have happened."

Jordan took a deep breath and held it.

"I should have told someone right away. I should have run to get the sheriff. But, see, them basketball boys told me if I helped them—if I stayed quiet—they'd get me a job at the resort. Vance Calwell's daddy was a big muckety-muck up in the manager's office. And Lee Burdette, his daddy was the groundskeeper—Lee's the groundskeeper now, I reckon you already met him. Calls himself 'Wesley' these days. Nobody in my family'd ever had a job at the resort. They just didn't hire Carpers. And anyway, they said if I did tell, they'd say it was me that hurt Alan, and everyone would believe them. I knew it was true."

"What happened next?"

"I ran home like a coward. Your mama came by that night, and my daddy made me tell her the truth. But by then it was late, and Alan had been layin' there hurtin' and bleedin' for hours."

"He didn't die right away?"

The man gave him the same funny look again. "Who said Alan was dead?"

"He's not?" Jordan felt the world tilt at an angle.

Mom's got all kinds of secrets.

"I can't rightly say if he's alive now, I ain't seen him since 1959. But for sure he didn't die that night. They took him to the hospital over the mountain, and he came back a week later walkin' with crutches. He and your grandma left town not long after."

"Left town? Where did they go?"

The man shrugged, not meeting Jordan's eyes. "You'll have to ask your mama." He looked up, and Jordan could see there were real tears in his eyes now, sliding down his face and wetting his white curdy cheeks. "When you see Doree, could you tell her I'm sorry? Tell her her brother was right. I know she's probably been blaming herself for what happened all these years, and I just couldn't live with it anymore. All these secrets, they eat away at you. If I didn't tell, I'd be nothin' but bones. The other week, Tommy Curry down at the garage says to me do I know that Doree's boy was working for a big newspaper. I reckoned it was a sign from God. I had to write to you."

CHAPTER 47

※

Doree

*D*oree approached the cemetery, her whole body trembling. The searchers had carried her brother out and laid him in the grass outside the fence. He wore his khaki army vest, the one he liked because it had so many pockets for pencils and black walnuts and roots and Lorna Doones wrapped in napkins. His eyes were closed. Thin streams of blood trickled from both corners of his mouth, making him look, in the shadows, like a marionette with a movable jaw. His right leg lay at an impossible angle and his jeans were dark with what could have been mud, urine, or blood, or perhaps all three.

Louis knelt over his son, patting the side of his face. "Alan," he said over and over. "Alan, my boy."

Suddenly, Alan twitched. Doree was certain she'd imagined it, but then it happened again. And then Alan moaned. She fell to her knees beside him.

"Call Dr. Sydenstricker!" someone cried. "He's alive!"

*T*he Greenbrier Resort doctor arrived first. Used to treating nothing more serious than hangovers and tennis elbow, he blanched at the sight of Alan's limp body. After taking Alan's pulse and peeling back his eyelids to shine a flashlight, he said something to Louis in a low voice. Louis nodded and stood up. "I'm going to go get the car," he told Doree. "We're driving to the hospital in Ronceverte. You'll need to sit in the back with Alan."

Johnny Burdette and one of the Level men picked Alan up and laid his limp body gently in the back seat.

Louis was usually the most careful of drivers. But that night he flew over Sewell Mountain so fast the car seemed to leave the dark road entirely. Doree knelt in the footwell, holding her brother's hand and studying his face in the moonlight. His eyes were twitching behind his closed lids. When they got to the emergency room of Greenbrier General Hospital and Doree stood up, she realized there was something gritty all over her knees. Lorna Doone cookie crumbs had been spilling from Alan's pockets like sand.

*T*he doctors said Alan should wake up the morning after the surgery, but he didn't. He lay in the hospital bed as the light outside the window went from milky dawn to golden to peach and back to black, his wan face reflecting the pale green of the hospital walls.

Sylvia sat at the edge of a metal folding chair by his bedside, her body trembling. "If my son dies," she hissed at Louis, "I will burn down every house in this valley."

"The doctors said he'll live." Louis sat with his eyes shut, his long fingers massaging his temples. He had closed the store. This was the first time it had been closed outside of a holiday since Sol opened Zelner's nearly half a century before. "It will all be all right."

"Says you, the one who says this town is just wonderful, that they don't hate Jews here, that we are all real Americans. Feh! They've never accepted us—not even you—and they never will."

"Sylvia, we don't know what happened yet."

Doree had folded herself into a corner of the hospital room, where she perched on a stool, a stiffly starched hospital sheet covering her legs. She gazed at her mother with a new coolness.

All these years her mother had been walking around with a scarlet letter on her chest, and everyone in town had pretended not to see it. Perhaps this was why she had no friends. Already convinced the townspeople hated her for her Jewishness and her foreignness, she had gone and given them reason to see her as deceitful and foolish. No wonder she held everyone at a distance. Her pride was armor—brittle armor. And no wonder she held the Greenbrier in such contempt. She had met him there, this, this . . . *Italian*.

Louis stood up. "I'm going to get a coffee, Sylvia. I'll bring you something to eat."

"No."

"You need to eat something."

"No."

Louis shrugged and left.

With her father gone, her mother seemed to remember Doree was in the room. Her eyes locked on Doree's. "Do you know who did this?"

Doree swallowed. Should she tell her mother it was Junior Carper? Her mother might do something crazy, like go over to the Carpers' house. Then what if Junior told her about the blackmail, about how Doree had stopped paying him, about how this was all Doree's fault? No. "I don't know," she said.

Sylvia's eyes were narrow and glittery. "Are you hiding something? Was it one of the boys you and Patty admire so much? Johnny Burdette's son? The Level boy?"

"I'm not hiding anything. But you are, aren't you?"

"What are you saying?" Sylvia sat up straighter, which made her seem to grow larger.

"Alan's father."

Sylvia stood up. In a flash, she had crossed the room and was standing in front of Doree. Her whole body was taut as an arrow, angled towards her daughter as if ready to fly at her. Doree was nearly overwhelmed with the urge to swallow her words. But she forced herself on, voice shaking. "The prisoner at the resort."

With those words, Sylvia seemed to deflate. She groped behind herself, looking for a chair, and finding none, staggered back a few steps to brace herself against the foot of the bed. "Who told you this lie?"

"It's not a lie, is it?"

Sylvia was silent for a long moment. "Who told you this?"

"Why does it matter?"

Sylvia didn't speak.

"Who was he? The Nazi."

Sylvia stared out the window. Finally, she spoke in a voice that had dropped lower and softer. *That sweet girl.* "He wasn't German. He was Italian. His name was Giacomo. I called him Jack. He wasn't a Nazi."

"Where is he now?"

"I do not know."

"You haven't seen him?"

"I have not seen him since the day I learned your brother was coming."

"But why? Why would you do that? Weren't you happy with Dad?" That wasn't the real question. Doree knew her mother wasn't happy with her father, had never been happy. The real question was *Why? Why couldn't you take what you were given and make the best of it? Grandma did. Were we not enough? Was I not enough?*

Sylvia seemed to collect herself. She looked at Doree with her black, glittering eyes and took a deep breath. "Because I am a fool. I have always been a fool. If there is one thing you must learn in this life, it is to not be a fool like me." Her mother's face was so close, Doree could smell her hair spray. "You must never think you are so clever you cannot be fooled. Because you're not so clever, no one is. Men can fool you. They will fool you."

Miss Cricket's warning rang again in her ears. *I saw you with one of those men.* Why would an A/V repairman need to know so much mathematics? No. It wasn't time to think about that, not now.

"How can you talk about fooling, when you're the one who's been fooling Daddy all this time?" She thought of her father with his tired face and his stooped shoulders, behind the counter of Zelner's all these years, smiling and chatting with customers who knew what he didn't. Her stomach twisted with pity.

"Your father knows."

"What? You told him?"

Sylvia snorted. "Someone wrote him a letter. Another Greenbrier prisoner. A woman. A drunk. She is jealous, I think. Bitter. She wants to stay in America, but they sent her back to Europe. Before she goes, she wrote to your father. *Klafte!*"

"What did he do?"

Sylvia's expression softened. "He asks me what I want to do. He says he wants me to stay and have the baby together, but he cannot make me."

"Why didn't you leave? If living here is so horrible, why didn't you just leave then?"

Sylvia shrugged. "I wanted to leave. But where can I go? Not back to Poland: There was still the war. Even after the war, I cannot go back to Poland: Everyone is dead. My brothers are killed in the camps or shot in the woods. My friend Ewa is dead of typhus in the ghetto. I wanted to go to Palestine, but I cannot: The British would not allow more Jews. My youngest brother is dead, killed fighting the British." Sylvia wiped at her eyes with a manicured finger, clearing away the crescents of smeared mascara. "Also, to take you from your father would have been too cruel, although I did not see that then."

"You were going to take me?"

"Of course. Should I have left my right arm? My leg? My heart?" Sylvia looked at Doree levelly. "But maybe I was wrong. Maybe, for you, it would have been better if I did leave. For your father too. I tried. I tried. I thought if I gave him Peter, it would make it right. Another baby—*his* baby. Though, you must understand, your father thinks of Alan as his son too. He always has. Your father is a good person. A mensch. This is not his fault. This is my fault. My foolishness."

"What about Grandma and Grandpa? Did they know?"

"No. Your father did not want they should be told. Why should we burden them with something when it is not necessary, he says."

The door swung open and a nurse walked in with a paper cup of medicine on a tray. "Oh!" she said, leaning over Alan. "When did you wake up?"

CHAPTER 48

❧

Sylvia

DECEMBER 1942

As if in a nightmare, the baby was coming, and Sylvia was back in a guest room at the Greenbrier Resort. The plush green carpet had been covered with removable tiling, and the mahogany desk carted away to storage along with the oil paintings of dogs and men on horses. The room had been partitioned by a white curtain on a rolling rail. But the old-fashioned chinoiserie wallpaper was the same. As each contraction tightened an invisible net of barbed wire around her abdomen, Sylvia stared at the peach blossom print on the wall next to her. As the pain grew, she imagined herself getting smaller and smaller until she disappeared into the flower's scarlet center. Then the pain would release, and Sylvia would return to the world, a world that offered little relief.

After the last of the detainees were sent home in August, the army had turned the Greenbrier into an army rehabilitation hospital. Soldiers walked the grounds with crutches and braces or pushed each other in wheelchairs. Their faces were light with relief. They could have died in muddy fields in France, but here they were, in this green valley, dining every night beneath chandeliers. The hospital was called the Ashford General, but they nicknamed it the Shangri-la.

The far end of the Virginia Wing was now a maternity ward, for pregnant wives who came to visit their convalescing husbands. So when Sylvia's time came, that's where she went. Her baby would be born kitty-corner from the room where it was conceived. Surely God was laughing at her.

Her labor began on a Monday, two weeks before Christmas. The baby was late, but only Sylvia knew that. It should have come at the end of November. She'd lied to Dr. Sydenstricker about when she first noticed pregnancy signs, to make it possible that the baby could be Louis's.

Now, as she lay on an army hospital gurney, pain rippling through the lower half of her body like being slowly crushed, she realized her lie might kill her. The baby might be too big. She'd die, and Pauline would get Doree anyway, and she'd never see the orange trees.

Everything she'd done had turned to drek.

A nurse came by to give her an exam. "Ooooh, you're getting close," she squealed, snapping off her rubber glove and giving Sylvia's arm a squeeze.

Everyone was cheerful here. The soldiers were cheerful because they'd done their bit for the war and they'd lived. The doctors were cheerful because this was a holiday for them, working in a hospital where nobody came to die, only to get better. The nurses were cheerful because the place was full of handsome young soldiers; according to Aggie, who'd been conscripted to give therapeutic massages to the patients, there was an engagement nearly every week. Now, nearing Christmas, the place was smothered in evergreens and lights and the staff was frenzied with holiday spirit. When Sylvia had first walked in, mid-contraction, leaning heavily on Louis, she'd been greeted by a nurse wearing a Santa hat.

Sylvia had wanted to tear it right off her head.

Another contraction. She counted and stared into the center of the peach blossom. When she got to thirty, the pain would peak and drain away. But she only made it to twenty-five before the tightening reached the bottom of her lungs and she had to gasp for air. She tried to remember her labor with Doree—had it been like this? It *couldn't have been*—but found only a blank spot in her memory, like a newspaper with the center cut out.

A doctor had come by with a syringe and a mask earlier, to start the twilight sleep, but Sylvia screamed at him. No medicines. No gas. The doctor, as cheerful as the rest, had held his hands up in mock surrender and backed away.

She would not be gassed.

She saw her brother, struggling to breathe. No. No. No.

She wanted her mother, *now*.

"Mama," she whimpered, as the remorseless wringing pain began creeping upward. As it peaked, in a dizzying blood-red wave, she began to scream. "Mama! Mama!"

Surely the war would be over soon. The Soviets were pushing back the Nazis at Stalingrad. Winter would finish them off. The British would remove the Jewish immigration quota for Palestine. Sylvia and Doree would cross a calm ocean. How good the sunlight would feel on her face.

"Oh dear." A nurse was standing at the foot of Sylvia's bed. The contraction had unclenched, and Sylvia became aware of a pulsing heat between her legs. There was a sound too, like bathwater slapping over the edge of the tub. She pushed herself up to see, but the nurse said, "Oh no," and pressed her back down. But it was too late: Sylvia had seen the spreading lake of blood on the floor.

Everything began to happen too quickly. Another nurse started mopping at the blood between Sylvia's legs with a towel while the first one pressed a stethoscope to her stomach. Then the cheerful doctor was back, though slightly less cheerful than before. "Well, Mrs. Zelner, it looks like we're going to the delivery room right away."

Suddenly things were in motion. Sylvia was rolled through the corridor she'd walked down so many times, the gurney's wheels clicking over the tiles covering the carpet. As she was pushed through the grand swinging doors of the ballroom—the operating and delivery room now—she saw Evangeline Curry in her gray hospital maid dress. Evangeline's eyes widened, and she gave Sylvia a small wave.

Sylvia turned her head away, filled with shame.

The ballroom had been subdivided by white canvas panels into several operating rooms. Sylvia was lifted from the gurney and placed on a table covered with a white sheet. Directly above her was the chandelier. The nine-foot Czech crystal chandelier everyone at the Greenbrier was so proud of. It glittered down spitefully.

"Forceps," said a voice.

Someone was doing something down there. Twisting, tugging, gutting. The pain was as brilliant as the crystals overhead. They were cutting her in two. They were killing her, like they'd killed her brothers.

Then it all stopped.

"Baby's out," someone said.

It was quiet. So quiet she could hear a pair of orderlies discussing a horse race in the next operating room. Maybe the baby had died inside her. Like her mother's baby, the one without a gravestone to leave pebbles at. You weren't even meant to say the mourner's kaddish for such a baby; its soul hadn't yet entered its body. For a moment, Sylvia felt relief.

But then there was a meaty smacking sound as the doctor slapped the baby's bottom, and a moment later a cry rose from behind the curtain.

"A boy!" called a nurse, poking her head around the curtain and beaming.

"Placenta previa and breech," said one doctor to the other. "In these mountains, a woman like this would have died giving birth at home if it weren't for us."

I'm not a mountain woman, Sylvia wanted to scream, but she found herself overwhelmed with an exhaustion so sudden and profound it might as well have been anesthetic. The last thing she saw before her eyelids fluttered shut was the beet-red foot dangling from the blankets as they whisked the baby from the operating room.

*I*t was two days before they brought the baby to her. She needed her rest, they said. She was back in a guest room, this time with two nattering army wives on adjacent cots. Sylvia lay on her side, eyes shut lest the wives try to ask her opinion of movie stars or curtain fabrics. Her arms ached, but for Doree, not this new baby, this backwards-turned boy.

By the second day, her milk had come in, and her breasts were as hard as apples, nipples fizzing. She awoke from a nap to find yet another cheerful nurse pushing a bassinet into the room.

"Look who's here!" the nurse cried in a bright, high voice. Was she talking to Sylvia or to the baby?

"Ooooh, your little boy!" said one of the wives. "What's his name?"

"He does not have a name," said Sylvia brusquely. The nurse exchanged a look with the wife. Obviously Sylvia had acquired a reputation as the difficult one. Well, good. Fine. She was. She would be. There was no reason to please anyone again, ever.

"It says 'Alan' here on his little name tag," the nurse said, lifting a bundle from the bassinet. "Alan Joshua."

Sylvia said nothing. She remembered Louis coming to her room the day before. He must have suggested "Alan." Had she agreed? She couldn't remember. His voice had been like a stream of water over rocks.

"I like it," said the other wife. "I imagine an Alan like a young handsome Irish soldier. Are you Irish?"

"Do I look Irish?" The venom was astringent on her tongue, like lemon juice. It felt good.

"It's a very nice name," said the nurse soothingly, coming towards her with the bundle. "You can call him 'Al' when he's bigger."

Sylvia wouldn't be there when he was bigger, but she hoped Louis and his parents wouldn't call the baby "Al." It sounded like a cigar-chomping gangster in a stupid film.

"Are you not feeling well enough to take him?" The nurse stood at her elbow, looking puzzled. She lowered the bundle to Sylvia's face.

Sylvia turned her head in the other direction, towards the peach blossom wallpaper.

"It's quite normal for a mother to feel blue for a few days after the baby is born, you know. Giving him a cuddle might help."

Because she wanted the nurse to stop talking to her in that syrupy voice, Sylvia reached out and grabbed the bundle. It wailed, and an arm sprang out, a tiny star of a hand clenching and un-clenching furiously. Feeling curious more than anything, Sylvia pushed the blanket back from its head.

Oh.

I'm sorry, I didn't know.

It's you.

The baby's pointed, translucent face shimmered up at her. He had Alfred's high forehead and delicate seashell ears, and the up-turned nose shared by Leon and the twins. As she continued to gaze, she registered new angles, new fragments of familiar faces. Faces of people who couldn't possibly be there. Moriz Mostowski's twist of a smile. The plump cheeks of the boy who drowned in Ludowy Pond, the one whose name she couldn't remember. The furrowed brow of Ewa's older brother, puzzling over a mathematic equation. Jack was there too—this was clearly his baby—a fact that Sylvia registered but simply moved past. The baby's grave, dark slits of eyes seemed to say, "I know. I know." It was as if he recognized her too. He recognized her, and he loved her anyway.

The Lord has other plans.

God hadn't punished her. The opposite. Despite everything, she had been blessed.

The baby's pink mouth opened like a cat's, so Sylvia tugged down her nightgown and put him to her breast.

"He's just had a bottle," the nurse said.

Sylvia barely heard her. The baby's lips closed around her nipple and began to suck, quickly finding a steady rhythm of sighs and gulps. Sylvia felt her milk release and her breast soften.

"Here, it's time for you to rest." The nurse leaned over and reached for the baby. "I'll take him back to the nursery."

Sylvia's hand shot out and shoved the nurse.

The nurse took a few stumbling steps backwards before regaining her balance. The army wives went silent.

"My baby stays with me," Sylvia said.

Gazing into the baby's unblinking eyes, she saw then with perfect clarity that this was her future and her destiny: to protect this tiny green shoot of a human, grown from a seed that had somehow survived the ravages of the past. Doree was an American; she would grow strong in any soil. But this baby came from somewhere else, somewhere between the New World and the Old, between this world and whatever lay beyond. He would need more from her.

Sylvia hadn't been able to protect her brothers, but she could protect this baby. She *would* protect this baby.

CHAPTER 49

Doree

JUNE 1959

Doree walked home from school with Patty, then waved goodbye to her friend at the top of Surber Road. Seemingly overnight, the trees of the Greenbrier Valley had burst into their summer foliage, their branches heavy with wet new leaves, the slopes of the mountains shaggy and tinged with yellow, the cows looking fatter and sleepier than usual.

Alan would be waiting at home on the porch in his wheelchair, a botany book on his lap. Sun was good for healing. There was a chance his broken leg would set crookedly and leave him with a limp, the doctors said, but they didn't want to risk more surgery, since "he's not athletically inclined anyhow." Because they'd removed his spleen, which had burst like a rotten fruit, he'd have to be wary of infection.

But when Doree turned the corner and the narrow blue house came into view, Alan was nowhere to be seen.

Inside, she found her grandfather sitting at the kitchen table, a half-drunk cup of coffee at his elbow.

"Hi, Grandpa," she said, giving him a peck on the cheek. "Where's Alan?"

"*Shaina maidel,*" he said. "Sit down."

She sat.

"Where's Alan?" she asked again, worry edging her voice. Was he back in the hospital? His spleen?

Sol sighed. "Alan is fine. He's gone with your mother."

"Gone where?" Alan could still barely walk with crutches.

Her grandfather's face was unusually still, with no trace of his usual twinkliness or smiles. "We don't know. We think—perhaps—Israel."

"*Israel?*" Doree searched her mind to remember if there was an Israel in West Virginia. There was a Rome and a London north of Beckley. Surely her grandfather couldn't mean the actual Israel, the one on the other side of the ocean.

"We think—perhaps—yes. Your mother ordered Alan a passport while he was in the hospital. Your father found the paperwork in her jewelry box. Her mother—your grandmother—is there. In Israel. It seems the most likely place they would have gone. Your father is trying to speak with someone from the embassy. I don't want you to worry."

I wanted to leave, her mother had said. *But where can I go?*

Anyone who was Jewish could go to Israel and become a citizen now. A poster in the Sunday school classroom at the synagogue in Beckley showed handsome young men and women dancing in a field, bandanas tied around their foreheads, palm trees in the background. *Make Aliyah: Move to Israel,* it said.

But imagining her mother actually doing this, actually leaving with Alan and not telling anyone—that was . . . well, the thought left an empty spot in Doree's mind. Unfathomable. Her mother was a woman of small, angry gestures—throwing gravy boats, slamming doors. Could she really have done something this immense? Could she really have left Doree and Pete behind? Bewildered, Doree began to cry, the tears forming so quickly she didn't realize what was happening until she saw the wet spots on the green kitchen table.

Her grandfather nudged his chair towards hers and put his arm around her. "Shhh, *zeeskeit*, it's all right," he said. "It'll be all right."

Her grandfather's arm on her shoulder, him calling her *zeeskeit*, the comforting smell of coffee—for a moment she felt like a little girl again, safe and protected. She leaned against him, sobbing.

Then her grandfather spoke again.

"I know things haven't been easy for you, Doree," he said. "Your mother isn't easy. Your grandmother being sick isn't easy. Being Alan's older sister isn't easy. But there's a phrase from the Talmud I've always loved—*Gam zu l'tova*—'even this is for the best.' Us Jews, we find strength in the hardships of life. Your struggles, Doree, have made you the strong young woman you are now. I'm so proud of you."

A sob tore Doree's throat. If only he knew what she'd done! If only he knew this was all her fault—Alan, her mother leaving, everything.

"Let me tell you a story," Sol went on, still patting her shoulder. "About my watch."

"What?" Doree said, trying to calm her breathing. She had never known her grandfather to wear a watch.

Sol turned his hand palm up, as if examining an invisible treasure. "It was a pocket watch. Silver. It felt good in my hand.

Heavy. It was the only thing I had of my father. You have his eyes, you know?"

"I do?" Doree couldn't remember ever hearing anything about her grandfather's father. Of course he'd had one once. But it had never occurred to her to ask about him.

"He died when I was very young. Your great-aunts Freya and Raisel, they remembered him. They said he had eyes the color of honey in summertime."

Doree had never thought of her eyes as anything but light brown.

"My mother gave me his pocket watch when I left Lithuania. I wore it in a pouch under my shirt. I wore it on the train across Europe. I wore it across the Atlantic. I wore it through the coal camps in McDowell County. Then, it was stolen by two men on the road." Sol looked down at his hands, as if still imagining the watch. "One of them was the one who bit off my ear. How I cried afterwards—for the watch, not the ear. I felt I had failed, that I'd broken the one link between me and my father. It was, at that time, the worst thing that had happened to me."

In her mind, Doree saw her young grandfather, tiny beneath his enormous pack. She saw a man loom over him, his teeth bloody. Then she saw Junior Carper, closing in on Alan, a two-by-four in his hand. A violent shiver shook her body.

"But losing that watch?" Sol went on. "It turned out to be a blessing, because the attack led me to quit peddling, led me to open the store, led your grandmother to see me as someone she might marry, led to my beautiful family. The watch, you see, really didn't matter. The things that connect us are not things at all. We're connected by people—our children, our grandchildren. One day you too will have children, and they'll connect me to the future, even though I'll be gone. That's what being Jewish is, a connection." He paused. "Alan may not understand this. He has an . . . an unusual mind. Pete, who knows? He's so young. But *you* understand, Doree. You will keep the connection whole." He was gazing at her with bright, watery eyes. "If I had my watch, I would give it to you."

Doree was flooded with shame like a poisonous chemical, hot and vicious. *She'd* be the one to keep the connection? She had tried to protect her family, and all she had done in the end was push Alan into harm's way, as surely as if she'd pushed him under a train. And for what? Because she thought she was better, cleverer. She thought she deserved something different, something special.

Sol went on, looking closely at Doree now, his eyes shining. "When I first held you, Doree, I saw the future. I saw the future and the past. In your eyes, the color of my father's, I saw the chain connecting us backwards, back across the ocean, back to our ancestors. And that same chain stretched into the future. I saw your children, Doree. I saw your grandchildren. This, to me, is what being Jewish is—not about keeping kosher, not about even believing in God. It's about being part of an eternal chain. An eternal chain that gives us the strength to go on even when we think we cannot."

A hot fat tear escaped Doree's eye. She wiped it away quickly.

She hesitated. She wanted so badly to tell him the truth. She hadn't protected Alan at all. She was the reason he was hurt! And the "eternal chain"? She'd flung it to the ground, hadn't she? *But why burden him?* Was this what it meant to grow up? To put all your confusion inside the puzzle box of your heart and lock it away?

Doree and her grandfather sat at the green enameled table for a while.

"I think I'll lie down for a spell," Sol said, pushing back his chair. He kissed the top of Doree's head as he tottered by. Then he disappeared into the darkened hallway, and Doree was left alone.

Doree slipped out of the house and walked down Main Street. Downtown looked smaller and shabbier than usual. She noticed for the first time how threadbare the purple curtains in Miss Cricket's upstairs apartment were, and thought of Miss Cricket sitting alone night after night with her dachshunds and her cigarettes. The awning of Zelner's was also looking worn, with a hole in the Z. Normally her mother would fix that. *Who'd do that now?* she wondered.

She turned up Laurel Drive. Tony was standing in the driveway, whistling and washing his car with a bucket and a large yellow sponge. Despite everything, Doree felt a shock of electricity, just seeing him.

"Doree!" he said, looking up, grinning. "How're you doing? How's your brother doing?"

"He's fine, I think."

"Good, good. I hope they get the little jerks that did this to him."

"Me too."

"Do they have any idea why someone would want to hurt him?"

Was it Doree's imagination, or was Tony's voice falsely casual? Did he already know exactly why someone would want to hurt Alan?

Will you please ask Tony about the urinals? Alan had said. *He's in charge down there.*

"He was curious about what was going on at the dig site, the new wing at the resort," Doree said, steadying her voice. "Some people thought he was too curious. They thought he was a danger to national security."

"Gosh," said Tony, the water from the sponge in his hand dripping down the side of his leg, leaving a dark trail on his Bermuda shorts.

"Why would people think that?" Doree moved closer. "What would a hotel foundation have to do with national security?"

Tony's face was uncharacteristically blank. He started to speak, then stopped himself.

"Tony, *is* it just a foundation?" She had the desperate need for him to say yes, yes, it was just a basement, to make everything go back to normal, to be the person he said he was. But she couldn't be foolish any longer, allowing herself to ignore the truth. She needed an answer.

"Officially, yes."

She stared at him. Then, slowly and deliberately, so her meaning was clear, she asked, "Tony, what exactly does an A/V technician do? Do you really just fix televisions all day?"

Tony was quiet for a long time. He turned his face towards the sky. She could see, again, the pulse flickering at the base of his throat, where the top button of his polo shirt was unbuttoned.

"No, I don't actually fix televisions all day," he finally said quietly, looking around to make sure no one was nearby. He went on, in an even lower voice, nearly a whisper. "I'd love to tell you about it, I really would. You'd understand—you're the only girl I've ever met who might really get it. You're so smart and everything. But I'm not allowed to talk about it. Not yet. Do you understand what I mean?" His dark eyes searched her face. "I'll tell you one day, I promise." He reached out to stroke her cheek, and, despite everything, her skin thrilled to the touch of his cool fingers. "I have a feeling we're going to know each other for a long time."

"Tony, I—" she began.

"Doree, you could come with me back to DC," he said. "There are lots of colleges there." He dropped the sponge in the bucket and stepped forward to touch her upper arm. "We could . . . we could get married. You want to, right?"

She froze. Married? She looked up at Tony's face. He hadn't shaved yet today, and the stubble stood out, blue-black against his olive skin. She wanted to reach up and touch it, to stroke the angle of his jaw. Then she thought of her grandfather's shining eyes, of the unbroken chain, and felt another flood of guilt. "Tony, we still hardly know each other. And we're . . . we're very different."

"It's kind of romantic, though," he said, a look of childish eagerness on his face. "Opposites attract, you know. I mean, the priest wouldn't marry us and my ma might have a heart attack, but I don't care. We could go to the courthouse. My uncle Rico married a French girl he met in the war and they didn't even speak the same language. But look, they've got five kids now, happy as clams."

"It's not that simple," she said, her eyes beginning to sting.

A look of confusion crossed his face. "But I thought, since . . . we . . . you know, went all the way. I mean, I wouldn't have if I wasn't serious."

"I know," she said. "I know."

"But . . ." He leaned heavily against the wet car.

Had it only been a few months since she was the girl who'd fantasized about marrying the first boy who'd give her his fraternity pin? How silly she'd been, how foolish.

"I'm sorry, Tony," she said. "It just wouldn't be right. But I'm so glad to have known you. You don't know what a difference it's made for me. I will never, never forget that. I will never forget you."

"Doree," he said, in a choked voice, reaching out his hand.

Every molecule of her body pulled towards him, as if magnetized. And yet, she pulled back. And yet, she walked away down the driveway, her vision blurred by tears.

CHAPTER 50

Sol

WHITE SULPHUR SPRINGS

*S*ol did well. The people in town called Zelner's "the Jew store," though it was meant—mostly—in a friendly way. He sold them everything they needed for their lives: sheets and towels and pots and pans, bangles and cigarettes and perfume, brassieres and dusters and overalls, washbasins and teddy bears and penny candy and coffee beans. They came to him for little white gowns when their children were baptized and for shoes when they were old enough for school. They came to him for Hershey's Kisses to apologize after they fought with their wives. They came to him for reading glasses when they began to get old. The town grew from three hundred to nearly two thousand as houses sprouted like mushrooms up the hillside and across the valley.

The resort, a splendid white palace like something from a storybook, opened in 1913 with much fanfare. Sol would take Pauline to stroll there on Sundays when the rest of the town was at church. Pauline would make slightly bitter jokes about how they only saw the outside, never the inside. They couldn't afford a room. *Maybe not*, Sol would say. *But our grandchildren will.*

Cecil Carper came every month for his five dollars and sat in the shoe-trying chair talking about fishing and cars and the stupidity of this law or that law, as if he and Sol were the oldest of friends. Sol wondered if Cecil actually believed that they were friends. Maybe he was stupid. Or maybe he was just lonely.

Sol and Pauline's first son, Louis, was born on the bed in the apartment above the shop. By the time their second son, Vincent, came, Sol had bought a blue-painted house on Spring Street with a proper kitchen and a parlor and a basement to store their baby chairs and bicycles and snowshoes for tramping through the winter woods. Neither boy had the gold-brown eyes of Sol's father; their eyes were the winter sky gray of Pauline's. But they were clever and sweet and they *belonged*, whooping through the streets of White Sulphur Springs on their bicycles with all the other boys. Happy, lucky, American children.

By 1920, Sol had enough money to sponsor his sisters Freya and Raisel and their families to come to Baltimore.

Dina was still in Lithuania, with her dolls and her dough. America didn't allow entry to the feebleminded. So Sol's mother didn't come either, of course. Sol even wrote to a lawyer in Baltimore, to plead her case, but the lawyer said it was hopeless, and wouldn't even accept a consultation fee.

See you soon, Dina had said, waving.

Dina died a few years before Sol's first grandchild was born. The child was a girl, and Sol would have loved to name her after his sister. "Dina" was a wonderful name, sweet and simple. But Louis and his dark-eyed young Polish wife had other ideas, *modern* ideas. The child was named Doreen, a name which grated against Sol's ears like a rasp on wood.

But the first time he held her in his arms and looked down at her tiny face, the eyes that met his were a honeyed brown color he'd only seen in his dreams for decades. He knew then that what the rabbi said at his wedding had been true. Here was the next link in the unbreakable chain connecting past and future, Old World and New, the dead and the living. She'd grow up both Jewish and American, the best of both. One day her children would lay pebbles on his grave.

So he'd lost a bit of ear and a watch to make it all happen. A small price to pay for eternity.

※

CHAPTER 51

Jordan

JANUARY 1992

Stepping out of the Volvo, Jordan's mother looked every bit the Baltimore housewife of Jessica's scorn. Camel coat, tennis bracelet, teased hair held back with a headband. She smoothed her slacks and handed her leather weekend bag to the bellman, then looked up at the Greenbrier with an expression of wonder, like a child gazing on a newly unwrapped dollhouse.

She drove all the way here by herself, Jordan thought with a pang of surprise. His mother hated to drive on the interstate. But he'd called her, and she'd come.

"Sweetheart!" she cried, spotting him. She rushed towards him so quickly one of her shoes caught on the edge of the front steps and she stumbled, then caught herself.

Jordan stepped down to meet her, and they embraced. She smelled like hair spray and familiar floral perfume. She gripped his upper arms and looked at his face. "Look at that five o'clock shadow! Like Richard Nixon! Did you forget your razor?"

"Nice to see you too, Mom."

"I wasn't criticizing. You always look handsome!"

The bellman lifted two suitcases from the trunk and a valet

slid behind the wheel. Jordan and his mother followed the bellman into the lobby, where his mother checked in and was handed keys to the room next to Jordan's.

"I thought it might be hard to get a reservation, but when I called last night, they said I could have whatever room I wanted," she said.

"It's the slow season."

She pursed her lips. "When I was young, there was no such thing as the slow season." She looked around the lobby with narrowed eyes. "That painting is new," she said. "And the couches are much larger than before."

"When was the last time you were here?"

His mother gazed around the room with the assessing look of a realtor. "Not since I graduated from high school, sweetheart. Nineteen fifty-nine."

They followed the bellman down the long green corridor, Jordan's mother chattering away about every small difference she noticed—a different armchair, a new wallpaper. "I'm going to change and powder my nose," she said, as she unlocked her room door. "Then lunch?"

"I thought we could talk," Jordan said.

"We'll talk! We'll talk at lunch." She was already halfway inside the room.

Jordan wasn't going to let her get away this time. He was going to treat her the same way he'd treat any other source. He was going to ask every single question he'd written down that morning in his notebook, even if the thought made him sweaty and nauseated. This was the biggest story of Jordan's life, in every sense. He wasn't going to fail now.

"Five minutes," he said. "I'll be waiting right here."

. . .

*I*n the nearly empty dining room, Jordan's mother dithered over the menu, asking question after question about the chicken pot pie, the tuna sandwich.

"I wonder if the chopped salad is premade?" she said, sipping her Diet Coke. "When I was growing up, everything here was from scratch. So nice." She looked up at the waiter, who looked barely out of his teens. "Is it premade?"

"No, ma'am," he said, without confidence.

She frowned and looked at the menu again.

"Mom!" Jordan was surprised by the vehemence in his voice. "Just choose."

"Okay, okay." She raised her hands in mock defensiveness. "I didn't know we were in such a big hurry."

"Sorry," he said instinctively. "It's just that you drove all the way out here to talk, and I want to talk."

"We can talk about whatever you want, sweetheart. But, oh, did I tell you about Rachel Golden? She's getting married! They're going to have the wedding at that Italian place on—"

"Mom!"

"Okay, okay." She took another sip of Diet Coke and looked up at the chandelier. Then she looked at Jordan and he saw her eyes had filled with tears. "Let's talk. What do you need to know?"

"I'll tell you what I know first, then you can tell me," Jordan said. He swallowed so hard he could feel his Adam's apple jerking up and down.

"All right." His mother ran a finger underneath her lower eyelids. "You're the big-shot reporter. You tell me what you know."

"So," Jordan began. "So, well, there's something under the hotel, under the West Virginia Wing here. You know this. They were building it when you would have been a teenager. Did you know what it was?"

His mother paused and turned her head slightly to the side. "We knew there was something happening," she said after a moment. "We all knew. The hole they were digging was too deep to be a basement, which was what the hotel claimed it was. But people didn't talk about it."

"It was a 'relocation facility' for Congress in case of nuclear war," Jordan said.

His mother didn't look surprised. "I suppose that makes sense."

"It's got room down there for all five hundred and whatever members of Congress," Jordan went on. "Dormitories, bathrooms, a cafeteria, everything. They never used it, obviously. But they've taken care of it all these years, kept it operational."

"I see." Her face was impossible to read.

"The man who takes care of the bunker," Jordan went on. "He knows you."

"Oh?"

"His name is Carl Carper, but he says people used to call him Junior."

His mother shivered and pulled her cardigan more tightly around her.

"He said he took money from you?"

"Yes," his mother said in a flat tone.

Jordan stared at her, waiting for her to go on. Finally, she continued. "Junior Carper took me for probably three hundred dollars, which was a lot in 1959."

"Why?"

"Oh, he was just a hillbilly—not that my family ever used that word—who wanted to spread rumors about my family, and

I was young and dumb enough to think money would stop him." She stared across the dining room, not making eye contact.

"What were the rumors?"

"Oh, just nonsense." His mother fussed with her tennis bracelet.

"Don't lie to me, please." Jordan had never spoken to his mother like this.

His mother looked up, her eyes wide and dark with—fear? Shock? "You sound just like your sister."

"Why can't you just tell me what happened?"

His mother made a frustrated exhalation. "It's such a horrible story. Why would I burden you with something like that?"

"It's not a burden." Jordan felt hot and shaky. "It's the truth. Jessica always knew there was something more going on, and you guys made her feel crazy for asking. And I knew too, I was just too well trained to ask. This is a puzzle, but I don't have all the pieces. I've told you what I know, so give me the rest of the pieces. Please, Mom."

His mother nodded. For a while she was silent. "You're right," she finally said, looking down at the tablecloth. "You're right. Do you know how to get in touch with your sister? Tell her if she comes home, I'll answer any question she—both of you—want. I'll tell you the whole story. Then you can do with it what you want. It won't be *my* story anymore."

❧

Doreen

BALTIMORE, MARYLAND

APRIL 1992

*D*oreen—she was "Doreen" now—held an envelope and walked into the post office. It was an airmail envelope, bordered in red and white. Inside was a newspaper clipping from the front page of the *Washington Post,* dated the day before.

> Decades-Long Secrets Revealed: Congressional
> Bunker Hidden Beneath Luxury Resort

Her son's first front-page story, above the fold.

Alan *had* been right about the bomb shelter, or at least close. This didn't surprise Doree, it simply confirmed the suspicions she'd long ago accepted and assimilated and chosen not to dwell on. But here it was, in black and white. With her son's name on it.

Who would have thought Jordan would be the one to shine light on these secrets after all these years? Jordan, who'd always been so good—too good, maybe. He reminded Doree of herself, before her mother left, before she had grown a harder shell, like a turtle. She was glad he hadn't listened to her when she told him not to go to the Greenbrier. She was proud that he'd followed his own mind.

Because he had been right, in the end. Keeping secrets hadn't helped.

On the envelope was her brother's address in Tel Aviv. She watched the clerk stamp it and drop it in the bin marked "International."

She closed her eyes and saw her brother dressed in his Christmas party outfit, standing at the edge of the West Lobby, staring down at the hole, enraptured.

It was she who'd been wrong, as her son had explained. It hadn't been Junior Carper who'd beaten up Alan. It had been Lee Burdette and the rest of the basketball team. It hadn't been her fault, not at all.

*A*t home, her children—her twins—were watching MTV together in the rec room. Had there ever been a more beautiful sight in the history of the world? Doree paused in the doorway, afraid any movement might interrupt the moment.

Jordan, sitting in the recliner with his giant feet on the ottoman, had her own father's gray eyes and sandy hair. But Jessica, curled like a cat on the couch—Jessica was her own creature. Her dark hair was shorn to stubble and her blue eyes—where did they come from, those blue eyes?—glowed in her thin, avid face.

It was Passover. Both her children were home.

After Jordan had called her from the Greenbrier that week in January, Doreen had made a decision. It was time to tell.

So she did.

For the first time in her life, she told her secrets without holding back, without trying to make it sound prettier or better or different: Her mother had had an affair with a detained Italian diplomat during World War II. Alan was the result. Her mother had left the family and taken Alan to Israel with her. She'd died, of cancer, when the twins were small. Alan still lived in Tel Aviv. He was a professor of mathematics.

"Do you talk to him, Alan?" Jordan had asked, plowing through a list of questions like a reporter. Which, of course, he was.

"We occasionally send . . . messages. Math puzzles."

"Math puzzles," Jessica had said, with her usual edge. "You haven't seen him in like thirty years, and all you talk about is math?"

"That's always been how we communicated best," Doree told her daughter. "Math is its own language."

*I*f only Jessica knew the rest. That part, Doree couldn't tell. It was a matter of national security, of course.

Doree did have a desk in a large office. She did have a slide rule, though just for nostalgia now—she used a computer to make most of her calculations, calculations about the trajectories of planes and satellites thousands of miles away. These days she was mostly checking the work of others, the ones who called her "ma'am." Things had quieted down in the office, since the end of the conflict in the Gulf. But there would be other conflicts. There always were.

"Mommy works in an office," she always told her children. And it was true, technically. But maybe if she could have told them the full truth about her work, Jessica would have been proud of her, instead of rolling her eyes at her boring mother with her boring job and her boring marriage. Doree hoped Jessica would one day learn life was never so black-and-white.

Gam zu l'tova, her grandfather had said. *Even this is for the best.* She'd cried for weeks over Tony. But if she hadn't met him, she never would have made a last-minute application to the University of Maryland, to study math. She never would have stuck it out when her male classmates rolled their eyes at her. She never would have gone to the government recruitment fair senior year.

And she never would have met Jonathan Barber, the gangly boy she'd long noticed on her morning commute. He'd always seemed so serious, always reading. Then on Halloween he'd stepped on the bus dressed as Marvin the Martian, and she'd burst out laughing. Jonathan was the first person—until recently, the only person—she ever told the truth about her mother and brother to. Who'd whispered, "There's nothing about your past that could make me not love you." Who she'd eloped with to Paris, and married in a tiny synagogue in Le Marais. Jonathan had made her laugh for weeks afterwards, imitating the rabbi's dubious English ("I promise to love and squish you all the days of my life"). He wasn't her first love, but he still made her laugh every day.

Without Tony, she never would have had the two beautiful children—beautiful adults—sitting together in the rec room.

The truth was, Tony *had* been her *beshert*—her destiny—just not in the way she'd first imagined.

(Imagine if she'd never met him and had actually become a math teacher! How horrible.)

She thought of those long-ago days in White Sulphur Springs when she was embarrassed to share an advanced math class with Alan. To think they were both mathematicians now, only on opposite sides of the earth. Life could be so strange.

For weeks after her mother left, Doreen would wake in the early morning dark to hear her father making phone calls to Israel, searching. It must have cost a fortune, but he never got through to Sylvia. He even closed the store for two days to drive to Washington and meet with someone at the Israeli embassy. Nothing but dead ends. He decided to fly over there himself, though Doreen knew they could hardly afford the ticket. Business at Zelner's had grown worse and worse, as if the scandal of Sylvia leaving meant Louis could no longer sell sundries. Plus, Sylvia had taken most of their savings with her.

In the end, Sol convinced him not to go. Alan would be eighteen soon enough, Sol said, and he'd surely come back on his own. And good riddance to "that woman."

No more *sweet girl*.

Louis seemed to age a decade in a month. Eventually he applied for a divorce on grounds of abandonment. He closed the store the following year, not long after a Ramsay's Price World opened on the western end of Main Street, where the rotting Carper's Travel Paradise had been demolished. For a while he drove to Beckley once a week to help Mr. Grossman with his menswear shop, just to make ends meet.

Pauline died a year after Sylvia left. By the end, the only person she recognized was Sol. When she could no longer get out of bed, Sol sat and held her hand from morning to night. Doree had watched them, studied the love in Sol's eyes. She knew that, if she was the first to go, Jonathan would hold her hand like that too.

Oddly, after his mother died, Louis seemed to unfold himself, like an indoor plant finally feeling the sun. When Doreen came home for winter break of her junior year, he told her he'd met someone—Mr. Epstein's cousin Louise, a widow in Huntington. Louis and Louise—Pete couldn't stop cracking jokes. They were married the following summer at the Huntington synagogue. In the wedding pictures, Louise gazed at Louis in unabashed adoration.

Sol lived to be eighty-two. He lived long enough to see Doree succeed—*We always knew you were clever, shaina maidel. My granddaughter, a mathematician!* She saved her Agency paychecks for years to buy him a present for his eightieth birthday: a pocket watch. It was silver with a Star of David, just like his father's. They buried him with it, attached to his three-piece suit with a thick silver chain.

As for Pete, he went to work as a trainee teller at First National Bank in Huntington right out of high school and worked his way up to senior loan officer. He married a local girl—a Methodist—and had a son and two daughters. Doreen attended all three of their baptisms in the old Methodist Church, whose stone towers and stained glass reminded her of the cathedrals she'd seen on her and Jonathan's wedding honeymoon in France. Sol was there too, in the front pew. He wasn't going to lose another grandchild, he said, fiercely, even if it meant sitting in a church.

Alan finally wrote, after years of silence. He addressed her so casually it was as if they'd spoken just the day before. He had a cryptogram he thought she'd like, he said. She solved it and sent him one in return. On it went, cryptograms crossing the ocean, the most fragile and tentative of links. They filled a hole in her heart she'd thought would be empty forever.

She'd been waiting to go until the children were grown. Then she was waiting to finish the next big project at work, or until after the High Holidays. Finally, she had to admit to herself that she was frightened.

Israel. The splinter of land that had taken half her family.

But it was time. She hadn't yet told her father and children, but she hoped they'd come too. She'd already spoken to a travel agent. She would see her brother again. She'd find out if he still loved Lorna Doones, and fishing vests with pockets, and perfectly sharp number 2 pencils.

And she would visit her mother's grave.

She had been wrong to think burying her mother's memory would make the pain go away. She had been wrong to think she could avoid passing on the pain to the next generation, to think her children wouldn't sense she was hiding from them. Secrets only grew larger in the shadows.

She'd visit Sylvia's grave. She'd leave a pebble on the headstone.

AUTHOR'S NOTE

Though the Zelners and other characters are imaginary, I've rooted historical events and places in fact wherever possible. As research resources, I owe a huge debt to Harvey Solomon's *Such Splendid Prisons: Diplomatic Detainment in America During World War II*; Garrett M. Graff's *Raven Rock: The Story of the U.S. Government's Secret Plan to Save Itself—While the Rest of Us Die*; Eli N. Evans's *The Provincials: A Personal History of Jews in the South*; Deborah R. Weiner's *Coalfield Jews: An Appalachian History*; Stella Suberman's *The Jew Store*; and Robert S. Conte's *The History of the Greenbrier: America's Resort*. The journalist who actually broke the Greenbrier bunker story was Ted Gup, then of *The Washington Post*, in May 1992.

ACKNOWLEDGMENTS

I am enduringly grateful to Kate Dresser at Putnam, Allison Hunter at Trellis Literary Management, and all the team members who helped shape this book and bring it into the world, including Tarini Sipahimalani and Natalie Edwards. Thank you to Marty Hebrank and Deborah Shlian for their excellent manuscript notes, and to Lindsey Alexander for her expert publishing advice. Thanks to Beth Hatcher for suggesting a road trip to West Virginia back when we were newbie reporters—it sparked the idea of this book. Thanks to my parents, who supported my writing from the very beginning. Thanks to Tess Pacanza for making the logistics possible. And thanks, as ever, to Jamin Asay, always my first reader, and father of our two beautiful boys.

Discussion Guide

1. *In the Shadow of the Greenbrier* is set in White Sulphur Springs, West Virginia, home to the opulent Greenbrier hotel. What did you learn about this place from your read?

2. The Zelners are the only Jewish family in White Sulphur Springs. Based on each Zelner's perspective, how does each family member feel about this fact? Discuss why Sylvia often finds herself at odds with the rest of the family.

3. Teenaged Doree is enamored with love, infatuated with boys, and desires social inclusion. What do her interactions with her peers, and particularly Tony and Patty, indicate about her worldview and self-perception? How are these beliefs carried through generations?

4. *In the Shadow of the Greenbrier* is both a multigenerational family saga and a complicated mother-daughter story. Compare and contrast Doree's respective relationships with Sylvia and Jessica. To what extent does Doree change as her role evolves from daughter to mother? How do the female characters' relationships differ from those of the men and boys in the story?

5. Sylvia and Pauline get married for security, while Doree aspires to both love and marriage. To what extent does author Emily Matchar depict love as separate from marriage?

6. Sylvia finds comfort in Jack's presence—a relief from the day-to-day burdens she's too used to carrying. What does Jack represent to Sylvia? Do you see the appeal of the relationship?

7. At one point in the novel, Sol tells Doree, "If only they could see the sweet girl inside," referring to Sylvia. Why do you think Sol sees Sylvia's sweet side?

8. Tony offers Doree more than just a summer fascination. In what ways does Tony challenge Doree's points of view? How do you think Doree's life would be different if she'd never met Tony?

9. At almost eighteen, Doree finds herself in a predicament, keeping a family secret safe. How would you have navigated the situation? How does Doree carry this experience into adulthood? In what ways does the story echo the past?

10. The Zelners harbor many secrets. Have you ever stumbled upon a family secret of your own? How did you react? How did it alter the way you viewed family?

11. *In the Shadow of the Greenbrier* is written in the perspectives of four generations. Whose story spoke to you most, and why? How does the story's structure help you understand how the family members relate to one another? What themes are carried through all the time lines?

12. Despite the novel's domestic focus, Matchar doesn't shy away from the gravity of the wartime backdrop. Have you read other novels about the home front during World War II? What themes arose, differing from novels set overseas at the same time?

13. Alan is a significant character in the novel, yet he doesn't narrate his own perspective. Discuss the impact of his limited presence on the page, and the role he plays in the Zelners' understanding of family and themselves.

14. Jordan and Jessica's generation allows them to offer their family history the most modern viewpoints. In what ways did their perspectives at any point in the story fail to align with what you deem "modern"? How are Jordan and Jessica's views of their family similar or different?

ABOUT THE AUTHOR

JAMIN ASAY

EMILY MATCHAR has written for an array of publications, including *The New York Times, The Washington Post, Outside, Smithsonian,* and *The Atlantic,* and is the author of *Homeward Bound.* Originally from North Carolina, she lives with her husband and two sons.

EmilyMatchar.com
🐦 @EmilyMatchar